IUNCTIŌ CŌPULA

# INNOCENCE
## TO THE
# MAX

## SJD PETERSON

DREAMSPINNER
PRESS

Published by
DREAMSPINNER PRESS

5032 Capital Circle SW, Suite 2, PMB# 279, Tallahassee, FL 32305-7886 USA
www.dreamspinnerpress.com

Innocence to the Max
© 2015 SJD Peterson.

Cover Art
© 2015 Reese Dante.
http://www.reesedante.com
Cover content is for illustrative purposes only and any person depicted on the cover is a model.

ISBN: 978-1-63476-369-1
Digital ISBN: 978-1-63476-370-7
Library of Congress Control Number: 2015943464
First Edition October 2015

Printed in the United States of America
∞
This paper meets the requirements of
ANSI/NISO Z39.48-1992 (Permanence of Paper).

To Becca, who opened the door to my writing as well as to my love for vampires.

# Readers love SJD PETERSON

## Ruin Porn (with S.A. McAuley)

"I really loved this one and thought it was so well done... It is a great collaboration between McAuley and Peterson "
—Joyfully Jay

"I wouldn't hesitate to recommend this one the next time you're in the mood for a beautiful disaster you can see coming a mile away, and have no intention of avoiding until you see it through to its finish."
—The Novel Approach

## Rival Within

"Wow. This book brought out some serious emotions in me, both good and bad. I love it when a book does that!"
—Love Bytes

"Well written intense at times story."
—MM Good Book Reviews

## BAMF

"This is quite different from everything else I have read from this author but it caught me in the first chapter and wouldn't put me down until I had finished it!"
—Prism Book Alliance

"*BAMF* was a delight for me to read... I think I can safely say; I enjoyed the hell out of this book."
—Boys in Our Books

By SJD Peterson

BAMF
Beyond Duty
Innocence to the Max
Leon
Masters & Boyd
A Night Never Forgotten
Plan B
Rival Within
*With S.A. McAuley*: Ruin Porn
Splintered
Tuck & Cover

GUARDS OF FOLSOM
Riveted
Pup
Tag Team
Pony
Roped
Mauled

WHISPERING PINES RANCH
Lorcan's Desire
Quinn's Need
Ty's Obsession
Conner's Courage
Jess's Journey

Published by DREAMSPINNER PRESS
www.dreamspinnerpress.com

*The Spanish name Francisco—from the Latin Franciscus, meaning "free man." A strange name for a boy who yearns for nothing more than to be owned.*

# PROLOGUE

FRANCISCO AGUILAR, known as Cisco to his friends and family, sat in the passenger seat of his best friend's car, staring out at the city of Mecosta as it passed by in a blur of color. It shouldn't have surprised him that he couldn't figure out where he wanted to go or how he wanted to celebrate his sixteenth birthday. Cisco had been waiting for something to happen for as long as he could remember. He had no clue what he was waiting for, but whatever it was, it would change his world, that much he was sure of.

Growing up in the burbs just outside the city limits of Mecosta, the first ten years of his life had been the picture-perfect all-American childhood. He was an only child, raised by loving and doting parents. T-ball games at five, Cub Scouts, schoolwork, he and Benny finding the same trouble that many young kids found, but even then there was always something missing. He'd felt it before his dad died when he was eleven, and he'd felt it afterward when he spent more time with his nanny than he did with his mom. The feeling had been there long before any of it. Cisco couldn't explain it; he only knew that deep inside, at his very core, he was waiting.

"Any idea where you want to go?" Benny asked as he turned down the radio.

They'd been driving around for the last hour and nothing had sparked even the slightest interest in Cisco. "I don't know. Why don't we head down to the strip and see if anything is going on?"

"Dude, nothing good ever goes down on the strip but trouble. I'm pretty sure that spending the night in jail or, worse, the hospital on your birthday isn't what you had in mind."

Cisco rolled his eyes at his best friend. Benny was the same age, but he always acted as if he was Cisco's protector or something, probably due in part to their different personalities. Benny was outgoing and loud while Cisco tended to be a little more reserved, quiet. The other part, he was sure, stemmed from the fact that at sixteen, Benny was already pushing six foot and his frame was large and thick with muscles—good

genes, as Benny's dad was well over six foot, as were two of his uncles—
while Cisco was celebrating reaching five foot four and a whopping one
hundred and ten pounds.

*You're a fricking runt!* Yeah, well, the birthday wish of a couple
inches and twenty pounds had obviously been ignored right along with
the wish for a Camaro convertible concept wrapped in Hugger Orange
pearl tri-coat paint with twin gunmetal-gray sport stripes.

"C'mon, Benny, we're not going to get into any trouble," he
promised. "I just like watching the people down there. We won't even
get out of the car."

"Yeah, okay, just lock your door."

Cisco rolled his eyes at his friend again, but he complied with the
demand and hit the lock. "Happy?"

"Not really," Benny huffed. But he turned the music back up,
The Fray blasting through the speakers as he turned the car toward the
downtown area.

They'd just pulled up at a light on the corner of Martin Luther King
Boulevard and Ninth Street and were trying to decide which direction to
go, when Cisco turned to stare out the window and the strangest feeling
overcame him. His heart started to hammer, sweat bloomed across his
brow, and he began to shake uncontrollably. Then Cisco spotted *him.*
*Leaning against a doorframe, partially hidden in the shadows, was a
tall, broad-shouldered man, dressed in tight black leather pants, thigh-
high black boots, and a white, elegantly ruffled nobleman's shirt. His
face was lost in the shadows, but Cisco could feel the man staring at him,
looking inside him. A chill ran down his spine and his skin tingled as he
felt the man's gaze like a soft touch against his skin.*

*What the hell is wrong with me?* He shook his head to try to dispel
*the odd feeling, but it only intensified as the seconds clicked by.*

*Cisco's breath hitched, the rush of blood in his ears blocking out
all sound, and his focus narrowed till everything but the stranger faded
away. Although Cisco knew he wasn't sleeping, it still seemed dreamlike,
some unknown force holding him rapt. Mine, a voice whispered inside
his head like smoke swirling, touching every part of him, the meaning
elusive, difficult to understand, and evading capture.*

*Before he had the chance to leave the car, still reaching for the
door handle with a trembling hand, the light turned green and Benny
stomped on the gas.*

*"No!" Cisco screamed, wrenching his head around, trying to keep contact with the mysterious man. "Turn around, Benny! We gotta go back."*

*"What the hell are you talking about?"*

*Benny kept driving, and Cisco lost eye contact. No, no, no! "That was him! Turn around."*

*Cisco grabbed at the door handle and yanked at it, but the door wouldn't open. Panic made his fingers clumsy as he fumbled with the lock, but before he could get it undone, Benny grabbed on to his arm and yanked him away from the door.*

*"What the hell has gotten into you? Jesus, Cisco, give me a minute and I'll turn around. Who did you see?"*

He met Benny's concerned gaze as panic continued to bubble just under the surface of his skin, causing goose bumps to bloom along his flesh and his hands to shake. Cisco shuddered. "I don't know," he admitted. "I just know it was *him.*"

By the time Benny could make it through heavy traffic and back to the corner where Cisco had spotted him, the stranger was gone. Tears welled up in his eyes and spilled over at the loss. Sixteen years he'd been waiting. As crazy as it sounded, he now understood what he'd been waiting for, but as a red light changed to green, he'd lost it before he even knew what it was that he had found.

BACK INSIDE his club, Maximilian De Ferrari leaned heavily against the closed door and shut his eyes. Behind closed lids, he could still see the dark, wistful eyes of the beautiful boy. Max placed a trembling hand over his now still heart. He could have sworn he'd felt a faint beat in his chest as he watched the boy. His heart hadn't beat since he'd been turned nearly a hundred years prior, and yet he could have sworn he'd felt it. As absurd as it was, the memory of it still lingered, leaving him dizzy.

Years before, he'd heard rumors about such a thing happening. Max had searched every text he could get his hands on, trying to find anything, a single reference to what was known as *Iunctiō Cōpula,* but in the end, he'd found nothing and concluded the rumors were false. A connecting bond between a vampire and his mate powerful enough to cause a dead heart to beat was ludicrous.

And yet....

As his mind had screamed *mine*, as he got lost in such an innocent soul, Max could have sworn he'd experienced something he had given up hope of ever feeling again.

"Angelo," Max bellowed as he pushed away from the door. He'd felt something, dammit, and he wouldn't rest until he knew who the beautiful boy was and what he had sparked deep inside a cold, dead heart.

# CHAPTER ONE

*Five years later.*

*MAXIMILIAN DE Ferrari, vampire and owner of Wicked Ground, is my destiny.* Cisco had been certain since that brief encounter all those nights ago, and tonight he was finally ready to go after what he wanted. He had tried in vain to get another glimpse of Maximilian. Though he hadn't had any success, he had the uncanny feeling that Maximilian was watching him. Periodically through the years, the hair at the nape of his neck would stand on end and an eerie feeling would wash over him. He'd felt eyes upon him numerous times. When he would turn around, however, there was never anyone there. But the feeling lingered as a tingling sensation on his flesh. The feeling had begun the same night he'd spotted Maximilian and he'd held on to the hope that it was indeed his stranger. That thought was what had gotten him through each day, that and his dreams of what meeting his Master would be like. Cisco wouldn't wait any longer, though. Tonight was his twenty-first birthday; Maximilian—Max—could no longer keep him out. Tonight, he would finally be able to step through the doors of Wicked Ground and enter Maximilian De Ferrari's world.

"Do you really think this is a good idea, Cisco?"

Cisco paused in his struggle with a pair of leather pants, which were possibly a tad more than a size too small, and looked up at Benny, who was sitting on his bed, biting nervously at his lip. How could he explain to his best friend that this was the only thing in his life he was completely sure of? Benny knew everything about him—they'd been best friends since first meeting on the playground while in kindergarten—but Benny didn't understand Cisco's obsession with Max. A day hadn't gone by that he didn't think about the captivating man, looking at him with eyes that seemed to pierce through the gloom of that foggy November night. Though there was an instant attraction to the mysterious man, there was something beyond just the physical. In just one look, Cisco knew he belonged to Max. That conviction had never wavered, only grown stronger over the years.

"C'mon, we've already talked about this a hundred times. I'm going."

"But… for Christ's sake, he's a vampire. Doesn't that scare you? It sure as hell scares the crap out of me! What if he drains you? What the fuck am I supposed to tell your mom?" Benny's voice rose with each word and his growing panic made his voice crack.

It was an idle threat and Benny knew it. He wouldn't be able to find Cisco's mom to tell her shit. After his dad died, Mom used the small fortune she inherited to constantly jet-set off to unknown ports with the new husband, her third, he believed, or maybe fourth, he couldn't keep up. She hadn't even bothered to send him a card for his birthday, but he did get a beautiful flower arrangement from his nanny.

Shrugging, then sighing in relief as the button on the leathers finally cooperated, he gave his friend a disbelieving look. "He's not going to drain me. You watch too many bad B movies. Vampires have publicly coexisted alongside humans for over twenty years. Did you know that statistically, humans commit murder more often than vampires? You have a better chance of being killed at that nasty go-go club you visit than I do walking into Wicked Ground."

Actually he had no clue as to the soundness of the statistics, but Benny got a little wigged-out about *bloodsucking freaks* so Cisco wasn't about to say anything that would send him off on another rant. Benny had never even met a vampire as far as Cisco knew, and as much as he loved the guy, Benny really was an idiot sometimes. If it was on the Internet, Benny believed it was real.

*Ah shit.* Judging from the look in his eyes, his protective friend was already geared up for a hell of an outburst.

"Well, I'm sure I have a better chance of defending myself against a guy who wants to play with my assets than you will from some supernaturally strong vampire that can control your mind," Benny argued.

"Listen," Cisco said, grabbing the harness that he'd ordered earlier in the week from its box. "You know the whole mind-control thing is crap, right?"

"Do I?" Benny responded, arching a brow. "You've been obsessed with this guy since the first time you saw him—how do you explain that? I mean, really, Cisco, who the hell waits five years for a guy to notice him? If it's not mind control, then the only other alternative is that you're seriously whacked and in need of a padded cell."

Studying the harness, Cisco ran it through his fingers, enjoying the feel of the soft leather. Unfastening the buckles and turning it over and over in his hands, he couldn't even begin to figure out how the hell it went on. Ignoring Benny's rant, he held out the harness. "Do you have any idea how this goes on?"

Benny threw his hands up, obviously a little more than frustrated if the heavy sigh coming out of him was any indication, but he still got up from the bed and took the harness.

He stared at it for a moment before declaring, "This is for a horse! Now, I know you think you're a stallion but…."

Snatching the harness back from him, Cisco gripped it hard in his fist, his face heating as anger surged through him. This wasn't a joke. "Go home, Benny. I'll figure it out myself," he said, turning away from his friend.

"Ah, c'mon," Benny said softly as he moved up behind Cisco and wrapped his arms around his waist. "I'm sorry, Cisco. I know this is important to you, but I'm worried. Are you sure I can't go with you?"

He shook his head. He knew Benny was worried about him and was only trying to protect him, but he also knew that he had to do this on his own. Besides, even though they were both gay, they were on opposite ends of the spectrum when it came to acting on their sexuality. His best friend seemed to be on a mission to bed every hot guy in Mecosta and the four surrounding cities, whereas Cisco was saving himself for Max. Benny was also a cocky son of a bitch, a total top, whose idea of a kink was what his back felt when he slept on the pull-out couch in Cisco's basement. Completely vanilla. Cisco wanted to submit to his Master. Wanted to be bound and at the mercy of his will, to feel the kiss of his leather against his skin, and to know that he was what his Master needed for his pleasure.

The image of himself chained to a wall, naked, hard, and aching as his Master entered him for the first time flashed through his mind. Picturing the way his body would feel, stretched and full, caused him to shiver and his cock to harden. The sound of his own voice, screaming his pleasure to the rafters, whimpering, and pleading, filled his ears, making him dizzy with anticipation and need. God, he wanted to be owned and loved by his Master.

Cisco took a few deep calming breaths and pushed away the images igniting him, then turned in Benny's arms and hugged him back. "I know you'd go with me if I asked, but I need to do this on my own. Besides," he said lightly to alleviate some of Benny's fears. "I'm not going to do anything but check it out. I'll call you the minute I leave, okay?"

Benny kissed Cisco's forehead, then took a step back. From the frown and furrowed brows, it was obvious he didn't approve, but he was letting Cisco make his own choices. "No, you have two hours from the time you enter that club to call me, or I'm coming in after you, got it?"

"Okay, Dad," Cisco teased. "Two hours, got it. Now will you either help me with this damn thing or get out of here so I can get ready?"

Benny took the harness, grabbed his hand, and led Cisco to stand in front of the full-length mirror. As Benny fiddled with the strips of leather and helped secure them over his shoulder and chest, Cisco studied his reflection in the mirror. He didn't look any different than he had yesterday. Same dark brows and buzz-cut black hair. Same dark brown, nearly black eyes, though they did appear to be a little wider, wilder, no doubt due to the excitement and anticipation that was rushing through his body. At five feet eight inches and yet to hit one hundred and fifty pounds, the tight leather pants only accentuated his small frame. No, he didn't look any different, but on the inside he was completely altered. The strength of his conviction that he *would* belong to Maximilian De Ferrari had changed him, completed him. After five years of waiting, his soul was ready to meet its owner.

The drive to the club was much the same: Cisco trying to convince Benny he would be fine and Benny, in turn, begging Cisco to let him come along. Stepping out of his friend's car and shutting the door, Cisco sighed in relief when Benny drove away, albeit with a frown marring his brow, but at least he had left with nothing more than a tight nod and a small wave.

Cisco stood and stared at the nondescript building, not having a clue as to what lay beyond. There was only a single black door in the middle of the red brick façade, no windows, and no flashing neon lights, nothing to indicate that there was a club on the other side of the brick and mortar. The research he'd done on the Internet as to the type of club Wicked Ground was had left him with more questions and little in the way of real knowledge. It was as if the entire scene was masked behind a veil of anonymity, very hush-hush. He'd only seen a few pictures, none of which came from the inside of a club, but from house parties thrown by members. Even those didn't give much information as they tended to be mainly of masked faces either posing with other members or in innocuous settings.

Though he hadn't found any photos of what lay beyond the door, Cisco wasn't completely benighted. He'd seen pictures of men in submissive poses, men in bondage, and various implements to cause pain, and had read quite a few books on the subject. He'd even gotten hold of a homemade porn flick once. *Once?* Okay, so he'd watched it more than a few times. He'd been enthralled by the way the Dom had moved against his sub. It had reminded him of a passage in a book he'd once read: "The slow sensual slide of bodies was like a symphony for the eyes." The Dom had been beautiful, but Cisco always imagined the Dom moving like liquid silver was his Master, his Max.

He'd seen enough and read enough that he wasn't completely unschooled, just inexperienced and untaught—but that *would* change tonight. He was sure of it!

Taking a deep breath and squaring his shoulders, Cisco pulled open the heavy door and stepped inside. The sudden darkness enveloped him, and it took a moment for his eyes to adjust. The foyer, as it began to come into view, was barely large enough for two men to stand in. The walls, ceiling, and floor were painted black, and the only light was a small glow that filtered through heavy black curtains in front of him. For long moments he couldn't move, his heart racing as the scent of leather and male sweat mingled with an overpowering coppery smell that robbed him of his breath. Fear raced down his spine and his throat went dry, making it difficult to swallow, but as frightened as he was, the scent was heady. His rapid pulse pushed his blood south, and his shaft began to swell in its leather confines. Arousal and desire won out over fear, and he pulled back the thick curtain and stepped into the club proper.

Though the lighting was subdued, most filtered through a haze of red silk and smoke, he found himself blinking his eyes and once again trying to adjust to the change of light. *They must do it on purpose.* It left a person vulnerable for a moment—not that Cisco needed a trick with lighting to feel vulnerable, he had already felt exposed and off balance before opening the first door. His determination was the only thing keeping him from turning on his heel and running.

"ID," a deep, harsh voice said from the left.

Turning, Cisco had to force himself to stand still and not take a step back. A huge—no, enormous, as in the size of a fricking full-grown grizzly bear huge—man sat on a stool with a beefy hand outstretched. His head was the only thing on him that appeared completely devoid of hair. He had a thick, well-trimmed beard, and his naked upper torso was covered in a thick mat of black hair.

As Cisco struggled to pull his ID from his back pocket, the giant bear leered at him with pale green eyes and a slight sneer curled his upper lip. The way the bouncer looked at Cisco, as if he were prey, added to the difficulty of trying to pull a small card from beyond-tight pants. Cisco shifted nervously, finally grasping the card between his fingers, and held it out to him. The door attendant's meaty fingers wrapped around Cisco's wrist as he plucked the card from Cisco's fingers with his other hand. He held on to him as he studied Cisco's face, ignoring the card in his hand. It felt as if he were a fly under a magnifying glass and at any moment he would have his wings ripped off. He couldn't stop the trembling that encompassed his body. He was scared shitless of the ginormous man.

*Breathe, Cisco, don't you dare pass out from lack of oxygen now. Breathe.*

Cisco ignored his warning to himself and held his breath as the man pulled him closer, leaned in, and whispered against his ear. "You be careful, little one. Don't make eye contact and don't talk to anyone except the one you seek." He squeezed Cisco's wrist in a crushing grip that made him gasp. "And unless you want to find out real quick just how much pain you can endure before you break, stay away from the back rooms."

Releasing his hold on Cisco, the bear held out the ID and looked at him with a softer, almost tender look in his pale eyes. His full smile showed elongated and wickedly pointed eyeteeth, leaving no doubt as to what he was. Cisco rubbed at the ache in his wrist, then took his card and slipped it back into his back pocket, nodding in understanding. He was robbed of his voice, not only from the warning but also from the realization that although he still wasn't convinced that a vampire could control his mind, he was pretty sure they could read it. He swallowed hard, finally dislodging the lump that had formed in his throat, and moved farther into the club.

Now past the darkened entryway, his eyes adjusted to the subdued light, Cisco could make out a modern bar that glowed invitingly. In time with the dull, thudding bass from within, twilight hues of cobalt, indigo, and crimson lights alternated throughout the club. The intoxicating scents that assaulted his nose in the entryway were stronger here, filling his nostrils as they floated heavily in the air. The color palette of black and red didn't surprise him; he had formed a mental picture of the club in his mind, so the gothic feel of the interior was expected, but the sleek modern décor wasn't. He'd imagined a dark, ancient dungeon with torture racks, iron maidens, and men chained to walls. Well, there were a few men chained from above on the large stage, so at least he had gotten that part correct. The rest of the club was clean, sleek lines, the black and red accentuated with highly polished chrome.

Passing the first table, his stomach roiled in revulsion as he witnessed a man, no bigger than himself, completely naked, hands bound, and at the feet of his Master, his mouth held wide open by a metal contraption that encompassed his shaved head. The Master was dressed in an expensively tailored Armani suit, giving off the impression of a cultured man. But when he used the smaller man's mouth as an ashtray, stubbing out his cigarette on his sub's tongue as he sipped from a wineglass, Cisco knew he was no gentleman and no one he wanted to know. He quickly moved away from the sickening sight.

Cisco wandered along the tables, careful to remember the bouncer's instructions and keep his eyes low. The moans of pleasure and screams of pain that filled the club, combined with the extreme assortment of men, were like a feast for Cisco's senses. His heart was hammering in his chest and he avoided looking at any one thing too long, remembering what he was told at the door. There were men in various states of dress from totally nude to barely dressed—with nothing more than small strips of leather covering various parts of their bodies—to completely encased in leather or vinyl. A dark mask with zippers covering the eyes, mouth, and ears worn by one bound man sent a bolt of fear through Cisco. His curiosity got the best of him, and he stopped and stared for a long moment at one sub kneeling, his head resting on his Master's thigh, his eyes closed, and a dreamy smile on his lips. The Master gently threaded his hand through the sub's light blond hair as he talked with another man. *That's what I want.* It wasn't so much the position of the sub that held his attention, but the tenderness of the Master and the look of pure bliss on the smaller man's face.

Cisco forced his gaze away from the beautiful sight and continued to move through the club. Though he could feel the stares of those around him boring into him, causing his skin to tingle, he avoided looking directly at anyone as he frantically scanned the area. Along one side wall, there were doorways covered in black velvet curtains. One curtain out of the five stood open and curiosity had him heading in that direction.

Cisco stopped dead in his tracks at the doorway, and his mouth dropped open. "Holy hell," he muttered under his breath. He hadn't noticed any women in the club, but here a shapely woman with large breasts, long, flowing black hair, and pale skin stood bent at the waist, her hands splayed flat on the table in front of her as a large, muscular man draped across her back pounded brutally into her. The man wore a long black trench coat that obscured Cisco's view of their lower halves. Though the woman was beautiful, she didn't hold his attention, his gaze fixed on the handsome man's face. He wished he could see more of the muscular man's body. Giving further credence to Cisco's belief that vamps could read minds, the muscular man turned his head to the side and met Cisco's gaze with hungry, lust-filled eyes. A sly smile curled the man's lip, and he threw back the long coat with a flourish.

Cisco gasped and his heart skipped a beat. Kneeling at the feet of the woman was a small man dressed in nothing but a wide leather collar around his neck with a silver ring attached at the back. A rope ran through the ring, down his back, and was secured tightly around his wrists, keeping his head pulled back into a perfect position. Each thrust by the muscular man forced the "woman's" very large, very thick cock down the sub's throat. Cisco stood transfixed at what was obviously not a woman, watching as the saliva-slick shaft slid in and out of the stretched mouth of the kneeling man. Stunned but apparently aroused, Cisco felt his cock lengthen to full hardness. When he looked back up at the muscular man's face, the other man smiled, revealing sharp teeth, and he winked at Cisco.

So engrossed in the sight before him, Cisco yelped, nearly jumping out of his skin, when a heavy hand landed on his shoulder and spun him around. He found himself staring directly at a smooth, massive chest. Slowly his gaze moved upward. *Good God, are all the Doms here required to be fricking huge?* This one was nearly as big as the bouncer, making Cisco feel even smaller and more insignificant.

"See something you like, boy?" a thick husky voice asked.

Cisco began to tremble under the heavy hand, and he tilted his head back to look up into red glowing eyes. He opened his mouth to respond and snapped it shut, remembering the bouncer's warning, but Cisco was unable to look away.

"Doesn't matter either way to me," the man grunted. He reached out with his other hand and grabbed on to the harness Cisco wore. "What the hell is this? You want to be a pony?" the man sneered. "Not too bright, are you, boy?"

Dread spread through Cisco as the man continued to laugh. He had wanted so badly to be part of Max's world, to impress him enough to get his attention. Tears of embarrassment burned the backs of his eyes as another man joined the first and they both laughed at him and taunted his inexperience. Cisco refused to let the tears fall and clamped down on his trembling leg that threatened to give out. He wouldn't be deterred from his goal no matter how ridiculous he felt.

"I doubt your scrawny little ass can handle being fucked and ridden hard," the first man snarled and shoved Cisco to the floor. "I'll teach you to be a good little pony. That is, if you survive."

"Don't break him too fast, Zeke. I want a chance to ride your new little pony boy."

Cisco struggled to regain his footing, fighting to free himself from the man's iron grip, but it was no use. It did nothing but to make the vampires laugh all the harder. Cisco's strength gave out and he was again forced to his knees, hands resting on his thighs as he stared at the floor. He no longer heard their words as they continued to rain down insults and jeers, too lost in his grief. For five years he'd been waiting and preparing to meet Maximilian De Ferrari, and it hadn't been enough. The pain in his heart overshadowed his embarrassment, and a single tear rolled down his cheek as others joined the first two men, surrounding Cisco while pointing and laughing.

# CHAPTER TWO

RESTLESS, MAX paced like a caged animal in the confines of his office. The calendar had mocked him for weeks; each day until November eleventh, when his Francisco would come of age, had seemed to drag on for an eternity. Since first spotting the beautiful boy, he'd watched him grow from a boy of sixteen to a handsome man. Max had protected him from afar during the day and watched over him as he slept at night. His desire for Francisco had grown unbearable until his yearning consumed him. Regardless of what others thought, Max knew he wasn't soulless, because as the days clicked slowly by, he'd felt the urge to claim what he knew was his within the pit of his soul. In fact, the demand became so overwhelming, he'd had to send either Darius, Silas, or Angelo to watch over his precious man, afraid he would no longer be able to fight the temptation. The last six months had been sheer hell. But he knew Francisco would come to him when he was ready, of this he had no doubt. He'd felt the connection, read the boy's emotions, knew Francisco had felt it too, the binding implanted within each of them.

Still, the waiting was torturous.

What had once brought him pleasure and satisfaction now seemed hollow and unfulfilling. When his fangs punctured the soft skin at the rapid pulse of a man's neck, Max would pull hard, sucking at the life-giving force, yet would feel nothing. Even the pleasure-filled moan his penetrating kiss elicited no longer moved him. There was only one man he wanted to touch, to hold in his arms. The only person he wanted to sustain him was his Francisco.

It had been the same every day over the last five years. He took the blood his body demanded, but he felt no joy in the act as he once had—it was nothing more than a necessity. The same could be said for mastering a submissive while on the stage of Wicked Ground. His followers demanded that he display his ability to take a sub, dominate, control, send him soaring as Max beat and fucked him. They still stared at him with wide, awe-filled eyes and bent low in respect when he approached, but again he was simply going through the motions. He was a master of not only those under him, but of illusion. To the outside world, those whom he ruled, nothing had changed. He was still the most powerful vampire in the area. But inside, everything had changed. He was in limbo, waiting to be complete.

"Sir, he's here," Darius called out as he burst into the room.

*Finally!* Max grabbed his waistcoat from the back of his chair and moved toward the door. "Is he alone?"

"Uh… well…."

"Goddammit, spit it out! Is he here alone or not?" Max yelled impatiently.

"Y-yes, sir, he came in alone," Darius sputtered nervously. "I warned him to be careful, not to talk to anyone or make eye contact. I kept an eye on him, but…."

"But what?"

Darius shifted from foot to foot, staring at the floor. "Zeke…."

Max pulled on his coat as he pushed past Darius, rushing from the room. "I'll rip that son of a bitch to shreds if he so much as lays a finger on him," Max roared.

Zeke was a wild card, on the verge of bloodlust and unpredictable. Panic rolled through Max's stomach as images of the broken and bloodless bodies of the sadistic prick's victims flashed through his mind. The thought of Zeke touching Max's beautiful boy spurred him on, and he broke into a dead run, tracing down the corridor toward the main club in a blur of soundless light.

The door nearly flew off its hinges as Max charged into the club. He scanned the room frantically, his gaze settling on a large crowd that had gathered along the far wall. As he approached the crowd, he stumbled when he felt a faint beat in his chest. He quickened his steps, shoving people out of his way. He found Francisco kneeling on the floor, grief and anguish rolling off him in waves and tears glistening on his cheeks. *Mine!* Rage filled him so completely, his vision turned red as a laughing Zeke reached out a hand toward Francisco.

"*No!* Damn you, no!"

In a flash of unbridled fury lasting mere seconds, three vampires lay broken and crumpled against the far wall and the crowd began to scatter. Max fell to his knees in front of Francisco, his vision clearing as he reached out and wiped away a tear. Dazed dark eyes looked up at him from under wet lashes.

As Max took Francisco's hand in his, the club disappeared and he was no longer aware of anyone except *his* boy. A smile grew on Max's face as warmth he hadn't felt in years spread through him. *Dear God! Iunctiō Cōpula has to be true!* It felt as if his soul had found its other half and with it the promise of life.

"Francisco," he said reverently as he looked into wide, stunned eyes.

Max leaned in and gently wiped away the rest of the tears, his finger tingling with the contact. Max knew with that one touch, he would always protect him, care for him, and put no one above him.

"You're mine," he whispered adamantly, holding Francisco's gaze.

CISCO, STILL light-headed from fear and the quick turn of events, leaned back slightly and ran his hand along his cheek where Max had touched him, awed at how warm his flesh felt from an ice-cold finger. He blinked, stunned at the magnificent man in front of him. *My Master*, whispered through his mind.

The piercing blue eyes he recognized at once—they were the same as he'd seen each night in his dreams—but the rest of Max's face was new to Cisco and it was even more handsome than he'd imagined. Lean with a strong, chiseled chin and cheekbones under pale skin, it would make Michelangelo weep at its perfection. His thick black hair was pulled back away from his masculine face, a single untamed curl against his temple.

Cisco hung his head, the tears still damp on his cheeks. He should have fought harder, screamed, kicked, bit, something. His cowardice was inexcusable and he was too ashamed to hold Max's gaze.

"Francisco, do not turn your eyes from me," Max said softly as he tilted Cisco's head back up with a tip of one finger.

"You… you know my name?" he asked, stunned.

"But of course," Max responded with a small grin. "You are my Francisco, the one I have been waiting for. My Iunctiō Cōpula, the one who will make my heart beat again."

Was it possible? Could Max have felt the same thing he had when Cisco had first been captured by piercing blue eyes? *But how…. Why?* Benny's concern came back to him. "Can…." He cleared his dry throat. "Do you control my mind? Is that why I came to you?"

"Of course not." Max chuckled softly as he pulled Cisco to his feet and wrapped his arm around his waist. "Only a heart has the power to rule a mind. Your soul cried out and mine answered. Come with me."

Cisco wasn't sure he understood what was happening, and he couldn't begin to explain it. That same dreamlike quality he'd experienced the first time he'd seen Max swirled around Cisco. Only this time he wasn't 100 percent sure he was awake. Everything was surreal. Still, he allowed Max to lead him across the club. The way Max was looking at him as if he were precious was all he needed to know at this moment. He loved the way his stomach fluttered pleasingly when Max looked at him, the way his skin tingled when Max touched him. How he felt free and consumed at the same time when Max was near him. It felt right, as if he was finally where he belonged after being lost for so long.

Max stopped near the large man who had checked Cisco's ID and given him the warning. With his eyes glowing red and standing at his full height, chest puffed out, he was even more imposing. Max must have sensed Cisco's unease since he pulled him closer to his side. A protective sensation surrounded Cisco, and he eased against the cold, rock-hard body as if it were a pillow.

"Darius, call Angelo and have him help you take those three downstairs. I'll deal with them later," Max ordered.

Darius rolled his shoulders without taking his gaze from the carnage in front of him, a wicked grin curling his upper lip and showing off his razor-sharp fangs. "Be my pleasure," he responded, sounding almost gleeful.

Silently, Max led them past a heavy door and down a dark corridor. Cisco could barely see a foot in front of him, but he was surprisingly unafraid. They stopped once again in front of a large wooden door. Max turned the knob—revealing the room within, completely devoid of any light—and ushered Cisco in. He jumped when the door closed behind him, the sound amplified in the blackness that surrounded him. His head spun, and he was off balance when Max released him briefly and then grabbed his forearms.

"Did they hurt you?"

Cisco could feel Max's gaze upon him even in the pitch-black room, inspecting him by rolling his arms, then spinning him, obviously checking his back for injuries. "No, Sir," Cisco responded, then yelped when he was pitched forward.

Strong hands caught him, steadied him, and then were gone. A chill settled over Cisco, and without Max near him, fear began to slither down his spine and kick up his pulse. "Maximilian, Sir?" Cisco called out meekly and wrapped his arms around himself, the silent blackness weighing down on him, crushing him, and he began to tremble.

"I'm here."

Cisco turned to face the disembodied voice coming from the other side of the room. He hadn't so much as heard a rustle of clothing. A light came on, and Cisco instinctively shielded his eyes.

"I apologize, I forgot you cannot see in the dark."

"Limited senses," Cisco replied, trying to shrug off the unease, and slowly lowered his hand.

Vampires were at the top of the food chain for a reason. They possessed lightning-fast speed and reflexes, ability to see their prey even in utter blackness, and a sense of smell that rivaled any predator. Add those physical traits to the fact that they had logical, rational minds, keen intelligence, and it was baffling they had not taken over the planet. Cisco was sure the only reason they hadn't was due to their low numbers—mortality rate nearly 90 percent during the change—and inability to withstand sunlight.

Max came to him, a slight grin on his handsome face. The smile lit up Max's face, softened his features, and if at all possible, made him all the more appealing. Cisco would do anything to keep that look on his Max's face, even give his soul. Max began removing Cisco's harness, and Cisco's cheeks heated in embarrassment.

"It's okay," Max murmured as he dropped the harness to the floor and laid a gentle hand on Cisco's shoulder. "I will teach you all you need to know."

"I am eager to learn."

Max cupped Cisco's face with both his hands and stared into his eyes, making Cisco's knees go weak. "Give me your innocence and I will teach you to please your Master."

Cisco stared back, mesmerized by the flecks of gold that swirled within Max's blue eyes, and in that moment, everything became perfectly clear. He lowered his eyes respectfully, fell to his knees, and pressed his face against the well-formed thigh of his Master.

With absolute conviction he said, "It is yours to master."

# CHAPTER THREE

HIS MASTER'S fingers were gentle against Cisco's scalp, and he enjoyed the sensation of ease produced by kneeling at Max's feet and the way Max touched him. But the moment did not last.

All too soon Max tapped him on the shoulder. "On your feet, boy."

"Yes, Sir," Cisco responded, trying his best to keep the disappointment from his voice when Max once again moved away.

"Have a seat," Max instructed, waving a hand toward an ornately carved wooden chair. Max sat in the other chair—more like a finely carved throne with red crushed-velvet back and seat—on the opposite side of a massive desk.

Cisco did as he was told, sparing a moment to take in his surroundings. The office was opulent. Bookshelves were filled with leather-bound tomes that looked centuries old. Scattered among the books were a multitude of small bronze statues, crystal globes, and brass bells, as well as many other eclectic but artistic treasures. The entire place was decadent, a fitting office for such a powerful man.

There wasn't a shred of doubt within Cisco that he belonged to Max, would do anything asked of him, anything to make his Master proud. Yet, somehow he felt as if it wouldn't be enough. He'd never been outside the boundaries of Mecosta, never had a lover, and lacked proper schooling. Hell, he couldn't even wear a proper harness. What did he have to offer someone like Max?

"Your willingness to learn and your loyalty are all I expect from you at the moment."

Cisco's head snapped back toward Max and he met his gaze, mouth wide open in shock. "You can read my mind. Oh crap, does that mean you can control it as well?"

Max grinned knowingly. "I was not lying when I said I cannot control your mind. Nor can I read it. Only a heart can do that, which I do not possess yet."

"Yet?"

"United soul mates who share a blood tie can to some degree read each other's thoughts. However, I can get a sense of what you're feeling and I'm very perceptive."

Holding Max's gaze, Cisco kept his features neutral and concentrated hard, bringing to mind the hilarious joke Benny had told him. "What am I feeling now?"

Max's brow furrowed into a deep frown and he glared at Cisco. "You will soon discover I absolutely do not do parlor tricks nor am I here for your entertainment. Is that understood?"

Cisco instantly nodded and shrank into his chair, lowering his head in shame. *Oh. My. God! How fucking stupid*, he chastised himself silently. Why in the hell had he done something so ridiculous, childish?

"I'm sorry, it was stupid of—"

"It's okay," Max interrupted, the scornful expression morphing into something less menacing but still serious. "But you must understand, this is a very dangerous world you've entered. In my haste, I made a very grave error, and leaving is no longer an option for you."

"What do you mean, leaving isn't an option?" Not that he had much to go back to. He'd somehow always known his place was with Max, but to never see Benny again? His best friend had been the one constant in his life, the one person he knew without a shadow of a doubt he could count on to be there. The thought of not having him in his life was too…. No, he couldn't even put it into words.

"Francisco, I am very sorry," Max said gently. "I made a huge mistake tonight. I have ruled the city of Mecosta for the past twenty years, and during that time I have made many powerful enemies that would love nothing more than to take the reins of command from me. The display out in the club tonight, the tenderness I showed you, was foolish."

He remembered the way the man in the suit had gently stroked the hair of the man kneeling at his feet, had witnessed the tender moment. "I don't understand any of this," Cisco admitted. "Affection isn't allowed here?"

Max shook his head. "Not from me. Not toward you. Not yet." He sat back in his chair and folded his hands in his lap, looking the part of the Master he was, but his eyes held a spark of compassion in them. "There are those within the clan who would like to see me destroyed. With power comes danger from those who lust for it and who will stop at nothing to obtain it. Tonight I showed weakness among those who want my throne, and as such, I have put you in great peril."

Excitement to fear, fear to embarrassment, embarrassment to hope, and now his very life might be in jeopardy. So many emotions and one-eighty twists and turns had left Cisco dizzy and struggling to keep up with the quickly changing events of the evening. The conflicting feelings swirled within him, fighting for dominance until he was numb.

After a long moment of searching, trying to figure out what he was feeling, thinking, needing to understand, he found no answers nor any calm. He asked the only thing he could, "What can I do to help?"

Cisco hadn't expected Max to laugh, but that's exactly what he did, a loud, boisterous sound that only added to Cisco's confusion.

"It appears I have been sent a brave little mate. Then again, it shouldn't surprise me. You've never backed down even from those much bigger and meaner than yourself."

Cisco blinked at Max. "Excuse me?"

"I have kept a very close eye on you since that first night I saw you all those years ago."

"I knew it!" Cisco had always believed Max was watching him, protecting him; it was why he'd tried to live a good and pure life since his sixteenth birthday. But he hadn't been sure, and most of the time he'd been able to convince himself he was simply loco or indulging in wishful thinking.

Now that he knew the truth, Cisco had to ask. "Then why didn't you come for me? Make yourself known? I would have gladly come to you sooner."

"The laws of my clan are very clear on the union of vampire and human. You had to discover the bond between us and act upon it on your own. I could not interfere nor try to influence you in any way."

"But I've always known," Cisco interjected. "Even before seeing you, I knew I'd been waiting for something. The night I saw you outside Wicked Ground, I knew. I knew it wasn't something, but someone. You!" His voice rose with his frustration.

"I know the wait was difficult while you were too young to enter my world. But I knew you'd come. I've seen you many times standing outside the Wicked Grounds. Your longing expression is one I know all too well."

"Difficult is an understatement," Cisco huffed. All this time he'd waited, wasted, when he could have been with Max.

"Yes, the ties between soul mates can be quite strong. So powerful, in fact, it could be all consuming." A thoughtful expression crossed Max's face and he tapped a finger against his chin. "Hmm, what about Iunctiō Cōpula? Would a human feel the linking webs like that of a vampire and at such a young age? Interesting." Max had a faraway look in his eyes, and Cisco was pretty sure he was talking to himself.

"You mentioned this injection copala out in the club earlier. Something about it being real. What is it?"

"Yoonk-TEE-Oh Kope-You-Lay," Max corrected, accentuating each syllable. "The rules that govern vampires are very strict, but from what little I have discovered about Iunctiō Cōpula, I believe its rules are even stricter," Max said and jumped to his feet.

Cisco watched him hurry to a bookcase at the far end of the office. He couldn't see what Max was doing, but suddenly the bookcase opened, revealing a passageway behind it.

"Hurry, come with me." Max waved him over, and Cisco scrambled out of his chair without hesitation.

The short hall behind the case led to stairs that appeared to descend into a pit of nothingness. Cisco had never been a fan of the dark, a fear he'd had since he'd been a young boy. But it seemed there was a lot of darkness in Max's world and he'd better learn to conquer his fears if he was to be a part of Max's life. *You can do this.* Cisco took a deep breath, foot poised on the top stair. He swallowed hard. *One step at a time.* Unsure of himself, he looked back toward Max for reassurance. With a wave of Max's hand, the candles in the sconces on the wall flickered to life. Cisco froze in shock as he looked back and forth between Max and the candles. *Holy shit, he's fucking magic.*

"Okay, I admit, that one may have been a parlor trick." Max chuckled. "But a useful one."

Cisco was in awe. There was so little he knew of his Master's abilities, and if he were wise, he'd pay attention and learn quickly.

Max held out his arm with a flair. "After you."

Cisco made his way down the stone steps, and a small chamber opened up, illuminated by a multitude of candles. In the center of the round stone room stood a podium and upon it was a large leather-bound book. It appeared as if a face had been worked into the material as well as many unfamiliar symbols.

"This is a copy of the book of lore, the one which governs us," Max explained as he went to the podium and ran his finger reverently over the cover of the tome. "It is said that the original is bound in the skin of the first, the creator of my kind."

"Fascinating, but kind of creepy," Cisco said, wrinkling his nose.

"Yes, I suppose deer skin is much less creepy. The words, however, are an exact match. It's the only known book that makes reference to Iunctiō Cōpula."

"But what does Iunctiō Cōpula mean?"

"Iunctiō Cōpula is Latin and means 'uniting link,' which I believe is what has begun to happen between us." Max opened the book to a marked page and pointed to some handwritten text. "It doesn't actually say it specifically. This makes reference to an inscription found in the year 110 AD but was written in Archaic Latin in 54 BC from textual fragments so it may or may not have been deciphered correctly. I've been trying to authenticate it for decades but only have lore and rumors to go by."

Cisco was so fucking confused. He rubbed at his throbbing temples. He didn't know what he'd expected to happen when he walked through the doors of Wicked Ground, but the incident with Zeke, the violence Max committed against Cisco's tormentors, bonding links, soul mates, learning he could never go home—it was all too much. The events of the day crashed down on him and the throbbing increased, his vision blurring. Cisco stumbled back and released a heavy breath. The room spun wildly, flickers of light danced across his vision, a deafening roar filled his ears from the rush of blood, and then blackness overtook him.

MAX FELT the nauseating feeling of distress coming from Francisco in waves before his eyes rolled back in his head. Max caught his boy a split second before his head would have hit the hard stone floor, then cradled him in his arms. Unsure of what happened or what was wrong with Francisco, Max rushed up the stairs and laid the unconscious man on the chaise lounge. Francisco had no wounds Max could see, his breathing was deep, regular, and his heart beat in a steady rhythm. It was as if Francisco had simply fallen asleep.

Max grabbed his phone and waited impatiently until Angelo answered. "Get up here now!"

"Little busy here, Max," Angelo answered, voice sounding strained.

"Drop what you're doing and get up here. Francisco passed out and I have no idea what to do for him."

"Darius and I are trying to get Zeke restrained before he comes to."

"Dammit, Angelo, I need you here now!" Max growled. "Get someone else to take over for you and get your ass up here." Max ended the call and returned the phone to his pocket, confident Angelo would follow his order.

This wasn't how Max had envisioned his first evening with Francisco. He'd planned to take his seat at the head of the club as he always did, and watch his boy. Slowly, over days, weeks, even months, integrate Francisco into the club. Allow Francisco to work hard and earn his right to be kneeling at Max's feet. He would have waited, groomed, taught, guided until Francisco was ready, for however long it took. He would have no other. Yet, after seeing Zeke and Francisco, all Max's good intentions had flown out the window. He'd reacted with pure unbridled fury without thought for his actions and now he'd put Francisco at risk.

And still, on some level, he felt no regret in having to keep Francisco close.

Max looked down at Francisco's sleeping face and ran a hand over his damp brow. It was such an odd feeling to care for this young man. For a century he'd only cared about his own needs and well-being and that of his clan. In the same amount of time, he hadn't had to deal with such emotional trivialities like love and compassion. He hadn't felt them since waking up on the floor of an abandoned shed, forever changed. No heartbeat, no breath, only an instinctual need to survive. Those early days had been hard; he'd been more animal than human, and to some degree that was still true. But he quickly learned that for his kind to survive, they must act civilized; chaos and anarchy meant certain death. Max ruled harshly but fairly, yet without sympathy or even empathy, completely unemotional.

That was, until Francisco.

The warming sensation of a faint heartbeat when he'd spotted Francisco had irrevocably changed him. After one hundred years, there was finally someone he would put before all others, even himself. The truth of it was even more intense now that Francisco had entered his world and he could finally touch rather than watch from afar. Yet the feeling was still foreign, unfamiliar in its newness as was the phantom sensation of his beating heart.

"You broke your new pet already?" Angelo asked as he rushed through the door.

"He is not my pet and I have not done any such thing. He passed out," Max snapped with frustration.

Angelo moved closer, gaze transfixed on Francisco, and Max tensed, protectiveness and possessiveness rearing up so quickly and unexpectedly he leaped from the chaise and put himself between Angelo and Francisco.

"Whoa there, boss," Angelo said in surprise and stepped back, taking a submissive stance, head tilted and presenting his jugular. "I wasn't going to touch him."

"Fuck, I know you wouldn't hurt him." Max shook his head, then scrubbed a hand over his face. "I don't even know where the hell that came from."

"Yes, you do. We've witnessed enough vampires losing their fucking minds once bonded. It can seriously make you do some crazy shit." Angelo smirked and rolled his neck. "All I can say is I hope I never meet mine."

"Right now I'm apt to agree with you. We haven't even completed the blood bond and already I'm seriously losing it, Angelo." Max returned to the chaise and carefully lifted Francisco's head, taking a seat and then laying it gently in his lap.

"You think he's okay? Should I call Dr. Heine?"

"There doesn't seem to be anything wrong with him, other than he's out cold. I could feel his distress and confusion, even experienced his panic like this choking sensation. I think he just short-circuited with all the new information I was giving him. How bad do you think the fallout from the display in the club earlier is going to be?" Max asked.

He didn't need to elaborate; Angelo had witnessed Max's show of weakness. Angelo had been his right-hand man for over fifty years, and knowing him as well as he did, Max suspected the man was already trying to work out a damage-control plan.

"The beatdown you put on those three vamps, no one will question. Everyone knows Zeke and his cronies are ticking time bombs and will assume they deserved it. Exposing Francisco as your blood mate before you have given him a chance to settle and establish his place, well.... It isn't one of the brightest things you've done."

Max ran his hand through his hair, closing his eyes briefly. "I know, I didn't think, simply reacted."

"That's not like you, Max. You're methodical in everything you do."

"I know," Max muttered and hung his head. "What a fucking mess."

Max briefly considered telling Angelo about his belief that Francisco was his Iunctiō Cōpula, but just as quickly decided against it. While Angelo was aware of Max's search for some truth behind the elusive lore, his best friend already thought he was crazy in his quest for an impossible dream.

"Yeah, well, let me reiterate, I do not ever want to come across my blood mate." Angelo shuddered, a look of disgust on his face. "I've seen what it's done to you these past five years and thanks but no thanks. I'll pass on that craziness, thank you very much."

"It's not like I went in search of him; it just happened. But now we have bigger issues to deal with. With the grave error I made in exposing Francisco, we need to figure out how to protect him and prevent bloodshed."

Angelo tipped his head back, staring at the ceiling, jaw clenched. After a brief moment, he lowered his head and met Max's gaze. "Only way to truly protect him and keep Zeke or any other power-hungry vamp from going after him is to turn him."

"No!" Max shouted, then lowered his voice when Francisco whimpered in his sleep. "Angelo, dammit, it's too dangerous. Unless you can come up with a way to do it that will guarantee absolute success, I will not risk it."

Angelo walked to the liquor cart without further comment. He poured two snifters full of brandy, handing one to Max before taking the seat across from him.

Angelo swirled the dark amber fluid and took a large gulp before he said, "Well, if you're dead set against it, then our only other alternative is to prepare for one hell of a fucking war."

# Chapter Four

A FOG of confusion scattered Cisco's mind as he struggled to climb up out of the blackness. Everything was a blur. Nothing made sense until Max's voice cut through the haze, reminding him where he was and what had happened. He remembered the heaviness and spinning, had known he was going to pass out but was unable to stop it or even warn Max. Embarrassment heated his face, his gut churned, and he started to scramble up but held back when he heard another voice... an unfamiliar voice.... Max had called him Angelo?

*Wait.* They were talking about turning him into a vampire? Cisco had never even contemplated the idea. Having read an article about the high mortality rate, he didn't think it would ever be asked of him.

"Well, if you're dead set against it, then our only other alternative is to prepare for one hell of a fucking war."

Cisco sat upright. "Do it. Change me." Both Max and Angelo gave him strange looks.

"Are you okay?" Max asked.

"I'm fine. I think the events of the night, coupled with the lack of sleep or food the last couple of days finally caught up with me. But—"

"Let me order you some food," Max offered and pulled out his cell phone.

"No, really, I'm fine," Cisco assured him. He then turned to who he presumed was Angelo. He was sitting in a chair across from them, large—which didn't come as a surprise after the others he'd seen in the club—long blond hair pulled back from his regal face. He looked imposing, his steel gray eyes cold, yet somehow he seemed warm, safe, which made no sense at all. "You can avoid war if Max changes me?"

"Not happening," Max interrupted.

"But why not, if it would prevent strife and bloodshed among your clan?" It seemed like a no-brainer to Cisco.

"The chance you'd survive is not good," Angelo remarked.

"Yes, I know, 10 percent success rate, but that's still a chance. If you go to war, it's guaranteed some will die, right?"

"No!" Max growled.

"Well, technically we're already dead, so…." Angelo grinned.

Cisco scowled at him. "You're walking, talking, and can be destroyed. Fine, call it a second death."

"Doesn't matter, it's not going to happen, but you *are* going to eat and then sleep so what do you want?" Max asked, holding up his phone. When Cisco didn't answer right away, Max added, "I've cut you some leeway as this is your first time here, but no more. You do not, nor will you ever, involve yourself in the decision-making process for this clan. You will simply obey me. Is that understood?"

The expression on Max's face and the look in his eyes were enough for Cisco to cower back. The conversation was over, and he knew better than to agitate or question Max further.

"Yes, Sir."

"Good, now tell me what you'd like to eat now, or I will choose for you. And you will eat it, I assure you."

"Umm… umm. I like meat and potatoes."

Max nodded, then stood and walked away as he dialed.

"You'll do well to remember your place and your position. You now belong to Max, and you must follow his orders without question." Angelo cut a quick glance toward Max and lowered his voice. "Everything he does is for a reason and for the good of our race. You can either help him in his mission or be his destruction. Those are your only options."

Cisco's pulse sped and his skin prickled as fear grabbed hold of him. What the hell had he gotten himself into? Had he seriously thought he'd waltz into Wicked Ground, kneel at Max's feet, and his life would be fulfilling and complete? Apparently he had. Instead, everything seemed incredibly frightening and it added to the weight of worthlessness that was still pressing down on him. Even so, the need to be near Max was still the most powerful force of all.

"I don't know why I'm not running and screaming in terror. I should be," Cisco muttered without taking his gaze from Max. "But I can't."

"Because in this you do not have a choice. He is your destiny."

Cisco turned back to Angelo. "That makes no sense. I'm a human; I don't follow your laws, hell, I don't even know what they are. So why is it I feel as if I no longer have free will? That I have no choice in this, nor have I ever."

"Ah, but you do have free will. We all do, no matter if we are human or vampire. You can choose to obey or not, make him stronger or be his undoing. However, the pull you feel is the need to be near him that cannot be severed. You were born to be his," Angelo said matter-of-factly.

"How is that possible?"

"Your dinner will be here shortly," Max announced, rejoining them. He waved a hand at Angelo. "Leave us."

"Yes, sir." Angelo jumped to his feet and was gone.

"How are you feeling?" Max asked.

Cisco watched Angelo leaving, wishing he could ask him more questions, find out what he meant by *You were born to be his*. The idea of the truth in it was frightening. He swallowed hard past his dry throat. He tried his best to appear calm, but he couldn't stop the trembling in his limbs.

"I'm fine."

"You will discover I loathe being lied to," Max said sternly and took the seat Angelo had occupied.

Cisco pulled his feet up under him. He held Max's cold gaze, the urge to wrap his arms around himself huge, but he resisted, trying his best to remain brave, although he felt anything but.

"Physically I'm fine, but in all honesty, I'm really confused and, after overhearing your conversation with Angelo, scared shitless."

"You don't have to be afraid. I will never let any harm come to you, and your confusion will fade in time."

"Can I ask why not turning me will cause a war?"

Max leaned back in his chair and pulled the leather tie from his hair, letting the dark locks spill over his shoulders. He then ran his hand over the back of his neck as if rubbing away the tension.

"I've made a series of mistakes in my haste, worst of which was exposing you to my enemies."

"Yes, I understand that, but if the solution is in changing me—"

"I will not discuss this further."

"But—"

"Silence!" Max shouted, a flash of red evident in his eyes.

Cisco snapped his mouth shut, his own tension growing by leaps and bounds.

"There will be plenty of time for questions later." Max retied his hair and stood. "Come with me. I'll show you where you can wash up before your meal arrives."

Cisco suppressed the shudder that threatened from the cold, hard edge in Max's voice. He followed him silently through a side door and down yet another hallway. This one was decorated in the same ornate, old-world feel as Max's office but was modernized with overhead electric lights. Covering the walls were numerous paintings, depicting various men from different times in history. They reminded Cisco of those he'd seen at the museum of the presidents, only these portraits were from a much older period of time, reminiscent of kings and court.

"This will be your room," Max announced as he opened the door at the end of the hall.

Cisco stepped in and whistled. A large king-size four-poster bed with luxurious linens in shades of red and gold dominated the left side of the room. The same color scheme was repeated in the décor of what looked like a large open apartment rather than just a bedroom, an office, sitting and dining areas as well as a small kitchenette adding to the impression.

"The washroom is through those doors," Max said, pointing toward the only other door within the room.

"It's amazing," Cisco commented in awe as he continued to take in the grandeur of the room.

"I had it designed with your comfort in mind."

"Really?" Cisco asked, wide-eyed. "You did all this for me? I don't know what to say except you shouldn't have. It's too much."

Max tilted his head and frowned. "If you'd prefer a different room...."

"Oh no, this is great. It's just... I don't know, I imagined a pallet on the floor next to your bed."

"I do not sleep, nor will you be allowed to be with me when I retire at dawn."

"I—"

"Please use the facilities. Your dinner will arrive soon."

Max turned away, and Cisco's heart fell to his gut. Max was so cold. Gone was the man who had rescued him from his tormentors, the same man who had shown Cisco the book of lore with such excitement. Although Cisco wished otherwise, Max was showing himself to be the stereotypical vampire Benny had warned against.

"Yes, Sir." Cisco sighed and went to the bathroom. He splashed cool water on his face, but it did little to help with the redness in his eyes or the dark circles beneath them. Maybe after some food and a little sleep, he'd be better prepared to deal with his new life. At the moment he felt more like a fish out of water, struggling ineffectively to find his footing and unable to breathe due to panic and fear.

Yet….

This was where he belonged. He knew it in the pit of his gut. It felt right, even if it was scary as hell. He belonged to a very powerful vampire; he'd be a fool if he weren't scared.

Once he'd used the facilities and cleaned up, Cisco dried his hands and face and stepped out of the bathroom to find Max standing near the door to the hallway. "Everything you need is here. If there is anything else you require for your daily needs, all you have to do is ask."

"Thank you."

"Yes, then, come along. Your meal is being delivered to my office." He turned and headed down the hall.

Cisco hurried to catch up and followed Max, not daring to say a word. Back at Max's office, Max held the door for him, then closed it behind them and pointed toward the chair.

"Have a seat," he instructed before taking his own chair. Cisco did as he was told.

He did his best not to squirm in his chair as Max stared at him without saying a word. He could tell by the thoughtful expression on Max's face that he was choosing his words carefully. Max opened his mouth to speak, but whatever he was about to say was disrupted by a loud buzzing sound.

Max jabbed a finger into the button on the intercom. "What is it?"

"Sorry to bother you, boss, but there is someone out here at the front door causing a ruckus. Can I drain him?"

"Depends, Silas. Who is it?" Max grumbled.

"Says he's looking for Cisco and refuses to leave until he sees him. I gotta give this kid credit, he's a brave little shit. So can I drain him? I'm starving."

Cisco jumped to his feet. "Oh damn, it's Benny. I was supposed to call him within two hours." When Max looked at him impatiently, Cisco rushed to the desk and, placing his hands upon it, leaned in closer and looked at Max imploringly. "Please don't let him drain him. It's my best friend. I gotta talk to him. Please!"

"Bring him to my office," Max said into the intercom and then released the button.

"Thank you. I promised I would call him after two hours. Oh God! I know he's got to be worried, probably freaking out, and it makes him a little crazy," Cisco explained, rambling as the panic caused his voice to come out as a squeak.

"Sit!" Max demanded.

Cisco jerked and stumbled back, falling into the chair, shocked at the venom in Max's tone. "I'm sor—"

"Not another word." Max rose to his feet, stormed to the door, and flung it open.

Cisco could hear the heavy footfalls along the corridor and Benny's voice complaining about the rough treatment. Max's reaction to Benny's arrival was extreme in Cisco's opinion. It made no sense. Benny wasn't a threat.

The instant Benny was through the door, he yelled, "Cisco!" Benny tried to break free from his captor, but the tall, thin man—Silas, Cisco assumed—jerked Benny back.

"Not so fast, you little pain in the ass," Silas spat.

"Okay, look, Mr. Tall, Pale, and Pasty, I've had just about enough of you manhandling me," Benny complained, glaring up at Silas.

Cisco started to giggle. He couldn't help it. His relief was so profound it made him giddy, plus Benny never had had the good sense to be afraid of anything.

"Enough!" Max bellowed. Apparently he didn't find the same amusement in the situation as Cisco did.

Silas and Benny froze, and Cisco clamped a hand over his mouth to stop the laughter.

Max pointed at Benny. "You, don't move." He shoved at Silas's chest. "You, out, and send Angelo in."

Silas stumbled back and shot an evil look toward Benny before spinning on his heel and stomping off down the hall.

"That's right, pasty man, just keep—"

"Silence!" Max yelled and slammed the door hard enough the walls shook. "Sit down."

Obviously there was a sliver of self-preservation in Benny because he clamped his mouth shut and took a seat in the chair next to Cisco. Their gazes met, and Cisco tried to convey he was fine, but Benny was shooting daggers at him from narrowed eyes. His best friend was totally pissed off and for good reason. He'd only seen that look in Benny's eyes once and that was a few years ago when Cisco had accidently backed into Benny's prized muscle car. The look on Benny's face at the moment was far worse.

"I'm sorry," Cisco mouthed. Benny's response was to cross his arms over his chest and continue to glare at Cisco.

Max took his seat behind the desk, his eyes glowing and angry as he looked back and forth between Cisco and Benny. Cisco held his breath and didn't say a word, luckily neither did Benny. From the look in Max's eyes, Benny might not survive if he threw out a smartass comment like he normally did.

"One of you want to explain to me what the hell is going on?" Max asked.

Cisco and Benny both began speaking rapidly at the same time. Cisco tried his best to apologize to both of them for his actions, but his words were lost in the jumble of each of them trying to talk over the other, voices rising.

"Stop!" Max demanded.

The room instantly fell silent once more. Max had a pained expression on his face as he rubbed his forehead. If Cisco didn't know any better, he'd have sworn Max had a headache. But that was preposterous since Max didn't have a pulse. A man had to have blood rushing through his veins to have a headache, didn't he? Cisco cocked his head and watched Max as he continued to rub at his head and eyes.

What the hell did he know?

He'd spent years researching everything he could on vampires, but was quickly realizing the notion *If it's on the Internet, it must be true* was complete and utter bullshit. He knew zilch about Max or how or what a vampire could feel. He was clueless about the actual biological process.

Curiosity overrode Cisco's fear, and he asked, "Do you have a headache?"

Max glanced at Cisco, then dropped his hand and began thrumming his fingers on the desk, staring at Benny without responding to Cisco's question. "What am I going to do with you?"

"What the hell is that supposed to mean?" Benny responded angrily.

"You cannot stroll into my club and create such a disturbance. There will need to be repercussions for your actions," Max stated matter-of-factly.

"Bullshit! If anyone needs to be spanked, it's this dipshit here," Benny spat and stabbed a thumb in Cisco's direction.

"Hey, I said I was sorry. I was a little preoccupied and forgot." Cisco shifted in his chair until he was facing his friend directly. "You have no idea the stuff I've seen and endured in the last few hours, so you want to cut me a little slack here?"

"You?" Benny said incredulously. "I was manhandled by a guy who threatened to rip my throat out—"

"You should be used to that threat by now! You get on a roll and you never know when to shut up. You go on and on and on."

"Screw you, Cisco! I don't even know why I bother. I should have just left you here all alone and let them drain you," Benny countered. "Not that they would have gotten much from your scrawny little ass."

"Yeah, well—"

"Jesus fucking Christ, *stop*!" Max slammed both hands down on the desk. "Have neither of you any sense of survival?"

# CHAPTER FIVE

*WHAT THE hell have I gotten myself into*, Max thought, staring up at the ceiling as if he could find the answers there.

It had taken the better part of a century to bring order out of the anarchy of vampire society and just as long for him to control the chaos within him. It took Cisco only a few hours to strip Max of his hard-fought restraint. Max glanced at the clock: only five hours till dawn and he had much to do before he could rest, the first of which was dealing with his unwanted guest and seeing to Cisco's security.

Benny and Cisco were staring at him with wide-eyed expectant expressions. Surprisingly, what was absent was any trace of fear from either of them. Max could sense their unease and their irritation, but not fear.

"Why are you not afraid of me?" Max asked Benny.

"I was plenty scared—scared you or one of your bloodsucking buddies had drained my best friend. Now that I know he's okay, I'm just pissed." Benny turned his angry glare toward his friend. "Dammit, Cisco, the club was full of delicious-looking frat boys. You are such a cock blocker."

"Benny, I said I was sorry and I meant it," Cisco responded, sounding sincere. "Things were happening so fast and then I passed out."

"You passed out?" Benny asked in alarm. "What happened? Are you okay?"

"I'm fine," Cisco said meekly.

Max didn't miss that the daggers Benny had been shooting at Cisco through his big green eyes were now trained on Max. Max held up his hands in defense. "It wasn't me. It appears your friend here has forgone both sleep and food for quite some time."

Benny shook his head and let out a heavy breath. "I told you he was an idiot."

Cisco suddenly looked all the more guilty and then muttered, "Now probably isn't the best time to tell you I forgot my cell in your car, is it?"

"Oh dear lord," Benny exclaimed and threw up his hands.

"You two talk amongst yourselves. I need a drink." *A stiff one—* Benny and Cisco began sniping back and forth once again—*make that a double.*

Max went to the bar and considered the brandy for a moment, disregarded it, grabbed the whiskey, and poured a good measure. He threw it back in one large gulp and then poured another. He swirled the amber fluid in his glass, longing for a time when alcohol had warmed his belly and dulled his senses. These days he got little more than a tingling sensation but enjoyed the taste and the memory of what it had once done, helping to calm him nonetheless. Perhaps one day he'd once again be able to enjoy such indulgences.

He glanced at Cisco, who was animatedly pleading his case to Benny, and even through Max's ire, he could feel the sensation of a faint heartbeat—or maybe it was only the memory of what once was, like how he remembered the alcohol. Perhaps one day very soon, it would be real, a dream come true.

God, to feel true warmth again. To hear his heart beating within his chest. To truly feel something other than anger, lust, and hunger.

A knock on the door pulled Max from his musings. He opened it to find Patrick outside with a large tray of silver-domed dishes. Max stepped back and allowed him entrance. "You can set it there on the table." Max pointed to the small writing table.

"Yes, sir," Patrick responded, keeping his gaze respectfully low.

Patrick was a couple years older than Cisco and had the same small stature, but where Cisco had dark hair and eyes with a deep olive complexion, Patrick was blond-haired, blue-eyed, and pale-skinned. Patrick belonged to Silas, was completely submissive, and a very good boy. *The perfect boy to see to Cisco's human needs*, Max contemplated.

"Thank you, Patrick. Would you mind if I ask a favor of you?"

"But of course, sir. You only need to ask."

"Do you see that dark-haired young man over there arguing with his friend?"

"Yes, sir," Patrick responded, looking toward Cisco and grinning slyly.

"He belongs to me."

"Really?" Patrick asked in surprise and looked up at Max with a shocked expression, but then caught himself quickly and hung his head. "Sorry, sir."

"Yes, yes, I know he's quite chatty, but he does indeed belong to me. Cisco will need three meals delivered to his apartment daily. Could you make sure his favorites are prepared and that he actually eats? I'll have a list sent to you and inform your Master of your new duties."

"It would be my honor, sir," Patrick responded and bowed.

"Very well, I'll make arrangements with security. You can begin tomorrow."

"Yes, sir. Thank you, sir. Will there be anything else?"

Max glanced at Benny and Cisco. "Not unless you happen to have a couple of gags in your pocket."

"No, sir," Patrick giggled. "I am sure I can find you a couple, though."

"No, that's all right. That is all, Patrick."

Patrick bowed again and hurried out the door. Max turned his attentions back to the two men. So engrossed in their conversation, Max doubted either Benny or Cisco had even been aware of Patrick's presence. Damn, Max wasn't sure how or if he could separate the two. He was going to need backup on this one. He pulled his cell out and dialed Angelo.

Angelo answered on the first ring. "Hey, boss."

"What's taking you so long?"

"Silas just gave me your instructions."

"You want to hurry? I have a bit of a situation."

"On my way." The line went dead, and seconds later, Angelo traced through the door. He stood in a combative stance, scanning the area wildly.

Max couldn't help it, he began to laugh. "Glad to see I can depend on you to be quick, but it's not that kind of situation." He pointed toward Cisco and Benny.

Angelo's nostrils flared, his expression going from wary to intrigued in an instant. "Who is that?" Angelo asked, gaze glued to Benny.

"From what I can gather from their insufferable babbling, he is more than simply Cisco's friend, but a best friend," Max responded, watching Angelo's reactions with interest.

"He smells amazingly delicious," Angelo murmured.

"Have you not seen him with Cisco before?" Max inquired curiously.

"No, I'm sure I would have remembered that scent." Angelo took in another deep breath and then shuddered.

Max considered Angelo's unusual response for a moment and then shook it off. He had other things to worry about at the moment. "I'm sure he'll be overjoyed another bloodsucker wishes to drain him," Max theorized.

Angelo looked as if he were in a daze as he continued to stare at Benny. *Great, now I must endure both the garrulous and the catatonic.* Max slapped Angelo on the chest. "Stop it. One situation at a time, please."

Angelo shuddered again and then turned his back on Cisco and Benny. "Sorry, it's been a while. I must need to feed," Angelo apologized.

Angelo Rigaud, noblesse d'épée—nobility of the sword—was a direct descendant from the house of Sebastiano-Amadeus and he took his heritage seriously. He was a warrior, steadfastly dedicated to law and order and rarely had time for "common folks" or giving in to temptations of the flesh. So it was astonishing—to say the least—that a young human man would elicit any type of response from Angelo.

Max motioned toward the duo with a wave of his hand. "C'mon and help me get rid of the jabber mouth, and then you may go feed."

Angelo pursed his lips, looking quite uncomfortable, but nodded his agreement.

Max laid a hand on Cisco's shoulder. "I hate to interrupt such lively conversation, but your dinner is getting cold and I'm sure your friend here would like to get back to his frat boys. Angelo will make sure you have safe passage out of the club, Benny."

Benny raked his gaze up and down Angelo's large body, a defiant expression on his young face. "I don't need a chaperone." He rose from his chair and looked at Cisco. "I'll give you a ride."

"I'm…." Cisco looked up nervously at Max. "I'm staying here, Benny."

"Cool by me. I'm dying to get back to the club. But come grab your cell out of the car so you can call me in the morning."

"That won't be necessary," Max interrupted. "I will provide one for him."

"Whatever." Benny rolled his eyes, obviously directed at Max, but he didn't turn away from Cisco. "So call me, yeah? There's a marathon of zombie flicks on TV tomorrow. We'll kick back, nurse our hangovers, and share details of our nights."

Cisco shook his head. "I'm not coming home, Benny."

"What do you mean?"

"I belong here. I won't be coming home."

Benny tilted his head. "Ever?"

Cisco shook his head again.

"What the hell, man? You don't even know this guy," Benny protested, stabbing a finger in Max's direction. He then pointed at Angelo. "Mr. Stick-Up-His-Ass there looks shady as fuck. I mean seriously, a night to get your freak on is one thing, but I don't think you should trust them, Cisco."

Angelo tensed, and Max moved slightly to put himself between him and Benny. He didn't know what was going on with Angelo, what was making him so on edge. If the man clenched his jaw any tighter, teeth risked being shattered. Max worried the situation was about to turn bad—quickly.

"It's time for you to leave," Max insisted and grabbed Benny's arm.

"Don't fucking touch me, bloodsucker." Benny jerked away, chest puffed up defiantly. "Who in the hell do you—"

"Benny," Cisco said imploringly, going to his feet and laying both hands on Benny's chest. "Please, just go home. I'll talk to you later."

"But—"

"I'll be fine, I promise. I'll call you in the morning, okay?"

Benny glared at both Max and Angelo, but then his gaze settled on Cisco and his expression softened. "Are you sure?"

"I am. Trust me, please."

"I trust you. It's the bloodsuckers I don't trust." Benny hugged Cisco.

*Mine!* Max fought the urge to rip Cisco away from Benny. He knew they were merely friends, logically knew Benny was no threat to him and Cisco, but instinct didn't give a shit about logic.

"Stop calling them that," Cisco chastised Benny and then shoved him back. "Now go have fun and stop being such a worrywart."

"Angelo will escort you to the door," Max informed Benny and then wrapped his arm around Cisco, pulling him in close to his side. Benny started to open his mouth, but Max held up his free hand. "I insist."

Benny stood still, the look of defiance never wavering. Max had to give the kid credit, he was brave, that was for damn sure. He also appreciated how protective Benny was of Cisco, even if his inner green-eyed monster wasn't real happy about it.

When Benny didn't look as if he were going to budge, Max added, "No harm will come to him. I promise you. I will protect Cisco with every ounce of my being."

Benny's shoulders slumped and he blew out a heavy breath. "Fine." He poked Cisco in the chest. "But you better fucking call me in the morning, or I'll be charging the gates again, got it?"

"Yes, Mom." Cisco chuckled. "Now go have fun."

"All right, Bloods—"

"Benny!" Cisco snapped.

"I mean, Mr. Stick-Up-His-Ass," Benny amended with a shrug. "Walk me out."

Angelo made a growling sound, but he didn't respond to Benny's rude name-calling. Max grabbed on to the back of Angelo's shirt as he started to go after Benny.

"What?" Angelo snapped.

"He is to make it out the doors without a hair on his head being harmed. Is that understood?" Angelo's glare was icy, but Max could practically hear the wheels in the vamp's head spinning. "Nor a single drop of blood is to be shed."

"You coming, vamp?" Benny called from outside the door.

Angelo growled again and stormed off.

"Not one hair, Angelo," Max reminded him.

"Yeah, yeah, yeah," Angelo grumbled and slammed the door behind him.

"Your friend needs to learn some manners," Max said coldly and then turned his back on Cisco to hide his grin. It would do no good to let Cisco think such behavior was tolerated. "Now come and eat before it gets cold."

"Yes, Sir."

Arms crossed over his chest, Max leaned his shoulder against the wall, watching Cisco as he ate and ignoring his own hunger, a feat nearly impossible with Cisco's sweet scent filling Max's nostrils and the steady *thump, thump, thump* of Cisco's heart filling his ears. His anger at himself, his growing hunger, as well as the guilt churning unpleasantly in his gut were all making it difficult to control his temper. He wanted to lash out, to roar in frustration, and to rid himself of the ache of hunger. If only he could have one small taste, a sip….

Max shook his head and pushed away from the wall so he could pace. He curled his hands into fists, opening and closing them several times as he struggled with the discord in his soul. Animal battling man.

"Would you like some?" Cisco asked cautiously as he pointed at his plate.

Max stopped briefly to look upon Cisco's meal and wrinkled his nose in disgust at the burnt cow flesh and cooked potatoes. "I do not eat food."

Cisco's shoulders slumped, and he averted his gaze, but not before Max witnessed the pain within them. "I'm sorry, I forgot."

Max sighed. "It is I who am sorry." He took the seat next to Cisco. When Cisco continued to sit motionlessly staring at his plate, Max reached over and lifted Cisco's chin with the tip of his finger. "It is not you I am angry with. It is myself."

"I don't understand," Cisco admitted and pushed away his half-eaten dinner.

Max shoved the plate back. "You must eat."

"I've had enough. My—"

"Cisco, it is imperative that you keep up your strength, which means you must eat as well as rest."

"I'll eat a big breakfast, I promise."

Cisco had a hard time holding Max's gaze. The dark circles beneath Cisco's eyes were also witness to the man's exhaustion. Max had already apologized and somewhat explained what had set off his ire. He and Cisco would have plenty of time to discuss it as well as what was expected of Cisco at a later time. For the moment, Max had other pressing matters he must attend to.

Max laid his hand against Cisco's cheek and brushed his thumb gently over the dusky hue beneath Cisco's eyes. "You need sleep."

"I don't know if I can," Cisco replied quietly.

"You must try." Max stood and held out his hand. "Come, I will get you situated in your room and we can talk later."

Cisco took Max's hand, allowing himself to be pulled along, but he sounded hesitant when he said, "You're not staying with me?"

"I'm sorry, but I cannot. There are matters that need my attention before dawn."

"What am I supposed to do while you sle—I mean retire?"

Max could feel the apprehension and fear rolling off Cisco in waves. He pulled the trembling man closer to his side as they walked down the hall. There were many new things both of them had to learn about the other, but once they set up a routine, he was sure everything would be fine. "I cannot change my wake patterns, so you will have to adjust yours to become a night owl like me. In the meantime, wait for me," Max said easily.

"Yes, Sir." Cisco yawned. "Always."

# CHAPTER SIX

MAX LEFT Cisco tucked away in his room, sleeping. Cisco was curled up beneath the covers, oblivious to the dangers that awaited him. His trusting nature triggered Max's protective instincts. He'd been watching the young man for a very long time, but never had he had him in such close proximity. Cisco's nearness elevated all Max's instincts, the most prominent his need to possess and protect.

"Mind if I make a suggestion?" Angelo asked as they walked down the underground passage to the dungeon area.

"You've never needed my permission to give me your opinion before," Max countered.

"Good point," Angelo chuckled. "But seriously, Max. If you're a wise man, and I know you are, Zeke will be meeting the sun come dawn."

Max stopped and faced his friend. "On what grounds?"

"On the grounds that he's a threat to everything we've worked so hard to accomplish. The strides we've made in integrating vampires into human society. It's not right that it could be undone by one vampire two steps away from bloodlust. No one around here would have a problem with Zeke being returned to the filth from which he came."

Max knew the truth in Angelo's statement. Zeke was a danger to anyone unfortunate enough to come in contact with him. The problem was Max had no grounds on which to condemn the man to death. Zeke hadn't actually broken any vampire laws. If Zeke were just any vampire on the edge of bloodlust, he might actually take Angelo's suggestions and carry them out. However, Zeke had very powerful friends on the council. His death would be investigated and the ramifications could be…. No, he couldn't risk it.

Max nodded and patted Angelo on the shoulder. "I'll take your suggestion into consideration."

"Max, dammit, I'm serious," Angelo stressed adamantly.

"I know, as am I. Come on, let's go see what Zeke has to say for himself."

Angelo fell back into step with Max, grumbling under his breath.

"What was that?"

"I just don't understand you," Angelo admitted.

"Me?" Max said innocently. "I'm an open book and you know me better than anyone. What else do you need to know?"

"Well, tell me this, what in the hell is the good in being the boss if you can't break a few rules once in a while?"

"Who says I don't," Max countered, then pushed the door open to the antechamber, holding it for Angelo. "After you."

As Angelo stepped past him, Max could have sworn he saw his sulking friend roll his eyes. Angelo would deny it; he found the act to be rude and uncivilized. Nearly two hundred years removed from his noble birth and Angelo still held on to his aristocratic ways.

"I think I'm finally beginning to rub off on you. Only took fifty years," Max teased.

"Help us all if that is true," Angelo tossed back over his shoulder.

The easy banter faded away as Angelo typed in the code for the interior chamber. Zeke was definitely no laughing matter.

Zeke and the other two vamps who had dared to taunt Cisco were secured to the wall by heavy ropes of hemp infused with lead and made an even more powerful tool against the unnatural strength of a vampire by being soaked in rosemary oil. Hemp, lead, and rosemary were all substances with properties intolerable to vampires; together they would keep the prisoners drugged and sluggish.

Zeke raised his head, wincing as the low wattage ultraviolet light trained upon him burned his eyes. He closed them before speaking. "About damn time you graced me with your presence," Zeke growled.

Max lowered his shades but was still careful to stand behind the lamps. "Ah, well, you'll have to forgive me, Zeke, I had more pressing matters to attend to."

"Coddling your new pet?" Zeke spat.

Max's anger began to burn hot within him, the memory of the sight he'd witnessed in the club rushing back to him. The look of grief contorting Cisco's features, the tears streaming down his face. Max clenched his hands into fists, fighting against the urge to rip Zeke's throat out or, better yet, to crank up the lights and fry Zeke's worthless ass on the spot. But Max was unwilling to stoop to Zeke's level, to give him a reason, proof that violence was the only way their kind would survive, thrive. Max picked up a pair of thick gloves from the table and slid them on.

"That is none of your concern," Max said nonchalantly, though he felt anything but.

"Well, stop fucking around and cut me loose. You have no right to keep me here. I've done nothing wrong."

"You created a disturbance within my club," Max reminded him. "Put your hands on something that did not belong to you."

"Oh bullshit. I did no such thing. I struck up a conversation with an unclaimed human, which was my right to do within the rules of your club." Zeke cocked his head, his lip curling into an ugly sneer. "That is unless you no longer wish to abide by your own rules?"

It was an old argument. The need for rules versus the desires of the strong to rule. Max and Zeke were on opposite sides of the debate. Their mission since first meeting back in the thirties was to prove the other wrong. Max refused to make it easy for Zeke or to give in to the son of a bitch.

"Lights please, Angelo," Max said as he cut the power to the UV lamps. They did not need the light to see; even a weakened vamp's vision was as acute in the dark as most humans' in the daylight. However, it would cause Zeke and his cronies Tim and Dan pain after the UV lights were extinguished and help to keep them under control.

Max removed the bindings from Tim first, who slumped against the wall, breathing harshly as soon as he was free but making no attempt to flee. Max then removed the ropes from Dan before addressing them both.

"I suggest you two find better friends to associate with. Now get the fuck out of my sight."

It was actually quite amazing how quickly the two vamps traced out of the room considering their weakened state. What wasn't surprising was that neither glanced at Zeke nor seemed concerned about what would happen to their friend. Max decided right then and there that Tim and Dan had no loyalty and could never be trusted in the future.

Max turned his attentions to Zeke and undid the tie around his left foot.

"What are you doing?" Angelo asked incredulously.

"Unfortunately, he is right. He's done nothing for which we can charge him or detain him any longer. Zeke has been punished for his slight and must be released."

Max removed the tie from Zeke's other foot.

"Then make something up," Angelo implored. "He's done enough shit in the past ten years you could charge him as a habitual offender. I mean seriously, Max, look at his eyes. You turn him loose and you'll be having the cops knocking down your door for harboring a fucking serial killer."

"Well, well, well, Angelo. I do believe you are afraid of me," Zeke said snidely.

In a flash Angelo had his hand clamped around Zeke's throat, their noses practically touching. "I don't fear you. I loathe you and everything you stand for," Angelo said, seething.

For a long, tense moment, the two vamps stared at each other, Max keeping close, ready to break it up before anything went too far.

"You're sexy as fuck when you get angry," Zeke murmured and planted a big sloppy kiss on Angelo's lips.

Angelo jerked back, a look of disgust on his face, and swiped his hand over his mouth. "You son of a bitch."

Zeke's laughter filled the chamber.

Angelo started to go at Zeke again, but Max blocked him. "Okay, you two, that's enough."

Max splayed his hands on Angelo's chest, felt the tension in the muscles, felt their trembling. Angelo glared at Zeke. It was quite obvious the fury ignited in Angelo by Zeke's laughter and taunt was blurring everything but the need for blood, including his position.

Max shoved him. "I mean it. Step the fuck down, Angelo."

Angelo continued to focus on Zeke for a second longer—eyes blazing with contempt—and then he abruptly spun and stomped away.

"That's right, noble boy, do as you're tol—"

Max rounded on Zeke, fisting his hands in Zeke's hair, tugging sharply. "You say one more fucking word to him and I will let him rip you to shreds, is that understood?" Max asked angrily.

Zeke hesitated, holding Max's deadly glare, no doubt contemplating his options. Zeke wasn't a complete idiot, he had to have seen the venom and conviction in Max's eyes and came to the only smart decision he could: he stayed silent and nodded.

Max released the grip he had on Zeke's hair and patted his chest. "Good boy," he commented without attempting to disguise the contempt in his voice.

Max removed the tie from Zeke's right wrist and then the left but held on to Zeke's wrist. "I do not want you to come within fifty feet of Cisco."

Zeke tried to pull away, but Max held fast. "Why the hell not? The rules clearly state any unclaimed boy entering the club is up for grabs. I saw him first."

Max's hold tightened until Zeke winced and tried to shrug away from the pain. "Cisco is mine," Max growled. "You stay away from him and you might survive another day."

Zeke's jaw was clenched so tightly it looked as if it would shatter, but he didn't back down. Somewhere he found the strength to overcome the pain and showed no fear in the face of Max's fury.

"It doesn't surprise me that you are finally dropping the bullshit about 'rules are made to be followed.' I told you we are not to be ruled and oppressed so stringently."

*Fuck!* Max released Zeke as if his touch had burned into Max. He would not play this game with Zeke, nor would he allow the bastard to make this an issue of the validity of his position.

"You seem to have forgotten the little clause in which any vampire can challenge another over feeding rights. I thought I'd spare you the agony of defeat, but if you wish to go ahead with the challenge, I'll be more than happy to oblige you."

"You're challenging me? You're willing to fight to the death for that scrawny kid?" Zeke responded disbelievingly.

"Only if you insist on taking me up on my offer." Max leaned in close, his tone seething. "I hope you do. It would bring me great pleasure to destroy you."

Zeke studied him for a moment, his glowing red eyes boring into Max. "He's not worth the effort," Zeke hissed.

"Nor are you," Max threw back and stormed from the room.

He had to come up with a legal way in which to ban Zeke or, better yet, something he could use against the man to have him condemned. Going to the king would do him no good; regardless of what proof he had, the king would side with Zeke. No, there were bigger issues brewing and he must tread lightly until he was ready to approach the council. Once he did, Zeke would no longer be a problem. In the meantime, he would make sure Cisco was sheltered from anything and anyone that could cause him harm.

Max pulled his cell from his pocket as he made his way through the labyrinth of tunnels. "Silas, get your ass down to the dungeon and make sure Zeke leaves the club," Max demanded as soon as Silas answered.

"Yes, sir. Who would you like me to get to watch the door?"

"I don't give a fuck, just do what you're told." Max ended the call and shoved the phone back in his pocket.

He stomped down the concrete tunnels, his angry footfalls echoing around him. He had half a mind to beat his own dumb skull in. What had he been thinking when he exposed Cisco the way he had? He hadn't been thinking was the fucking problem. It shouldn't be Zeke, Angelo, or even Silas who had to endure Max's wrath, but his own foolish self. Blame assigned, now he only needed to figure out what the hell to do next.

The easiest solution would be to complete the blood tie with Cisco, establishing his exclusive rights to his boy, but he couldn't. Not yet. He needed more information on Iunctiō Cōpula, as he had no idea whether it could only be achieved by nonbonded blood mates. Perhaps it was part of the process, to be completed at a specific time and place.

No, he couldn't chance it. He'd need to be vigilant in his protection of Cisco, as he had no doubt Zeke would make it his mission to steal Cisco from him.

Unease danced along Max's spine, and he quickened his steps. He'd waited five years for Cisco. Truth be told, he'd waited for his beautiful boy since the day he'd been turned, only he hadn't known it at the time. He'd been looking for something, anything to take away the pain and the ugliness of his new—he couldn't call it a life as he no longer had one—existence, and he'd finally found what he'd sought in Cisco.

Max rushed through the door of Cisco's room as the panic reached a fevered pitch and then nearly collapsed in relief when he spotted Cisco curled up on his side, still fast asleep. Silently, he moved to stand over Cisco and gently ran a finger across his brow.

Somehow he was going to have to teach Cisco how to protect himself against a being that could snap him in half like a twig, while at the same time teaching him how to kneel at Max's feet in a display of complete submission. Cisco would be pushed to extremes on both sides of the spectrum.

*I hope you don't end up hating me for what I'm about to put you through.*

# CHAPTER SEVEN

CISCO AWOKE surrounded by a soft, comfy cloud of down and silk. He stretched his arms above his head, yawned, and then buried himself beneath the comforter, snuggling into the mattress. Sleep beckoned him to return, the warmth and softness too alluring to deny.

A shuffling noise and what sounded like glasses clinking had Cisco grudgingly peeking out from beneath his cocoon of blankets. It took him a second before his eyes adjusted to the bright sun-filled room enough to make out a small figure setting out dishes on the dining table. The scent of bacon and warm bread caused his belly to growl.

"That smells good," Cisco commented, pushing down the covers and sitting up, resting his back against the headboard.

"Oh!" The stranger turned quickly, dropping the mug in his hands, but it only bounced a couple of times before he got hold of it once again.

"Good thing you hadn't already poured coffee. That could have been quite painful." Cisco chuckled.

"I know, right?" the stranger said, sounding relieved. "I'm sorry. I didn't mean to wake you, but Max insisted your breakfast be delivered promptly at 8:00 a.m. I'm Patrick, your personal waiter and bringer of sustenance."

"I'm not much of a morning person," Cisco admitted. "I don't normally eat breakfast, but I'd love a cup of coffee, maybe some juice."

"You gotta eat," Patrick insisted as he poured a steaming mug of coffee. "Cream and sugar?"

"Yes, please, two of each, but really, coffee is enough."

Patrick added the cream and sugar and then brought the coffee to Cisco, who accepted it happily. Cisco inhaled deeply, the rich aroma helping to burn off some of the fog of sleep. The first sip worked even better.

"Skipping breakfast is not an option," Patrick remarked, going back to the table and removing silver covers from plates. The scents of bacon and yeast became even stronger in the room. "You can eat, or I can feed you, your choice. But either way, you're eating. Boss's orders."

It did smell delicious, and who was Cisco to go against the boss's orders? He had a feeling to do so would be futile. In the short time he'd been with Max, Cisco already knew the vampire was not the kind who took no for an answer. While he'd glimpsed a softer side to Max, Cisco had quickly figured out that the man had a short fuse. Max could go from calm to raging mad in less than a second. He'd witnessed the icy glare, the violence, the danger. He didn't ever want to be the cause of any of those reactions ever again.

"I'll eat at the table." Cisco set his mug on the bedside stand and threw off the covers.

Patrick glanced Cisco's way and grinned. Only then did Cisco look down and realize he was butt-ass naked. His cheeks heated and he snatched the covers back over himself.

Patrick's smile grew and he shrugged. "You ain't got nothing I haven't already seen. Your red cheeks are cute as hell, but sadly they won't last long."

"I don't know about that. I've never been much of an exhibitionist."

Patrick gave him a disbelieving look and then laughed as he shook his head. "Well, aren't you just too adorable for words?"

"What can I say?" Cisco shrugged. "I haven't had a lot of experience with flashing my junk."

"You will soon enough and you better learn to like it, or at least get used to it. Most of the Doms in this club, including yours, rarely allow their boys to wear much in the way of clothing. Now c'mon before your breakfast gets cold."

Cisco quickly scanned the area looking for his pants, then sighed when he spotted a stack of clothes sitting on the end of the bed. He pulled on the T-shirt, boxers, and sweatpants. All were brand-new and fit perfectly, as if they'd been bought specifically for him, which was ridiculous considering Max had only left him a few hours before dawn and not many stores were open in Mecosta at 3:00 a.m., and none that sold clothes.

He picked his mug back up and made his way to the table, sitting down in front of a heaping plate of eggs, bacon, hash browns, and toast. A second plate was filled with pancakes and still another with fresh berries and melon.

"Damn! You planning on feeding an army?" Cisco asked as he laid a napkin across his lap and picked up the fork.

"Nope, just you," Patrick responded.

"No way can I eat all this."

Patrick took the seat across from Cisco and poured a cup of coffee, blowing on the steam before taking a tentative sip. "Better try," Patrick said and took another sip. "I'm to stay with you until you eat it all."

Cisco picked up the plate of pancakes and set them down in front of Patrick. "Then you better help me, or we'll both be stuck here for a damn long time." Patrick looked nervous as he considered the plate and then Cisco. "Go on, it will be our little secret. I'll tell Max I ate it all," Cisco encouraged. "It's either that or I'll be flushing it, because seriously, dude, I can't eat all this." Cisco handed him the fork from the fruit plate.

Patrick hesitated for a second, but finally took the offered fork. "What the hell. I don't mind a few extra swats."

"What? You're going to get hit if I don't eat everything? Are you serious?"

Patrick cut a hunk of pancake and stabbed it with his fork. "Don't look so alarmed, I get off on it," he said, then popped the food into his mouth, chewing behind his grin. "Master Silas has a very good hand."

"Is that your man—I mean vamp—ugh! I mean Dom?" Cisco sputtered, stopping his silly babbling by taking a big bite of egg.

"Don't worry about it, you'll get used to the way in which to address them. I belong to Silas, he's my Dom and Master. Max rules us all and deserves to be addressed with the utmost respect. Oh, and they hate the term bloodsucker or undead. I also suggest you never, ever refer to Max as a vamp, at least not where he can hear you, unless you get off on pain too."

Cisco considered Patrick's words carefully. Did he like pain? Would he be able to handle it, or would he break quickly? And if so, would Max find him unworthy? Cast him aside? *Oh fuck! What about being bitten?* Did it hurt? Would he be left feeling drained? What about recovery time?

The sound of his fork hitting his plate echoed around the room as Cisco grabbed his cup of juice, taking a big gulp to try to wash down the bile that rose up in his throat.

"Hey! You okay?" Patrick sounded concerned. "You're as white as a ghost."

Cisco tried to respond but couldn't, the nausea intensifying, and he took another big drink and then a deep breath. He took another, then another before he could answer. "Yeah, I'm okay, I think. I just realized I am in way over my head. I don't know shit about the life here or even what is expected of me."

Patrick reached over the table and snagged a strip of bacon, munching on it as he spoke. "Don't sweat it. You have the honor of belonging to the most powerful vampire in town, also the hottest. Don't tell anyone I said that, especially Silas. He can be a wee bit jealous. Anyway, just do what you're told and everything will be fine."

Cisco began to tremble as the enormity of his new life overwhelmed him, and Patrick's blasé attitude did nothing to help. "What if I can't? I have no idea what to do, what I should and shouldn't do or say. Jesus, Patrick, I've never even met a vampire before last night."

"Wow, you're really in for a treat."

"What do you mean?"

"Eat and I'll fill you in on the joys of living here," Patrick offered.

"I don't—"

"It's not open for negotiation. You help me by keeping my word to Max, and I'll tell you what I can about him."

Cisco picked up his toast and took a bite. It felt like sludge on his tongue and his stomach roiled in protest, but he forced it down. He needed all the help he could get before he made a damn fool out of himself. He took another big bite.

"Wise decision," Patrick remarked with a curt nod. "So, as the human sub to a vampire, you'll be expected to follow every command he gives you without hesitation and without question. Please him and feed him are your only purposes in life. In doing so you will be rewarded beyond your wildest dreams."

"Does it hurt?" Cisco asked meekly.

Patrick cocked his head and stared at Cisco as if he'd grown a second head. Patrick then shook his head. "You do realize you're in a BDSM club, don't you? You know, leather, cuffs, floggers? Bullwhips? Dom, sub, pleasure versus pain?"

"No, I thought I was at Disneyland," Cisco responded sarcastically. He might not have ever experienced the lifestyle, but he wasn't a complete idiot, he'd done his research. It was the biting thing he was clueless about. "You'll have to forgive me here, but not too many clubs have members with supernatural strength and razor-sharp teeth who want to feed off me."

Patrick laughed and raised his mug. "Touché."

"So does it?" Cisco pressed.

"Have you ever been denied an orgasm? You know for a really, really long time, all the while being teased unmercifully until you think you'll lose your mind? And then, when he finally fucks you through the mattress and you're allowed to come with him, you lose your mind because it feels so goddamn good your head explodes. This one"—Patrick pointed to his crotch and then to his head—"and this one feels like it could."

Cisco wasn't about to admit he was a virgin. He had a very vivid imagination, a capable hand, and he wasn't inexperienced when it came to toys. He nodded because he did know what a good orgasm felt like. When he closed his eyes and imagined it was Max fucking him, it damn sure made his dick explode and his toes curl.

"The vampire kiss is even better. It's different, it's not going to make you orgasm, though it certainly could, but it's the only thing I can think of to compare how much pleasure I experience when Silas feeds."

"Jesus."

"Yup," Patrick said with a wide grin. "You don't have to fear his bite. What you need to worry about is getting addicted to the high it produces. A V-junkie will willingly allow a vampire to drain them. Chasing the BBH."

"BBH?"

"Bigger and Better High," Patrick clarified.

"Ah, got ya." Cisco munched on his toast absently as he pondered Patrick's statement. It really must be one hell of a high if a person was willing to die for it. Then again, many had died with a needle in their arms chasing the high. Still, Cisco couldn't ever imagine anything that felt good enough that he would be willing to die for it. "Does that happen a lot? I mean the draining thing."

"From what I understand, it used to happen quite a bit. It's one of the things Max and Angelo have worked so hard to stop. Not just for the humans' sakes, but for the vampires' as well. A vampire who gives in to bloodlust is a very dangerous being, one that cannot be controlled. It's like a rabid animal, the only thing you can do is put it down." Patrick shrugged. "Or in this case, set it out to meet the sun."

"I'll keep my fingers crossed I never come across one of those."

"You already have."

"What?" Cisco asked in alarm and choked on his toast.

"Easy there," Patrick said and handed him his juice.

Cisco got his coughing under control and took a sip of juice to wash down the stuck food. "Who? When?"

"Zeke."

Just the mention of the man's name who had approached him in the club made Cisco shudder. The way the vamp had looked at him, the sickening look on his face. "Wh-why hasn't he been put down?" Cisco shuddered again.

"Technically, Zeke isn't in bloodlust, but he's certainly on the verge of it. You can always tell one by the color of their eyes. If they are deep red, stay away from them, better yet, fucking scream and I guarantee Max will be at your side in a blink of an eye. Whatever you do, don't try to run from one, that just excites them, and trust me, you can't outrun a vampire."

Cisco glanced down, surprised he'd cleaned his plate. He set it aside and grabbed his coffee mug, wrapping his hands around it as a chill settled over him. "I've seen Max's eyes turn red. Does that—"

"No, and neither is any other vampire in this club," Patrick interrupted. "Vampires' eyes will flash red when they are really pissed off or while feeding. Those in bloodlust are always red."

Cisco huffed out a pent-up breath. "That's a relief."

"Yeah, you don't have much to worry about as far as your safety is concerned while within the walls of Wicked Ground. Max has a very impressive security system."

"Is that true during the day as well?"

Patrick took the mug from Cisco, set it aside, and then plopped the plate of fruit in front of Cisco. "Eat."

Cisco gave him an exasperated look but shoved a large piece of melon in his mouth, chewing noisily and showing off the food. Patrick stared at him with an arched brow but didn't comment on Cisco's piggish behavior. Cisco realized he was being stupid, stopped the childish behavior, and took another piece of melon. Only then did Patrick answer his question.

"Obviously, Max isn't the only one who is unavailable during the day. No vampire can resist the call of the grave at dawn. While they are below ground, we have a security force that rivals any SWAT team and it's easier to break into Fort Knox than it is this place. You are totally safe. Silas explained that you got thrown into this world without a lot of info. I can answer some of your questions as far as the daily routine of the club, ease some of your fears. But for the really big questions like what's expected of you, how to behave, favorite positions, implements, you'll have to ask Max those." Patrick yawned and poured more coffee into his mug and then topped off Cisco's. "Sorry, I'm usually in bed at this time of day so I'm a little sluggish."

Cisco finished the last of the berries and held up his empty plate. "All done, now you can go to bed."

"No can do," Patrick responded. He stacked the empty dishes, silverware, and plate covers.

"Why not?"

"I'm to see to your needs, and while it's an honor to serve Max, do you mind learning the ropes quickly and getting on Max's schedule? I'm so not a morning person," he explained and yawned again.

"I won't sleep until Max does at dawn tomorrow," Cisco assured him. "I'm not usually a morning person either."

"Good man. I have a few errands to run for Silas before lunch, but we can pick up our conversation then."

"Sounds good." In fact it sounded really good. It gave him plenty of time to take a nice long shower, shave, and process what all had taken place since walking through the doors—he glanced over at the clock. Wow, had it only been just over twelve hours? So much had happened. No wonder he was still feeling off balance. He probably would for some time to come.

Cisco helped Patrick load the cart and then followed him to the door. He was a little taken aback when Patrick rapped his knuckles against the door, even more surprised when the door was opened by an unfamiliar man dressed in a black T-shirt, cargo pants, and holding a large gun that was strapped around him.

Cisco took a step back. "What the hell?"

"I told you Max had an impressive security team." Patrick chuckled. "This is Andrew. He's your personal bodyguard today."

"Nice to meet you," Andrew said with a curt nod.

"Hi." Cisco waved and then leaned over to whisper in Patrick's ear. "Am I locked in here? Like a prisoner."

"Of course not," Patrick assured him with a small smile. "You can leave the room and Andrew will follow you wherever you go. But honestly, I wouldn't advise it. This place can be a little difficult to navigate without a tour guide. Go take a hot bath, relax, I'll be back at noon, okay?"

"Yeah, okay. See you then."

"Don't look so freaked-out." Patrick patted Cisco on the back as he passed.

"I'll try not to."

"You are about to embark on the greatest journey of your life. Smile," Patrick tossed over his shoulder.

"Will there be anything else, sir?" Andrew asked.

Cisco shook his head. "No, not at the moment, thank you."

"Very well, just knock if you need anything. I'll be right outside the door," Andrew informed him and then closed the door, the lock engaging with a resounding clunk.

Cisco leaned against the wall. His legs were like rubber and his heart was beating fast. He slid down the wall and wrapped his arms around his knees. "Servants, people forcing me to eat, sleep, crazy red-eyed vampires, and armed guards? Jesus, this place is going to be harder to get used to than I thought."


THE THICK steam swirled around Cisco as he wiggled his toes, the bubbles tickling as they popped and dispersed. Lying back against the tub, he grabbed his new cell phone from the ledge and dialed Benny's number.

"Hello? Cisco, is that you?"

"Yeah, it's me. Sorry I didn't call earlier, I thought I'd let you sleep in. I figured you'd need a little recovery time from your frat-boy bash."

"Don't play cute with me. You knew I'd be too worried to enjoy my evening. You owe me big-time, you little shit."

"I was totally safe. You should have gone and enjoyed yourself. Max promised nothing bad would happen to me."

"Oh, and I'm supposed to trust the word of a stranger, a bloodsucking freak, no less."

"Benny," Cisco snapped in irritation. "Stop calling him that. I don't expect you to trust him, but can you at least give me a little credit? Trust me a little?"

There was silence at the other end of the line, but Cisco didn't press. He wouldn't stop trying to alleviate Benny's fears, but his best friend was going to have to get used to the fact that he'd chosen to be there of his own free will. Benny would either have to respect that or... well, he also had to convince Benny he was committed to his decision and that it was the right one for him.

"I don't know, Cisco. I'm just really not comfortable with all this stuff, ya know?"

"I do know, Benny. But he's kept his promise so far. He's provided me with a cell phone and obviously since I'm calling you, nothing bad has happened to me. In fact, I have this amazingly elegant suite with anything and everything I could possibly want. Hell, Benny, I even have my own personal waiter and bodyguard. Nothing is going to happen to me." When Benny didn't respond, Cisco added, "I'll tell you what, I'll talk to Max tonight, set up a time for you to come over, let me show you around and see for yourself the security he has in place."

"Yeah, if you're committed to this craziness, then I guess I have to trust you."

"Thanks and we'll get together soon, I promise."

"Hey, Ben, have you seen my shirt?" asked a faraway voice Cisco didn't recognize.

"I don't know where your clothes are, look under the bed, sheesh." Benny's voice was muffled as if he'd covered the phone with his hand.

"Too worried, huh?" Cisco teased.

"Shut up," Benny grumbled. "This isn't about me, it's about you causing me gray hair."

"Uh-huh."

"Hold on, let me get rid of… umm…. Hey, you, what's your name again? Ow! Hey, baby, stop throwing shit, I was just teasing. Cisco, I'll call you right back."

"Okay," Cisco snorted.

"Stop laughing and I mean it, I'll call you back."

"I'll be here."

Cisco set the phone aside; still laughing, he slid down into the tub until the bubbles tickled his chin. If he knew Benny, and he did, his friend wouldn't be calling back right away. If Benny liked the stranger enough to let him stay the night, he would want to get his freak on again this morning before he let the guy leave. Cisco had plenty of time to soak in a nice, quiet, peaceful tub. Considering Benny had called the guy baby, Benny and what's-his-name were definitely going to get their freak on. If the guy believed Benny's bullshit, that was.

# CHAPTER EIGHT

THE INSTANT the sun disappeared beyond the horizon, the grave released its hold on Max and his eyes flew open. His first conscious thought was of Cisco and his need to be with him, the desire nearly crushing him. Max pushed up from his bed and sat on the edge as he fought the urge to race from the room and check on Cisco. No, he could no longer give in to instinct. Angelo was right, he had to act logically, ensure his planning was methodical as it always had been. To think any other way was sure to have deadly consequences.

Forcing one foot in front of the other, Max walked into the bathroom and stripped out of his clothes. Following his usual morning routine, he set the taps on the shower just this side of scalding and stepped beneath the hot spray. He was so cold he shivered even with the heat. He stayed where he was long after he'd washed his body and hair, but the heat of the water couldn't reach the chill that settled within him nor did it do any good to combat the heaviness weighing down on him. He sluggishly stepped from the shower, wrapped a thick towel around his shoulders, and used a second one to run down his torso and legs. He dumped the wet towels in the hamper, still shivering, even once dry.

His stupidity in not having fed last night caused his hands to tremble, and he struggled to pull on his pants, his fingers clumsy as he fastened them up. He was momentarily disoriented when the material of his shirt covered his head and he fell heavily onto the bed, the room spinning out of control. Max squeezed his eyes shut and grabbed his head with both his hands.

"I must feed."

The thought of feeding from anyone but Cisco was unappealing, yet he must. He couldn't put his boy or his clan at risk because of his foolishness. He wouldn't be able to protect, lead, or function in his weakened state.

Summoning the last of his strength, he put on his knee-high boots, fingers protesting and clumsy. Nevertheless he managed it as well as tying his hair back with a leather strip. The effort was almost too much, and he doubled over as pain shot through his stomach. Dammit, he'd waited too long. He stumbled to the door, swaying as he pressed his hand to the lock. The light from the print scanner burning his eyes, he turned his head to shield them and then stumbled through the door when the lock disengaged.

"Whoa there." Angelo grunted as Max's weight crashed into him.

"I—"

"Don't talk. Let's get you back in your room."

"I must get to Cisco." Max clung to Angelo, the pain maddening, robbing him of his strength. Angelo dumped him on the bed, but he didn't even have enough strength to pick up his head.

"Cisco is safe. How long as it been since you fed?"

"A day or two," Max slurred.

"Bullshit. What the hell is wrong with you, waiting so long to feed? Can you imagine what would happen if one of your enemies saw you in this condition?"

"That's why I have you," Max retorted. His gut cramped and his muscles contracted painfully, causing him to cry out in agony.

"I'll be right back."

"No. You can't bring them here." No one was allowed in his chamber. Angelo was the only one to have ever seen the interior. He couldn't risk it.

"I wasn't going to bring them here." Angelo sounded offended. "I was only going to bring you a small fix."

"That won't be necessary. Help me up."

"Max."

He pushed past the agony and weakness and pulled himself to a seated position, but not without great difficulty and pain. "I did this to myself. The least I can do is to suffer a bit and get my ass up."

"For fuck's sake, you're a stubborn man. You know what I should do is sit back, watch you struggle, and laugh my ass off at your foolishness. Maybe remind you that I did tell you so."

"Yes, but finding humor in my discomfort is below you, dear Angelo."

"Yes, well…."

Max grinned when Angelo slid an arm around Max's waist, giving him his strength as they made it out of the room and down the hall. "You're so good to me."

"Lucky for you, I like you." Angelo sniffed. "We'll take the back passage to your office."

Max was aware of his feet moving, but he struggled to understand what was happening, going in and out of awareness, flashes, blurs of light, muffled words, pain, hunger, consuming. Death clawed at him, pulling him down further and further until there was only misery. Max no longer knew head from toe, hand from foot, his entire body made of torment.

A glimmer of light, faint heat. *Cisco.* The thought of his boy was enough to push Max through the sludge, work his way to the surface. Warmth, glorious warmth. Fangs piercing flesh. Max clung to the heat, the coppery scent arousing him, the first pull, sparks on his tongue, igniting him. He sucked in earnest, took the life-giving substance into himself. Each pull, each drop, chased away the cold, the pain, the blackness.

"Max."

Max held his prey tighter, sucked harder.

"Goddammit, stop!"

Max roared, snapped his teeth when the heat was pulled away. *Fight.* He lashed out, battled to regain his meal, spurred on by the memory of the agony that only seconds ago had threatened to destroy him. *More.*

His head slammed against something hard, pain flaring, and he wrestled to free himself from the tight binds. He fought harder, screamed, snapped, but he couldn't throw off his attacker.

"Max, stop. It's okay, it's me."

Max stilled, a familiar voice cutting through the fury.

"That's it. I've got ya."

"Angelo?" The binds on his arms loosened and the weight against his back eased.

"Jesus, Max."

Max's vision cleared and he stumbled back in shock. A ghostly pale young man with a look of terror on his face was on his knees and held a hand to his neck, blood seeping from around his fingers.

"What the fuck have I done?" Max rushed to the boy, who tried to scramble away. "Wait, stop. I won't hurt you." *Stupid thing to say since I've obviously already hurt the man.* "Let me see."

"I got this, Max. You go get washed up and I'll take him to Dr. Heine's."

"I...." Max looked up at Angelo and then back at the young man, fear still shining in his eyes. "I don't know what came over me."

"Everything will be fine," Angelo assured him. "Get yourself together and I'll be right back."

Max nodded. He pushed to his feet and fell back into his chair. He was losing it at a time when he couldn't afford to. He'd made one stupid mistake after another in the last few days. His lack of control put everyone at risk. He'd nearly killed that boy. The reality of it was sobering, the realization that it could have been Cisco, frightening. He must put aside his selfish quest for Iunctiō Cōpula until he reestablished his control and power. The one thing he couldn't ignore or change was his desire for Cisco, but he could control it, let it propel him to do the right thing and prepare his boy, provide for his safety, and crush any challenge to his ownership of Cisco.

Eager to get back to Cisco, Max pushed up from his chair and began to pace. He needed a plan, a clear-cut way to reestablish his power and ensure Cisco's safety. First he must begin to prepare his boy for his role at his side. His followers would demand he show his ability to rule and that included his ability to control that which was his. Cisco. He must become the perfect submissive. Those he ruled would accept nothing less. If he couldn't dominate his own house, how would others be confident in his ability to rule them?

They wouldn't.

That was it. He had to establish Cisco's place within the clan, which was at his Master's feet. Secondly, he had to remove any seed of doubt that might have been planted within the club in reference to his ability to rule. A show of strength. Then and only then could he continue with his quest for Iunctiō Cōpula.

Max stopped midstep as Angelo reentered the room. "How is the boy?"

"Dr. Heine says he'll be fine, and I've wiped all memory of the event. But how are you doing?"

"I'm far from okay, but I will be," he assured Angelo. He grasped his hands behind his back and began pacing again. "We need to reestablish my power. Quash any doubt. Set up a regular feeding schedule. Make sure you procure plenty of willing humans. I do not want to feed from the same person twice. If worse comes to worse, please make sure Dr. Heine has a full stock of donor blood. I will be quite busy preparing Cisco. I don't believe I will allow him in the club tonight, but for sure tomorrow night. He must be seen at my side. And I want to know immediately of any rumors of a challenge to my claim on him. Is that understood?"

"Good to hear you sound more like yourself." Angelo smiled and took a seat on the couch, hands behind his head. "What are you going to tell Cisco?"

"Cisco doesn't need to know anything but his place."

Angelo's smile widened. "What else do you need me to do?"

"Cisco will need a proper collar, cuffs, and attire. Be sure to send the leatherworker in to see me tonight, say… three. That should give me plenty of time to get the club's affairs in order."

"Yes, sir."

"That will be all," Max informed him dismissively, already working out his plan for Cisco in his head. "If you need me, I'll be in Cisco's apartment."

He didn't wait to hear Angelo's response, tracing out of the room and to Cisco's door in a blink of an eye. He started to open it and then thought better of it. He cut a glance at Andrew, who was guarding the door. "You are relieved of your duties."

"Yes, sir."

Once Andrew had disappeared down the hall, Max rapped his knuckles against it instead. Next time he wouldn't knock; Cisco would be expecting him and waiting.

"Umm… Andrew, is that you?"

"No, it is Max."

The door flew open. "Please come in, Sir. I've been waiting for you."

"Good evening, Cisco. I hope your day was acceptable," Max remarked as he entered the room. He smelled the remnant odors of food, soap, and a hint of Patrick, but it was Cisco's scent that was most rewarding.

"Yes, thank you, Sir. Patrick made sure I was well fed and not without company. Thank you for arranging it for me."

"And did you get some rest today?" Max asked as he continued to survey the room, looking, watching for anything out of place, hints of a breach in security.

Cisco stood in the middle of the room, looking unsure as he wrung his hands nervously. "Yes, Sir."

"And you had proper nourishment?"

"Yes, Sir. Patrick was quite insistent that I eat everything."

"Patrick was merely following my orders. He's a good boy." Max took a seat on the couch. "Join me." He waved a hand to the chair opposite the couch.

"Yes, Sir," Cisco responded without hesitation and hurried to the chair. He sat erect, hands in his lap, head held high and gaze respectfully low.

Max leisurely took in his boy. Cisco was dressed in the clothes he'd requested Patrick set out for Cisco. Black leather pants, white silk dress shirt, and his feet bare as Max had ordered. Cisco had also bathed; Max could smell the hints of sandalwood soap and the scent of the citrus shampoo. It was frustrating having his boy's scent masked.

"I don't like your smell being hidden from me. From now on I wish for you to only bathe with unscented products. I will make sure they are at your disposal."

"Yes, Sir. Sorry, Sir."

"From this moment on, you will no longer be sleeping at night. You must adapt to my schedule quickly and without question. Is that understood?"

"Yes, Sir."

Max could feel Cisco's unease growing, filling the room with a bitter aroma. The last thing he wanted to do was cause his boy distress, but… "It will do little good for me to apologize again for the situation you now find yourself in. It bothers me that you are upset, and if I could change it, I would. However, there are more important things to attend to. The most pressing is keeping you safe, and in order to do that, I must prepare you to take your position at my side. Is that understood?"

Cisco nodded. "Yes, Sir."

The unease didn't dissipate from the air, but as tough as it was, Max couldn't dwell on it. As Cisco became more familiar with his surroundings and his new role, at least the confusion and fear of the unknown would ease.

"At the moment there are things that need my immediate attention." Max pushed to his feet. The thought of leaving Cisco even for an hour didn't settle well with him. He would have a difficult time focusing. Yet he didn't dare take his boy into the club. He wasn't prepared, too many variables, too many things could go wrong. No, he could not take Cisco into the club, but…. An idea forming, he smiled. He could spend a little more time with Cisco, an opportunity to begin to teach his boy his place. "Have you had dinner?"

"Yes, Sir."

"Very good. Come along, then. You'll accompany me to my office."

"Yes, Sir."

Max wrapped his arm around Cisco's waist and pulled him close as they made their way down the hall. He was most content when he was touching his boy, something he hadn't felt in a very, very long time.

"I know everything is a little disorienting right now, but I promise you, I am going to do what I can to ease your confusion. Just know that you are the most important thing in my world and everything I do from this moment on is for your own good. Understand?"

A wide grin spread across Cisco's face and the happiness filled the air around them. "I understand, Sir. That means a lot to me."

At the door to his office, Max stopped and turned to look down at Cisco. He used the tip of his index finger to lift his boy's chin until his face was upturned. "Look at me." Cisco slowly raised his beautiful dark brown eyes. "I need you to trust me."

"I do, Sir."

Max leaned down and pressed a gentle kiss to Cisco's lips. It was the last show of kindness he could indulge in until they were again alone. Max opened the door and ushered him in.

A PARADE of both vampires and humans came in and out of Max's office, all the while Cisco knelt next to Max's chair, hands clasped behind his back, eyes low. He'd tried to pay attention to the conversations, but they'd begun to run together, and to be honest they were quite boring. Ordering food from the local distributor, beer and liquor from another, paper supplies from yet another. Then there were the updates from the security team, the accountant, and from a physician. The last did grab Cisco's attention. For the first time, Max had moved to the other side of the room, instructing Cisco to remain where he was, as Max spoke to the doctor in whispered tones that Cisco couldn't make out. Still, he hadn't dwelled on it for long.

An ache had settled in his lower back from keeping his posture so rigid and his knees throbbed painfully. He didn't dare shift his position or ask Max if he could perhaps stretch out on the couch, which would have been heavenly. This was a test. He was sure of it. He had been instructed to assume a display position, not to move and not to speak until Max released him. He could do this. Somehow he had to figure out how to overcome the small aches and pains, endure them.

This was only a small sample of what was sure to come now that he belonged to Max. He'd done his research, gotten a glimpse of others within the club, the act behind the curtain. It was a preview. Cisco's heart sped as he remembered the large muscular man pounding into what he'd originally thought was a female. Remembered how his arousal had grown, his cock hardened when her true identity was revealed. The way her hard dick had slid in and out of the submissive's mouth while the other slammed into her. He couldn't wait to be the source of Max's pleasure. To feel his Master's cock against his tongue, taste him, drink him down. Cisco clamped down on the shiver that threatened as his body heated, his cock hardening as he imagined himself on his knees, Max fucking his mouth. Cisco closed his eyes, the images in his mind vivid. His pulse sped faster, a rush of blood roaring in his ears, body thrumming.

His eyes flew open when Max's hand landed on his head and began stroking his hair. In that moment he remembered that Max could feel his emotions and his cheeks heated. He snuck a glance in Max's direction out the corner of his eye, but Max's expression was neutral as he studied the papers before him.

*Okay, no more mind porn.*

He took deep breaths in through his nose and blew them out slowly, willing his rushing pulse to slow. It was a struggle to keep his mind clear and get himself under control, but he finally obtained a reasonable calm. The effort paid off in other ways as well. His knees were numb and the kink in his back quiet. He bit his lower lip to keep from smiling. He'd figured out one way to deal with pain. Imagining Max naked and aroused was enough to block out anything and everything but Max.

# CHAPTER NINE

THE CLUB was packed as Max strolled through the door. Before he could take two steps, a young human male—Mario, he believed the man's name was—with big green hopeful eyes rushed toward him and dropped to his knees.

"Is there anything I can do to please you, Sir?" Mario asked, clutching Max's thigh.

The man stunk of arousal and desperation. With a flick of his wrist, Max sent him flying across the room, crashing into a table. No one was allowed to touch him without his permission. He'd seen Mario numerous times in the club, the man obviously knew the rules, but his addiction to the high of a vampire kiss had made him reckless. In Max's opinion, they—like a vampire lost to bloodlust—were worthless and a danger to the fragile peace among the two species.

Each step he took, men dropped to their knees, but Max ignored them all. He wasn't in the mood to play the game tonight. The sooner he got this over with, the sooner he could get back to Cisco and start preparing him to be the one kneeling at Max's side. Having Cisco in his rightful place would disappoint many of the subs who had all been vying for the position. However, it would also stop the swarms of boys buzzing around like annoying gnats.

Standing at the end of the bar, Max summoned Silas, who was serving a customer at the other end, with a wave of his hand.

"Good evening, Max," Silas said in greeting.

"Evening. How is everything?"

"Club's hopping, good mix," Silas commented. "So far we haven't had any problems."

"We may have a potential one brewing. Could you make sure someone escorts Mario out of the club? I believe he has forgotten himself and the rules. Be sure he is reminded of his place before he leaves."

"Yes, sir."

Max glanced around the club, not finding anything that grabbed his attention, nor did he find the one face he was looking for. He hoped the bastard had gotten the message and was smart enough not to return anytime soon. Never would suit Max just fine, but he knew that wasn't going to happen.

"Have you seen Zeke tonight?"

"He's in there," Silas said, pointing to the second room in the line of private chambers.

Max frowned, still staring at the drawn curtain. "Who's he in there with?"

"Cora and some new kid looking for the double-V treatment."

Corcoran—Cora Cockblock, as she would come to be known—started her acting career as a young boy playing female roles in the early nineteenth century, and decades later, after she was turned, went on to become the star of a successful drag show in New Orleans. She occasionally performed for the members of Wicked Ground. That Cora was in the back room having a threesome wasn't unusual, but that she was back there with Zeke rather than her lover, was.

"What's all that about?" Max asked, frown deepening as his wariness increased.

"Don't know, but you could ask George. He's down there."

Max followed where Silas was indicating with a nod, and found George sitting at the end of the bar, throwing back a shot. "Thanks. I won't be staying long. If you need anything, contact Angelo. I am not to be disturbed," Max ordered without taking his gaze from George.

George Wheeler was the complete opposite of his lover. Cora was outgoing, educated and loved sparkly things. Her motto: the shinier the better. George was gruff and unrefined, a bit of an introvert. The only shiny thing he liked was the chrome on his Harley. Yet the two had connected instantly when they'd met and had become inseparable. Whatever was going on, it couldn't end in any other way but bad.

Max slid into the seat next to George. "How's it going?"

"Fine," George grumbled and slammed his glass on the bar. "Silas, bring me the whole fucking bottle."

"Doesn't sound like things are fine."

"I said I was fucking fine," George snarled and raised his glass again.

Before George could slam the glass down on the bar again, Max grabbed his forearm. George glared at Max, his eyes flashing red with rage.

"Take it down a notch," Max said, keeping his voice low and calm, a tone that broached no argument. "You do not want to do this."

George continued to glare at Max until the red began to dissipate and the tension in his arm eased. Only then did Max release him. George turned away and hung his head. "I'm sorry, Max."

Keeping his movements slow, Max laid his hand on George's back. "You want to tell me what's going on?"

"Just paying off a debt."

"You made a deal with Zeke?" Max asked incredulously. "That's like making a deal with the devil himself. Hell that's worse."

"You don't think I know this? I haven't dealt with him in a long time, but the bastard has a very long memory," George responded sadly.

Max was curious as to what kind of debt George was into Zeke for that he'd agree to share his lover with him. George and Cora had been lovers for over twenty years and often added a human submissive into their play. Cora had explained that since they both had Dominant tendencies, it was fun to bring in a third on occasion. And a vampire had to feed, so why not make it pleasurable for everyone. But George hated Zeke almost as much as he hated sharing Cora with other vampires. However, although Max's interest was piqued, he wouldn't ask the details. It wasn't his business.

Silas brought over a bottle of whiskey, filled George's glass and then set the bottle down. He gave Max a questioning look, but Max didn't have time to acknowledge it. A roar of cheers and clapping had Max whipping around to see what the commotion was all about.

"Fucking hell," Max growled through gritted teeth.

The curtain to the room Zeke and Cora were in was now wide open. It was difficult to see what was happening as many of the club patrons were now on their feet, trying to get a look, but Max got glimpses of a sight he knew was going to cause one hell of a reaction in George. Zeke wasn't fucking Cora, which was a good thing; he was pounding into the submissive. What wasn't such a good thing, in fact was a really, really bad fucking thing was that Cora was on her knees, hands behind her back, while each thrust of Zeke's hips shoved the human's cock into her mouth. It was a humiliating position for any Dominant vampire. Proof that Zeke was doing it on purpose was the big grin on his face as he looked out at the crowd.

George knew it too. Max caught him around the waist at the last second before he could rush to the room. George was like a wild man in his arms: screaming, snapping, and snarling. Max had a hard time holding on to the man. Luckily, Silas jumped the bar and stood in front of George, hands on his chest pushing him back and blocking his view of what was happening.

"Let me go," George howled.

It took both Max and Silas to hold on to George when Zeke's boisterous laughter filled the club. "Close that fucking curtain," Max bellowed. He couldn't do anything about Zeke's behavior since he wasn't actually doing anything wrong. George had given him permission to have sex with Cora, and she had to have agreed or she wouldn't be there.

"George, man, c'mon, look at me," Silas said calmly. "He's trying to rile you up."

"I'm going to kill him," George responded, still struggling in a futile attempt to free himself. "How dare he disrespect her like that?"

Max and Silas held on until George wore himself out and gave up the fight. He wrapped his arms around Silas and rested his forehead against Silas's shoulder. "That's it, man, let it go," Silas said soothingly and stroked his hand across George's hair. "He's not worth it, man."

Max continued to hold George until he was sure he wasn't going to start fighting again. He met Silas's gaze. "I'm going to go take care of this. You got him?"

Silas nodded.

Rage simmering deep inside his gut, Max stomped over to the room, pushing his way through the crowd. At the door, he pointed at Zeke. "Get the fuck out of my club."

Zeke smiled, then pulled up his pants and fastened them. "Good evening, Max," he said smugly.

Max's fury burned bright, and his hands itched to make contact and wipe that look off the bastard's face. Instead he curled them into fists, fighting the urge. With the large crowd still gathered around, he couldn't afford to lose control. "I'll tell you one more time to get out of my club before I have you removed." He took a step closer to Zeke, eyes blazing. "It's the last choice you'll get."

Zeke studied him for a moment while he continued to straighten his clothes. "Not because you told me to, but I'll leave for now. I have other things to attend to." He shot a disgusted look toward Cora and then pushed past Max, bumping his shoulder as he went.

"Zeke," Max called out.

The arrogant asshole stopped but didn't turn around in a show of complete disrespect. The crowd began to whisper to each other, no doubt shocked at Zeke's out-of-control behavior. Zeke had thrown down the gauntlet, and Max scooped it up. In the blink of an eye, his chest was pressed against Zeke's back, his hand clutching Zeke's throat.

Max squeezed hard as he leaned in and whispered against Zeke's ear. "Challenge accepted."

Zeke tensed with apparent surprise but recovered quickly. It was what Zeke wanted, and Max was done playing fucking games. He had to take care of the threat Zeke posed once and for all.

"What challenge is that?" Zeke drawled, trying to sound nonchalant, but Max heard the slight tremor in his voice. Whether it was from fear or anticipation, Max wasn't sure. If the man was smart, it was fear, but Zeke had never been too bright.

"You want my power, come and get it. But until you do, you will obey me. That's two strikes. You create a disturbance in my club again, and I will personally take you out. Is that understood?"

Zeke turned his head just enough that Max could see his grin. "Understood," he said with a wink. "Now do you mind taking your hand off my throat so I can obey your order and leave?"

God, it would be so easy to rip Zeke's throat out. Tear him to pieces and leave him to suffer until sunrise. Zeke was nothing more than a rabid mongrel, and if he didn't have such a powerful family, the deed would have already been done—years ago. Max grudgingly released his hold on Zeke and took a step back.

Zeke squared his shoulders, made an exaggerated show of brushing off his clothes, and strolled casually out of the club. By the time Zeke disappeared out the door, Max was already regretting his decision not to give in to the urge and end Zeke's miserable existence.

When Max turned back around, Silas had released his hold on George, who now had his arms around Cora, kissing her face where they stood near the room that Zeke had chosen to humiliate George. Max was sure the two of them would work out what had transpired, but the wound was deep and Max didn't kid himself to think George wouldn't want revenge. It had been one thing to allow Cora to go with Zeke, but it was a completely different animal to allow the entire club to witness his humiliation as well as Cora's. The club once again in order, the shaky balance reclaimed, Max sighed. He needed a little comfort and reassurance of his own. Knowing the only place he'd find either, he made his way back to Cisco's rooms.

AFTER SOME self-discovery and a boring couple of hours in Max's office, Max, to Cisco's relief, had sent him back to his apartment. Max had explained he had to make a brief appearance in the club and instructed Cisco to be "properly" waiting for his return. He had just enough time to shower using the new unscented products Max had delivered and be in his display position—in nothing but his jeans as requested. His knees bothered him, but nothing that wasn't bearable. He could imagine that this was something he'd better get used to and he no doubt would develop calluses on his knees.

*Can you even get calluses on your knees?*

He'd have to ask Patrick the next time he saw him. There were still a lot of questions he hoped to ask Patrick. Cisco felt slightly better after Max's declaration that he was the most important thing in his world. The sentiment had hit Cisco directly in the chest and made him happier than just about anything ever had. That didn't mean he wasn't still nervous. He wanted so badly to make Max proud. Having a game plan and a little more inside information on how to go about it would definitely work to his advantage.

The knob turned and Cisco instantly adjusted his posture to the perfect position. Max stood near the closed door not saying a word. Out of the corner of his eye, Cisco got a glimpse of Max's face. His gaze was on him, but his expression was hard to read. Cisco couldn't explain it, but Max seemed stiffer, agitated maybe. He wasn't sure, but the aura around him seemed different, tense. Max continued to stare at him without moving or saying a word. Cisco's skin prickled and his pulse sped as the moment dragged on. Anticipation, both good and bad, surged through him. As Cisco's unease started to outweigh his excitement, Max walked across the room to where Cisco knelt and began to circle him.

"You did well tonight."

"Thank you, Sir."

"I'm not sure what kind of fantasies you've had about my life or yours as my submissive, but you'll learn that it can be… shall we say… less than exciting. It can also, at times, feel quite isolating and restrictive. However, I will do my best to make sure your service to me is rewarded. Rewards that I hope you will find pleasurable."

"Your pleasure is all that matters, Sir."

"Those are pretty little words, Cisco, but I don't think you believe them."

Cisco stiffened. "But I do. I would never lie to you."

"That's good, since lying to me would be futile. I do trust that you want to please me, but eventually you will learn not only how to, but to find your own pleasure in doing so. Stand up."

Cisco came to his feet, still contemplating what Max had said. But then it didn't matter because Max was touching him, fingertips sliding down his shoulder to his back, then around to his hip.

"You are a virgin, are you not?"

Cisco's cheeks heated. How the hell could Max know that? He'd experimented. Some. After all, his best friend since childhood was also gay. "Not technically," he responded. He and Benny had done a little rubbing off on each other, mutual blow jobs, hand jobs, the usual adolescent exploration. He knew how to pleasure himself, had prepared his body for Max.

"Not technically?" Max repeated, sounding confused.

Oh Jesus, his cheeks were going to melt off his face, they were so hot. "I've been touched," he responded, being as vague as possible.

Max ran a finger down Cisco's chest to his navel. "Apparently," Max chuckled. He cocked his head, studying Cisco, who did his best not to squirm under his scrutiny. "Why are you embarrassed? I simply want to know what sexual experiences you've had."

*Because I'm a twenty-one-year-old virgin.* He'd never been good at hiding his reactions, especially when it was something he felt strongly about. Benny always said he was an open book, one just had to read it on his face. Cisco drew in a lung full of air and blew it out slowly. He should have known this issue would come up. There was nothing he could do about it now but tell the truth, as painfully embarrassing as it was.

"I've experimented a little with stuff, like hand jobs… you know… stuff." He huffed out a breath. "I've played with toys but I've never had… well… you know, anal sex with a partner."

"See, you are already pleasing me." Max began walking around Cisco, touching him randomly as he moved.

"Really?" Cisco asked in disbelief. "I would have thought someone of your position would prefer a lover with a little more experience."

"Experience is one thing, it definitely has its advantages," Max agreed with a nod, still moving, footfalls measured and sure.

Touch. Touch. Touch.

Cisco's skin tingled with each swipe of Max's finger, making it difficult to concentrate on the conversation. A shoulder, hip, forearm, back, none of them sexual, per se, but still each one ignited his arousal. The heat from his cheeks and ears was making a mad dash south and settling in his groin. Cisco gave himself an internal shake. He forced his focus away from his rising libido and back on the conversation.

"Are there any advantages to being less experienced?"

"Oh yes. There are many I can think of, but the most important are, one, I will have the honor of showing you such pleasures, and two, I am quite the possessive man, as you can imagine." Max stopped behind Cisco and leaned in, his lips almost brushing Cisco's ear. "It would drive me insane if I knew another man had been your first," Max whispered, his tone deep and seductive.

Cisco shuddered, once again proving he didn't control his reactions well. With Max, it was even harder, futile even. "Suddenly I don't feel quite so bad about being a virgin," he admitted.

"You shouldn't. We'll take it slow. I have no desire to damage you," Max commented, the seductive tone gone, becoming more matter-of-fact as he once again began to pace around Cisco.

Christ, the man could change moods like flipping a switch. It was disorienting, and Cisco was convinced he did it on purpose to keep people unbalanced. It worked. Cisco's head was swimming.

"Strip."

Cisco's hand flew to his button, and without hesitation he undid his pants and shoved them down. He stepped out of his jeans and kicked them away before quickly returning to his display position. His erection strained up and away from his body, and his cheeks began to heat again.

"Once again you are embarrassed. Interesting. You'll get over that soon enough," Max commented, sounding assured. He stood in front of Cisco, arms crossed over his chest as he raked his eyes up and down Cisco's body.

Cisco didn't feel quite so confident, especially when Max added, "I wish to watch you pleasure yourself."

# CHAPTER TEN

THE FLUSH raced up Cisco's chest, his neck, and infused his cheeks. Max hadn't been kidding that his boy would lose his embarrassment when it came to such things quickly enough. But part of Max would miss it. Cisco's innocence, his unsure movements, and the sweet blush were all things he would surely hate to see go.

Still Max refused to make this easy for Cisco, and he held his position, arms across his chest and his features neutral. Cisco must learn to follow his orders—all of them—without hesitation. This was a simple test, albeit one Max would take great pleasure in viewing. It also had a purpose. He would learn much of what his boy liked, where his sensitive spots were, whether he liked it hard and fast or slow and languid. Sure, he could discover those things for himself, but why not allow Cisco to give him a show?

Cisco exhaled deeply as he looked down at his straining cock. His boy might be embarrassed, but apparently his dick had no issues with Max watching. Cisco wrapped a tentative hand around it, giving it a few quick pulls.

It didn't take long, a few more strokes, and Cisco's eyes fluttered closed. "Oh yeah," he groaned.

Max allowed Cisco to do as he wished for a moment, giving him time to settle into his rhythm, for his arousal to build, before he spoke. "Open your eyes and look at me."

Cisco's eyes flew open, a look of alarm on his face, and his hand stilled.

"Keep stroking yourself."

"Sir?"

Max took a seat in the oversized chair, kept his demeanor relaxed, less intimidating. "I'm enjoying the show very much," he praised. "Continue."

Cisco shifted his feet, widened his stance, and began to stroke himself again, following Max's order to keep his eyes open. Max watched as the apprehension and embarrassment began to seep from Cisco as his pleasure increased. Before long Cisco's hips were beginning to move, a slight sheen of perspiration glistening on his forehead. His breathing quickened, as did his heartbeat.

Cisco licked his lip, his hand moving faster, gripping tighter. "I don't know how long I'm going to last," he warned.

"Talk to me," Max encouraged softly, his voice deep and seductive. "Tell me what you're thinking, what you're feeling."

"I… I don't know if I can," Cisco responded, sounding unsure, the flush showing itself once again on his cheeks.

"Stop thinking of yourself, where you are, and concentrate only on me. Do it because it pleases me."

A glint of determination shone in Cisco's eyes, and Max knew he'd said the right thing. His boy was so eager to please him. Max rested his elbow on the arm of the chair, propped his chin on his thumb, and hid his grin behind his fingers.

"I like pleasing you, Sir." Cisco groaned and started to pump his cock in earnest. His chest rose and fell rapidly, and his legs trembled. Cisco's need was beginning to burn off the last traces of any embarrassment.

"That's it," Max murmured. "Show me how you like it. I want to see and hear how badly you want to please me."

"Since the first moment I spotted you, I've thought only of you. What it would be like to be with you. When I stroked myself, I always imagined it was you touching me." Cisco blew out a heavy breath and his eyes fluttered closed, but he caught himself quickly and opened them again, holding Max's gaze with dark, lust-filled eyes. His pupils dilated, blowing out any trace of the warm chocolate color. His hand moved steadily, but his fingers relaxed, not putting any real pressure on his cock, no doubt in an attempt to not come too quickly.

Max briefly wondered when Cisco had last come. Had it been so long that he was simply needy, or was it that Max was watching him or his need to please Max? He supposed it mattered little which. Cisco was a sight to behold, his body damp with perspiration, skin flushed as he gave in to his pleasure. Max's cock began to fill, the feeding he gorged himself on still coursing through him, warming him.

The trembling in Cisco's limbs increased, as did the wild beat of his heart. The effort it took to keep control was physically evident and his voice was tight. "I crave your touch, want it so bad," he grunted and opened his legs wider. "Would do anything to please you… to be what you need. You're on my mind all the time, always have been. Can't focus on anything but you.

I couldn't wait to come here. I've been so lonely, needed you so much, only you and… oh God.…" His fingers tightened and he started to pump his cock faster, his thumb smearing the come that was leaking from the small slit on each pass. With his free hand, he reached down and began playing with his balls. He rolled them in his hand, tugging them just a little.

"I need you, Sir," Cisco panted. "I've waited so… ah… fuck… so long. Waited to have your hands on me. Feel you entering me, fucking me, loving me."

"Soon," Max promised. And it would be soon. Max might be able to keep from feeding on Cisco—although not without difficulty—but there was no way he'd deny himself the pleasure of Cisco's gorgeous, tight, and simply perfect body. A body he felt he'd already waited too long… so long… to enjoy.

"I can feel a knot forming in my back, my balls tightening. Burns, pressure, starts in my—" Cisco tipped his head back and his jaw clenched momentarily as he fought to keep control. "—in my groin, moves up to my belly and down my thighs, everything trembling, tense. Everything coiling tighter and tighter, making it hard to breathe. Need to… ah, I need to come. So bad. Sir, please, I can't hold it back. I need to come!"

Max swallowed, his body suddenly tense. "Come for me, boy. Show me," he whispered.

"Yes, thank—" Cisco's voice cut off as his back arched, head tilted up, completely still for a few heartbeats. "Sir!" he cried out as the first blast shot up over his fist, rope after rope soaking his stomach as if he'd been holding back for much too long. Perhaps he had.

"Ah.…" Cisco gasped, stunned and speechless and at last completely spent.

Max jumped, catching his boy at the last second before his legs gave out, and pulled him into his arms. Panting and weak, still trembling with the aftershocks, Cisco allowed Max to hold him until his pulse slowed, panting breath easing as he came back to himself.

"That was beautiful," Max told him. "The way you gave in to your passion, gave it to me to witness and enjoy."

Cisco pressed his face into Max's neck with a sigh and leaned on him heavily. "Thank you, Sir." He clung to Max for a few more moments and then lifted his head and met Max's gaze. "What can I do for you to thank you properly?"

Max gave Cisco a little leeway for not addressing him as Sir. Cisco would learn those shows of respect soon enough; they would, in fact, become second nature. Max was glad his boy's first thought was Max's need and pleasure. He held those sincere dark eyes and grabbed Cisco's hips and pulled him forward.

"Good boy. You've made me very happy, and I'm about to show you my appreciation with my dick down your throat."

Cisco groaned at the contact and swallowed hard. "Yes, Sir. How would you like me?"

Max nipped at Cisco's neck, mindful of his sharp teeth, careful not to break the skin. It would be a temptation he would not be able to resist. "Come, boy."

Max grabbed Cisco's hand and led him to the couch. Max slumped down onto the buttery soft leather, spreading his legs and getting comfortable, and ran his hand over the thick bulge in his trousers as he looked up at his boy's eager face. He didn't miss the way Cisco's gaze was glued to Max's crotch as he continued to run his fingers along his length.

Max tried not to smirk as he leaned back a little more, resting his head and shoulders, settling farther into the couch. "On your knees, boy."

"Yes, Sir." Cisco knelt slowly in front of him on the floor. He put his hands on Max's thighs and slid them along the fabric, over his hardness, his hips, until he reached the waistband of his pants. Cisco worried his bottom lip with his teeth as he worked. His hands hovered over the button as he looked up from beneath long dark lashes. "May I?" he asked, his voice relaxed, teasing.

"Boy," Max warned, his voice tight as his arousal grew. Cisco popped the button and slid the zipper down.

Max was impatient to get Cisco's warm, wet mouth on himself. Cisco might be untouched in some things, but he'd admitted his mouth was not as virginal as his ass. Max wouldn't have to go slow, he could take what he wanted, needed. And oh how he needed Cisco. The warm blood from the donor surging through him, heating him, was making him needy.

"If you'd lift your hips just a little, Sir, I could get these restrictive garments out of the way," Cisco suggested, and when he did so, Cisco slid Max's pants down over his ass and down his thighs, far enough to free Max's straining erection. Cisco gasped and then licked his lips. "Oh, you have quite the impressive cock, Sir," Cisco breathed, lowering his mouth to Max's lap and brushing his warm lips over the flared cockhead.

Max groaned in response to the teasing touch. He arched as he settled his hand on the back of Cisco's head, pushing it down. "Suck me," he demanded.

Cisco opened his mouth wide, lowering it over Max's cock. He hummed as if the first taste pleased him and then gripped Max's prick and stroked it with soft warm fingers. It was slow and steady, and so damn maddening. He wanted to thrust, to ram his cock down Cisco's welcoming throat. Cisco sucked and licked, his tongue caressing the shaft, teasing the head… but it wasn't enough. Max wanted—no, he needed more. Feeding, the excitement in the club, watching Cisco come had ignited a fire within him and left him inflamed. He found himself wanting to move, to take. He heard an animalistic rumbling and realized it was from his own chest.

Cisco must have heard it too, in tune with Max's desire, because he relinquished his hold on Max's body and clasped his hands together behind his back, handing control over to his Master. The weight of Max's hand forced Cisco's head lower, made his boy open his throat as Max pushed his cock deep. The grunt from his boy was satisfying, and Max had to clamp down on the urge to thrust, to go deeper, take even more.

Max rocked his hips, short, quick thrusts, careful not to choke Cisco, but when Cisco's breathing evened out and he swallowed, the constriction around the head of Max's cock nearly caused him to come. Only by years of practice and pure stubbornness was he able to rein his orgasm in. Cisco's hot, wet mouth surrounded Max's cock, the slick wall creating the perfect friction. But all too soon, need and hunger surged through Max and he knew he wouldn't be able to keep his release back much longer. He grabbed Cisco's head in both hands and pulled him off his cock with a pop. Cisco whimpered pitifully as if he'd just been denied his favorite toy. Max wouldn't deny him for long, though, he couldn't.

"Kneel up," he demanded, pushing himself to his feet.

Cisco hurried to move, confusion plain on his face. "Sir?"

But his confusion quickly turned to understanding when Max once again grabbed the back of Cisco's head, pushing his face against Max's cock. "Open up, boy." The instant Cisco's lips parted, Max shoved his cock in, taking what he wanted, what he needed, thrusting, fucking, claiming.

Cisco moaned, the vibration sending shockwaves through Max from the head of his dick down to his toes, making them curl. He shoved in hard, felt Cisco's throat tighten around him, stroking Max's flesh, and he growled with the sensation.

"Fuck, yes, that feels good. That's it, boy. Take it, all of it. Show me how much you want to please me. Prove it to me."

Cisco slid his hands around Max's body to his ass, digging his fingers in, encouraging Max to move. He happily obliged him, snapping his hips, holding the back of his boy's head, going balls-deep with each thrust. Cisco's body was at ease. He took deep breaths through his nose and relaxed his throat. Cisco sealed his lips around Max's slick cock, adding the perfect amount of pressure and friction.

Tight and wet and warm and God, the way Cisco had given himself over to Max. The greedy slurping sounds, the moans coming from Cisco, the sounds he pulled from Max with his talented tongue as it pressed against the underside of Max's cock with each pass added to the eroticism and pleasure. Max couldn't look away from the way his slick cock slid past Cisco's red, swollen lips. The lust and eagerness in his boy's eyes was heady. Although he'd given up control, Cisco wasn't passive, he sucked and licked and moaned as he feasted on Max's cock.

"What a good little cocksucker, such a talented mouth," Max praised. Cisco sucked harder, hungry, fingers massaging the flesh of Max's ass. "Ah, yes. That's it. Make me come, boy."

Obviously emboldened by Max's praise, Cisco moved closer to Max's crease, ran a single finger up and down it, adding pressure with each pass, closer and closer to Max's hole. Max stiffened; he wasn't used to anyone touching him in such a way, yet to his surprise, it caused a thrill to course through him. He thrust harder. Cisco's bold touch excited him, and when Cisco began tapping the pad of his finger against Max's hole, it nearly tipped him over the edge. Before his change he'd enjoyed his ass played with, had loved being fucked, but since taking over power, he couldn't put himself in such a vulnerable position, nor had he ever been with anyone who would take such liberties. Cisco, whether due to his innocence or his ability to read Max's body, continued to put pressure against Max's hole, pushing in just a little.

"Fuck," Max gasped. "Close." He thrust again and again, reaching for his orgasm, cock rock-hard and throbbing.

Cisco pressed harder and abruptly shoved the tip of a dry finger in, just past Max's muscle. But it was enough to push Max over the edge, and he roared his release, coming in spurts, holding Cisco's head still as he shot his load down his throat until he swallowed every last drop. With a shudder Max pulled away and fell back onto the couch, boneless.

Cisco sat back on his calves, reached out, and laid a hand on Max's knee, squeezing it lightly as he panted. When he'd caught his breath, he ran a hand over his face, wiping away the sweat that dampened his brow.

"That was so fucking amazing, Sir," he moaned. "God, I never knew…. Never been so turned on as I was while sucking you. The way you forced me to take it, held me, your flavor… just…. You have me so fucking hard again it hurts."

Max didn't say a word for a moment, enjoying the way his body continued to tingle as he came down from his orgasmic high. He raked his gaze over Cisco's lean form; he was indeed hard, his erection straining and ruddy, the head glistening with fluid. Cisco didn't beg. He kept his head down and silently waited for Max to respond. Max didn't draw it out any longer than was necessary—he wasn't a cruel Master—just long enough to bask in the glow of his orgasm for a bit.

"Stand up, boy."

Cisco scrambled to his feet, his hands instantly going behind his back, his chest pushed out, still rising and falling with his rapid breaths. Max grabbed Cisco's hips in both hands and jerked him forward as he leaned up, taking Cisco into his mouth and sucking hard.

Cisco cried out, going up on tiptoes, his hand briefly landing on Max's head, but he caught himself quickly and returned to his display position. Max hummed his approval, tongue swirling around the bulbous head, licking, tasting, and savoring.

"Ah, Sir. Feels so good…." Cisco shuddered and shook his head, muscles tense. "So, so, good."

Max continued to feast on Cisco's cock for a few more minutes until his boy began to babble incoherently and his body trembled with the need for release. When he sensed Cisco wouldn't last much longer, he pulled off his cock and grasped it in his fist, pumping Cisco's slick shaft several times until Cisco thrust into his hand. Max ran his lips over the head, dipping his tongue into the small slit, lapping at the delicious flavor that seeped from Cisco's cock.

"That's it, boy. Want to taste you. See you come."

Max kept steady pressure on Cisco's cock, knew how he liked it as he sped his hands, his mouth still working the sensitive cockhead. Cisco moaned, then suddenly stilled, held his breath to stave off his release, draw out the pleasure as long as he could. Max wasn't having any of it. He was greedy. Wanted to taste it right then.

"Come for me," he demanded, putting a snap of authority into his tone.

Cisco threw his head back, spine arching as he cried out Max's name. The first spurt landed on Max's lips. He opened his mouth and took Cisco deep, greedily gulping down his boy's hot seed till he'd sucked him dry.

Cisco shuddered one last time, and Max sat back and pulled Cisco onto his lap. His boy buried his face in the side of Max's neck, breathing harshly. It was the second time Cisco had displayed this particular behavior. Was it something he did as a comfort measure, or was he hiding his face, perhaps his embarrassment? Max allowed him to cling for a few minutes, ran a soothing hand down his back, enjoying the heat of his boy's body. He'd learned more about his boy in the last hour and two orgasms than he had in all the years of watching him from afar. Cisco was a sensualist, loved to be touched and caressed. Max filed that knowledge away. It was something he could use as a reward or deny as a punishment.

Max laid his head back on the couch and wrapped his arms around Cisco. Content and happy for the first time in what felt like forever, he began considering his own future, his own happiness instead of that of the clan.

# CHAPTER ELEVEN

THE NEXT night was a repeat of the one before. Cisco knelt at his feet while he took care of paperwork and then he sent Cisco back to his rooms to wait while Max made his appearance in the club. He'd planned on allowing Cisco to accompany him, but after the fiasco with Zeke the night before, he wasn't ready to chance it. Thankfully, Zeke hadn't been stupid enough to show his face again, and the club had been quiet. Well, there had been no disturbances, but it was far from quiet. The club was growing in popularity among both vampires and humans. With the rising success came greater profit, greater presence of a positive atmosphere, where humans and vampires could interact in a safe and mutually beneficial setting. But with success also came difficulties. To keep everyone safe—Max's first priority—he'd need to visit the Coalition of Vampire and Human Coexistence to inquire about a possible transfer of more vampires to Mecosta. Only a certain number of vampires were allowed in one area at any given time. To break those rules risked heavy fines and even possible expulsion of all vampires from the area. He could hire more human staff, but they simply weren't as effective as a being with supernatural strength. Plus, with the influx of new human submissives and a growing waiting list with even more wanting admittance, they simply didn't have enough vampires to keep up with the demand of subs looking for Doms. Until he could obtain such approval, he'd have to be watchful of any possible problems and quash them quickly.

It was a tentative peace they had with the government and local police force. He dared not break any laws. Yet to go without security was also skirting disaster. Hopefully, between himself and Angelo, they'd be able to charm both the CVHC and the local law agencies.

Either way, Max knew where his priorities lay at the moment. It wasn't a matter of *if* Zeke would act up again, but *when*. He had to have his boy ready. Max would stand up to any and all challenges of his rights to Cisco, but if he failed….

Max shook his head. He wouldn't even entertain the idea. He wouldn't fail.

With riding crop in hand, he pushed through the door to Cisco's apartment and found the boy standing in the center of the room just as he'd instructed.

"Everything you do is a direct reflection upon me. If I cannot control my boy, I will be viewed as weak, and I promise you, I am far from weak. Failure to follow my rules exactly will be dealt with swiftly and harshly. Is that understood?"

"Yes, Sir."

"You will be confined to your rooms until I am confident you can be allowed in public. Learn quickly and you will please me. Fail to try and suffer."

"Yes, Sir. I will please you," Cisco responded in a strong, confident voice.

"Good boy."

"Thank you, Sir."

"Strip and kneel," Max demanded, pointing to the center of the rug in the middle of the room.

Cisco instantly shoved down his sweatpants and removed his shirt. He folded the garments quickly and placed them neatly upon the bed before going to his knees with his hands clasped behind his back in the spot Max had directed.

Max felt the familiar stirring of heat in his groin, the stimulation pleasant, but without blood, he could not achieve an erection. He would feed as soon as he was done with Cisco's lesson. Every passing day, the thought of sinking his fangs into anyone but Cisco revolted him further, but he couldn't allow for his strength to wane. How he wished he could bind himself to Cisco in blood, but he'd have to continue being patient. Angelo had a donor waiting for Max, and he'd learned his lesson after the last time he waited to feed. To wait too long could have dire consequences for both himself and the donor. He couldn't allow that to happen again. But first….

Max tapped the crop against Cisco's thigh. "Knees shoulder-width apart. Back straight. Head up, eyes down." He tapped him on the chest. "Chest out, shoulders back."

Each command was instantly followed. Max viewed Cisco's perfect posture with pride, but he kept it out of his voice, keeping his tone neutral. It would do neither him nor Cisco any good if he were to be soft. This was a simple, basic task, not one to be praised.

"When you are following me and I stop, you are to instantly drop to this display position. Any other time you are kneeling at my feet, you are to be in this display position. Your chest is to be in perfect line with my chest when I am standing, in the middle of my thigh while I am sitting. Think of yourself as merely an accessory to my wardrobe. You are to be seen and admired and worn in such a fashion as to impress."

Max began to pace in a circle around Cisco. "You never lift your eyes. Do not *ever* look anyone directly in the eye, nor are you to speak unless I give you permission or ask you a direct question. Is that understood?"

"Yes, Sir."

"I know you have researched the BDSM lifestyle. Throw everything you think you know out of your head right now. It means nothing between us. There are no safewords, no contracts. You simply and completely belong to me and will do as I tell you. You must put your complete trust and faith in me. I know what you can or can't handle. I can hear your heart beating, the rush of your breath from a hundred yards. I can smell your pleasure and your fear. I will either choose to stop when you have reached your limit or you will die."

Cisco gasped, his anxiety causing his heart to race. Max leaned in slightly before Cisco's level of distress turned to panic and whispered, "I would never deny myself the pleasure of having you as my boy." Cisco's relief was immediate, and Max heard the barely audible sigh, the tension in the air dissipating.

Max once again paced around Cisco, tapping the crop against his hand. "You must learn to tune out everything. To focus on me and nothing else, including the needs of your body. You may find yourself in this position for extended periods and may want to shift—don't. Your fingers may cramp and you wish to stretch them—don't. You must learn to rise above your physical form and endure any amount of pain simply because it pleases me. You do wish to please me, don't you, boy?"

"Yes, Sir, more than anything."

Max could sense the truth in Cisco's conviction, and smiled. "Go kneel next to the ottoman."

Without a word, Cisco pulled himself to his feet. Keeping his posture perfect and his hands firmly clasped behind his back, he walked to the ottoman and went gracefully to his knees.

"Bend at the waist and rest your chest against it, head turned to the right."

Cisco did as he was told. The ottoman was the correct height to put Cisco's taut ass perfectly on display. Max set the crop on the dresser and pulled open the armoire, considering the tools within. He settled on a short-handled deerskin flogger. Picking it up, he ran the soft strands through his fingers and nodded his approval. It was perfect for Cisco's first experience as it was very light and had minimal thud or sting. Eventually he would work his boy up to a more intense flogger such as a thick buffalo or bull leather, but for now, the pain would build from the repetition of the blows rather than the strike itself. Cisco must learn to master his body before he could truly hand it over to Max to command.

Max ran the tips of the flogger along Cisco's spine, down to his ass and thighs, and then back up. "You may scream or cry if it becomes hard to bear, but you cannot move from this position. Understood?"

Cisco took a deep breath, letting it out slowly as he seemed to sink further into the leather of the ottoman. "Yes, Sir, I am not to move." His words held conviction, but the nervous energy zinging around him wasn't something Cisco could yet control. In time he'd learn, the nervousness replaced with anticipation, excitement, even pleasure.

"Take each blow and feel it, process it, and then push it away. We begin." Max started with light slaps to Cisco's shoulder blades, working the flogger in a figure-eight pattern, moving down as Cisco's skin began to turn pink. Never staying in one spot too long, he utilized Cisco's entire back. Cisco stayed calm, his heartbeat and breathing slow and steady.

His boy took to the new sensation well. He was a natural. Max could hear the low moan that began rumbling in Cisco's chest. Max moved down to the untouched flesh of Cisco's ass, heard him suck in a breath, his pulse increase. Max moved farther down to his boy's thighs, working the flogger until Cisco once again settled into the sensation, took it in, processed it, and then moved above it.

A thrill of excitement surged within Max. His boy really was a natural, his need to please Max the driving force. Cisco wasn't holding his breath, wasn't tensing or bulling his way through the pain. He truly was following Max's instruction to the letter. He used that knowledge to make the decision to take his boy to the next level.

He walked to the armoire, returned the deerskin flogger and picked up a soft bovine leather one. He hadn't expected to need it so quickly, but he was beyond ridiculously happy that he did. When he turned back around, he could see the tension in Cisco's muscles, hear the slight hitch in his breath. But Max didn't coddle him. He was curious to see if his boy would take to the heavier flogger as well as he had the one made of deer hide.

Before beginning, he critically inspected the flesh of Cisco's back, ass, and thighs. His skin had a nice pink coloring, but it merely looked warmed. Max ran the flogger tails along Cisco's back, letting him feel it, know what was coming. He was about to take the warmth to a new level of heat.

"Are you comfortable?" Max asked once more as he inspected the new flogger.

"Yes, Sir. I am," Cisco answered.

"Good." Max widened his stance a little and looked down at the naked body before him. The pink flush of Cisco's skin, the heat radiating off him, and the relaxed manner as he awaited the blows to resume all brought a large smile to Max's face. "This new flogger is a bit more intense. You are permitted to talk, scream, even beg—in fact, I'd enjoy hearing all three. However, I will remind you this one time of my rules. You may not move or interfere with my pleasure in any way. Your body is mine to do with as I wish. Do you understand?"

"Yes, Sir, I understand. My body is yours to command," Cisco confirmed.

Without another word of warning, Max began. Cisco gasped with the first slap of the flogger, his muscles tensing, but he kept his position. With the flick of his wrist, Max laid another blow to Cisco's other shoulder, which produced another sharp intake of breath. Confident with the weight of his blows, he worked the flogger in the same pattern as he had with the one made of deer, his strokes only slightly heavier, giving his boy a chance to get used to the new thud.

"I like the way your skin looks all warm and glowing," Max murmured.

"Thank you, Sir. I like the way it feels too." Cisco had an edge of surprise in his tone, but no strain in his voice at all.

Max continued to lay down the flogger, the blows steady and rhythmic. "You sound a bit shocked that you're enjoying this."

"I am, Sir. I was nervous...." Cisco worried his bottom lip with his teeth. "Anxious really that I wouldn't be able to handle it, that I'd upset you, embarrass myself."

"I knew you could handle it," Max said adamantly. "You are stronger than you think you are. Simply being here proves that."

"Thank you, Sir. I—" Cisco's speech was interrupted by a slap of the flogger, and he grunted, arched a little. He took an audible breath before he continued. "I wasn't sure, but I guess what matters is that you are."

"You're right," Max commented, his arm moving easily. "What I think, what I say, what I want are the only things that matter."

Max rained down the slow, steady blows, enjoying the deepening blush that bloomed on Cisco's flesh and the way his boy responded to each strike, the small grunts and gasps. He spread the blows out, moving closer to Cisco's ass, the tips dragging over his skin with each stroke. Max was overwhelmed with the urge to touch the forming red patches, to press his lips against them, feel the heat rise from the smooth skin and sink his teeth into the tender flesh, but with an iron will, he pushed the urge away.

"You should see your back," he said softly. "The way it responds to the leather is quite a sight to behold."

"I'm glad you like what you see, Sir," Cisco answered quickly, and then his breath caught in response to a stinging blow.

Max wondered briefly if his boy even realized how much he was getting off on the pain, that it was hardening his cock. Max moved down to Cisco's pink ass, the tops of his thighs.

"Oh God," Cisco groaned, arching into the blow.

Max didn't change the speed or weight of the flogger, concentrating on the steady blows until he'd pulled another deep groan from his boy and then stopped. Max let his hand hover over Cisco's back, not touching, just soaking in the heat radiating from his boy's skin. His boy seemed relaxed, but he was breathing a little quickly past his parted lips.

"Are you thirsty?" he asked.

"Yes, S—" Cisco swallowed, cleared his throat. "Yes, Sir, I am."

Max walked to the kitchenette area, pulled down a glass from the cupboard, and filled it at the sink. He brought it back and held it out to his boy.

"May I sit up, Sir?"

"Yes, you may." Max grinned, pleased Cisco had asked permission to break his position.

"Thank you, Sir." Cisco sat back on his calves and accepted the glass. He tipped it up, taking a large gulp. His erection was thick, a lovely ruddy shade, curling up toward his navel, bobbing as he continued to drink. Max watched his throat as it worked, but forced his gaze away when the urge to bite nearly overwhelmed him. When Cisco had drunk his fill, he wiped a hand over his mouth and handed Max back the glass. Only then did he appear to catch sight of his erection, his expression evidence of his shock, as was the blush that reddened his cheeks.

Max set the glass on a nearby table without taking his eyes from his boy. "There is a fine line between pleasure and pain," Max said by way of explanation and then crouched down and took Cisco's beautiful cock into his hand, stroking it lightly.

"Oh." Cisco hissed and pushed into Max's hand. "I would never have thought." Cisco moaned, swaying a little, seeking out more friction.

Max allowed it for a few more strokes and then abruptly pulled his hand away. "Back into position." Max retrieved the flogger while Cisco did as he was told, but not without a whimper of loss.

Again without warning, Max resumed his strokes, beginning in the sensitive area of Cisco's ass, the tight mounds too tempting to ignore.

"Ah!" Cisco flinched, shying away from the blow with a groan as the first stroke hit his already reddened skin. Max kept the blows steady, consistent, and before long Cisco eased back onto the ottoman.

Max worked Cisco from his shoulders to his thighs. Max was careful to evaluate the response to each blow, the speed of Cisco's heartbeat, his breath, the way he'd shift or recoil, watching and listening for any evidence his boy was reaching his limits. On one downward pass, the tails of the flogger dragged across Cisco's balls, causing him to stiffen and cry out.

"Oh fuck!" His voice strained and his body coiled with tension.

Max moved away from Cisco's ass, returning to his reddened shoulders, easing the weight of his strikes. Once again Cisco responded beautifully, taking deep breaths, blowing them out slowly as he worked to rise above the pain. When he seemed to settle once more, Max moved downward, keeping the slaps light, bringing his boy down a little.

Cisco was rocking against the ottoman beneath him, humping a little. As Max continued to work Cisco's back, his boy's movements became harder, more desperate, and he gripped the ottoman, rutting against it.

"So hard," he groaned. "I need…. Ah God, Sir, you're going to make me come."

"You are not to come. Still yourself," Max demanded, keeping the flogger steady.

Cisco groaned and whimpered, his knuckles turning white where he gripped the ottoman, the lean muscles of his back bulging. He was holding his breath in an attempt to follow Max's order. But Max knew his boy wouldn't be able to hold on for much longer, and he eased the strength of his blows till they were merely tickling touches, bringing his boy down further until he let out the pent-up breath and stretched his fingers as the urgency dissipated.

Max smiled. He was sure when they had begun the session that Cisco hadn't ever thought he'd get off on it to such a degree that he was aching to come simply from the sting of the flogger and a little friction from the soft leather of the ottoman. Hell, Max hadn't seen this coming. He'd have thought for sure that Cisco would have begged him to stop hitting him. It was an unexpected but very pleasant surprise indeed.

His boy deserved a reward. Feet on either side of Cisco's legs, he dropped the flogger and bent at the waist, laying his hands against Cisco's back, pressing his fingertips lightly into his heated flesh. Cisco hissed with the touch, his hips reflexively snapping against the side of the ottoman. Max slid his hands gently down Cisco's back to his ass and massaged the taut mounds, pushing Cisco's erection against the leather, giving him a little of the friction he'd been seeking.

"Is this what you want, boy? A little pain with your pleasure?"

"Yes, feels so good." Cisco pushed into Max's hands with each thrust of his hips, his breath speeding as well as his heartbeat. A fine sheen of perspiration covered his back, causing the red marks to glisten in the light.

Max leaned down farther still and licked a path up from between Cisco's shoulders to the base of his neck, tasting the sweet salt of Cisco's skin and causing him to shudder with the contact.

"I can taste your need," Max whispered against his boy's flesh.

Max continued to massage Cisco's ass as he licked and kissed the soft flesh of Cisco's neck. He rubbed his cheek against the soft hair on the back of Max's head until his own need began to overwhelm him. His teeth ached, his stomach clenching. He leaned back and gritted his teeth, clamping down hard on the desire until he was able to rein it in. Regretfully he'd need to end the session, no longer trusting himself. The sooner they moved to the club, the sooner he could feed. The thought didn't settle well with him, but he'd do what he had to, whether he liked it or not.

Once he was in better control of himself, Max slid a hand between the ottoman and Cisco's body, wrapping it around Cisco's cock, pumping it a few times.

Cisco shoved his ass back, giving Max more room to work, thrusting with short quick snaps of his hips. "Love your hands on me," he moaned. "Ah, Sir… feels so good."

Max slid the hand he had on Cisco's ass to his hip and jerked him back, his ass slamming into Max's groin. Cisco arched as his hands scrambled for purchase on the ottoman. Max placed his palm against Cisco's chest, then pulled him back till he was sitting up on his knees. Cisco snapped his head around and looked.

Two more hard pulls and he smiled down at his boy. "Come for me."

Cisco made a strangled sound, his eyes nearly rolling back in his head as warm wetness fountained over Max's hand. Max watched his boy's beautiful face, slack with pleasure, and couldn't resist pressing his mouth to his boy's panting lips, taking in his breath as he continued to pump every last drop from Cisco.

When Cisco was spent and had gone limp against Max, Max placed a soft kiss to Cisco's lips and then eased him back down to lie on the ottoman once again. "Such a good boy," he praised and placed another kiss on the back of Cisco's head before moving away.

"Th-thank you, Sir," Cisco replied sluggishly.

Max went to the kitchenette and washed his hands, then ran a soft cloth beneath the cool flow of water and wrung out the excess. He brought it back and stood over his boy, studying him for a moment, enjoying the sight of his work as well as the blissed-out look on Cisco's face.

"This will be a little cold," he said soothingly and carefully spread the cloth over Cisco's back.

Cisco gasped, tensing for a second until he got over the initial shock and then let out a long breath. "Whew, you weren't lying. That *is* cold." Cisco chuckled.

"Too much?"

"No, it's fine. Feels good, Sir." Cisco turned his head so he could see Max. "I still can't believe I did that."

Max tilted his head and stared at him. "Did what?"

"That I got so turned on. I mean, I've been looking forward to it, but I was a little scared too. I wasn't sure if I would be able to handle it, but getting hard, getting so turned on I had to fight back my orgasm." He shook his head slightly. "Nope, I never would have expected that."

"You're a natural. You gave me exactly what I wanted tonight and tomorrow you'll do it at my side in the club." He held his hand out to Cisco. "C'mon, let's get you cleaned up and fed, shall we?"

"Yes, Sir. Thank you, Sir," Cisco responded, sounding excited.

He hadn't lied. Cisco had been stunning and had given Max what he wanted most: his submission. That Cisco had found such pleasure in it made it all the better. Tonight had been yet another test, and his boy had passed with flying colors. He couldn't wait to show Cisco just how boundless the pleasure and rewards could be as he pushed his limits and taught him to fly.

# CHAPTER TWELVE

DRESSED IN tight black leather pants, a black silk T-shirt, and black heavy-soled boots, Cisco knelt in the center of his room, waiting to be inspected by Max. He didn't worry about those things; he'd showered, dressed, knelt, and waited as per Max's instructions. It was what would happen after the inspection that had his belly flip-flopping. He was being allowed in the club that night, albeit for only a short visit. Cisco was nervous as hell.

Max entered the room and took a seat on the couch, silently studying him. He was used to Max watching him, but it always caused his pulse to speed in anticipation and, to be honest, a little fear he'd screw up. He didn't know if that would ever completely subside as he became more familiar with his surroundings and with Max, but for now he used it to motivate himself to please.

"There are a couple things I want to discuss before we enter the club. A list of rules and expectations. Ready?" Max asked.

Cisco concentrated on keeping his breath slow and even, doing his best to push aside the jittery feeling and focus on Max's words rather than his own discomfort. It took a few seconds but he calmed himself, finding the right headspace, and he nodded.

"Ready, Sir."

"First, you will not speak unless I give you permission. I doubt anyone will be so bold, but they might. If someone addresses you, whether Dominant or submissive, you wait for me to reply or give permission for you to answer, understand?"

"Yes, Sir."

"Secondly, I expect you to remain at my side at all times. We won't be there long, so there will be no reason for you to stray. You will walk at heel, head high, eyes low, and your posture perfect. If I stop, you are to drop to your knees and go to your display position at my side. The only time you should not be on your knees is to walk behind me. Any questions so far?"

"No, Sir."

The room went silent. Cisco could feel Max's eyes boring into him and it was a struggle not to squirm. Even harder was not looking up to see the expression on Max's face, get some hint as to what Max was thinking, but he didn't. It wouldn't do much good anyway; he rarely could tell what Max was thinking behind the neutral expression he so often plastered on his face.

"I won't lie to you, boy. The club is a very dangerous place to be, especially for you. If there is any kind of disturbance, I want you to stay close and do everything I tell you without question. You are not to leave my side for any reason. If you have any concerns or questions, ask now. Once we leave this room, you will no longer be able to speak."

"I'm to be silent unless given permission to speak, kneel at your feet each time you stop, and if there is any disturbance, I am to stay close and do exactly as you say," Cisco repeated his instructions, making sure he hadn't missed anything and letting Max know he had in fact been paying close attention.

"Very good." Max went to his feet. "Make me proud, boy. Come along, then."

"I'll try my best, Sir." Cisco quickly stood and followed Max out the door and down the hall.

A modern bar glowed invitingly, with dull bass thudding in time with the twilight hues of cobalt, indigo, and crimson lights that alternated throughout the club. The intoxicating scents, the color palette, the sleek décor rather than torture racks, iron maidens, and men chained to walls of an ancient dungeon. It was all familiar, yet Cisco felt as if he were walking into Wicked Ground for the first time. He trained his gaze on Max, watching his every move, trying to anticipate them rather than scanning the club. Nothing around him mattered but Max. Cisco had to please his Master.

"Good evening, sir."

Max stopped to speak to someone, and Cisco easily went to his knees at Max's side. He didn't recognize the voice. He dared not look up and see who it was addressing Max; it didn't matter. He kept his gaze trained on the heavy black boots in front of him and his attention on Max's voice as he spoke.

"Good evening. I haven't seen you in ages. How have you been?"

"I was summoned to London, family business," remarked the stranger. "The club looks great, a lot of new faces."

"Yes, we've had quite the spike in membership lately. I have a few moments before the show. Let me buy you a drink and catch up on old times," Max offered.

"You honor me."

Max began to move, and Cisco rolled to his feet instantly and fell into place behind him, walking to heel at precisely the distance Max had instructed. The muscles in his neck and back coiled with nervous tension; he couldn't screw this up. Max had told him that how Cisco behaved was a direct reflection on him. *Sheesh, nothing like putting pressure on a guy.* Although he'd found a good headspace while kneeling in Max's office and again while preparing for the evening. Unfortunately he'd lost it the moment they walked through the door of the club. He was trying his best to get back to that place, but he was finding it difficult without the quiet of Max's office and his Master's fingers threading through his hair as he worked. The sights, sounds, and the pressure were distracting as hell, so much so that he nearly ran into Max when he stopped at the bar. Luckily he caught himself at the last possible second. He had to swallow down the grunt of pain as his knees connected with the hard tile and pray like hell his momentary lapse of focus hadn't been witnessed by anyone other than Max. Even when his eyes weren't upon Cisco, he always somehow knew exactly what Cisco was doing or, more importantly in this case, what he was feeling, so the discomfort in his knees and his nervousness had surely alerted Max.

*Focus, Cisco*, he told himself and took a few deep, calming breaths. He was where he wanted to be, where he needed to be, and he had to prove it not only to himself but to those around him.

"I heard rumors that you have bonded. I can see now those rumors were in fact true."

"Ah, Jacob, the truth comes out as to your sudden reappearance after such a long absence. You haven't come to see me but to catch up on the latest gossip. You wound me, old friend."

FOR THE last five years Max had kept Cisco's existence a secret from everyone except those within his inner circle. He'd hoped, by doing so, he'd have given Cisco plenty of time to settle in and learn what was expected of him, and the opportunity to choose once he had all the knowledge. Max's reaction after finding Zeke tormenting Cisco…. Well, it had changed everything. Therefore, he wasn't surprised that people would be interested in Cisco.

"I would never dishonor you, Max," Jacob assured him and bowed his head in respect. "But I admit I am curious as to who has earned a permanent spot at your feet. I was beginning to think you'd never take on a human of your own." Jacob's smile was broad.

Max returned the smile. He'd known Jacob for a very long time. There would be many who would feel the same way. "No one is more surprised than I." *At least five years ago I was.*

"May I see him?"

Max's first thought was to use his body to shield Cisco from Jacob, which was completely ridiculous, but even knowing it was, he still struggled to tamp down on the possessiveness that rose up in him. "Stand, boy. Master Jacob wishes to see you."

Cisco rose to his feet with catlike grace and stood on display, his posture perfect.

Jacob looked Cisco over carefully, clinically, and Max noticed the tug of a smile as the man admired Cisco's body. "Oh, he is quite the striking creature, isn't he?" Jacob remarked, scanning over Cisco's lean form.

"That he is." *And all mine.* When Jacob licked his lips, it was more than Max could handle. He discreetly slipped between Jacob and Cisco and waved Silas over.

"Yes, sir?" Silas asked.

"Will you make sure Jacob gets whatever he wishes?"

"But of course, sir."

"I do believe I'll have a shot of scotch. Good drink, good conversation, and good friends," Jacob said pleasantly.


CISCO LISTENED as the two vampires caught up on old times, talking of family and a time long ago. It was small talk really, but Cisco was surprised at how easily Max laughed with Jacob, teasing each other. Cisco couldn't help but envy Jacob. To have known Max for so long, to have the ability to make him laugh so easily and freely…. Cisco yearned for such a connection. A deep one, the kind only lovers could achieve.

Cisco still paid close attention to the conversation, and when Max said "It was good seeing you my old friend. Please stay, enjoy yourself" and went to his feet, Cisco quickly followed.

"Thank you, I do believe I will," Jacob replied slyly. "I'm famished after such a long trip."

"I hope it will be worth it."

As Max moved away, Cisco right on his heels, Max heard Jacob remark, "It already has been."

Cisco kept his head high, his gaze low, and his posture tight as he followed Max to his chair at the front of the club. Cisco could feel all eyes upon him. He was filled with a mixture of both pride and concern. Such a strange combination of emotions, but one that was becoming familiar. He'd known there would be much to learn if he was to fit in there, deserve his place of honor. Max took his seat and Cisco went to his knees, adjusting his position so that he was in direct line with Max's thigh. The anticipation twisted and churned in his gut from both wariness and excitement. Max must have sensed his unease because he laid his hand upon Cisco's head, petting, and before he realized it, Cisco was pushing into that soothing touch. It grounded him instantly, calmed him. As they waited for the show to begin, Cisco cut a quick glance toward Max, who was thoughtfully surveying the room, no doubt looking for any hints of danger.

Cisco followed his gaze, witnessed how many members nodded in acknowledgment as they caught Max's eye, the subs lowering their gazes quickly. There was a buzz in the club, everyone talking about him, about the boy at Max's side as they kept looking at him, some pointing, others watching him as they spoke to each other behind their raised hands. Cisco shifted slightly, making sure that those who stared saw a perfectly displayed sub. The tension grew, the spotlight becoming uncomfortable, and he was beyond relieved when lights dimmed and the curtain rose.

Cisco froze and he gasped as he caught sight of the man standing in the center of the stage. He was beyond massive; his arms outstretched. He was covered from head to toe in tight leather; the only things visible were his eyes and mouth. When he opened his mouth to bellow "Welcome to Wicked Ground," Cisco knew the man was in fact a vampire from the glint of light off his fangs.

The crowd roared, cheering and clapping. They instantly went silent when two other men, dressed in much the same manner as the first, except without gimps covering their heads, danced seductively onto the stage. It was a strange dance, alluring, the flow of their bodies both hypnotizing and disconcerting. It took Cisco several seconds to realize these too were vampires. The disconnect was due to them tracing; it gave the appearance similar to that of a video feed going in and out, only without the static. One millisecond they were there, the next somewhere else, the speed so quick it was smooth but… Cisco couldn't find the right words but it was mesmerizing.

The first vampire stood still, in his original stance, as the other two continued to dance, working their way around the first, using his body to thrust against, to hold on to as they bent themselves backward. Slowly the large vampire lowered his arms, the movements of the dancers becoming quicker, erratic, frenzied. And then they were gone in the blink of an eye. The large vampire's arms were back in their original position so quickly Cisco questioned whether they had ever moved and if the dancers had been there at all.

The crowd once again cheered and applauded.

Out of the corner of his eye, Cisco saw Max nod and a second set of curtains opened to reveal a man completely naked, his wrists and ankles bound by shackles. Heavy chains pulled the man's limbs away from his body until his lean muscular body was displayed in an X position.

Cisco's first thought was how beautiful the man was, with his long flowing blond hair, chiseled features, and full lips. Cisco's second thought was how painful it must be to be stretched and suspended in such a manner. However there was a look of bliss on the man's handsome face. The Dom on stage began walking back and forth, his muscular thighs bulging with each predatory step, beautiful yet dangerous.

The deadly combination should've frightened Cisco, yet his blood heated and his cock hardened. The thrill of anticipation caused his pulse to speed, the scent of leather and arousal, the sounds of low moans and shifting bodies, heightening the excitement.

The Dom picked up what looked like small metal clamps attached to a length of delicate chain. He ran them through his fingers as he continued to move before the bound man. Then without warning, his hand shot out and attached one end of the chain to the man's left nipple, causing him to cry out. There was a second cry as the other clamp was attached. The Dom then pressed his face to the man's chest. Cisco couldn't tell if he was biting or sucking, but the look on the submissive's face told Cisco that whichever it was, he was enjoying the attention.

Moments later the Dom picked up a second set of clamps, and Cisco held his breath as one length was attached to the man's sac, the cry of pain echoing off the walls of the otherwise silent room. The Dom attached the other end to the center of the chain that was attached to the sub's nipples. When a third set was produced, the man moaned and grunted, his expression switching back and forth between pleasure and pain as the Dom strung the chain over the one attached to his chest, evened out the lengths, and then to Cisco's horror and the sub's scream of pain, attached both clamps to the head of his cock.

The Dom turned around in a flair of showmanship and raised his arms, working them up and down to the increasing roar of the crowd. "More," someone yelled. "Yank them off," said another. "Make him scream," yelled another still. Once he'd worked the crowd into a fever pitch of applause and cheers, the Dom walked to the edge of the curtain and reached for something out of the view of the audience. Before revealing it, he turned his head out toward the crowd, a wicked grin exposing his even more wicked fangs, before revealing a wand, glowing with purple light and a length of electrical cord attached.

The crowd went wild.

Cisco tensed as the Dom began moving the electrical device, hovering it over the man's bare chest. He knew what it felt like to be shocked, having had a mishap while helping Benny do some renovations on his kitchen. It had hurt like a motherfucker and he had a new respect for the power of electricity. He was held rapt by the scene before him, holding his breath as if he were the one about to receive the jolt.

The sub grunted, his body bowing at the first contact with the wand, and then whimpered when the device was withdrawn. Jesus, Cisco hoped like hell Max never asked him to take such treatment. He would; he'd do anything for Max, but… yeah, he hoped Max never asked him to endure that.

"I want your mouth."

So enthralled by what was happening on the stage, it took Cisco a few heartbeats to realize Max had spoken. He turned his head to find Max with his legs splayed out, his pants undone, and his hard cock in his hand, stroking himself. What had been happening between the Dom and his sub had been exciting, but it couldn't hold a candle to the beauty of Max's arousal.

Cisco sucked in a harsh breath and, without thinking about it first, looked around to see if anyone was watching. He'd never had any kind of sexual contact in public before. He'd thought about it, knew it would be expected of him. But now that the moment had arrived, the thought of an audience made him a little nauseated.

"Boy, that's one strike," Max said with a hint of a growl in his voice.

Cisco jerked his head around and scrambled to Max, his cheeks heating. He pushed up Max's white dress shirt, his palms sliding over the hard ridges of Max's cut stomach. With his free hand, he wrapped a fist around the thick shaft and stroked it as he lowered and sucked the flared head into his mouth. At the first hint of Max's flavor on his tongue, Cisco's embarrassment, along with the club and the world, melted away and he relished in pleasing his Master. *Nothing else matters but Max.*

Cisco bobbed his head as he continued to slide his fist up and down Max's cock, twisting his hand on each downward pass. He tried to get clues from Max, a moan, a tensing of muscle, some indication of what ministrations brought Max the most pleasure. Max stayed rigid, still, keeping his secrets to himself. It didn't deter Cisco, but rather ignited his determination. He slid his hand down Max's cock and tightened his fist around the base as he took it deep into his mouth, sucking hard, tongue working the underside of the thick shaft.

As Cisco pulled back, Max finally gave up one of his secrets. He laid his hand on the back of Cisco's head and pushed it back down. Cisco gagged when the head pushed into his throat and his eyes watered, but he recovered quickly. He relaxed as best he could and gave himself over to Max, allowing him to set the pace.

Cisco released the hold he had on Max's cock, sliding his fingers down to caress the soft skin of Max's balls. He knew he'd hit the right spot when Max thrust up slightly as he pushed Cisco's head down. Max's reaction coupled with the sounds of the crowd as well as the cries and moans from the sub on stage were a heady mix, and Cisco pleasured Max in earnest. His own cock was hard and throbbing for attention, but he ignored it, lost himself in Max's pleasure.

They worked in perfect harmony, Cisco easily giving up control to Max but working hard to increase Max's pleasure.

"Enough." Max pulled his hand away.

Cisco, lost in the moment, continued to suck, working hard to bring Max to release.

The back of his neck was gripped painfully. "I said enough," Max snapped and shoved Cisco away. "That's strike two."

Cisco landed on his ass, panting harshly as he stared at Max in confusion. Max ignored Cisco; instead he stood, fastened up his pants, and strolled away. Cisco had to scramble, nearly running to catch up.

Tears burned his eyes as he went to heel, following Max. He could tell by the heavy steps and jerky movements that Max was angry.

*What the hell just happened?*

He'd been so lost in Max, tried so hard to please, yet somehow it had all gone terribly wrong in a blink of an eye. He wanted to apologize for whatever it was he'd done wrong, to beg forgiveness and ease Max's anger. But he knew better than to speak. He hadn't been given permission.

His trepidation and dread grew with each step. By the time Max led him back to his apartment and slammed the door behind them, Cisco nearly fell to the floor and started blubbering. But he locked down on his trembling legs and choked back the sob that threatened and went to his display position in the center of the room.

"You were given specific instructions. You informed me you understood what they were. I gave you an opportunity to ask questions. You declined. I am now to assume that you simply have chosen to disobey me."

"I'm sorry—"

"Strike three," Max snapped. "You have not been given permission to speak. Perhaps we should return to the club and give you the chance to break the rest of my rules. Go for the fucking trifecta of disrespect."

Max crossed his arms over his chest and pressed his back against the closed door as he stared at Cisco. Cisco's heart was hammering in his chest, his grief trying to bubble up to the surface, but he gritted his teeth and blinked away the tears before they could fall. He'd fucked up and he'd take his punishment like a man.

"I gave you one simple command: do exactly as I tell you. Did you not tell me you understood?"

"Yes, Sir."

"And yet, you disobeyed me. I can hear your heart beating from several yards away, as can every other vampire in this club, so I guarantee, they also heard and saw your disrespect."

*Oh fuck!* He hadn't even realized, too focused on his own need to please that he completely ignored Max's need. Cisco hung his head; he had no excuse.

"Everything I do is for your own good. I will push you to your limits. I will make you work harder than you have ever worked before. What I will not do is ask you to do something I don't think you can handle. That being said, I demand the utmost respect, I deserve it. Tonight you denied me what I deserve, and you will have to be punished."

Cisco straightened and held his head high, ready to take his punishment. He'd gladly endure anything if Max forgave him.

"You are to remain in your room. You have until I return tomorrow night to think about what you have done and give me a good reason why I should allow you to return to the club with me."

With that, Max spun on his heels and strolled to the door. With his hand resting on the doorknob, he looked back at Cisco. "Remember I asked you to throw out everything you thought you knew about BDSM?"

"Yes, Sir."

"It wasn't a flippant statement. This is not your typical club, nor am I a typical Master. Out there, in your world, you can safeword—as a submissive you have the most power. But not here, Cisco. My kind are but animals with a tentative hold on humanity. Here, you fuck up, you die. I won't let that happen."

Staring at the closed door, Cisco's heart sped painfully as the full weight of his actions slammed into him. Alone, he could finally fall to his knees and give in to his grief. He did neither. He went to his desk, pulled out a pen and pad of paper from the drawer, and began to write. He went over every moment of the night, pouring his feelings out in a messy script. When Max returned, he'd take his punishment, and come hell or high water, he'd convince him why he deserved another chance, and mean it.

Max had been harsh, just as he had warned he could be, but now Cisco had a better understanding of why. Max not only had to teach Cisco how to live in this new world but also protect him. Considering Cisco was a tempting prey to many vampires, and even more so to those out to hurt Max, Cisco wouldn't make the same mistake twice. He refused to let anyone use his innocence to get to Max.

He would obey. It was the very least he could do in honor of the man who had just vowed to keep him alive.

# CHAPTER THIRTEEN

"I TOTALLY fucked up," Cisco blurted out as soon as Benny answered his phone.

"Yeah, you did. You called me at five in the morning. Have you lost your goddamn mind? Call me back at a decent hour," Benny complained sleepily.

"No, wait! Please I need your advice," Cisco pleaded.

"Jesus, Cisco, you know my brain doesn't work at this time of the morning."

"I know and I promise to make it up to you, but I really need to talk to you. I messed up last night. Max took me into the club for the first time, and I didn't obey his rules. He is beyond pissed at me."

"I'm proud of you."

"I'm serious."

"So am I. You're a grown man, dude. You don't have to take orders from your man. Haven't you ever heard the saying that compromise is the success to any long-lasting relationship?"

"It is a compromise, Benny. I know you have a hard time understanding it, but through pleasing him, I get pleasure. I'm not like you. I'm not aggressive or dominant. I want to serve him."

"You're right, I don't understand. What the hell do you mean you want to serve him? You barely know him," Benny countered.

"But I do know him. At least part of me does. It's like when you see someone and in that moment, you just know there's this connection. Only deeper, like soul-deep, almost magical in the way you're drawn together. That's what it's like with Max. I know I'm exactly where I belong and I'm really trying, but everything has been happening so fast, I'm having a hard time focusing."

"Well, if you have this magical connection, then he'll understand and give you a bit of time to adjust to everything. I don't see the problem."

"Well… umm…. You see…."

"Would you just spit it out? I want to help, but fuck I'm exhausted. I didn't get to bed till two and I have to get up in a couple hours for work. So if you don't mind…."

Cisco gritted his teeth and blew out a breath. Benny was going to freak. "I have to learn quickly because apparently Max accidently put me in danger and—"

Cisco pulled the phone away from his ear to keep Benny from rupturing his eardrum as he screamed. "I knew it. You need to get your ass home pronto!"

"I can't."

"Why the fuck not? I warned you that those bloodsuckers were going to end up killing you. If you're in danger, get the fuck out. Problem solved."

Cisco sighed. He should have known Benny wouldn't understand. It had been a mistake to call him, an even bigger one to tell him he was in danger, but he needed to talk to someone. He was feeling as if he were drifting in an ocean of uncertainty. He could use a damn lifeline, and he really needed Benny to be it.

"At this point I'd be in even more danger if I left. It's not from Max or his staff, it's from outside forces who want Max's power for themselves. Trust me, right now I'm better off here with Max than home."

"Fine, you won't listen to me about obeying. You won't listen to me about getting the fuck out of Dodge. Tell me again why you're calling me?"

"I guess I just needed to work it out in my head and have someone listen. Oh and because I love you."

"Uh-huh, don't try to suck up now," Benny grumbled. But Cisco could hear the hint of a grin. "So tell me what happened last night."

Cisco stretched out on his bed, sinking into the soft mattress as he recalled for Benny what had transpired in the club and the reason for Max's strong reaction. Cisco had already worked it out through his journal what he'd done wrong, what he had to apologize for, and why he should be allowed back in the club, but he wanted reassurances. Benny was always quick to point out the obvious, everything was black or white with him, but in the end he gave great advice. He also had Cisco's best interest at heart.

"Dammit, Cisco, I warned you not to go to that club. But you didn't listen and now you've gone and put yourself in danger. You don't have a choice but to obey him at this point."

"I know, but…. Ugh, this is a lot harder than I thought it would be."

"That's because you didn't fucking think!"

"You've always known I was a little bit of a scatterbrain," Cisco laughed nervously, doing his best to ease Benny's obvious anger. Another not so bright thing to do.

"Are you seriously going to crack jokes? Aren't you fucking scared? Jesus, Cisco, you could die!"

"Of course I'm scared and confused and a hundred other fucked-up things. But I also believe in Max and I have to prove that to him. I know he can keep me safe if I put my trust in him."

"Do you really?"

"Yes," Cisco replied without hesitation.

"And yet, you said you were comfortable in this submissive role, but he gives you very specific instructions and you break two of the three main points."

"I know, but that's before I truly understood just how grave the situation was and what Max was willing to do for me," Cisco sighed. "But I know now, the problem is with everything going on, I'm having a really hard time focusing."

"Ask him for help. He's this big ol' bad Dom. Isn't it his job to teach you?"

"It's…. I mean, I know I should tell him, but…. Benny, he's everything to me and it's really important that he sees me as someone who is worthy to belong to him."

"So you'd rather fail him and yourself and end up pushing up daisies? That makes a shit-ton of sense, Cisco." Benny's tone was full of exasperation, and Cisco didn't have to see Benny to know he was rolling his eyes.

"No." Cisco sighed again and then stifled a yawn.

"You already know what you have to do."

"I know. I just needed to hear you say I was on the right track."

"The right track would be to bring your ass home and forget all this nonsense, but since that's no longer an option, you need to suck it up, apologize, and start fresh. You must talk to Max about your difficulties."

"I will and thanks for listening, Benny. I knew you'd help."

"I don't know how much help I've been but you're welcome. Please be careful, Cisco."

"I will," Cisco promised. "I'll talk to you soon. I miss you."

"Miss you too, brat," Benny said sadly, and the line went dead.

Cisco turned off his phone and set it on the bedside table before lying back with his arms folded beneath his head and staring at the ceiling. It had been selfish to call and worry Benny as he had—he was doing that a lot lately. But no more. Beginning tonight, he was going to be the man he knew he could be, not only for himself, but for Max and Benny too.

THE FAMILIAR urge of wanting to rush to Cisco the minute his eyes opened was present, but once again Max resisted it. He didn't want to leave Cisco hanging too long, but it would do no good to make it easy on the boy either. Cisco must learn, must realize how imperative it was that he learned, and learned quickly. It was the only way Max had any chance at keeping his boy safe. He pulled himself from his bed and padded across the room to the bathroom. He set the taps to hot and stepped beneath the flow. He washed himself thoroughly, including shampooing and conditioning his hair. He took care to dry, brush his teeth and hair, and pay the same meticulous attention to his hygiene and attire as he normally did.

As he dressed in black slacks and a white linen shirt, his thoughts wandered to the night before. It had started out perfectly. He'd enjoyed his visit with Jacob, the club was full, exciting, and without any disturbances. He'd also noticed the way many of the members of the club looked at Cisco. Some with awe, others with disappointment it wasn't them at his side, but the one thing that stood out was it was plain to see that everyone saw Cisco as the attractive man he was. It had triggered Max's pride; his boy looked good at his side, complemented him. Yet his jealousy had always been just below the surface. He knew it was something he would have to learn to deal with and accept as a part of his life. He'd learned to control his impulses when he'd first turned. He was confident he'd learn to control this one as well.

Cisco had started out as the perfect sub, kept his posture straight, his head high and gaze low. He'd heeled beautifully, and the envious looks Max had gotten from the Doms and the longing looks he'd gotten from the submissives had made his pride swell. Unfortunately Cisco had made mistakes that were more than likely witnessed by others. He'd overreacted. It hadn't been the minor infractions that had ignited his fury but perceived threats, and he'd allowed them to dictate his actions. It was stupid, but at the same time, it was imperative that Cisco listen to him and follow his orders without hesitation. He believed Cisco desired to be with him, but he must also be smart. He had to take the dangers seriously. The best way to keep his boy safe was to know he could depend on him to follow his instructions to the letter.

He sat on the edge of the bed and pulled on his knee boots, tucking his pants into them. He then stood before the full-length mirror and inspected his image. It was the same one that had stared back at him for a hundred years, preserved perfectly, forever thirty. He wouldn't age— no wrinkles, no graying of his hair, never changing. Being immortal had its advantages, yet he often wished for mortality, even more so now. He wanted to grow old with Cisco; he did not wish to watch his boy age, wither away, and eventually die. He had faced many deaths during his long existence; however, Cisco's was one death he knew he might not recover from. Knowing that, Max would follow Cisco into the dark.

He tied his hair back with a leather thong, gave his reflection one last once-over and stepped out of his room. Angelo, Silas, and Darius were waiting for him in the antechamber.

"Good evening, gentlemen."

"Evening, Max," they all responded in unison.

Max held out his fist to Darius. "Hell of a show you put on last night."

"Thanks." Darius grinned and bumped his fist against Max's.

Silas draped his arm over Darius's shoulder. "C'mon, rock star, let's go see what Patrick has lined up for your morning snack." He stopped and looked at Max. "You're welcome to join us if you'd like?"

"No, you two go ahead, I'd like to have a word with Angelo."

As soon as the other two were gone, Angelo turned to him. "What's up?"

"Let's go to my office."

Once in his office, Max went to his desk and pulled out a thick file from his drawer. He slid it across the desk to Angelo. "I need you to take this to the council."

Angelo frowned as he picked up the file. "I thought they were already considering our request for more vampires?"

"They are. It's not the CVHC I need you to address, but the vampire council. I've been thinking a lot about what you said, and you're right, we have to do something about Zeke. I need you to work your magic and convince Egnatius to sign a death warrant for Zeke."

"Jesus, Max." Angelo whistled. "You do realize how hard it is to get an audience with him, don't you?"

"Of course I do," Max replied. Egnatius was the supreme ruler over the entire race of vampires, the oldest of their kind and last surviving vampire to have been turned by the father of their race. But he was their only hope of having the warrant issued. "We can't take it to the state council. Zeke has too many supporters. There are many who have grown restless with the slow progress we've made in integration and many more who agree with Zeke's ideologies of taking over the human race rather than becoming a part of it."

Angelo thumbed through the file, his scowl deepening as he examined it. "I agree we can't take this to the state, but you do realize a lot of people are going to be pissed that you didn't follow the chain of command."

"I don't care," Max retorted and pushed a button to reveal a hidden compartment within the drawer. He pulled out a file and slid it across the desk, holding Angelo's questioning gaze. "Once Egnatius reads this, I doubt the state council will have enough time to complain about whether I have broken the chain of command or not."

Angelo studied the closed file suspiciously before picking it up and opening it. Angelo scanned across the first page, and Max knew the moment the extent of his mission hit him by the way his eyes widened and he looked back up at Max.

"If this is proven to be true, it won't be only Zeke who will be meeting the sun. You sure you're prepared for the fallout from this?"

Max nodded gravely. There were many who would be affected, destroyed, even his own maker. But Max had no choice but to proceed. He had to protect his coven. He'd been gathering information for years, debating as to when to reveal the dark secrets he'd uncovered. Now with Cisco safely behind the walls of his compound, it was time.

"I won't demand that you do this. I will still expect you to garner a warrant for Zeke, but as for the issues with the state leaders, I'll leave that to you. Read over the file before you make your decision. The ramifications will affect us all."

Angelo closed the file and stacked it with the other on Zeke. "I don't need time to read it over. You believe it is time to take it to Egnatius and that's enough for me. When do I leave?"

"Tomorrow at nightfall." Max stood and held out his hand. "You honor me, old friend."

Angelo shook the offered hand. "And you honor me with your trust with this matter."

Max slumped into his chair after Angelo left and scrubbed a hand over his face. What was done was done, and there was no going back now. A storm had been brewing for quite some time and it was about to slam down on them. Lives would be forever changed, some lost, even within his own house.

As difficult as the decision had been, Max knew it had to be done. He could only hope that once the storm passed, their foundation would still be strong enough to rebuild upon.

# Chapter Fourteen

Max pulled the key from his pocket, unlocked the door, and swung it open to reveal the room inside. A large Saint Andrew's cross was the focal point of the room, and he knew the second Cisco spotted it from the small gasp he made. Max smiled and led his boy into the room, a space he'd had designed for his and Cisco's private times; everything new and fresh. The thrill of finally having Cisco there, the opportunity to finally enjoy it, caused his arousal to grow.

"You may inspect the cross," Max instructed. "Become familiar with it as you will no doubt be spending a lot of time bound to it."

"Yes, Sir."

Cisco was timid as he made his way closer to the cross. He ran his hands over the black leather and wood as well as the iron rings secured to the cross at wrist, neck, and ankle, testing each one for their strength. A look of awe mixed with apprehension crossed Cisco's face as he rattled the metal shackles that hung from the ceiling.

Max walked over to the armoire, pulled open the doors, and picked up a small crop, testing its weight against his thigh. "So, boy," Max said as he walked up close to Cisco, "there is the matter of your punishment we must address."

Cisco's shoulders slumped slightly, but he caught himself quickly and corrected his posture. "I have thought a lot about it, Sir. I am ready for my punishment."

"And what are you being punished for?"

"At first I thought it was because I hadn't listened, had disrespected you by not following your orders." Cisco worried his bottom lip with his teeth for a moment, a thoughtful expression on his face. "Which, come to think of it, was foolishness on my part and I have no excuse for my misbehavior. But I realize it comes down to one thing that caused the problem and which I need to be punished for."

"And that is?" Max prompted.

"For not trusting you, Sir. I was so worried about what was going on around the club, what others might think of me, what you might think of me, and I even put my own pleasure above yours. I should have trusted that what you were asking of me was the right thing for me and not cared what others thought. I didn't trust you and in doing so I displeased you. Not only did I displease you but I put you and myself in danger. I understand how serious this situation is and I promise to do better. I want to make it up to you, Sir. I promise I will try harder if given the opportunity to prove myself to you."

"It sounds as if you've thought quite a bit about your behavior."

"Yes, Sir, it's all I thought about. I even started a journal to help me work through the events of the evening, and I will use it as a reference to learn from."

"That's good, very good," Max praised, a smile tugging at his upper lip, which he didn't even try to hide from Cisco. His boy had done well, had thought about his actions, and was ready to make amends. "While it is true a Dom's job is to earn a submissive's trust, we do not have the luxury of time in which to earn it. You must simply choose to trust me or not, to obey or not, to please me or not. They are all your choices to make, but you must remember that each choice will have a consequence. Kneel."

Cisco dropped to his knees, squared his shoulders, and pushed his chest out, and he had a confident and determined expression on his face as he settled into his display position. Max took his time, leisurely raking his gaze up and down Cisco's body. He really was quite the exquisite creature. He might be on the smaller side, but his muscles were firm and well defined beneath his smooth olive skin. Not only was Cisco sexually appealing, but he was also intellectually appealing. He was shy, innocent, but beneath that head of dark hair was a quick mind. Even if Cisco could be a bit exasperating at times with his insufferable babbling, Max couldn't have asked for a better mate. And he did have a hell of an array of gags at his disposal so he doubted Cisco's babbling would be a real issue.

Forcing his gaze away, Max stepped directly in front of Cisco. "As you learned last night, punishment is easy to earn. Tonight we will begin with your punishment, but in the future, each evening will start with discipline and end with any punishment that you have earned."

Cisco's face scrunched up in confusion.

"Do you have an issue with this?"

"No, that's not it, Sir, it's just… I don't understand the difference. When I was growing up, my parents used the two words interchangeably. But honestly, they both felt like the same thing to me."

Max thought about Cisco's concern for a moment. He could see where his boy would be confused. He would need to keep in mind that Cisco had no real experience within the lifestyle and would need to be acclimated quickly.

After considering his words carefully, he said, "It takes a lot of self-discipline to submit, so think of it as a tool that gives you the opportunity to settle into the proper headspace before the evening gets under way. Punishment is about learning from the mistakes you've made. Once administered, it gives you a clean slate. Your mistakes are made up for and forgiven and I will not ever use them against you unless you do not learn from them and continue to make them. Now do you understand the difference?"

"Yes, Sir." Cisco nodded. "I understand, Sir. I want your forgiveness, want to learn, want to please you."

"Then go face the cross so we can deal with your mistakes and move on."

"Yes, Sir. Thank you, Sir." Cisco approached the cross, started to reach for the wrist cuffs, then jerked his hands back and shifted from foot to foot, unsure.

Max didn't let him struggle. He stood behind him, dropped the crop to the floor with a small thud, and took his right wrist, securing it with the cuff before doing the same with the left. Max then slid his hands down Cisco's body. As he moved, he caressed Cisco's back, his ass, his thighs, enjoying the way his touch pulled a low moan from Cisco. He secured Cisco's feet to the cuffs at the bottom of the cross, completing the X with Cisco's body. As Max rose, he gave in to the urge to taste and licked his way from Cisco's low back up to the base of his skull.

"You taste good," he murmured against Cisco's ear as he pressed his body against his boy's.

"Mmm, thank you, Sir. You feel good," Cisco murmured.

Max wished he'd had Cisco remove his pants before he'd bound him to the cross. He would have loved to have explored his boy's luscious body with fingers and tongue, pull more of those sweet sounds from Cisco, indulge in a little pleasure, maybe find a little release for his aching cock. With a sigh he grudgingly took a step back.

Cisco whimpered and turned his head to look at Max over his shoulder, a look of disappointment on his face.

"Eyes on the cross, boy," Max ordered as he retrieved the crop.

Cisco jerked his head, obeying Max immediately. "Sorry, Sir."

Max tested the crop against his thigh once again, happy with the sound it made and the weight of it in his hand. It would work nicely for Cisco's first experience with punishment.

"You will take a stroke for not trusting me, another for speaking when you were ordered to remain silent, and a third for failing to put my pleasure above your own. Take them for me."

Cisco shifted his stance as best he could, tested the strength of his retrains and blew out a heavy breath before settling against the cross and responding, "Yes, Sir."

Max took another step back and swung quickly.

"Ow!" Cisco yelped as the first blow connected with his right shoulder.

Max watched as a red welt began to rise on Cisco's skin. Satisfied with the strength of the blow and the result, he swung again, placing a matching stripe on Cisco's other shoulder.

Cisco cried out and hunched his shoulders in a futile attempt to escape the blow. Max could feel Cisco's tension increase, heard the harsh intake of his breath and couldn't miss the way his legs were beginning to shake.

Max stepped close once again, careful not to make contact with Cisco's shoulder but close enough to give him reassurance. "Deep breath. Take the pain into yourself, welcome it and know through the pain you are not only learning from your mistakes but being forgiven."

Cisco took a few more deep breaths as he opened and closed his hands and then seemed to settle once again, his breathing slow and even. "Thank you for your forgiveness."

Max took one step back at the same time he swung and added another stripe just below the first one. Cisco went up on tiptoes, his body tensing as he held his breath, but he didn't cry out. After a few heartbeats, he blew out a breath and the tension seeped from his body in a rush. Cisco's first experience with punishment produced a smile from his boy, no doubt from both pride and relief. Max's initial belief his boy was a natural sub was confirmed.

Max dropped the crop and pulled his shirt off, tossing it haphazardly behind him. He pressed his chest to Cisco's back, causing him to hiss as Max made contact with the stripes. Yet even with the sting, he pressed back against the contact. Max adjusted his stance as he slid his hands along Cisco's arms until he reached his bound hand and entwined their fingers. They were pressed chest to back, thigh to thigh and hand in hand in the same X position.

"Punishment is easy to earn, but if you learn from your mistakes, try hard to better yourself, then you please me," he whispered against Cisco's ear as he pressed his growing erection against his boy's ass. "If you fail, try again."

"I want to please you," Cisco moaned and tried to thrust his ass back against Max's groin but could do little more than wiggle in the limited space between Max's body and the cross.

Max licked a path from the juncture of shoulder and neck up to the soft, warm spot below Cisco's ear. His flavor, the sweet scent of his flesh, and the steady rhythm of his pulse caused Max's gut to clench and his mouth to water. He scraped the tips of his fangs against Cisco's skin. His boy tilted his head, offering himself to his Master. Max was dizzy with need, his desire for blood overshadowing his arousal. So tempting. He pressed his mouth a little harder, felt the skin dip in, start to give.

*No!*

Max spun away at the last second, putting some distance between himself and Cisco. He couldn't risk it. He bent, hands on his knees, and closed his eyes as he struggled to rein in the animal within him. For the time being, he'd set aside his quest for Iunctiō Cōpula, but that didn't mean he would abandon it. He couldn't, his need to discover its truths even more important now.

"Sir?" Cisco asked in confusion.

It took a few more minutes to lock down his need before he could finally straighten and take care of his boy. He'd have enjoyed exploring his boy's body, rewarding him with pleasure, but the beast within had been awakened and until it was fed there was no way he could keep it contained.

Without a word, Max inspected Cisco's wounds, making sure the skin wasn't split. Satisfied his flesh was merely heated, Max removed the cuffs from Cisco's wrists, then bent to remove the cuffs from his ankles.

"Sir? Have I displeased you somehow?" Cisco asked with a shaky voice.

"No, you did very well taking your punishment. I'm proud of you, boy."

"Then… I don't understand."

Max removed the last cuff and then stood, taking a step back. He no longer trusted himself to be close to Cisco. He curled his hands into fists to keep from reaching out and taking what he wanted, what the beast demanded.

Max started to snap at Cisco. It wasn't his place to question Max, but the sadness and confusion were palpable and it wasn't fair to allow his boy to think he'd done something wrong.

"It is nothing you have done. I simply must feed, and until I do so, I cannot be trusted to take care of you properly."

Cisco rubbed at his wrists as he slowly turned around. "It would be my honor to feed you, Sir."

Going to the armoire, Max pulled out a small container of salve and put a dab on a gauze pad. He then walked around Cisco and tended to the wounds. The strong antiseptic scent covered up Cisco's, making it bearable for Max to be near him.

"That is not possible."

"I was talking to Patrick, and he said Silas takes blood from him."

"That is because they are bonded," Max informed him and threw the pad in the garbage. "Come along, boy."

"Yes, Sir."

"You will wait in your room until I return," Max instructed as they walked down the hall toward Cisco's apartment. "There is no need for you to wait in display for my return. You may use your time to reflect upon your punishment."

"Yes, Sir. Permission to speak, Sir?"

Max rolled his neck and opened the door, ushering Cisco in and then closing it behind them. "Yes, as long as you are respectful and remember your place."

"Of course, Sir. I'm just curious about the bond. You said Silas and Patrick are bonded and it is why Silas can feed from Patrick. But you talked of a bond between us and yet you cannot."

Max went to the bar and poured himself a snifter full of brandy and brought it to his nose, inhaling deeply. It too helped mask Cisco's scent, easing the clawing in his belly, but only slightly. Cisco had the right to know such details, but it was more complicated than a simple answer and might take longer than he could keep the beast at bay.

He threw the brandy back in one large gulp. "I will explain everything upon my return." He walked over to Cisco and ran his knuckles along the boy's soft cheek. "Do not worry. Our bond is strong, and one day you will be all I need in all things. Understood?"

"Yes, Sir," Cisco responded with a relieved tone and pushed into Max's touch. "Thank you. I will look forward to your return."

The hunger flared again, ripping through Max's stomach like a sharp knife. He stepped past Cisco, averting his eyes, knowing they would be glowing red. Without another word, he traced from the room before he lost all control.

# CHAPTER FIFTEEN

WITH ONE hunger satisfied, another flared brightly in Max. His cock was hard, his desire for his boy now demanding it be sated. He'd promised Cisco they would talk and they would, but as he walked into Cisco's room, finding him sitting on the couch dressed in nothing but a pair of black boxers, it was too much of a temptation to deny himself.

"Come here, boy," Max demanded.

Cisco scrambled to his feet, and as soon as he was within reach, Max grabbed him and pulled him into an embrace. "I have need of your body," Max murmured, his voice low and husky with desire.

"It is yours to control," Cisco moaned as he slid his hand around Max, fingers digging into his back, kneading.

"Kiss me."

Cisco leaned forward, pressed his lips against Max's, and flicked his tongue out, licking, asking for admittance. Max opened to Cisco, allowing himself to be kissed and touched, letting Cisco set the pace for a moment. Cisco was heavy against him, his boy's mouth hot and wet, and the smell of arousal wafting in the air.

Cisco explored Max's mouth with tentative swipes of his tongue until Max thought he'd go mad if he didn't deepen it. Impatient, Max took control of the kiss, dominated it, sliding his tongue along Cisco's lips, teeth, and tangling with his tongue. He slid his fingers through Cisco's short hair, grasping it and angling his head as his tongue slid deeper, pulling a needy moan from his boy.

With his free hand, he trailed his fingers over the warm skin of Cisco's back, tracing lean muscles that flexed at his touch. He moaned into Cisco's mouth as their erections pressed against each other from the rolling rhythmic sway they had begun, their bodies in perfect sync. Max was awash with need, hungry, although it wasn't a thirst for blood driving him but the sweet aroma of arousal and the warm, firm body against his.

Max ended the kiss, leaving Cisco breathing harshly and clinging to Max's shoulders as he moved down the lithe body. He closed his mouth over one of Cisco's nipples, teeth grazing and tongue sliding. Max nibbled and suckled at his skin. As he continued the assault on first one then the other nipple, Max steered them toward Cisco's bed. When his boy's calves hit the mattress, Max pushed Cisco down and covered his small body with Max's larger one. He propped himself up by placing his hands on either side of Cisco's head, staring down at Cisco as he rolled his hips. Cisco arched his back, a low rumbling moan pouring from him. As Cisco stretched and swayed beneath him, he bared his neck, the pulse pumping the promise of life, calling to Max like a siren's song. He ducked his head, letting his open mouth trail over blood pumping close to the surface. His boy willing, wanting it, would make the taste all the sweeter. Right there, right beneath his tongue, he could feel the life, could feel the ties of their bond tightening.

With the last sliver of his will, Max leaned back. Now was not the time. This was about Cisco, his rewards, about reassurance after what had taken place in the playroom.

"One day, I will feed from you and only you."

"I want that," Cisco moaned, his body still arching, still swaying. His erection hard and throbbing against Max's groin.

"You must trust me," Max murmured against Cisco's lips. "Everything I do, every action, every thought, is with you in mind."

Max forced his hand between their bodies without taking his gaze from Cisco's eyes. His fingers slid smoothly over Cisco's engorged cock, pushing down the cotton material of his boxers. The silky skin of Cisco's cock was warm against his palm.

"So good to me," Cisco moaned and thrust into Max's fist.

Max shifted to lie next to his boy, hand roaming over the smooth, hot skin, stroking, teasing. Cisco's eyes met his as he arched into Max's touch. Dark eyes full of passion and hunger.

"I can be very good to you," Max whispered, increasing the pressure on Cisco's cock, quickening his strokes. "I can give you such unimaginable pleasure and a peace within yourself few ever find. Trust me with your mind, body, and soul. Give me your submission, and I can make you whole."

"Want you.... Oh... oh God I want that. So bad...."

Max kept his strokes strong and steady. "Then give it to me, boy. I'll make you feel so good."

"It's.... Ah God, it's yours. All yours," Cisco whimpered breathlessly. His hips were in constant motion, thrusting and rolling as he chased his orgasm.

Max shifted again, situating himself between Cisco's spread legs. He continued to jerk his boy off, his other hand teasing the sensitive skin of his balls, sliding back farther to tease at his opening. Cisco tensed.

"Trust me," Max murmured. "I know what you need." It took a few heartbeats, his boy still unsure, before he relaxed, rocking up into Max's touch. Max pressed harder, not penetrating, just pressure. "That's it."

"Close... ah so close... hard... I ache," Cisco babbled, his face flushed. Moans, whimpers, and disjointed words poured from him as he began to thrust in earnest.

"Come for me," Max demanded as he thrust the tip of his finger inside Cisco's ass.

Cisco's back bowed up off the mattress, every muscle in his body tensing for a split second before he shouted out his release. Rope after rope of hot seed landed on his stomach and chest. Max jerked him until the last drop dripped from the flared head and Cisco slumped against the bed, gulping for air, his heart fluttering.

Max stared at him in awe. His boy was spent, drenched in sweat, and the evidence of his hard release glistened on his flesh. Cisco was so beautiful when he gave in to his pleasure. A small smile curled Cisco's lips as he came back down from the heights of his orgasm.

"Thank you, that was.... Sir, that was amazing."

"It looked amazing from my vantage point as well," Max replied with a wink.

Cisco propped himself up on his elbows and looked down at the mess on his torso. "Looks messy," he chuckled.

Max ran a single finger from Cisco's breastbone to his navel, then pressed his come-covered finger against Cisco's lips. Cisco hesitated for only a split second before his lips parted and Max pushed his finger in. Cisco sucked on the digit, his dark eyes watching Max.

The scent of sweat and semen wafted up, filling Max's nose. His cock throbbed, but he ignored it. The unfamiliar urge to curl up and hold Cisco overpowered his need to fuck. A feeling he'd never experienced till now. It wasn't unpleasant or unwelcome.

"Let's get you cleaned up a bit," Max suggested and crawled off the bed.

"Please, Sir. Is there something I can do to show my gratitude?" Cisco asked, his gaze on the thick bulge in Max's pants as he licked his lips. "Repay your kindness."

Max held out his hand. "Yes, you can come get cleaned up as I instructed." He winked, letting his boy know he was not upset, just a little bit of a tease rather than criticism. He felt good, really good. Which considering his cock was hard and going untouched, sort of boggled his mind. However, he didn't dwell on it long. He had a messy boy to clean up.

HE WAS warm and flushed from his recent shower, and still boneless from the orgasm Max had pulled from him. There was soft music playing. Cisco should have been able to relax into the soft cushions, especially with Max's arm around him, holding him close. But he couldn't relax. He wasn't sure if he was dreaming or not, and he was afraid to move, afraid to take his gaze off Max, who was resting next to him with his eyes closed, for fear he would disappear.

He'd always fantasized about submitting to Max, pleasing his Master, the beatings, the fucking, the service. But the really good ones, the ones that made him happiest, were the ones like he was currently having. With Max's hard, cold body against his heated one, he should be shivering. But that's how he knew he had to be asleep. He was infused with warmth.

"What are you thinking about that has you so tense?" Max asked without opening his eyes.

"I was thinking I don't want this dream to end," he admitted honestly.

Max opened his eyes, his head lolling to the side to meet Cisco's gaze. "You're having a good dream and yet you're tense? That doesn't make a whole lot of sense, boy," Max chuckled.

"You're right," Cisco said, returning Max's smile. "It makes no sense. I'm just being mushy and sentimental."

"Would you like to hear a secret?"

"Yes, Sir."

"Before I was turned, I used to have a bit of a mushy side myself. Most would argue that point, but I had my moments. Of course I will deny it if anyone accuses me," he said with a grin.

"And now?"

"I no longer have such emotions."

"I don't believe it."

"Alas, it's true." Max laid his head back and closed his eyes. Max was denying it, but there was a look of tenderness on his face as he spoke. "It's one of the pitfalls of being immortal. I try to hold on to some of my human nature, but each passing year, it becomes more and more difficult to recall those feelings."

"I don't see a whole lot of difference between humans and vampires. So you have the superhuman strength and the whole living forever thing going on, and I don't go around sucking blood out of people." Cisco laughed. "Okay, so we are different, but well, you look human, you talk like you're a human."

"It is not what you think, Cisco. I behave civilized, demand it from my followers, strictly for the survival of my race. Not because of any sentimental reasons. Trying to maintain a footing in two worlds is very difficult. It is why I demand your absolute obedience. If you are to be a part of my other world, then you must keep your hold on both just as I must do. I admit it is very difficult to balance both, but unfortunately it is a requirement and one at which you cannot fail." Max's brow furrowed. "The repercussions are quick and brutal."

"Yes, I understand that, Sir. I'm not afraid."

Max rolled so quickly to his side that Cisco jerked back and gasped in surprise. "You should be. You should always have some sliver of fear within you at all times. But rather than let it cripple you, you must use it to make yourself stronger. That includes fear of what I could do to you."

"Why… why must I fear you?" Cisco stammered.

"Because I am an animal. Any wild animal that is wounded, feels cornered, or is starving will lash out and attack. Remember that, Cisco. Vampires live by instinct. We can only hold back the beast within us to a certain degree. You must always hold on to a shred of that fear and treat the vampires within my clan as you would any wild animal. Understood?"

Cisco began to tremble slightly, his throat dry. He nodded rather than try to speak past his constricted throat.

Max ran a soothing hand along Cisco's back, pulled him in close once again. "I don't say these things to upset you, but to prepare you. With regular feeding a vampire can control most of his urges, but without blood, he soon reverts to pure animal. It's why blood-bonded vampires have an easier time walking the edge of both worlds. It's the most intimate act that a human and vampire can share. It goes even deeper than the intimacy of the sexual act."

Both longing and jealousy rose up in Cisco. The idea of Max sharing that kind of intimacy with another person made his chest tighten. He wanted to be the only one Max shared such things with.

But he couldn't ask, couldn't demand it of Max, although he did want to understand so he asked, "Seeing as you've taken me on as your submissive, would it not make things easier on you if we were to have that bond?"

"Yes, but as I said, our bond is a bit deeper, I believe. Remember me telling you about Iunctiō Cōpula?"

"Yes, a bonding link or something."

"Yes, that's it. I must learn more about the ritual as the taking of blood for the first time may be part of the process." Max shook his head. "I don't even know if it's real, but I have to believe it is. The hope of what it could do is what has kept me sane all these years."

"I would think it would be great to live forever. Doesn't dying scare you? I know it does me," Cisco admitted. It had since he was a young boy. Having lived through the death of his grandparents, father, other close relatives, friends, he'd always feared it. Would it hurt, what happened after death, was heaven real, and if it was, did that mean hell had to be real as well?

"Ah, but I am not living, Cisco. Just like the line I walk between the two worlds of human and vampire, I also walk that same fine line between life and death. The only way to get off that tightrope is to fall into real death. If I was given a chance to live again, even if only for a short time, I'd welcome death."

Cisco was beginning to understand Max better. It had to be so hard to navigate all the worlds he must exist in. As difficult as it would be to know Max was feeding from someone else, he'd endure it, he'd endure anything if he could help him obtain his dream of living again. To give him that one true pleasure. Now that he had a better understanding, he wanted to know everything about Max.

"Tell me about your life before you were turned."

Max pulled him in closer still and glanced at the clock before saying, "You better get comfortable, this may take a while."

Cisco draped his arm over Max and laid his head on Max's chest, snuggled against him. Getting comfortable for a long night against Max was no hardship at all.

# CHAPTER SIXTEEN

"I WAS born in Philadelphia, Pennsylvania, on Christmas Day, 1877. My parents had immigrated there ten years before my birth. From what I understand, they had tried numerous times to have children, but unfortunately each pregnancy had ended in miscarriage. They were ecstatic when my mother was finally able to carry a child past her fifth month. In December of '77, she was eight months pregnant and they were looking forward to my arrival."

"So your mom had you early?"

"Yes, but my birth was not to be the celebration they had hoped for. My father was a police officer, and he was stabbed severely while in the discharge of his duty. He died of his wounds before a physician could be fetched. My mother in her aggrieved state went into labor and I was born later that night."

Cisco shifted closer, laying his head on Max's shoulder, and ran a soothing hand along Max's chest. "How awful," he said, sounding earnest. "Did they ever catch the man that killed your father?"

"Oh yes, they paid for their crime."

"They?"

"Joseph Rebman had been my father's charge. His twin brother Jarvis had assisted him in the escape. They fled to New Jersey. Having learned that the officers of the law were in pursuit, they committed suicide by drowning. At least that is what the official report stated. I'm inclined to believe the officers handed out a bit of justice by becoming judge, jury, and executioner. But either way, my father was avenged."

"So what happened with your mom? It must have been difficult to raise a child on her own."

"We shall never know. She died when I was three."

"Jesus, Max," Cisco said and jerked upright to look down at Max with tears brimming in his eyes. "That's the saddest story I've ever heard. How can you not be crying your eyes out while remembering it?"

"Ah, Cisco," Max responded gently and ran the back of his knuckles across Cisco's cheek. "It was a very long time ago, and I have told you, I no longer feel such emotions as love and sadness."

"I don't believe it," Cisco retorted. "You act like a big ol' bad vampire Master, but I know you have the capacity to care. I see how hard you fight for your clan and I've seen you in action. You don't fool me."

"When it comes to what I do for my clan, it is simply out of duty and a deep instinctual drive to survive, and my—shall we call them affections—for you are…." Max tried to find the right words. Displaying emotions and feeling them were two completely different things. Yes, he was fond of Cisco, but instinct drew him to the man and possessiveness wasn't the same as love. Max gave up trying to explain. "Let's just agree to disagree on the subject of my feelings." He encouraged Cisco to lay his head back down upon his chest.

"Yes, Sir," Cisco complied, sounding resigned, but Max knew the subject would come up again. He'd seen the glint of defiance in his boy's eyes.

Max held Cisco, enjoying the warmth of his body and the peace in the quiet. But his curious boy didn't stay silent for long.

"How did you become a vampire?"

"Well, I moved to Chicago in 1900 and followed in my father's footsteps, becoming a police officer. It was actually a pretty boring job. Hell, the average officer on a beat only made about thirty arrests a year, roughly half for disorderly conduct, drunkenness, or vagrancy. But I was still proud of what I did, considering my humble beginnings in an orphanage. I couldn't have known then just how close those footsteps were."

"You were murdered," Cisco asked, sounding incredulous.

"Yes and no." Max shrugged.

"Okay, that's a strange answer. How does one get murdered but doesn't?" Cisco chuckled.

"I see your point. The city had experienced a rash of bombings, and I was hurt during the investigation. I was sent to a private hospital outside the city to convalesce. My wounds became badly infected and I was stricken with fever. Dr. Bragdon was sure I would die and, under the cloak of darkness, had me transferred to a private home. I don't know if I would have died from my injuries. Perhaps. But I did die that night. So come to think of it, either way you look at it, the person who detonated the bomb did commit murder."

"I understand now why you're such a good leader and disciplined. It makes sense that you would be... I don't know... the sheriff of the vampires. Was Angelo in law enforcement too?"

"Don't let him hear you ask that," Max laughed.

"Really? Why is that? I would think it would be an honorable job."

"Angelo... shall we say, comes from much more notable beginnings than I. He is a noblesse d'épée, meaning nobility of the sword. He's a direct descendant from the house of Sebastiano-Amadeus. He believes in law and order, but he's a warrior and much, much older than I."

"Wow, he must be ancient."

"As a matter of fact, he is," Max said curtly.

Cisco jerked up again, his eyes wide. "Seriously?" Obviously Max wasn't able to keep his neutral expression or Cisco was learning them, because he narrowed his eyes, a disbelieving expression on his face. "Stop teasing me."

"What? Eighty years is much older than I am."

"Uh-huh. I bet you're teasing about the nobility part too. Wouldn't he be like the head guy or something?"

"Angelo doesn't wish the job. He is content with being the protector of the ruler, rather than ruling."

Cisco yawned big and snuggled closer into Max's side. They'd had a busy night, his boy no doubt exhausted. "Okay, let's get you tucked in. I'll be retiring soon."

"I hate it when you leave," Cisco mumbled and then yawned again.

"You're sleeping when I'm gone. How can you hate it?"

Cisco extracted himself from Max and then stood near the couch and held out a hand. "I don't know. I just do."

His boy was obviously more exhausted than Max had thought. He wasn't making any sense. Max took the offered hand and then led Cisco to the bed, pulling back the covers and holding them until Cisco slid beneath the sheets.

"Can't you stay for just a little bit longer, Sir?" Cisco asked, his eyes already closing.

"Not this time, boy. Now go to sleep." Max tucked the covers around his boy and brushed a finger along his warm cheek. Cisco sighed and within seconds his breathing deepened, becoming slow and even. Max switched the light off and quietly slipped from the room, a smile on his face and that strange warmth tickling his belly.

MAX SAT in his office, staring at nothing. The pleasant calm he always experienced when lying with Cisco was gone. His boy's curious mind brought back unwanted memories. What he hadn't told Cisco was when asked about his past the first thing that came to mind was blood.

Those early days had been nothing but blood. His need for it. Nothing else had mattered. He'd been ruled by it. Now at times like this, when he closed his eyes, he could see them. His victims.

Horror-filled eyes stared at him accusingly from pale faces surrounded by a halo of blood.

Always blood.

How many had he killed? Ten? Twenty? A hundred? He knew not.

The days and months after he'd changed had been a haze of agony. He'd been so hungry. God, the blood.... He scrubbed a palm over his face and then hung his head in his hands. So much blood.

He didn't know who his victims were, what kind of devastation he'd left their families to deal with, but he knew their eyes. He would never rid himself of the image of those dead eyes.

*Do you feel guilty?*

A woman's voice, a familiar one.

This had been the same voice that had spoken to him through the haze of red that had marked those early days. He didn't know who the disembodied voice belonged to, perhaps his mother, his conscience, or simply the imaginings of a ravished mind.

Did he feel guilty?

As Max sat there, he tried to recall what it felt like to experience it, but it was difficult. He knew anger, rage, hunger, desire, hate, but guilt? No, he'd done what he'd had to do to survive. He knew he should, yet he did not, the feeling absent just as love was. But how could he hate but not love?

It was the same question he'd been asking himself for years without ever finding the answer. It seemed odd that he could so readily feel hate, could taste its bitterness on his tongue, but have such difficulty recalling love. The more he thought about it, the new sensations Cisco brought out in him, he questioned if it were in fact part of the curse that denied him love, or was it he simply had never experienced it before, either in this life or his past one.

*DON'T LOOK back, he'll find you.*

*Run.*

*Don't stop.*

Cisco did, straight to Benny's door, calling to him like a light at the end of a dark tunnel. Pounding. Bloodied knuckles. Harder now. Hurry, hurry, hurry. No one came. Locked.

Panic bubbled up within him, heart pounding. But then words were whispered, soft breath against his ear lulling him like a lover's seductive tone: *Run.*

Cisco turned, the darkness closing in on him. No stars. No moon. No hope.

*Run!*

He sprinted across the lawn, rocks and twigs cutting into the tender flesh of his bare feet. He ignored the sting of pain. Ran. Max had taught him. He could endure it.

*Max!*

He had to find his Master. Max would protect him. But where to run?

*Blackness.*

*Nothingness.*

*Hopelessness.*

Muscles straining, breathing labored, he raced through the dark. Branches scratched his face, his arms, and his chest, pulled his hair. He was in a forest, dirt and leaves beneath his feet.

Was he going mad? There was no forest near Benny's home, only concrete, buildings, cars, people. Dizzying. He swayed with disorientation.

Laughter? A growl? Someone was behind him, closer now.

He didn't stop, legs pumping, feet screaming, flesh torn.

Cisco slammed into something solid, his hands reflexively coming up to protect his face—brick? He didn't have time to contemplate it, he was flailing, struggling for purchase, but it was useless. He hit the floor with a thud.

Pain exploded and then he had a brief reprieve of floating. No, he was swimming.

Definitely gone mad. Nuts. Insane.

Cisco kicked, worked his arms, swam to the surface, broke through, and sucked in a great breath of air.

*A hand shot out and grabbed him, pulled him along. Cisco opened his mouth to say something, to scream, but nothing came out. He tried to get a look at his captor but nothing, he was blinded to the stranger's face.*

*Dark corridor. Heavy wooden door. The faceless man unlocked the door and opened it, then shoved him into the room with such force, his feet couldn't keep up, his hands coming up just in time to protect his head from smashing onto the cold stone floor. Too stunned to move, too confused to process what was happening, Cisco lay upon the cold floor, looking up at a black wall covered in frightening weapons and devices. Light glinted off the blade of a twisted knife, a battle-ax, mace, and scythe. There also appeared to be restraining devices, barbaric-looking medical tools, gags.*

*Everything was blood splattered.*

*Cisco began to shake uncontrollably.*

*He turned away, closed his eyes, but the images of the torture devices were seared into his mind, never to be unseen.*

*Screams, agonizing screams, came from somewhere far away, and he jumped to his feet, turning in wary circles. What was this place? His first thought was that he'd been dropped into hell. Only there were no flames, no heat, only fear and dread, for surely the devil would soon appear.*

*And he did.*

*"I have been waiting for you. I do not like to wait," a deep voice in the shadows said.*

*Cisco spun, following the sound, but the man remained faceless, hidden deep behind the darkness.*

*"Wha—" Throat dry, constricted, he was forced to swallow down his fear before he could get the words out. "Who are you?"*

*Red glowing eyes appeared from out of the dark, and then the light glinted off a mouth full of razor-sharp teeth. No, just two razor-sharp canines. Vampire.*

*Not just any vampire, but one that caused Cisco's blood to turn to ice within his veins.*

*Zeke stepped from the shadows and studied Cisco with an intensity only a predatory animal could achieve.*

*"Do you not wish to run? I always enjoy a bit of a fight from my meal."*

*Cisco was frozen in place, his feet refusing to move, and he could scarcely breathe.*

*Zeke stepped closer still, his lips curling into a wicked grin. "Do you not wish to scream?"*

*He couldn't. His throat was constricting. It was harder to breathe. His heart beat erratically. Still he tried. He opened and closed his mouth several times. Tried to get enough air into his lungs so he could, but it was useless. No sound came out.*

*Circling Cisco, Zeke kept his gaze intently upon his prey. Each pass got closer and closer until Cisco could smell the pungent odor of decaying flesh. As if realizing Cisco was in fact no threat, Zeke stopped and stood directly in front of Cisco, their noses nearly touching.*

*Zeke ran a finger up Cisco's neck, ghosting it over his useless lips. "You seem to be struggling there, boy. No matter, I will help you." He pressed his lips against Cisco's. "I can make you scream."*

Cisco jerked upright, wildly scanning the area as he searched for Zeke. As his vision adjusted to the darkness, the familiarity of his room came into focus. *Just a dream.*

And yet....

Cisco trembled uncontrollably as the nightmare held him, refusing to release its claws. He lay down on his side, pulled his knees up, and wrapped his arms around himself as he stared at the opposite wall. He was too afraid to go back to sleep, afraid to step back into the nightmare. Only it didn't feel like a nightmare, but a premonition, a look into the future. It had been too real to be just the imaginings of his sleeping mind.

He shivered again.

# CHAPTER SEVENTEEN

THE ROBUST flavor of the Fuente Don Arturo AnniverXario cigar filled Max's mouth, and he blew it out slowly, watching the thick cloud of smoke swirl in the air around him. The once calming act did little to soothe the tempest raging within him.

Angelo was on his way to Europe with information that would irrevocably change all their lives. Whether for better or worse remained to be seen. Max supposed it would depend on who was left standing when the last battle was fought. Angelo had been correct when he'd remarked about preparing for war, only it wouldn't be started on such a minor issue as whether or not he changed Cisco.

He rolled the cigar through his fingers and then took another pull, blowing out the smoke slowly as he stared at the red embers. He couldn't help but chuckle at the irony. He was enjoying a cigar given to him by someone he planned to destroy. He doubted the gifter of such a fine cigar would find the same humor in it.

No, this battle had been brewing for years. It had begun when Max had taken the seat of power instead of Zeke. Perhaps longer. The exact moment it began was unclear, as time had a way of becoming meaningless when one lived forever. However, with Angelo now on his way—in his possession evidence of Zeke and Liam, the king of California, plotting to further the vampire race by taking over and enslaving the humans—time now seemed of the utmost importance. A takeover was why it had been imperative that Zeke strip Max of his power. Liam knew Max would never agree to such madness. Those holding seats of power needed to be loyal to the cause of integration rather than elimination. King Liam, however, had already begun rectifying that. A single accident would go unnoticed, perhaps even two, but by the third, Max knew there was more to it. They'd started in the small jurisdictions, but he had no doubt there were more to come. It hadn't taken him long to discover that Liam would stop at nothing to remove those who would oppose him and scorn his ideologies of grandeur, and then to insert those who agreed with him into their vacant seats.

Max hadn't planned to expose King Liam and Zeke yet, not until he'd had the opportunity to identify all those involved. His stupidity in exposing Cisco as his weakness had forced his hand. Zeke would stop at nothing to use that weakness to achieve his ultimate goal. It was another reason Max hadn't taken Angelo's advice and put Zeke out to meet the sun when he'd dared to touch Cisco. Max didn't know how many members Liam and Zeke had recruited. There could be hundreds for all he knew, perhaps even some in his own house. To kill Zeke then would have ignited Liam's rage, and until he could inform Egnatius of the plot, Max couldn't chance it.

Max took one last hit, then stubbed out the cigar and got to his feet when there was a soft rap on the door. It was time to feed. Normally he could go days, even weeks without feeding and still be able to maintain control. But with the threat of takeovers and his desire for Cisco, he had to keep up his strength. He pulled on his waistcoat, straightening his clothes as he made his way to the door.

The instant he opened it, a young man fell to his knees at Max's feet. The scent of need and desperation wafted from the man and hung cloyingly in the air. Max recognized him at once. In disgust he realized it was Mario, the same man he'd informed Silas to remove and make sure he knew his place. Obviously it hadn't been done.

"What the hell are you doing here?" Max spat angrily and took a step back from the disgusting creature.

"I'm here to service you, Sir," Mario said meekly.

"The fuck you are."

"Please, Sir. Please allow me to take care of your needs."

Max stormed over to his desk and grabbed his phone.

"Wait. Please, Sir," Mario said imploringly. "Silas said if I failed to please you, he'd kill me. Please…." He hung his head and began to sob. "Please, I beg of you."

Max stilled, his finger hovering over the call button. "Silas sent you?"

"Yes, Sir. The donor Dr. Heine had procured for you wasn't feeling well. His iron was low from what I understand, and I was rushed over. Please don't let him kill me, Sir. Please, Sir, I beg of you," Mario cried, his body trembling.

Max could smell the bitter scent of fear overpowering the stench of desperation. Junkies like Mario disgusted him, and the thought of feeding from him had Max wrinkling his nose. And yet he hesitated. It wasn't the tears; he'd seen plenty of those without giving a shit as to the reason for them. It wasn't the begging—again, he'd experienced plenty of men begging, hell, he made them beg. But something stopped him from tossing the worthless man from his office. Something that whispered to him, yet he couldn't make out what was being said, couldn't understand it, but it was powerful enough to demand he listen.

Even as he thought better of it, he set his phone aside without dialing and found himself moving toward Mario as if being pulled along by invisible strands. "Stand up," he ordered.

Mario stood on trembling legs, his rail-thin arms going behind him, doing his best to display, but the shaking in his limbs made it difficult to achieve and he swayed even as he tried to stand straight and push out his chest.

Max's mind was screaming to stop even as he leaned in closer. His gaze was riveted to the pulse throbbing at the man's neck. Max's stomach clenched and his mouth went dry. Life. Just below the pale skin was life. It called to him. The steady rhythm—*thump thump thump*—a beautiful symphony. The sound, the call, the need, the hunger, they all swirled and mingled together to quiet the voice in his head. The alluring song was enough to drown out the unpleasant smell of fear and desperation. Enough that his lips made contact with warm flesh, fangs piercing, and he pulled the melody into his body. He swallowed it down in great gulps, relishing the heat that filled him, soothing the clenching in his gut, and chasing away the coldness in his chest. Life, it was the only thing that mattered.

A KNOCKING sound had Max looking up from the smoke swirling up from the end of his cigar. He stared at the door, a fog of confusion encompassing his mind. The knock sounded again; it was coming from outside his office door. Shaking his head to dispel the strange feeling, Max stubbed out the nearly spent cigar and leaned back in his chair.

"Come in."

"Good Evening, Sir," Michael, the head of IT Security greeted as he came through the door waving a manila folder. "I have the reports you asked for."

*Reports?* Max didn't remember asking about any reports. He glanced at the clock, his confusion only growing further. He'd been awake for nearly an hour and yet he barely remembered anything past lighting up his cigar. He must have really been lost in his thoughts, yet he couldn't even recall what he had been thinking about.

"I've finished installing the new software, been running data for the last twenty-four hours, and I gotta tell ya, it's some of the most impressive technology I've ever seen," Michael commented, dropping the file on Max's desk.

Right, right, the updates to the security he'd demanded. "Have a seat." He picked up the file and scanned the first page, a bunch of numbers that made absolutely no sense. "What am I looking at?"

"It's the output of random sequences—"

He looked up at Michael and met his gaze. "I don't speak geek. Give it to me in layman terms."

"Sorry. Basically what it means is that this new software is able to take in all the data from alarms, camera feeds, sensors, door locks, hell the damn cash register, analyze it in a nanosecond, and not only alert us when there is a security breach but in some instances correct the problem. Say if someone was to try to use your prints to access your chamber while you were knocked out, or God forbid had cut off your hand, the system would recognize the slight difference as to how you normally press your hand against the panel and wouldn't allow access. It can also do face recognition from the camera feeds and the system knows who is allowed access to certain areas and who isn't. It really is quite brilliant and has improved our already kickass system to off the charts."

Max was doing his best to pay attention. He was getting the gist of what Michael was telling him—security system upgraded to brilliant—but a nagging feeling kept him on edge. He'd lost an hour of time, and the whole experience wasn't sitting well with him.

"I thought you'd be more excited, considering how fanatical you are about security."

"No, it's great." Max glanced at the clock once again and then the smoldering cigar. He was losing it. It was the only explanation. "Do you mind if we do this another time?" he asked distractedly.

"Sure." Michael tilted his head a concerned look on his face. "Are you okay, sir?"

"Yes, yes, I'm fine," he said with a dismissive wave. He put the file in his desk drawer and went to his feet. "I have something I must attend to. I will call for you at another time."

"Yes, sir."

The instant the door was closed behind Michael, Max traced to Cisco's apartment. He hesitated with his hand on the knob, schooled his features, and pushed aside the unease before opening the door.

"SHIT, SHIT, shit." Cisco turned off the taps and stepped out of the shower. He could say he'd woken to find his clock flashing, the power must have gone out at some point, explain about the nightmare and his difficulty in falling back to sleep. But they were merely excuses. He should have planned for something like this. Ugh! Why the hell hadn't he set a second alarm? He could have used his phone. Dammit, he'd just made up for his mistakes and here he was making another one. Max was going to be pissed. Cisco wrapped a towel around his waist, quickly brushed his teeth and rushed from the bathroom, still dripping wet as he ran a towel over his head and face. Hopefully he could get dressed and be kneeling before Max came in.

No such luck.

"Oh," Cisco squeaked and took a step back when he spotted Max leaning against the door, arms crossed over his chest. Yup, he was pissed. Cisco caught himself quickly and dropped to his knees and displayed. "Sorry, Sir. I slept through my alarm."

"Have you had your breakfast?"

"No, Sir. I don't need anything. I'm ready for whatever you wish."

"I wish for you to have breakfast," Max said and pushed away from the door. "Take a seat at the table; I'll have it brought up."

Cisco scrambled to his feet, nearly tripping on the wet towel on the floor, but righted himself before he could face-plant and snatched up the towel.

Max took the phone away from his ear. "You may get dressed first," he said to Cisco and then went back to his phone conversation.

Cisco rushed to the chair next to the bed, where the clothes he was to wear were laid out for him as usual. He had quickly learned what his plans for the evening would be by which types of clothes were waiting for him. Leather, they would be going to the club; jeans, they'd be staying in, and if there was nothing or only a pair of boxers, they'd be going to the playroom. Tonight there were black leather pants, black fishnet shirt, as well as black socks and heavy-soled black boots. A thrill ran through

Cisco as he pulled the articles on and then sat on the edge of the bed to put on his socks and boots.

Just as Max finished his call and slid his cell back into his pocket, Cisco hurried to the table and took his seat, hands folded in his lap, and awaited his instructions.

"It will be here shortly," Max informed him as he took the seat across from Cisco. Max didn't say anything further, only stared at Cisco with an unreadable expression on his face as he thrummed his fingers on the table. The tension within Cisco coiled until he felt like an overwound clock that was about to burst. Was Max thinking of what punishment he should dole out? Would he still allow him to accompany him to the club?

*Will my head explode if Max doesn't say something soon?*

He was saved when there was a knock on the door and his breakfast was brought in on a rolling cart. But Cisco's relief was short-lived. As soon as the food, coffee, and juice was set on the table, the silent and unknown waiter gone, Cisco's tension ramped up once again as he tried to choke down the eggs, hash browns, and toast. It felt like sludge on his tongue, his gut revolting against it, as Max sat silently across from him, watching him. But he knew better than not to eat.

Max's eyes were on him, but Cisco couldn't help but feel as if Max wasn't really looking at him. He seemed distracted, as if he were lost in his own thoughts, his own world. Cisco was curious as to what had Max distracted, but once again, he knew better than to ask. The one thing he was sure of was whatever Max was thinking about, it was deep, went beyond something more substantial than whether Cisco had overslept.

Forcing down the last bite, he dropped his fork onto his empty plate, picked up his napkin, and wiped his mouth. One last drink of his coffee before Cisco straightened his shoulders and dropped his hands into his lap, lacing his fingers together to keep from wringing his hands. Waiting.

Max could read his feelings, but he either ignored Cisco's unease or didn't care, because he made no comment, allowed the tension in the air to grow until it filled the room, suffocating and thick.

Max shoved his chair back. "Let's go," he said out of the blue and went to the door.

Cisco scrambled to catch up, to fall in behind Max and walk to heel as they headed down the hall. His head swam with the sudden turn of events. He would be the first to admit that he knew very little about Maximilian De Ferrari or the world in which he ruled. However, he knew enough to know that Max's sudden change in attitude wasn't only confusing Cisco, it was scaring the bejesus out of him. Something was up, something big.

The club gave no clues. The tables and bar full with Doms and subs, vamp and human. A show of a Dom's prowess with a bull whip on the stage held many of the patrons' attention. Cisco tried his best to get a reading of what was going on by the expression on the Doms' faces, but nothing seemed unusual. Everyone appeared to be having a good time. No ruckus, nothing that would give him a hint as to what was the cause of Max's strange behavior.

His focus on the club, Cisco nearly slammed into Max when he suddenly stopped, but thankfully, with barely a split second to spare, Cisco dropped, his knees hitting the hard floor with a painful thud. He swallowed down his cry of pain, biting on his lip till it nearly bled. Once the sharp pain eased, Cisco looked up and met familiar eyes. Max had stopped to talk with Silas, who must not have been working the door or the bar, as Patrick was at his side.

"What's going on?" Cisco mouthed silently.

Patrick cocked his head slightly, no doubt making sure Silas wasn't paying any attention to him before he whispered silently, "At dawn."

Cisco gave a slight nod, letting Patrick know he understood and turned his focus back to Max, trying to decipher without success what he and Silas were talking about. Before long, Max moved to his normal place of honor, taking his chair and sitting stiffly as he surveyed the club. The only hint Cisco got that Max knew he was even there was when Max's hand landed on his head, fingers rubbing soothingly over his scalp. In that instant, his belief was confirmed that something much bigger than his own little slight of sleeping in was happening. This wasn't about him, or even Max. There was some heavy shit going down among Max and his vampire followers, and whatever it was, it was causing them to be wary. The longer he knelt at his Master's side, the more the idea solidified. He noticed the small nuances of Max's close staff, their eyes constantly shifting as if looking for someone or something, and the tension in each of them was noticeable by the way the muscles in their necks, arms, and chests bulged with tension.

Something was coming.

Something bad.

Images of Zeke suddenly assaulted him. He could feel his hot breath, smell the stench of death on it. Bile rose up in Cisco's throat, and he had to swallow several times to force it back down. His head was swimming, the tendrils of fear trying to take a hold of him. It took every ounce of will to clamp down on it and hold his position. The return of Max's hand to his head, his gentle fingers petting, helped and soon Cisco could take a full breath.

Now as he looked around the room, Cisco began to wonder if it was paranoia making him see things that weren't there, but he quickly dismissed the notion. No, there was definitely something bigger than a simple nightmare. Something that would have a major impact on Max and thus on Cisco himself, as well as everyone else within the club. Cisco didn't know how he knew, he simply did.

Something bad, very bad, was headed to Wicked Ground.

CISCO JERKED with surprise at the rap on his door even though he was expecting Patrick. Fuck, his nerves were shot.

"Mr. Aguilar, are you expecting a guest, sir?" Andrew asked through the closed door.

His legs were shaking, heart hammering as he rushed over and slung the door open. Patrick stood next to Andrew with a silver dome-covered plate. He caught on quickly. "Yes, Andrew, I didn't eat much for dinner. Thank you."

"I told you," Patrick grumped. "Like I'm going to attack the man with a pie."

Andrew didn't look the least bit apologetic. He was just doing his job, and with Max for a boss, he certainly wouldn't want to screw it up. "C'mon in, Patrick. I was hoping you could help me for a minute with my new harness. I have no idea how these things are supposed to go on."

Patrick walked past him. "Thank you, Andrew, we won't be long," Cisco said before closing the door.

"Okay, so what the hell's going on around here lately," Cisco blurted out as soon as the door was closed.

"Shh, c'mere and eat and I'll tell you what I know."

"I'm not hungry." He looked down at the cream pie, and his stomach flip-flopped. "I'd puke if I tried."

"You got to eat it. Mr. Prison Guard out there is going to check."

There was no way he could even attempt to eat the dessert. He grabbed the plate, took it into the bathroom, and dumped the contents in the toilet before flushing. He brought the plate back out, set it down, and met Patrick's gaze.

"Talk."

Patrick scanned the room and then grabbed Cisco's wrist and, with his free hand, covered his lips with one finger. Patrick led him to the TV, turned it on, and then went to his knees, pulling Cisco down to his.

"I don't know if the room is bugged, but I'm not taking any chances," Patrick said quietly.

The churning in Cisco's gut only intensified. "You're scaring me," he admitted.

"You should be scared. I don't know what's going on, but something's not right. Silas has been acting edgy, even more protective than normal. Tonight was the first time he's let me in the club in days. From what I can gather, a lot of the other subs are being kept on a short leash as well."

"Have you at least heard any rumors? Anything that might explain it?"

"The vamps are being pretty hush-hush, but I've heard Zeke's name mentioned more than once. I'm pretty sure it has something to do with that psycho. He's gone missing, which is really weird for him. Zeke loves to cause shit, loves even more to push Max to rage. Darius thinks the guy finally got the message and is staying away. I don't believe it and neither does Silas. Zeke seems to have simply vanished and no one knows where he is. That creepy prick is up to no good, mark my word, and no doubt everyone will stay on their guard until they have found him."

The mention of Zeke's name caused Cisco's skin to crawl. "That explains Max's attitude tonight."

Patrick cocked his head. "What do you mean?"

"He barely said five words to me. At first I thought he was mad at me for oversleeping, but he never mentioned it, nor did I get my daily discipline. He seemed really distracted."

"Wait, you woke up late too? Was your alarm flashing like the power had gone out?" Patrick asked. Cisco nodded. "Shit, I was hoping I just had a faulty clock or something, but if yours went out too…."

"Maybe we did have a power outage."

"That's impossible. We have a backup system. Even when we were hit with some major storms a few years back, the entire town without power, we never had a blip in our service. Besides, our clocks aren't attached to an electrical outlet, they're all wireless and controlled by the security system. When you have a bunch of vamps running around, you can't have a breach in timing that shuts this place down at dawn."

"You think someone did it on purpose?"

"I don't know, but the second Silas wakes up, I'm going to let him know about it and you need to let Max know as well. I got to get back. Just stay in your room and don't come out till Max comes for you. Got it?"

"Yeah, I got it. You be careful too."

"I always am." Patrick pecked him on the cheek before rolling to his feet. He grabbed the empty plate and knocked on the door. "Hey, Andrew, I'm finished." He turned his head in Cisco's direction and whispered, "Be safe."

"You too," Cisco responded past his dry throat.

He shut off the TV and then plopped down on his ass, pulling his knees up close and hugging them to his body. He knew whatever was going on was bad, but he didn't know just how bad. If Zeke was behind it, then it wasn't only bad, but terrifying.

# CHAPTER EIGHTEEN

THE SLOW, soothing rhythm of Josh Groban's voice should have been enough for him to drift off to sleep. Yet, an hour after Max had retired for the day, Cisco's thoughts were still racing. He shifted in bed again, for what? Hell, he had no idea how many attempts at trying to find a comfortable position that would make. He'd been tossing and turning since he'd crawled into bed. Although Max had assured him the clock going out was a nonissue—Michael had installed a new software program that had taken everything off-line for a while—Cisco couldn't help but feel Max was placating him. There had been real concern in Max's eyes when he'd told him about the clock failing, and although he'd recovered quickly, had a ready explanation, Cisco knew it had upset Max.

He bent his arms behind his head and stared up at the ceiling, his racing thoughts not allowing him to settle. God, he wished he could talk to Benny. Benny always knew what to say, calmed his neurotic thoughts.

Five years he'd spent dreaming of joining Max in his world, and now that he had, he missed talking to Benny every day, seeing his silly smile. Hell, he even missed the exasperated looks Benny was constantly throwing Cisco's way when he spent too much time talking about Max—he'd done that a lot—or when he'd do something Benny disapproved of—he'd done that a lot too, come to think of it. Poor Benny, maybe he was better off without Cisco pestering him every day. The thought made his chest ache.

He wasn't sure what he'd thought was going to happen between him and Benny, how the move would affect their relationship. Apparently he hadn't considered it. In his rush to join Max he hadn't been thinking of what he was leaving behind. After being awake all night with nothing but sadness for company, he knew exactly what he'd left.

Rolling onto his side, he glanced at the clock—eight o'clock in the morning—and sighed. Benny was just arriving at work, and if he wanted to talk to him, he'd have to wait till noon. Benny wasn't allowed to take personal calls while working, unless it was an emergency. Pulling Benny from the OR suite, where he worked as a surgical assistant, because Cisco missed him wasn't what he'd call a family emergency.

Another thirty minutes of tossing and turning and Cisco groaned, then grudgingly threw off the covers. He headed to the bathroom, peed, washed his hands and face, and considered the big tub for a moment. A soak might relax him enough, but he pushed the idea aside. It wouldn't do anything to ease his frazzled nerves or the heaviness in his chest.

Not one to drink much—he liked to keep his wits—Cisco went to the stocked bar and poured himself a good measure of bourbon. He swirled the amber fluid in his glass, contemplating it. He didn't have to worry that Max would need anything. It was hours away from sunset. But if it could help him settle enough to get some sleep….

"Fuck it, it can't hurt," he grumbled and threw back the contents in one big gulp. He coughed and sputtered as the alcohol burned its way all the way down to his gut. Shaking his head, he blew out a ragged breath and then poured another. It wasn't supposed to taste good; it was supposed to help him sleep. He took his drink, settled down at the desk, and fired up the computer. The security on the system was ridiculous, and Cisco found the last time he'd tried to use it that surfing the web was nearly impossible. But he could at least send Benny an e-mail.

He pulled up his e-mail server and typed Benny a quick note, telling him he missed him and would call later tonight. He'd just hit Send when there was a rap on his door. Cisco jerked in surprise, his arm hitting the glass, but he caught it and righted it before it could spill onto the keyboard and only a small amount sloshed over onto his hand. As he made his way to the door, he sucked the alcohol off his fingers and wrinkled his nose at the harsh flavor.

"Hello? Andrew, is that you?" Cisco asked through the door.

"Yes, sir. Sorry to bother you, but Patrick is here. Is it okay if he comes in?"

Cisco didn't hesitate. He turned the deadbolt and threw open the door. Something slammed into him the second the door was opened, sending him flying back. His head hit the hardwood floor with a sickening thud, pain exploding across his skull. The edges of his vision went dark, and stars danced behind his closed eyes. What the hell? But before he could figure out what was happening, something was placed over his mouth and nose, a putrid smell filling his nostrils and then nothing.

Something that sounded like metal being scraped against stone and a damp, moldy smell like he'd experienced in his grandparents' hundred-year-old basement were the first things Cisco became aware of as the darkness released him. He groaned as nausea was the next sense to come online and his head lolled to the side as his mouth watered, stomach clenching painfully. He was going to puke. He then wished he was still in the peace of nothingness when his head began to throb painfully and he started to retch.

Slowly, with more effort than it should have taken, Cisco rolled to his side. He had to get up, find a toilet, a toothbrush, but his movement halted. He forced his heavy lids open and tried to see what was holding him where he was. The flickering light burned his eyes, made the throb in his skull intensify, and he closed them again and laid his head back down against the cold surface beneath him. He was lying down, but he didn't understand why the bed was so hard, so cold. Nothing made sense.

Cisco struggled to remember what had happened, the last thing he remembered, but everything was scrambled and the effort did little more than make his head hurt worse.

"Ah, are you finally going to wake up?" The deep, baritone voice was unfamiliar.

Cisco struggled to place the voice with a face. The man apparently knew him. However he couldn't seem to grasp what was going on or even who was talking to him. His head was swimming in a heavy fog. He tried to speak, to answer, but his tongue felt swollen and dry, his throat raw and painful.

"Wait, don't try to speak yet. I'll get you a glass of water. The effects of chloroform can be quite difficult to deal with, but it will wear off soon enough."

Chloroform? Had he heard the man right? He couldn't have. Why would he be suffering from the effects of chloroform? It made no sense.

Cisco raised his head and tentatively opened his eyes. He blinked rapidly for a few seconds until his vision began to clear and the light no longer made it feel as if hot pokers were being shoved into his pupils. It took him a moment to realize the flickering light was from a candle, which didn't make any sense. He had candles in his bathroom, but even through the haze, he knew he wasn't in the tub, nor in his bathroom at all. The strong scents of mold and earth made him think he was underground, perhaps in a basement. His ears were ringing, head throbbing, and his stomach was still flip-flopping, nausea still threatening. The effort it took to try to sort it all out hurt his head, and he let it rest back against the cold surface and closed his eyes once again. He sighed when the blinding pain began to ease slightly.

"Here," the stranger said, and then Cisco's head was lifted and something pressed to his mouth.

He opened his eyes once more and gasped as fear grabbed hold of him and robbed him of his breath. Zeke's bright red eyes stared at him. He tried to pull away, but he couldn't move. It was then that he realized with a sinking feeling that he was bound with restraints around both his wrists and ankles. There was a sound like a chain clanking as he continued to struggle. His fear increased to outright terror. He was chained to a cold metal table at the complete mercy of a powerful vampire who had tormented and taunted him when he'd first stepped through the doors of Wicked Ground. A vampire he'd since learned wanted to see nothing more than Max's complete and utter destruction.

"The shackles are made from pure iron. You'll only hurt yourself if you continue to struggle. Escape isn't possible," Zeke said, sounding almost gleeful.

Cisco's heart was slamming against his chest, thumping wildly, and the roar of blood in his ears was deafening. Bile rushed up, burned his throat, and he barely got his head turned to the side before it spewed from him. Tears burned his eyes and spilled from them as wave after wave clenched his gut and he continued to retch and puke. The pain in his head so extreme, the fear, the burning, the tears, it was all too much. His entire being was one big bundle of raw, agonizing pain, and he began to pray it would end.

How long he'd stayed in that miserable place, Cisco didn't know. He only knew when it ended, was aware of the cool liquid in his mouth, swallowing, relief, and then blessedly peaceful blackness.

BLOOD SEEPED from between Max's fingers where they tightened around vulnerable flesh, an unprotected throat, cutting off Andrew's breath. "I'm going to ask you one last time. Where is he?"

"I don't know," Andrew mouthed, unable to get a breath and unable to speak.

Silas laid a tentative hand on Max's shoulder. "Max, if you kill him, we won't be able to question him."

What Silas was saying was true, logical, but Max didn't want logic, he wanted Cisco. The urge to watch the life drain out of Andrew's terrified eyes was so overpowering he felt his fingers tighten ever so slightly, an almost gleeful feeling coming over him as Andrew's face turned a brighter shade of red, eyes bulging. Andrew had failed, he'd allowed someone to take Cisco, and he deserved nothing less than death for his inadequacy. At the last second, a flick of his wrist sent Andrew flying across the room instead. He landed against the wall and grabbed his throat, gasping for breath.

Max stomped away, curling his hands into fists, and clamped down on the urge to finish the job. "Where the fuck is Angelo," he bellowed.

"He didn't answer his phone. I've left a message for him," Silas informed him, keeping out of Max's path, choosing to stay close to the far wall and not attempt to impede Max's temper tantrum in any way. Smart man.

"I want every person who was in the building: security, housekeeping, the fucking dishwasher, in my office *now*!"

"They are waiting in the club. Shall I have them come in one at a time, or would you like to address them all at the same time?"

Max shot a look toward Andrew, who was still on his knees, retching and coughing. "Bring that piece of shit with you," Max snarled and traced to the club.

The lights were subdued, as was the mood in the room. The stench of fear burned Max's nose. The club was eerily silent, many of those in attendance scarcely breathing.

He leaned down next to a young Hispanic girl, who had wide brown eyes and stunk of fear. "Do you know where my Cisco is?"

"N…. N…." She shook her head, the color draining from her face, heart fluttering wildly. He heard the truth in her statement and spared her his wrath.

A couple dozen or so people had pushed tables together and were sitting around them, looking scared out of their minds. Good. Fear he understood. He could use it to his advantage. Max made his way around them slowly, looking at each one with a critical eye. Someone here had to have information. With the security measures he'd had installed within Wicked Ground, he was sure it was an inside job. If he had to torture each and every one of them, he would. Nothing mattered, not their fear, not their pain, not their deaths. The only thing that mattered was Cisco being returned to him.

"You," Max snapped, pointing at a young man—Jonathan he recalled was the man's name—"Are you not the kitchen manager?"

"Yes, sir, I am," he responded with a shaky voice.

"Did you notice anything unusual, anyone in the club that didn't belong?"

Silas came in, half carrying, half dragging Andrew and set him in a chair at the end of the table. There was a collective gasp from the group, but Max ignored them, keeping his attention on Jonathan.

"No, sir. There hadn't even been any deliveries prior to the alarm sounding. We had a skeleton crew of myself, Angela, and Connie. They entered the club when I did at six this morning, and I don't think either of them ever left the kitchen."

"You don't think?"

Jonathan frowned, a thoughtful expression on his face, obviously trying to recall the events of the morning. He finally shook his head. "No I'm sure neither of them left the kitchen."

Satisfied the man was telling the truth, Max pointed to him. "You and the ladies may leave."

Jonathan, the young lady he'd already spoken to, and an older gray-haired lady jumped to their feet and rushed from the room. Max continued to study the people left at the table. As he passed a young blonde-haired girl with wide horror-filled blue eyes, Max got a slight whiff of blood. He grabbed her ponytail and jerked her head back. She screamed as Max's gaze settled on the fresh puncture wounds.

"Who has fed from you," he demanded angrily.

Tears spilled from her eyes, and she began to shake uncontrollably. Her mouth opened and closed several times, but no sound came out.

Max tightened his hold. "I asked you a fucking question. Answer it. Now!" he roared.

"I don... I don't know who it was, sir," she sobbed.

"Would you recognize him again? Was anyone here with you that would know?"

"No, I wasn't here. I went to a rave last night."

Max released her hair and slammed his hand down on the table in front of her, making her and everyone at the table jump. "You let a stranger feed from you?"

She shook her head. "I would never."

"Bullshit, you've obviously allowed someone to bite you. Were you drunk?"

Again she shook her head. "I only had water. Please, sir. I swear…
please. I didn't drink. I swear it. I don't even remember leaving the club.
I woke up this morning with…." She put a shaking hand to her throat,
sobbing uncontrollably.

Max arched a brow at Silas, who was standing next to Andrew, his
arms crossed over his chest, taking it all in. Silas shrugged. Max then
settled his gaze on the fresh puncture marks on Andrew and rushed to
him. "Who bit you?"

"I don't know," Andrew responded huskily past his raw throat.

Max spun around. "Who else here is bitten?"

Three men and two women raised their hands.

"Are any of you donors for vampires here at the club?"

Two men he knew were maintenance workers raised their hands. "Do
you know who bit you last night?" All three of them shook their heads.

What the hell was going on? He had at least five humans who had
been bitten with no recollection of who had done it, one of whom had no
memory of the rest of the night. Fuck! What a mess. After being bitten by
a vampire, the prey could be tracked, even influenced. A survival instinct
at its finest. It might take up to a week for the bond to be broken.

Max rubbed at the tension settling at the base of his skull as he
began to pace. He had to get to the bottom of this. That five members
of his staff, possibly more, had been all bitten by an unknown vampire
couldn't be a coincidence. Whoever was behind the strange attacks had
to have had something to do with Cisco's disappearance.

"You five"—he indicated the people he meant with a wave of his
hand—"in my office. The rest of you don't move. Silas, go check and
make sure Jonathan and the ladies haven't been bitten. If they have, bring
them to me."

"Yes, sir. Right away, sir."

Max ushered the five into his office. Andrew had recovered enough
that he was able to make it on his own. "Have a seat," Max ordered, then
went around his desk and took his seat. He picked up the phone and
dialed Heine's office.

"Dr. Heine," the doctor answered by way of greeting after only
one ring.

"It's Max, I need you to come to my office."

"I was right in the middle of—"

"Now," Max demanded and slammed the phone down.

He understood that people had lives, jobs to do, commitments, but none of that mattered to Max. The fucking world could stop for all he cared. It didn't deserve to spin until Cisco was back where he belonged and Max got the opportunity to make the culprit pay a very heavy price for his stupidity.

Max thrummed his fingers against his desk in impatience, looking at the members of his staff who all sat stiffly on the couch and chairs looking scared shitless. A thought occurred to him, and he jumped to his feet, causing the staff to shy away and gasp.

Jesus H. Christ, why hadn't he thought of him sooner? Of course it was Zeke behind this. He rushed for the door, nearly knocking Dr. Heine down. "Have a seat, I'll be right back," he tossed over his shoulder as he rushed to the club.

He spotted Darius entering the club. "You, have you seen Zeke?"

"No, sir. I haven't seen him in…." Darius scratched at his longish beard, looking up as he tried to recall.

"C'mon, man, when?"

"For better than a week, I'd say. Been quiet around here without that bastard."

"He's taken Cisco."

"What? When?" he asked, looking shocked. Max instantly could tell his shock was genuine.

"Find Silas, he'll bring you up to date. I need everyone on this. Every loyal member needs to be in this club, now!"

Max didn't wait for a response. He rushed to the security room and threw open the door.

"I've already pulled up the video tapes," Henry informed him.

"And?"

"Nothing. Clint here"—Henry stabbed a thumb toward the ex-SWAT leader who now worked in Max's control room—"was working the day shift. He didn't see anything, no alarms, no intruders, nothing. I've looked over them personally, and I agree with his assessment. Fuck, Max, I didn't even catch anyone at Cisco's door until you strolled down the hall and found Andrew on the floor. One minute Andrew was standing guard and the next he was on the floor as you stepped up to him. It's the damnedest thing. It makes no sense whatsoever."

Max squeezed his eyes shut, the image of Cisco's pleading eyes assaulting him. How the hell had he let this happen? How had he allowed someone to come into his house and take his boy?

# CHAPTER NINETEEN

*"THEY BROUGHT to me a knight with a sore on his leg; and a woman who was feeble-minded. To the knight I applied a small poultice; and the woman I put on diet to turn her humour wet.*

*Then a French doctor came and said, "This man knows nothing about treating them." He then said, "Bring me a sharp axe." Then the doctor laid the leg of the knight on a block of wood and told a man to cut off the leg with the axe, upon which the marrow flowed out and the patient died on the spot.*

*He then examined the woman and said, "There is a devil in her head." He therefore took a razor, made a deep cross-shaped cut on her head, peeled away the skin until the bone of the skull was exposed, and rubbed it with salt. The woman also died instantly".*

*Usama ibn Munqidh 1175*

"I UNDERSTAND that Max has been training you?"

Max? The mention of his Master's name was enough to encourage Cisco's consciousness to swim up out of the sludge that was surrounding it. He fought his way to the surface, breathing harshly as he struggled. It took him a few seconds to understand his surroundings, the flickering light, the damp earth smell, the familiar voice. Zeke.

Cisco tried to lift his arms, then his legs. He was still bound, the hardness beneath him cold. With a sinking feeling, he realized he hadn't been dreaming, but he was in fact captive in some underground chamber, at the mercy of Zeke. His heart began to hammer and the bile rose in his throat, but he clamped down on his panic. He would do himself no good to start puking or crying. He had a feeling it would only excite the sick bastard. Cisco had to be strong, use his training, be brave, and somehow escape his capture and get back to Max. If he couldn't, then he simply had to endure whatever Zeke had planned until Max came for him. And Max would come. There wasn't a shred of doubt in Cisco's mind that Max would rescue him if he couldn't free himself.

"I asked you a question, boy."

Cisco gritted his teeth at being referred to as *boy* by anyone other than Max, but he pushed away the urge to tell Zeke to fuck off. It wouldn't help his situation. "Yeah, he has."

Cisco's jaw was grabbed with such force, he thought the bones would shatter. It took everything he could muster not to react; instead he met Zeke's blazing red eyes.

"When you speak to me, you will refer to me as Sir. Is that understood," Zeke spat.

Cisco swallowed, his throat dry and raw. "Yes, Sir," he responded, tamping down on his contempt.

Zeke stared down at him, his lip curled into an ugly sneer. The stench of something rotten, like decayed flesh, wafted around Cisco and his gut roiled. He swallowed several times, his mouth watering, and he worried he would vomit. Hell, it would serve the fucker right if Cisco did upchuck right in his face. The problem was, in this position, he'd probably end up aspirating the shit and he'd be the one stinking of rotting flesh within hours.

Zeke patted Cisco's face. "Good boy. Do you know who I was in my former life?"

*An asshole* was the first thing that popped into Cisco's mind, the anger and contempt for Zeke burning off the fear. He still knew better than to say it out loud. "No, Sir."

Zeke released him and moved away. Cisco tried tracking him with his gaze, but he stepped out of sight. The same strange scraping sound he'd heard the first time he had woken echoed around the room. Steel against stone?

"I entered the Scuola Medica Salernitana in thirteen hundred and four. It's quite fitting that I was referred to as Master Henry Ezekiel Sherman when I completed my studies ten years later, and now I am once again referred to as Master. Although, the reference is for a completely different reason now. You see, I am no longer allowed to practice medicine." Zeke chuckled darkly. "At least not legally. It would appear my licenses are no longer adequate. But no worries, the skills I learned in my previous existence come in quite handy in my new role."

A chill ran down Cisco's spine. He didn't know much about doctors during the medieval period, but he had seen a documentary on the evolution of medicine and knew the dark ages was a scary time to be sick or hurt. Some of the more common practices were bloodletting, trepanning, and boar bile enemas. Cisco shuddered again when he recalled the part in the show that talked about the unlucky souls who suffered from hemorrhoids. Poor bastards were sent off to the monks— who would put a red-hot iron up their ass. Cisco didn't even want to think about it, the notion too awful to consider.

Vampires didn't feel compassion, sympathy, or empathy. Or at least that was what Max had told him. Cisco didn't believe it. He'd experienced Max's excitement, his compassion, and his tenderness. Max worked tirelessly to keep the peace, he cared about the vampire race, and perhaps Max wouldn't call it love, but he did have strong feeling for him. Maybe, if he could reach that more human part of Zeke, force the vampire to see him as someone that mattered, perhaps he had a chance to survive long enough for Max to come.

"What happened? I mean how did you become a vampire?"

*Scrape. Scrape. Scrape.*

"Does it matter?"

Cisco tried turning his head to the sound of Zeke's voice, but his restraints didn't allow for much movement. All he got for his effort was a painful throb in his head. He laid it back down on the hard steel and took a few deep breaths. Whatever drugs he'd been given were finally wearing off, his brain firing—yet the throbbing in his temples, burning in his nose, and dry raw throat remained. He tried to figure out where he was, but the room was dark, the only light a flickering candle on a table next to him, the rest of the room hidden in complete blackness.

"I suppose it doesn't matter," Cisco finally responded. "I was only curious. It had to have been hard being a respected member of the medical establishment—you were obviously a very smart man—and then to become an outcast."

"A respected member." Zeke laughed, his face materializing before Cisco's, his expression angry, intense, ugly. "Do you know what it's like to watch every member of your family, all your friends, and a good portion of your community die? There was no respect, there was nothing but death, disease, rot, and loss. King Liam saved me from hell, gave me a second chance." Zeke smiled, his long, sharp teeth reflecting in the candlelight. "Just as I am going to give you a second chance."

The enormity of what Zeke was telling him hit Cisco directly in the chest. Zeke had lived through one of the worst plagues in human history—the great pestilence. A period of time when a large number of the population had died, some estimates as high as two hundred million people who succumbed to the disease. Jesus, to have not only survived such a catastrophic event but then to witness the aftermath as an immortal had to have left a great mark on Zeke's soul. No wonder he was so bitter.

For the first time, Cisco thought about all the changes someone like Zeke would have witnessed throughout the long years since he'd been born. He'd have seen great world wars, an abundance of violence, and never-ending death. No wonder vampires had such a hard time making connections to humans. The life expectancy of the average man was just over seventy years. How many people had Zeke watched die in his eight hundred years of existence? Had he cared about any of them, and if so, had he contemplated turning them? Had he tried, only to watch them die during the change?

"I'm sorry," Cisco said sincerely.

"What the fuck for?" Zeke spat.

*Scrape. Scrape. Scrape.*

"It must have been horrible to have watched so many people you cared about die. I don't know… I guess I'm just sorry you had to go through that."

"Well, aren't you just the sweetest little thing," Zeke said sarcastically. "There is nothing for you to feel sorry about. I rarely think of that time and when I do, only with the fondest of memories. I did not have to suffer like the rest of the mortals, rather, I fed on the survivors. Oh, and what easy prey a human is. Especially one who is grieving. They just invite anyone into their home, looking for scraps of food, an inkling of human kindness, something to make their wretched fucking lives bearable."

The tone of Zeke's voice was chilling. It was as if he was remembering the destruction with glee, reveling in his memories of it. *Fondest of memories?* How could anyone with a shred of decency think of such a horrible event with fondness? Could Zeke really be so cold, so heartless?

The answer was an unequivocal yes. Cisco knew the truth of it when Zeke appeared before him once again, an eerie grin on his face as he held up an old iron knife. The first slice was to Cisco's stomach. He screamed in agony and then in terror when Zeke rubbed his lips against the wound and then threw his head back, laughing boisterously as he licked the blood from his lips.

MAX SCOWLED at the display on his cell phone and then pushed the On button. "Why are you calling me? You should be here."

"I'm sorry, Max, I cannot leave. I am about to address the council. What's going on?"

"He's taken him," Max growled as he paced, running his hands through his hair in frustration.

There was a pause, and then Angelo's tone sounded confused when he asked, "Who has taken whom?"

"Zeke"—even the name upon his lips enraged him—"he's taken Cisco."

"What? How is that possible? Our security is impenetrable."

"Apparently it's not as fucking impenetrable as we thought," Max spat. "He waltzed right in here and not only taken my Cisco, but the son of a bitch has bitten at least five members of our staff."

"Are they okay?"

"Yes, yes," Max responded impatiently. "Dr. Heine has quarantined them until he can figure out how to break the connection. If he can't, they will have to stay quarantined until the effects wear off." They would not be happy about being held for a week, but that wasn't Max's concern at the moment. At least they would be safe, warm, fed, unlike his Cisco who....

No, he couldn't think of what was being lavished on his boy at the moment. It would serve no purpose other than to drive him mad with rage, and he must keep his wits. He must figure out how to find Cisco.

There was a rustling sound through the phone line and then Angelo's voice was muffled when he called out, "Yes, Sir, I am coming." His voice was clearer when he once again addressed Max. "I'm sorry, Max. I've got to go. I will do my best to hurry this along." His voice dropped lower, as if he was being careful not to be overheard. "Should I tell them the most recent developments?"

Max considered it briefly. Although he knew beyond a shadow of a doubt that Zeke was behind Cisco's kidnapping, he had no proof. He could not go to the council with gut feelings. Plus, the last thing he needed right then was for the council to believe him weak and paranoid, especially not with the other matter Angelo had to deal with. He didn't know if anyone on the council was in league with Liam and Zeke. If they were, Max couldn't let it get out that his house had been penetrated. No, he'd have to deal with this one on his own for the time being.

"No," he finally told Angelo. "Just present the case you have now and get your ass home."

"Yes, sir. And Max?"

"What?"

"We will get him back. I promise you."

The line went dead, and Max slumped down onto Cisco's bed and dropped his head into his hands. A sadistic vampire had his sweet boy and Max was powerless to do anything. He'd broken his promise to Cisco. He'd promised he was safe, that no harm would come to him. He'd vowed he wouldn't let anything happen to him and he'd failed.

How could this have happened?

How!

Max scrubbed his hands over his face and flopped back on the bed. He stared up at the ceiling but saw nothing but Cisco's face, mocking him. His dark eyes accusing, tears rolling down his face in disappointment.

"I'm so sorry," Max whispered.

The image of Cisco morphed into a familiar one: he was kneeling on the floor, grief and anguish rolling off him in waves and tears glistening on his cheeks. Only this time it wasn't Zeke who was his tormentor, but Max, those beautiful dark eyes so full of sorrow and pain. "Help me," he mouthed silently.

Max jerked upright. He had to do something. Lying on Cisco's bed and grieving his loss wasn't going to help his boy. Filled with a burning determination, he moved around the room, his gaze scanning every inch— messed bedsheets, a glass of liquor, and the computer turned on. Cisco had been awake, but why? Had he heard something? Was someone with him? Max picked up the glass and smelled it. The strong scent of bourbon wasn't enough to mask Cisco's scent. Curious, Cisco wasn't normally a drinker. Max set the glass back down and continued to scan the room.

His nostrils flared as he moved, took in every scent. Andrew's blood was the most powerful, making it difficult to detect smaller traces of scents. He went to his hands and knees, scanning the room from a different level, looking for missed evidence. He got a waft of chloroform. They had knocked his boy out. Of course they had. Cisco would not have gone willingly and there were no traces of a struggle. They surprised him, drugged him, and took him. But where? The clues were here; he must figure it out. Somehow, some way, Zeke or one of his associates had gotten past his security and into his most inner private chambers without being spotted. How was this possible? *Goddammit, it couldn't have been Zeke who actually took him, you moron!* It had been daylight so it had to have been a human doing Zeke's bidding. But who?

"Think, damn you, think."

Max stood up and turned in a slow deliberate circle. Camera feeds could be hacked; no machine designed by man was infallible. Computers failed, systems broke down, and he got that. But no one had seen Zeke in a week, and from what he'd gathered, nor had anyone spotted any strangers in the club, at least not vampire. Max sighed in frustration. He'd been right to worry about all the new activity and growing popularity of the club, but in his arrogance, he hadn't taken the proper precautions. Still, how could a human have pulled off such a feat?

Humans couldn't trace, couldn't use mind control, nor could they brainwash someone in the blink of an eye. They damn sure couldn't achieve invisibility. So how the fuck had he or she done it. It made no sense. Was it possible that he'd been arrogant to think vampires were the only species who had higher powers than that of an average human?

Leaving Cisco's room behind, Max traced to the chamber beneath his office. If there was reference to any type of being that could achieve such things, he'd find it within the pages of the book of lore. It was a long shot, but at least it was something to go on.

He searched until dawn encroached and was forced to give up, having found nothing, a waste of time. Once again he had failed Cisco.

# CHAPTER TWENTY

MOMENTS AFTER the sun had set, Max was sitting at a banquet table cursing the limitations of his body. He'd been unable to hunt for Cisco for the past ten hours, his only solace that Zeke too would have been at the mercy of the grave. Still, he couldn't help but wonder where his Cisco was. He wasn't restricted to the same limitations as the vampire. Had he lain awake all day? Had he been cold? Was he hungry? Had he been in pain? The thoughts assaulted him, inflamed him, yet resolve and determination burned brighter. His Cisco was strong, brave. He could endure hardship for a little while, and then he'd soothe Cisco's wounds with the screams and blood of his tormentors.

Max looked around at the members of his security force, human and vampire, as well as every other vampire in his inner circle, examining each one carefully, looking for some kind of hint, a clue as to their guilt or innocence. However, no matter how he tried, he couldn't concentrate, his thoughts drifting back to Cisco.

He was getting nowhere. Might as well lay it on the table.

"One of you, perhaps more than one, knows what has happened to my Cisco. If you return him to me now, I shall make your death quick. If I must find him on my own, and I assure you I will, you will beg for death," he said with deadly seriousness.

Everyone in attendance began looking at each other, but no one spoke up. Max tried his best to pick up on something, a scent, a look, anything that would give away their culpability, but once again he couldn't detect so much as a hint of malicious intent.

"Very well, we shall do this the hard way," Max reported with disdain. He turned his attention to Michael, the security technician. "What have you discovered?"

The tension in the room waned slightly, each man's focus now on Michael.

"Our camera system was definitely hacked. Whoever did it is a fucking genius. Somehow they were able to make a seamless loop, manipulating the images in real time, right down to simulating the breathing of those on film. I've never seen anything like it. It's like Star Wars kind of fucking tech and impressive as hell. On top of that, as impossible as it should be, they did it remotely, meaning he or she didn't do it from within the compound. We're running programs now trying to trace where the infiltration originated from, but it could take hours, days even."

"Any way we can speed up the search?" Max inquired.

Michael shook his head. "No. Then again, until last night, I'd have sworn the technology to manipulate our camera feeds didn't exist. I've put out a few calls, looking for anything, even undeveloped shit that might help. Right now, though, it's a waiting game."

"Keep searching. You're excused. And take your techs with you." He waved a dismissive hand toward the men who worked under Michael. Max believed Michael wasn't involved, and his tech nerds were so scared, they were ready to shit themselves. They weren't involved. Max had picked up on the awe Michael had at the technology he was talking about, felt the disbelief, and it seemed genuine. He'd been wrong before, but he didn't think so this time. Besides, sitting around this fucking room all staring at each other wasn't going to get his Cisco back.

"Yes, sir," Michael replied and hurried out of the room.

"Dr. Heine, bring me up to date on the bites."

The old doctor pulled his glasses down from the crazy white hair atop his head to set them on the tip of his nose as he read from the papers in front of him. "From what I can decipher, none of those bitten had any recollection of the event. They weren't drained to an incapacitating level, simply bitten. My guess would be this was done so the vampire would be able to track their movements. They'd need to know where certain people were before entering the club, and so if I were you, I'd look to the five victims, figure out their movements, how they unwittingly helped the culprit."

"Makes sense. Any way to figure out who the biter is?"

Dr. Heine pushed his glasses back up and sat back in his chair. "I've swabbed the bites, but even if I am able to pull a DNA sample, I'd have to test it against a known subject, and at that time, the point may be moot, wouldn't you say?"

"So basically you're telling me nothing new," Max grumbled.

"Pretty much," Dr. Heine responded with a nod.

Max slammed his hand down on the table in frustration. "Does anybody have anything to add besides I got fucking nothing?" After a long, drawn-out silence, the tension in the room growing to a level that it nearly exploded, Max looked to Silas.

"What about Zeke, any leads on where he is?"

Silas started to open his mouth to say something, then shut it again.

"Well?" Max growled.

"You said you didn't wanna hear I got fucking nothing, but yeah, I got fucking nothing. I've been to every known hangout, his home, and I can't find him. I even tried getting into the king's compound, but I didn't have a fucking appointment."

"I've put a call into the king as well," Max admitted, "but I have still to hear back from him." Fucking bastard, no doubt he was stalling. Based on what Max knew, it wouldn't be impossible that Zeke had Cisco at the palace or another destination Liam had ownership of. Zeke was a sadistic prick but not the brightest. He had to have help, and Liam would give Zeke what he wanted if in return, Liam took control of Max's clan.

"I don't mean to interrupt here," Darius said, "but shouldn't Angelo be here?"

"He won't be back until tomorrow night," Max informed him.

"But if anyone knows the coming and goings of Zeke, it would be him. He's been watching him closely for years," Darius pointed out. "Don't you think, given the gravity of the situation, the hunt would be more successful if—"

"Goddammit, don't you think I've thought of that? He can't fucking be here," Max roared, his rage and despair over the situation nearly blinding him. He surged to his feet. "Everyone but Darius and Silas, get the fuck out!"

Humans and vampire alike began scrambling to escape Max's fury as he struggled to get it reined in. As soon as everyone left, Max slumped back down into his chair, his anger leaving him like a deflating balloon, until there was nothing but hopelessness.

"Angelo is addressing the council tonight with some urgent matters. If he is successful, one of the benefits will be a death warrant for Zeke."

"Wait a minute," Silas piped in, a confused expression on his face. "Zeke stole your blood bond. You don't need council approval."

"I am not bonded to Cisco, so technically he hasn't broken the law. Breaking and entering, even into my home, isn't grounds enough to obtain more than a public flogging. The sad thing is, Angelo has been trying to convince me to kill Zeke for years, but would I listen? My fucking obsession with law and order—" Max laughed bitterly. The irony of it was painful rather than amusing.

"You can't blame yourself for this," Silas said. "You're a big part of the reason we've been able to integrate into human society. Without the strict law and order you've upheld, that wouldn't have been possible."

It was little consolation at the moment. He couldn't help but wonder if he'd just done as Angelo had suggested and sent Zeke out to meet the dawn, consequences and law and order be damned, then his Cisco would be safe.

"It's true, Max. There are a lot who look up to you, respect you. We just need to get the word out—"

"No! We can't let this out to the general pop," Max said adamantly.

"Why not?" Silas asked. "The more people out hunting Zeke the better."

"Then those who do know will just have to work harder. If it gets out that someone was able to not only get past our security systems, but make it to the innermost areas and steal my mate, it will serve no purpose but to strengthen our enemies. They'll use the knowledge to turn others against us, set doubt in their minds, and in the end won't help me find Cisco." Max shook his head. "No, we need to keep this quiet for now. Silas, have the human staff been kept here?"

"Yes, sir, but they are getting antsy. They have families they need to return to."

"I need you to make sure the human staff we've eliminated as suspects have no memory of Cisco's disappearance. The others who have not been eliminated, as well as the five bitten, will need to stay here for now. Nothing we can do about the few vampires who know. I can only hope none of them are the ones assisting Zeke."

"I'll take care of it," Silas assured him. "Do you really think one of us has helped Zeke?"

"I don't know anymore," Max admitted. "It's the only logical explanation for how Zeke obtained entrance. He had to have had help."

"There is another possibility," Darius said. "Michael said the technology used was like out of Star Wars or some shit. What if it's not alien technology but magic?" When both Max and Silas stared at him without saying a word, he added, "I know you think I'm crazy, but what is crazier than the fact that we exist? We're dead, for fuck's sake, but here we are. If you ask me, that's some heavy-duty magic."

Darius didn't belong to an era that was ruled by superstition, one before the age of technology. He'd been turned less than thirty years. He did, however, grow up in the French Quarter of New Orleans, the son of a woman who claimed to be a genuine palmistry and tarot counselor. Having an analytical mind, Max had blown off Darius's passion for magic, chalking up his beliefs to being raised by a nutjob. Another irony hit him, yet this one was rife with humor. Witches, warlocks and magical spells were bullshit hocus-pocus, but a race of undead and a connecting bond that could restart a dead heart was totally plausible.

Christ, he'd been a fool.

For so long his single driving force had been securing the clan's position, integrating them into human society, assuring their survival. For the past five years, he'd worked even harder at it in preparation for Cisco to join him. Everything he'd done, his sole purpose, he realized, was not for the good of others but for a much more selfish reason.

Then a thought occurred to him. Fuck! Why hadn't he thought of this sooner? "Get Michael back down here now!" Max bellowed.

Silas pulled out his cell phone instantly and dialed as Max began to pace.

"What's going on?" Darius asked.

"You were right! Why the hell hadn't I thought of it?"

"You think it's a magic spell or something?"

"No, the alien technology or rather, in this case, vampire technology."

"What?" Darius asked with a confused expression.

"He's on his way," Silas announced as soon as he ended the call.

"Never mind, Darius, I'll explain it when Michael gets here, but I think I just figured out how they manipulated our system." It had nothing to do with magic and everything to do with newly installed software. Now he just had to learn where Michael had gotten it and who created it, and it would lead him right to the bastards who had dared to enter his house and take what was his.

They would pray for death.


SO FAR the new software looked legit; Michael hadn't found anything that would suggest otherwise. But Max knew it was the key to finding Cisco. If he'd thought it would help, he'd have still been glaring over Michael's shoulder while he searched, but it had only served to make the man nervous and his fingers clumsy as they moved over the keyboard, which was counterproductive, and hence Max found himself in the last place he wanted to be.

He sat rigidly in his rightful place of power at the front of his club, but he felt anything but powerful. He could hear the murmured conversations, each patron talking about the disappearance of Cisco. He should have known it was futile to keep it a secret. Still, he tried to keep up appearances before his enemies, and at this point, not knowing who was loyal, every one of the patrons were potential threats, conspirators.

A loud commotion followed by a familiar voice shouting "Get your hands off me, bloodsucker!" had Max jumping to his feet and tracing to the entry door.

Benny stood glaring up at Darius, completely oblivious to the potential danger he was in, or perhaps he simply didn't care. When he spotted Max, he tried to jerk away from Darius's hold on his forearm, but Darius held tight.

"Would you tell your help to get his hands off me," Benny demanded.

"Look, you little fucker," Darius growled. He grabbed Benny's other arm and lifted him off his feet. "I'm going to enjoy draining every last drop from you."

Max laid his hand on Darius's shoulder, halting his movements. "Benny, why must you constantly torment my brethren?"

"He started it," Benny responded defiantly without taking his gaze from Darius.

"And now I'm going to finish it," Darius snarled.

"Darius, put him down."

"Max—"

"You heard him, bloodsucker, put me down," Benny demanded.

Darius's eyes flashed red, and for a tense moment, Max feared Darius was going to defy him. With everything else going on, the last thing he wanted to do was make an example of Darius.

Thankfully, Darius came to his senses and released his hold on Benny with a grunt, letting him fall to his feet. Max caught Benny by the scruff of his neck before he could stumble back. Benny started to open his mouth, but Max jerked him away, tightening his grip.

"Not another word until we're in my office."

Benny must have heard the dangerous warning in Max's voice because he clenched his mouth shut till the door behind them closed. "What happened to Cisco?"

Max shoved him down into a chair. "What makes you think something has happened to him?"

"Don't yank my chain, Max. I get an e-mail from him—"

Max whirled on him, laying his hands on the arms of the chair and getting in Benny's face. "When?"

"What's going on?"

"When, goddammit! When did you hear from him?"

"Three days ago."

Max squeezed his eyes shut, anger and disappointment swirling around within him.

Benny fisted his hands in Max's shirt. "What the fuck is going on? Cisco e-mailed me saying he missed me and would call when I got out of work and then nothing."

Max lifted his gaze, unable to hide his grief. He stumbled back, forcing Benny to release him, and fell back onto the sofa. "He's gone."

"Gone?"

Max scrubbed a hand over his face. What the hell was he supposed to say? The truth? A lie? He'd assured Cisco's best friend that no harm would come to him.

"What the hell do you mean, gone?"

"I've let him and you down," Max admitted.

In true Benny fashion, he jumped up and, without fear, got in Max's face, stabbing a finger into his chest. "Stop your cryptic bullshit and tell me what happened to Cisco."

"He's fallen into the hands of my enemies."

Benny held his gaze for a moment, unblinking as if he were trying to process what he'd just heard and then simply said, "Get him back."

*Fuck!* If he knew where he was, he'd already have him back, but he didn't know and he'd never felt as impotent as he did at that moment.

"Did you hear me? Get him back!" Benny screamed.

Anger coursed through Max. Anger he could deal with; he understood it. The hopelessness was what had him sitting there like a worthless piece of shit but the anger....

"You don't think I'm trying?" Max snapped. "Cisco is my reason for existence. The reason I can dare to believe again. You don't think I'm trying?" Max shoved to his feet, glaring down at Benny. "I'd scour the fucking Earth for him, but that would waste precious time. So as hard as it is, I'm trying to be patient and not make the same fucking mistake twice, you got it? Now sit the fuck down and, instead of acting like an idiot, give me some solutions."

Benny obviously had at least some smarts, realizing that screaming and throwing around accusations, no matter how deserving, weren't doing a damn thing to help get Cisco back.

"Alright," he conceded, running his fingers through his hair and blowing out a huffed breath as he returned to his seat. "Tell me what happened."

Max had no choice. He recounted every painful detail since first discovering Cisco was gone. While doing so, he worked through every minute detail in his head, searching for a hint, the smallest of clues he might have missed, but found none. By the time he finished, he was frustrated as hell and no closer to finding Cisco.

"I need a drink," Benny muttered.

"Do you really think that will help?"

Benny glared at him. "No, it won't fucking help, but it may take care of this throb in my head you just gave me."

Max walked to the bar. "Beer or—"

"Beer's not going to help this," Benny interrupted and rubbed at his temples.

"Whiskey it is." Max dropped a couple ice cubes in a glass and brought it and the bottle, setting them on the coffee table in front of Benny.

"Thanks." Benny filled his glass, threw back a good measure and then refilled the glass.

"Any chance Cisco has reached out to anyone else, another friend? Perhaps a family member?"

Benny shook his head. "Cisco doesn't have any family to speak of, and if something was going down, something that upset him or he was scared, he'd get a hold of me."

"Can I ask what was the nature of the e-mail you received from him?"

"He just said he couldn't sleep, that he missed me and he'd call later when I got out of work." Benny stared down into his glass, shaking his head. "He never called."

Max tapped his fingers on the arm of his chair. What had kept Cisco from sleeping? Had he had a premonition? Had his poor boy known something wasn't right and hadn't been able to come to him to have his fears eased?

A loud banging on his office door had both him and Benny jerking in surprise.

"Max! It's Andrew, I remembered something. Max!"

Max rushed to the door and threw it open to find Andrew breathing harshly, his face lit up, eyes wide. "What is it?"

"I… I don't know if it's a memory or a dream, but it popped into my head and I rushed right over."

"Dammit, Andrew, what is it?" Max asked impatiently and glanced at Benny who joined him at his side.

"Right before Cisco disappeared, I remember knocking on the door and asking him if it was okay for Patrick to come in."

"Find him and Silas, now!"

"Who is Patrick?" Benny asked.

"The man who just may lead us to my Cisco."

# CHAPTER TWENTY-ONE

HANDS AND feet long ago having gone numb from the tight binds, Cisco no longer had the strength to wiggle his fingers and toes to keep the blood pumping. Zeke had subjected him to unimaginable horrors during the night, his servants forcing him to stay awake during the day.

How many days had it been?

He couldn't even begin to guess as they had long ago run together into a perpetual state of agony. He wasn't even sure what was real anymore. Was he truly experiencing this or dreaming, seeing hallucinations of his ravaged mind? The fear the giant spiders crawling over the walls produced was as real a fear as that of Zeke's knife as it sliced through Cisco's flesh. Memories of Benny's smiling face and soothing touch were as real as the snarling face and rough treatment of Zeke. The line between reality, dream, and nightmare had become blurred.

The only thing Cisco was sure about anymore was he was ready to die. He'd silently prayed for it, begged for it, and it seemed his desire for death was finally being answered. He knew it was coming for him. In life Max was the only thing he'd ever truly wanted, and now, even the idea of his Master wasn't enough to make him want to stay. He was beaten and exhausted.

Broken.

"Are you ready to go?" a voice whispered to him.

*Yes.*

"Open your mouth, drink."

He didn't think he had the strength, but he must have found it somewhere, because suddenly his mouth was filled with something warm with a coppery flavor. He swallowed, his raw throat protesting, but then fingers were in his hair, stroking him soothingly, encouraging.

"Come to me," Death beckoned. "Serve me."

Cisco let go, the allure of peace propelling him into the dark.


SILAS WAS like a stone statue, his expression blank, with a visibly trembling Patrick kneeling at his feet. Max stood before them, as still as Silas, giving nothing away and letting Patrick continue to worry and stress. Patrick's heart was beating butterfly quick, and his breathing was nearly as rapid. It was normally more difficult to read the emotions of a blood-bonded human, but one didn't need to have any sort of powers or skills to read Patrick's. He was scared nearly to death, and if his heart beat any faster, said death would be sooner rather than later. With Patrick experiencing such an extreme emotion, even if Max was to question him, it would be hard to decipher if it was fear or deception that was causing his reactions. What he needed was for Patrick to be calm and Silas to prove he still had control over his boy before Max began his interrogation.

"Silas, get your boy under control."

"Yes, sir."

Silas laid a hand on Patrick's shoulder and leaned down to speak to him. Max ignored them, stepping back to lean against the wall, giving the two a moment alone. The waiting was difficult to say the least. Each tick of the clock was a painful reminder of Max's inability to protect Cisco. Everything was falling apart. His ability to rule, to protect—he was even beginning to question his conviction and loyalty to his race. None of it seemed to matter if he didn't have Cisco, and therein lay the problem. A true leader couldn't put his selfish needs above the greater good. History had proven over and over how dangerous such a trait was in a ruler.

"Max, Patrick is ready to answer any questions you may have of him," Silas announced.

Max turned around to find Patrick's chest pushed out, posture perfect, and head held high. The look of fear as well as the trembling was absent. It had only taken a few moments for Silas to calm his boy and Max could not deny the strong bond that was still present between Master and boy.

Max stood looming over Patrick, but the boy's demeanor didn't change. He was completely at ease at his Master's feet. "You have spent quite a bit of time with Cisco. Has he ever confided any of his concerns?"

"Yes, sir. The last night we were in the club, he was nervous and I could tell something was weighing heavy on him. He asked me to come see him. I told him I'd come at dawn."

"And did you?" Max asked.

"Yes, sir." Patrick looked up at Silas. "I'm sorry I disobeyed you, Master. Cisco was worried, and I was only with him a few minutes, then I went straight to my room and locked myself in."

"We will address your disobedience later. Pay attention to Master Max and answer his questions honestly," Silas responded sternly.

"Yes, Sir," Patrick said, shoulders slumping, but he caught himself quickly and straightened his posture.

"Wait a minute," Max said abruptly. "You saw Cisco at dawn?"

"Yes, sir."

"Then you were the last person to see him!" Max grabbed Patrick by the arms and jerked him up till they were face to face. Silas stiffened, but he didn't interfere nor did he say anything. "What did you do with my Cisco?"

"I... I...." Patrick stole a glance toward Silas, and then he went limp, but his expression was confident and his voice strong when he continued. "I didn't do anything with your Cisco, sir. I wouldn't. It was the day before that I went to Cisco. He was worried so I told him what I knew, and then I left. However, before I left, I did warn him to lock his door and not to come out or open it for anyone but you."

"Do not lie to me, boy," Max warned. "Andrew said the last thing he remembered on the day Cisco disappeared was asking Cisco if it was okay if you came into his room."

Patrick shook his head vigorously. "I wasn't there. Ask my Master. After I told him about the power outage, he became alarmed. I was locked up with him before dawn."

"It's true, Max. Regardless of what Andrew said, my Patrick could not have been there the morning Cisco disappeared. He has no way of escaping from my chambers, I assure you."

The spark of hope drained from Max, and he gently eased Patrick back down onto his knees and patted his head. "I'm sorry, boy." Max scrubbed his hand over his face, frustration and sorrow seeping back in.

"It's okay, sir. I understand you're scared. I am too. Did Cisco tell you about our alarms not going off? We both got up late that day because our alarms were flashing like the power had gone out. I told him that was impossible because of the generator system."

"Yes, but unfortunately I assured him it was nothing, that he was safe. I explained Michael was installing a new software security system. I am now sure the breach came while the software was being installed. You're lucky you have such a good Master who took it seriously and took the proper steps to protect you," Max said dejectedly. With a heavy heart, he trudged back to his desk and flopped down into his chair, placing his head in his hands.

Gentle fingers ran across Max's hair. "Sir, Cisco has a good Master too. You can't blame yourself for the evil others do," Patrick said softly.

"I can," Max replied without looking up. "It was my job to protect him, to keep him safe and I failed him."

"You only fail him if you give up. He's strong, and he'll endure anything in order to get back to you. You must keep fighting, must keep looking for him because he's out there waiting for you."

"Listen to him, Max," Silas added. "If they wanted to simply kill Cisco, they wouldn't have taken him but simply killed him in his room. Zeke is using him to get to you, and if Cisco dies, he loses his leverage."

"I don't know where else to look," Max said as he looked up at the two men at his side.

They both stared back at him with concerned looks, and then suddenly Patrick blurted, "Oh shit! Why didn't I think of that?"

"What?" Both Max and Silas asked in unison.

"Mario! Oh. My. God! I ran into him in the passageway between the kitchen and your office. He had this smug look on his face and muttered something about enjoying being Silas's bitch while it lasted. I ignored him at the time because that asshole is always trying to rile me up ever since I became Silas's mate instead of him."

"When was this?" Max demanded.

"The night before Cisco went missing."

"Mario doesn't have clearance to be in the kitchen or any other of the inner areas of the club," Silas pointed out.

"I didn't think so either, but I didn't question him when he knocked on Max's door. I figured he'd been summoned," Patrick responded with a shrug.

Max cocked his head, brows furrowed as he stared at Patrick, trying to recall Mario coming to his office. He'd been a bit crazy lately, but he'd have remembered Mario being there and he damn sure would have remembered tossing the little urchin out on his ass.

"Mario has never been to my office," Max explained in confusion.

"Yes, he has," Patrick insisted. "Before I stepped into the kitchen, I heard you ask him something."

"Impossible," Max retorted, going to his feet. "I'm telling you, I never summoned him nor would I have allowed him in my office."

"You sure of the time and day?" Silas asked Patrick.

"I'm positive, Master. Just as positive as I am I heard your voice and you didn't sound happy to see him. I didn't think anything of it. In fact I think I laughed because it sounded like the little tool was about to get a reaming from you and not the good kind."

A spark of memory flickered inside Max's mind. He couldn't quite make it out, as if the images were hidden behind a thick veil, only flashes of movement but nothing solid or meaningful. He concentrated harder, doing his best to recall the evening in detail. He'd been in his office, enjoying a cigar, waiting for the donor, but he couldn't recall the donor arriving or even whether he fed that night. Fuck! That was the night he'd lost a full hour of time.

"Silas, did you send me a donor that night?"

"Of course, sir. You made it very clear to have a different one sent to your office every night. I have a list of thirty willing donors already scheduled and working on finding more."

"Do you happen to know who you sent that night?"

"Carlton. Did he not show up?"

"I don't—"

"Carlton Monty? The housekeeper's son?" Patrick interrupted.

"Yes," Silas confirmed.

"That's impossible. Or rather, it's not possible that Carlton fed Max that night. He died in a head-on collision earlier that evening around five. Poor Mrs. Monty is devastated to have lost her only son."

"Did you know about this?" Max asked Silas.

Silas frowned and shook his head.

"So you didn't send another donor, and yet Mario was seen coming to my office," Max clarified. Silas nodded again. "I have no recollection of Mario coming. In fact, I lost a full hour that night," Max responded, confusion infusing him.

"Holy fuck! You mean to tell me there is someone or something powerful enough to wipe a vampire's memory?" Silas asked in apparent shock.

"Only one thing I know of—" Max pushed to his feet and grabbed his jacket. "—a very old, very powerful maker. Silas, I want every available person looking for Mario. Call me the second he is found." Max headed for the door.

"I'm on it," Silas confirmed. "Where are you going?"

"I'm going to go see someone I haven't seen in a very long time." He stopped just outside of the door and turned back. "I almost forgot. Patrick, will you see to Benny? He's in my office."

"Yes, sir."

"Let him know that I got a lead and I'll have Cisco home soon."

Max didn't wait for a response. Within minutes, he was entering his private plane, the engines roaring to life. Since he couldn't trace from California to Chicago without completely depleting himself of energy, he'd have to rely on the next best thing.

# CHAPTER TWENTY-TWO

AS FANGS pierced his neck once again, Cisco squeezed his eyes shut and tried to block out the cold lips working against his flesh, as well as the loud satisfied moans and slurping sounds emitting from Zeke. Patrick had told him that the vampire kiss was better than any orgasm, but Cisco didn't experience even a sliver of pleasure. Still, feeding Zeke wasn't as disgusting as when Zeke forced his putrid blood down Cisco's throat. Cisco had been in such agony the first time Zeke had done it that he'd thought death had come for him and he'd willingly let go. But it had been a trap. It hadn't been death that had come for him but the undead. Once he'd realized what was happening, he'd tried to fight, had vomited the putrid blood, but that had only resulted in enraging Zeke.

Cisco gritted his teeth and squeezed his eyes tighter, still holding back the tears that wanted to fall. He was so fucking weak, a failure. He'd broken after only a single night of torture. Now with each new feeding, he could feel his tie to Max slipping away, being replaced by a need, a sickening desire for Zeke. Cisco struggled to hold on to the last strands of Max, worked so fucking hard to keep the images of Max vivid in his mind, pretend it was he who was taking from him, but he was slipping away and Cisco was left grasping at smoke. It was Zeke who was beginning to consume his thoughts, his soul, his very being.

Soon, all traces of Max would be gone and with him, Cisco knew he'd lose all sense of himself. The tendrils of evil were already digging into his flesh, penetrating muscle, seeping into organs, and with each sip, the hold strengthened.

"Your blood and sorrow get me so fucking hard," Zeke grunted against Cisco's neck as he licked the wounds.

Cisco didn't respond, resigned with what would come next. When he was suddenly flipped onto his stomach and his hips grabbed in a bruising grip, Cisco stayed pliant. It wasn't only his body and mind that were broken, but his spirit as well.

SITTING ON the front porch of his small country home, Dr. Bragdon looked up from his book and smiled when he saw Max standing on his steps. "Max! It's good to see you. To what do I owe such an unexpected gift?"

"I'm sorry I didn't inform you I was coming. I need your help."

Bragdon sat his book aside and leaned forward, brow dipping into a deep frown. "What's the matter?"

Max briefly explained what had been happening with Cisco and the mission he'd sent Angelo on. He even went as far as to admit he'd suspected Bragdon might have been somehow involved with Zeke and Liam's plot. The entire time Max spoke, Bragdon stared at him with a thoughtful expression, listening intently without interruption, his fingers tapping against the arm of his rocking chair.

"Since you are here, am I to assume you no longer believe I am involved?" Bragdon asked once Max had gone silent.

"I don't know what I believe anymore or even who I can trust," Max admitted. "All I do know is there is a vampire who was able to bite and influence my staff and he is one extremely powerful son of a bitch if he was also able to wipe my memory clean."

"I do not possess such power over you, and even if I did, what would be my motive?"

Max thought about it carefully. As far as he knew, Dr. Bragdon had never turned a single person to vampire unless he believed them to be terminal. With most of his patients, he never even attempted such an extreme measure unless he felt there was something special about them. To an extent Max believed Bragdon was still playing God with people's lives, but there was also something good and pure in his motives. However, he had been close to Liam and had helped him obtain his throne.

"You were instrumental in Liam obtaining his seat of power."

"Something I grew to regret," Bragdon replied. "Liam became quite radical in what he envisioned for the future of our race. The last time I spoke with him, I expressed my objection to his goals and he responded with an ultimatum."

"Which was?" Max inquired.

"I was either with him or against him. I don't like ultimatums." Bragdon sat back in his chair and smiled. "I haven't spoken to him in a very long time."

Max ran a hand through his hair and then across the back of his neck, rubbing at the tension that had settled there. "Then once again, I have hit a dead end. I have been fucking up one thing after another, and for my sins, Cisco suffers."

"I don't know about that. Sounds like you've been very busy and been doing everything you can."

"It's not enough, and I have no idea what to do next."

"This whole helpless attitude doesn't sound like you. The Maximilian De Ferrari I know wouldn't give up so easily."

"Easily?" Max spat bitterly. "I have wracked my fucking brain, tormented my staff, my friends, hell I nearly fucking killed one trying to get information, not to mention I have a small army out searching for Zeke, but it hasn't done me a damn bit of good."

"Well, it's good you're here, then, huh?"

"Look, Bragdon, I'm in no mood for games or riddles. If you know something that can help me find Cisco, then let's hear it. If not, I'm out of here."

"Simmer down. You going off half-cocked without a plan isn't going to do you or your Cisco a damn bit of good. Now I may not have talked to Liam, but I assure you I know what that bastard has been up to." Bragdon pushed to his feet. "Follow me."

Max's interest piqued, he followed his maker into the house and into his office. The place hadn't changed a bit in the years Max had been away. In fact it looked exactly the same as it had the first time he'd been here. Heavy wood desk, shelves lined with medical texts, the same musky scent as if it had been frozen in time just like its owner.

"Have a seat," Bragdon said and pointed to the chair on the opposite side of his desk. He then pulled out a thick file from a drawer and slid it across the desk to Max. "I wish you would have come to me before going to Egnatius so you had all the facts."

Max flipped the file over, scanning the pages at the back first. Bragdon had definitely done his homework, his files appearing to go back even further than Max's own. The early pages were basically a diary of Bragdon's thoughts and concerns about Liam. He'd been keeping a close eye on Liam and Zeke's activities. Bragdon was aware of the plot and kept meticulous notes on the conspirators' comings and goings. Halfway through the file, Max spotted a name that caused him to freeze. It was one Max hadn't uncovered during his own search and, had he discovered it, might have caused him to think twice before going to Egnatius.

Gilad Deschanel.

As Max continued to read about how deeply Gilad was involved, actually....

"Gilad? Are you fucking kidding me?" Max gasped in horror.

"I wish I was," Bragdon responded, sounding full of regret.

Max now knew exactly who had been behind his memory loss, and with Gilad's power, an hour of lost time would have been obtained with a mere flick of his wrist. No one was 100 percent sure how old Gilad was, although some claimed he was one of the first. Max didn't know if the rumors were true or not. At the moment, what did matter was he'd sent Angelo alone to meet with Egnatius with information that would doom Egnatius's maker.

*Oh shit!* Why hadn't he thought to ask sooner? "Is Egnatius involved in this?"

"No," Bragdon replied, sounding completely confident. Still Max needed to know.

"You sure. One hundred percent sure? I sent Angelo to see him."

"Angelo is safer there than you are within your own walls." Bragdon took the file and thumbed through the pages, pulling one out. He looked up at Max with a concerned expression and then held out the paper.

Max stared at the paper with trepidation as if it were an asp ready to strike. He knew beyond a shadow of a doubt he didn't want to read what was printed on it and yet he knew he must. Resigning himself, Max took it and read.

*September fourth 1921, George Wheeler stalked and killed Milton Warman. The obscure newspaper clipping attached below from the New Orleans Times is the only known record of the crime. According to the article, Milton was set on fire and burned alive.*

Max scanned the newspaper article but saw no mention of George or any other suspect. "Who is this Milton Warman, and why would George kill him?"

"Milton was Cora's first love, and he wasn't burned alive, well not technically since he was a vampire. George was determined to have Cora for himself, but the bond between her and Milton was unbreakable."

"So George killed him. Does Cora know?"

Bragdon shook his head.

"What does this have to do with Liam's plot?" Max asked, unease and dread settling into his gut, already working out where the breach in his clan was based and fucking hating it.

"Apparently there was a witness, some guy named Jon who was a human lover of both Cora and Milton. Jon told Cora that George had tied Milton up and left him to bake in the sun. When she confronted George, he was very convincing in his declaration of innocence and he also had an alibi."

George's words came back to Max. *"Just paying off a debt."* "Let me guess, Zeke?"

"You got it. On Liam's orders, Jon was given to George to punish for being falsely accused. George declined, whether out of guilt or to spare Cora, I don't know. I also don't know if George had anything to do with Jon's subsequent disappearance, but I suspect he either set it up or at the very least had knowledge of it, considering the last time Jon was seen alive he was spotted with Zeke."

"Son of a bitch," Max grumbled and crushed the paper in his hand.

"Easy there," Bragdon soothed, laying a hand on Max's forearm. "You might need that bit of information."

Max jerked his arm away. "It will be useless anyway once George is dead," Max countered but did drop the paper on the desk before pushing to his feet. Motherfucker was going to meet the same fate as Milton come morning.

"Max, wait!" Bragdon called out and followed behind Max. "What the hell did I tell you about going off half-cocked? You want to save Cisco, then I suggest you think about what you're about to do. If you rush back and kill George, you may be destroying useful information he may have."

Max didn't need George's information. He had enough proof to bring Liam, Zeke, Gilad, and the rest of their group down. What Max needed was vengeance. He wanted to hear George's cries of pain, to witness his suffering for his treachery. Max's shirt was grabbed and he spun to lash out, his vision going red, but pain erupted in his chest and he cried out in agony as he fell to his knees.

"Max!" Bragdon shouted in alarm.

Max reached out to his maker, but the misery gripped him, caused his muscles to contract, robbing him of his ability to control his body, and he fell to his side. Max lay in a fetal position, unable to move or scream and completely at the mercy of the pain that held him as icy tendrils penetrated his soul.

# CHAPTER TWENTY-THREE

THE LEASH attached to Cisco's collar as he was led into Wicked Ground wasn't the only thing that kept him from fleeing. It was as if something had completely taken over his body and fused it to his tormentor and new Master and he was unable to break free. Other than a mellow tune playing from the overhead speakers, the club was eerily silent. Each person Cisco passed had a shocked expression on their face. A blond man close to his own size whispered Cisco's name as he passed, but Cisco had no recollection of ever meeting the man or how the man knew his name.

In fact, beyond his name, he had no idea who he was. He had no memory of his childhood, his parents, his friends. It was as if he'd been born only days ago, birthed for one purpose. The only thing that kept his heart beating and his body animated was his Master, Zeke. Without Zeke, Cisco would fail to exist. There was nothing but Zeke.

His Master sat upon an ornate chair of carved wood and red velvet, a seat worthy of his power, and Cisco instantly fell to his knees at his side. He moved a fraction of an inch closer until his arm came in contact with Zeke's thigh, needing the contact like he needed the very air in his lungs. His lifeline. Cisco clasped his hands behind his back, pushed out his chest, and pressed his chin to it. He was rewarded with his Master's touch. Zeke silently praised him by running his fingers through Cisco's hair, petting him.

"Who the fuck do you think you are?" someone asked, but Cisco didn't dare raise his head to see who the angry voice belonged to, instead focusing on the heavy black-soled boots, and tensed, waiting for Zeke to strike.

Surprisingly his Master did no such thing. "Good evening, Silas," Zeke responded, seemingly unaffected by the stranger's venomous tone. "Considering I am sitting in the seat of power, I would have thought even you could figure it out."

"You have no right to that chair, and I'm going to take immense pleasure in seeing Max remove you from it and rip you limb from limb."

Once again Zeke didn't seem concerned by Silas's angry tone or his threat. Zeke's voice sounded almost jubilant when he said, "I am sorry to deny you of your desire to see me so messily dispatched, but I am simply obeying the orders from our king."

"Max won't—" Silas's words were cut off, and he awkwardly fell to his knees, his body contorted.

"You will kneel in respect when I enter the room," demanded a booming voice. The snap of undeniable authority from the stranger caused Cisco to tremble.

"Easy, boy," Zeke murmured and ran his hand down Cisco's neck to his back in a soothing manner.

Cisco welcomed the heavy fog that settled down over him and obscured everything but his Master's touch.

THE LAST hint of the sun's rays dropped below the horizon, and Max's eyes flew open and he jerked upright. He scanned the unfamiliar area until recognition finally hit him. He'd spent many nights waking in this familiar place, returned to it numerous times at dawn. But for several ticks of the clock, he couldn't figure out why he was in Bragdon's private chamber or how he'd gotten there.

"You okay?" Bragdon asked, rising from his bed.

"No. What the hell am I doing here?"

"I brought you here. You don't remember?"

Max shook his head. Something was amiss, and for the first time in decades, he had woken feeling dazed, not all his synapses firing, and he struggled to sort out his thoughts.

"I'm not sure what the hell happened to you. One minute you were hell-bent on killing George and the next you were screaming in agony. I've only seen that kind of reaction when…."

If Max hadn't been sitting when the memories of the night before slammed into him, he'd have been knocked on his ass.

*Zeke.*

*Liam.*

*Plots.*

*Betrayal.*

*Cisco.*

Max clutched his chest and stood on shaking legs. "I can't feel him!"

"I was afraid of that," Bragdon said grimly.

"Why can't I feel him! It's like my heart has been ripped out of my chest and there is this huge hole that Cisco had once filled. But...."

Max stumbled back, his legs hitting the side of the bed, and he sat down heavily upon it as they gave out. "He's dead. My Cisco is dead." Max hung his head, completely beaten.

He'd brought Cisco into his world, had promised to protect him, and he'd failed. It no longer mattered if Liam and Gilad started a war. It was no longer his concern or his fight. Zeke had taken away his everything. The thought of Zeke caused Max's vision to turn red with rage. He was ready to follow Cisco into the dark, but before he did, he would send that son of a bitch to hell in a blaze of agony.

Max traced from Bragdon's chambers to his private plane. "Get me home now!" he bellowed as soon as he entered the plane.

The pilot looked both shocked and frightened by Max's sudden appearance, but luckily for him, he recovered quickly and scrambled to the cockpit without a word. Max engaged the lock on the door and pulled his phone from his pocket as he took a seat. He dialed Angelo's number; it went straight to voice mail. Max started to leave a message but then snapped his mouth shut and hit the Off button. Angelo knew what needed to be done if anything happened to Max.

The engines roared to life and the plane moved down the runway. Minutes after they took off, Max's phone vibrated and the display showed the main number for Wicked Ground. "Who is this?" he said by way of greeting.

"Max, it's Patrick. He's here," Patrick remarked in barely a breath of sound.

"Who the hell is there?" he demanded.

"Zeke. Come through the service door." The line went dead.

Max pushed away the images of Cisco and the memories of what Zeke had stolen from him before they could crush him. He couldn't allow them to weaken him or distract him. He'd be with Cisco soon enough, or he'd simply cease to exist. Either way he'd have peace. For the moment, Max focused on what Zeke's death would be like. He laid his head back, a smile curling his lip as he imagined what Zeke's cold black heart would feel like as he crushed it in his fist before Zeke's wide, stunned eyes.

The flight seemed to last an eternity. With each passing minute, Max's excitement grew until he was literally shaking with the need to get his hands on Zeke. The plane barely touched down when Max threw open the door and in the next second was standing a block away from Wicked Ground. Only then did he muster the strength to rein in his rage. He wasn't a complete idiot. He'd heard Bragdon, and Max wasn't about to rush into the club like a wild man. No, he needed to use his rage, let it propel him toward his goal rather than let it consume and control him. He no longer cared about his own safety. He'd lost the one thing that mattered to him. But dammit, he could make the bastard who killed his Cisco suffer.

Max tried the service door and found it unlocked. Patrick had either been able to open it or he was leading Max into an ambush. Either way Max wouldn't be deterred. He stood just inside the door, scanning the area with a critical eye, looking for any hint of danger, listening for any indication of anyone being near. Only after determining that he neither heard nor smelled anything out of the ordinary did he cautiously make his way farther into the club. Keeping to the shadows, he moved silently through the kitchen until he was standing at the entrance to the main room. The stench of human fear clung cloyingly in the air, and he heard the faint beats of several rapid hearts, rustling of movement, murmured whispers, and John Mayer playing through the sound system. Max inhaled deeply, trying his best to decipher the different scents, searching for familiar ones, but they all swirled together. The fear and anxiety permeating throughout the club masked everything and made it impossible to know who all was on the other side of the door.

Max was so focused on the room beyond that he didn't hear anyone approach until it was too late. A hand landed on his shoulder, and he spun, taking a defensive stance to find Darius standing behind him with a single finger over his pursed lips. He nodded to the right, indicating Max to follow. Still anticipating an ambush and no longer sure who he could trust, he warily followed Darius to the far end of the kitchen.

"Zeke is sitting upon your throne and Liam is standing behind him, making sure everyone complies with Zeke's orders."

"What's the chance I can get my hands on Zeke without being stopped?"

"Zilch," Darius responded grimly. "Liam got Silas on his fucking knees and catatonic within seconds. He's sporting some hard-core mojo."

"Then how the fuck is it you're here," Max asked suspiciously, his body still coiled for attack.

"Because Liam is not my maker and the arrogant fuckers didn't even bother to check the security booth. The two of them strolled in here like they owned the place, and with the way all the other vamps are acting, they very well may."

Liam and Zeke had powerful ties over many vampires, even those who hated them. For the average vampire, going against his maker was nearly impossible. But Max wasn't an average vampire and although Liam had ties to him, Bragdon was his maker, thus making the influence less severe.

"Do we have anyone else we can trust that's not catatonic?" Max inquired.

"I've put out an alert, a few are on their way but not enough to take out Liam and Zeke. At least not yet."

"What about Angelo? Have you heard from him?"

"He was the first person I called, but with the difference in time zones, I don't think he's awake. I did leave him a message, though."

"Shit! Okay, give me a minute to think here." Max closed his eyes and began working through scenarios that would give them the best chance to succeed. He had no idealistic notions that he could take out Liam, but he'd die with satisfaction knowing he destroyed Zeke first. However, he couldn't come up with a plan to get his hands around Zeke's throat before Liam stepped in. Darius wasn't powerful enough to take on the king by himself and the thought of waiting for others would drive him mad.

"Fuck. I need someone, anyone who can control Liam for a few minutes."

"Will I do?" Bragdon asked, stepping out of the shadows.

"Where the hell did you come from?" Max asked in surprise. Jesus, that was twice within a matter of moments someone had snuck up on him. He needed to get his shit together, or Zeke would win the ultimate fight. Something that was completely unacceptable.

"I was waiting for you," Bragdon replied with a sly grin. "Brought a few friends too."

Max searched for the few said friends, but couldn't detect anyone nearby. "Who?"

"You let me worry about that. You just worry about taking Zeke out."

Max wanted nothing more, but he'd learned his lesson and he'd be damned if anyone else would get the upper hand on him. What happened after Zeke fried, Max gave no fucks about, but until then he had to have a solid, well-defined plan.

"Unacceptable," Max informed Bragdon. "You may trust them, but until I know who in the fuck is at my back, I won't be going through that door."

Bragdon studied Max for a moment and then smiled broadly. "You're learning. I am ineffective in taking down Liam. He'll stop me in my tracks before I make it halfway to him, but Darius could with the help of Constantine and Malaki."

Max's eyes went wide. "How in the hell did you get Egnatius's personal bodyguard and physician?"

"Malaki had... shall we say, an affliction Constantine couldn't deal with. Plus he thoroughly enjoys visiting Chicago and seeing Malaki suffer was a bonus."

Holy fuck! Malaki and Constantine were in the running with Gilad for old age. They would certainly be more than capable of taking down Liam. Hell, the two of them working in tandem could cut Gilad's feet out from under him. The problem was, the two hated each other so whether they would actually work together as a team was an unknown variable.

"How can I be sure the two won't start bitch-slapping each other rather than taking out Liam?"

"You can't," Bragdon responded with a shrug. "However it's your only option and the fact that they hate Liam even more than they hate each other... I'd say the chances are pretty good that they'd take the king out before the bitch-slapping commenced. But ultimately this is your call."

Max thought about it. He had zero chance of success if he and Darius burst through the door. Constantine and Malaki were wild cards, but at least it gave him a chance. Without them he would fail.

Max looked back and forth between Darius and Bragdon and then nodded. "Alright, let's do this."

Darius gave a fist pump, but the more refined Bragdon merely smiled. Bragdon then gave a signal with his hand and Constantine and Malaki materialized before him.

Max pointed at Bragdon. "You stay here. The rest of you follow me."

"The hell I will," Bragdon protested. "I'll be damned if I'm missing this show."

"Fine, you stubborn shit," Max conceded in exasperation. "On my command, I go after Zeke, the rest of you take Liam."

"Can I disembowel him?" Malaki asked, sounding way too fucking gleeful at the prospect.

"Sure. Darius and Constantine can hold him down for your psychotic ass."

Constantine snorted when Malaki frowned. "Fuck you both. I owe that bastard a little payback," Malaki retorted unapologetically.

"Liam stole his favorite toy," Constantine clarified.

It was enough to bring Max's thoughts back to what Zeke had stolen from him. But once again he pushed them aside, refusing to give in to his grief at the loss of his Cisco. It would all be over soon enough and the agony forgotten in the peace of death.

Max pinned Malaki with a hard glare. "I don't care what your reasoning is, just take that fucker down. Got it?"

"It will be my pleasure," Malaki said with obvious glee.

Max moved to the door of the club, hand poised over the knob, and looked back over his shoulder at the four men behind him. "Ready?"

When all four nodded, Max threw open the door.


THE CROWD within the club erupted into screams of terror. Cisco tried to figure out what had everyone so frightened. He'd felt the wind, saw flashes of light and movement, but he was unable to bring all the random events together to make any sense of what was happening. And then suddenly everything went still and quiet as wide piercing blue eyes met his. Cisco knew those eyes. Somewhere in the recesses of his scattered brain, a spark of recognition fired. Yet try as he might, he couldn't grasp the memory, couldn't recall the face or the person they belonged to and then they were gone. Lost to the wind that swirled around him and in the screams that were loud enough to shatter eardrums. Cisco laid his hands over his ears to block out the pain-filled cries. Lights flickered, the unusual wind ruffled his hair, but he did his best to ignore what was happening around him as he struggled to remember where he'd seen those amazing blue eyes.

His heart was pounding wildly, a tickling sensation in the pit of his stomach. Those eyes, it felt as though if he could only remember to whom they belonged, he'd be free, but no matter how hard he searched for the answer it eluded him. His task was made all the more difficult by the commands of his Master. Commands he wanted to ignore but was unable to deny. His body moving without conscious thought. Cisco was on his feet. How he got there he didn't know, nor did he understand why he was retrieving the small dagger his Master had strapped to his ankle.

Gripping it in both of his hands, Cisco drew the weapon back over his head, his Master's gaze holding him rapt.

A large man was leaning over his Master, hands around his throat. "Kill him," his Master mouthed silently.

Unseen hands wrapped around Cisco's and an unfamiliar voice whispered in his ear, "Do it. Kill him."

Cisco hesitated for a mere heartbeat and, as he stared into the glowing red eyes of his Master, allowed the hands upon his to guide the dagger through flesh and bone.

# CHAPTER TWENTY-FOUR

THE SHOCK at seeing Cisco kneeling at Zeke's feet when Max had burst through the door had caused him to hesitate for a split second, enough time to give Zeke the upper hand. Max found himself slammed against the wall with Zeke's hand reaching for his throat. His shock at seeing Cisco quickly turned into determination, giving him the power to throw off his attacker and regain control of the situation. Zeke was an equally matched adversary, but Cisco's presence and the lifeless look in his boy's eyes spurred Max's rage, giving him an edge. He gave himself over to the animal within him.

Flesh tore, muscles strained, and gnashing teeth pierced skin as he and Zeke rolled around the club. Zeke grabbed a handful of Max's hair, wrapping it in his fist at the same time he snaked his other hand beneath Max's knees and flipped him. Excruciating pain shot through Max's back as he landed on the table, splintering it, the shards embedding deep into his muscles. Max pushed past it, needing revenge, wanting to eradicate the vile creature. He rolled to his feet, pulling a large piece of wood from his back and slamming it into the center of Zeke's chest.

Zeke was propelled backward with the force and crashed into Max's chair. Before Zeke had a chance to recover, Max was on top of him, hands tightening around Zeke's throat. Still, Zeke wasn't about to go down easily and fought with brute force born of desperation to survive in the face of Max's fury. For long, drawn-out moments, they were at a stalemate, powerhouses matched and met. Max tightened his hand around Zeke's neck, fingernails piercing flesh. Max saw Zeke's mouth working, but he had no fucking desire to figure out what he was saying. There was nothing he could say to save his worthless existence.

Something out of the corner of his eye caught Max's attention, and he tensed for an attack and eased his grip on Zeke's neck. It was all Zeke needed, and he snapped at Max, fangs threatening, when a dagger was plunged through his right eye, stopping him cold. A bloodcurdling scream filled the air, loud enough to shatter eardrums. The agony in his Cisco's cry nearly crushed Max, but he knew he had mere seconds before Zeke recovered from his wound, so Max took advantage of the situation and ripped Zeke's throat out.

Fighting raged around Max, but the only thing he could think of was getting to Cisco. Max caught him before he crumpled to the floor and cradled him in his arms. His boy was limp, but his heartbeat was strong. As much as it aggrieved him to do so, he had to leave Cisco and help the others, but where to leave him? Max scanned the area. Silas had snapped out of his catatonic state and was jumping into the fray. Everywhere around them was danger, hordes of Zeke and Liam's followers coming out of the woodwork and flooding the club with nefarious intent.

Patrick! He could trust Patrick. Max pulled Cisco tighter into his chest and, dodging around the chaos, made it to the kitchen. He scanned the area wildly. "Patrick!" he bellowed. There was no answer, no scent, or any other indication of Patrick's presence. He rushed to his office and barreled through the door. Max spotted Andrew across the room with gun fixed on Max, Patrick standing slightly behind him. Max took a step toward them when he heard the sound of a shotgun being pumped. Seconds later, cold steel was pressed to his temple.

"Fuck, Max, you scared the shit out of me," Benny complained and dropped his weapon as his gaze settled on Cisco. "What happened? Is he okay?"

"Yes, I have no time to explain." Max rushed to the bookcase and disengaged the lock to the hidden chamber beyond. "All of you, get down there, now."

Patrick didn't hesitate. He did as he was told, as did Andrew. Benny was the only one to stand his ground. "What's down there," he demanded.

"Your safety." He shoved Cisco into his arms. "Now go!" Benny grunted with Cisco's weight and stumbled back into the passage. The second he cleared the door, Max sealed the entrance and traced back to the club.

The club was awash with the sounds of the wounded and dying and the scent of blood and carnage was thick in the air. Max ran headlong into the fight, and red eyes met his gaze, but they were not the ones he sought. Suddenly his back met the floor, his legs kicked out from beneath him. Zeke glared down at him, black sludge leaking from the gaping wound on his neck, and snapped his teeth at Max.

Max rolled in time to avoid the razor-sharp teeth and jumped to his feet. Zeke just as quickly was on his, standing before Max. Rather than strike, Zeke then took a step back. "I will feed and… heal. Grow stronger and I will return. Next time it won't be your boy's tight, warm ass I fuck, but his cold, dead carcass."

"Touching him was your first mistake," Max spat and, in a flash of unbound rage, ripped Zeke's heart from his chest and squeezed it in his fist before Zeke's wide eyes. "Threatening to do it again was your last." Max then sent Zeke flying across the room.

Suddenly, like a pack of ravenous dogs, Darius, Silas, Cora, and George jumped on top of Zeke and in a flurry of movement, Zeke was ripped apart.

"Silence!"

Max spun as the booming voice filled the club to find Egnatius standing near the door, arms stretched out wide, and in the next second, there was complete silence. Not a moan, a rustle of clothing, a heartbeat, as if Egnatius had frozen time.

Surprisingly it was Angelo who broke the silence when he stepped out from behind Egnatius with a wide grin, gaze on Max. "I leave for a few days and the whole place goes to shit."

Liam, who had his hand around Bragdon's throat and was being held by Malaki and Constantine, mistakenly took Angelo's joke as an opportunity to speak. "Egnatius, my lord, I was—"

"Silence," Egnatius demanded and pulled his right hand into a fist. Liam fell to his knees, his face contorting in agony.

Even with the destruction beneath his feet, Egnatius strolled gracefully across the room to stand before Liam. He ran his hand over Liam's bowed head and then grasped his hair, forcing his head back.

"You have disappointed me, my son. More importantly, you have disgraced yourself and our kind." Liam's eyes bulged from his head as Egnatius continued to stare at him, Liam's expression one of pure torture, his pale skin going from white to a fiery red a split second before his head exploded.

Egnatius wiped the blood and gore from his hand and the front of his shirt as if he were wiping away dirt, his expression calm, almost carefree in the face of the horrors around him as he surveyed the room.

His gaze then settled on Max. "It would appear that my services are no longer needed here. You seem to have your house under control."

Max swallowed down his snort of laughter. Jesus, there was blood, body parts, and death surrounding them, and Egnatius thought this was under control? Max didn't even know how to respond, but apparently Egnatius wasn't expecting him to. Instead he pulled an envelope from his inside suit pocket and handed it to Max.

"Your death warrants. Carry them out as you see fit." Egnatius then turned abruptly and headed out of the club. "Malaki, Constantine," Egnatius called over his shoulder and the three were gone.

"You couldn't have waited to start the party until after I got here?" Angelo asked. His words were light and teasing, but Max saw the way his brows dipped and the look of displeasure on his face as he took in the club.

Max felt the same way. Such a waste. There was no pleasure in death. His gaze landed on what was left of Zeke and Max amended his thoughts. There wasn't pleasure in Zeke's death, but it was an event to be celebrated.

"Sorry you missed the festivities," Max told him with a slight grin. "But I'm glad you showed up in time for the cleanup."

"Damn, I should have timed my arrival better." Angelo's matching grin then faded. "How is Cisco?"

"He's safe," Max responded curtly. He wasn't ready to tell Angelo what had happened to his boy. He dared not even think about it for fear it would cripple him, and there was much to do before dawn. Knowing Cisco was safe, Max quashed the urge to run to him. He had to attend to those who were loyal to him and dispose of those who were not.

Over the next hour, with the help of Dr. Bragdon and Dr. Heine, the wounded vampires and humans alike were tended to while the remains of vampires who'd fought against them, including Zeke, were taken outside to meet the sun at dawn. Those disloyal who were still standing were rounded up and bound. Max stood before them, searching their faces. He hated that so many of his kind would be destroyed, but they had made their choices to follow Zeke and Liam and now they must follow them to the end. He looked at each of them and realized one from the group was missing. Max searched the crowded room and found George near the bar tending to Cora's back.

As Max approached, George looked up at Max and must have known his secrets were no longer buried because he sounded resolved to his fate as he said, "Can I have a moment to say good-bye?"

"Good-bye?" Cora asked, turning to stare at George in confusion.

George set the salve aside and wiped his hands on his shirt. "It was me who helped Zeke obtain access to the security system."

"You what?" Cora cried out. "Why? Why would you do that?"

There was true pain and regret in George's eyes as he stared at his lover. But, like the others, he had chosen his fate.

"I'll give you five minutes," Max informed him. He then checked his watch—twenty minutes till dawn.

Max went and spoke to Silas and Darius. "How are Patrick, Cisco, and the others?" he asked Silas.

"They are in Cisco's apartment, safe and sleeping," Silas responded.

"Very good. I've given George a couple of minutes to say his good-byes, and then we'll secure him and the others outside before we retire."

Both vampires seemed shocked by Max's statement, but they didn't question him, only nodded in understanding.

"I'm sorry I had to be the one to tell you," Bragdon apologized as he joined them. "He fought valiantly against our adversaries and will die having regained some of his honor."

"Thank you, old friend," Max said sincerely. "For everything."

A few moments later, George appeared, his shoulders back and head held high. "I am ready to face my punishment and hope my death gives you peace. I ask for your forgiveness."

Max held his gaze. "Bragdon has informed me you fought against the intruders. You dishonored me but atoned for the deception with your gallant effort fighting alongside us. It is Cora you must seek forgiveness from."

"I already have," Cora blurted out. "He's told me everything and I forgive him. If he is to die, then I shall follow him."

"Cora, no!" George said in horror.

Cora laid her hand against his cheek. "It is my wish. You saved me time and time again, and if I cannot save you, then I shall follow you. I cannot endure your loss."

Cora, knowing what she did, would still follow George to his death rather than exist without him? The wish wasn't animal driven but something much deeper. Perhaps Max had been wrong. Maybe vampires did possess the ability to love. It was the only thing more powerful than instinct. The driving force behind George's choice hadn't been instinct, nor greed or power but out of a fear of losing that love. With his secrets exposed and Zeke dead, George was no longer a threat. There would still need to be punishment, perhaps exile, but Max would not execute George or Cora for loving each other.

"Cora, take your man home. I will deal with his punishment later."

"Thank you, Max," Cora squealed and threw her arms around Max's neck. She kissed his cheek and whispered, "I promise you won't regret this."

As the sun inched closer to the horizon, death called to Max, but unlike those who would meet the sun, Max would return at nightfall to the man who meant the world to him and the promise of love.

# CHAPTER TWENTY-FIVE

CISCO JERKED awake, blinking rapidly at the red, yellow, and gold colors dancing across the ceiling. It was a welcome sight after the black despair of the nightmare he'd been trapped in.

He ran his hand over his burning eyes and sighed in relief. "Just a bad dream."

"It's alive."

Cisco turned his head to find Benny sitting at the small table, feet propped up on a chair.

"Hey," Cisco said and winced. His throat was raw, making him sound like an old man who'd been a lifelong smoker.

"I was beginning to wonder if you were ever going to wake up."

"What time is it?" Cisco asked and sat up, groaning when his stiff muscles protested.

"Five," Benny informed him and then brought over a bottle of water. "Sounds like you could use this."

"Thanks." Cisco downed half the bottle. His voice sounded much more like his own when he said, "Man, I had the worst nightmare."

"Worse than Zeke kidnapping you and torturing the fuck out of you?"

"How the hell…?" Cisco jerked up his T-shirt and his heart stopped dead in his chest. The angry red scars on his chest and stomach were proof that it hadn't been a dream. He began to shake and his lungs seized up as the horror of what he'd been through came rushing back. It had been real, the torture, the rape, the feeding. So much blood. Oh God, it was all real.

"Cisco!"

Benny shook him, crying out Cisco's name over and over, but he couldn't respond. He couldn't move, couldn't fucking breathe. He'd been weak, had allowed himself to be taken over and broken. Worse, he'd lost hope in Max. He'd lost Max, the one thing in his life that had mattered. The one thing that had completed him.

"Goddamn you, Cisco, breathe!" Benny screamed in his face and then hit Cisco in the chest.

Reflexively Cisco inhaled sharply, and the instant air entered his lungs, hot tears streamed down his face. "I failed him," he sobbed. He brought up his knees and wrapped his arms around them, hugging himself as he rocked.

"Max?"

"I was so fucking weak and I broke. I let him down."

Benny sat on the bed and grabbed Cisco's chin. "You didn't fail him, and you are so fucking brave. I wish I had balls half the size of yours."

"No, I'm not. You don't get it! I'm not strong or brave. I couldn't handle the pain, the torment, and I—"

"Stop it right now!" Benny's hand tightened on Cisco's face. "From what I've been told, what you did this morning is nearly impossible."

Cisco's despair was so profound he couldn't see or think past the pain of knowing he'd lost Max. "I…. It doesn't matter what I did. Nothing matters without Max."

"The hell it doesn't matter," Benny countered. "You went against a command given to you by a vampire you were bonded to by blood, and not only did you go against him, but you very well may have saved Max's life."

Benny's comment caused Cisco to jerk back in surprise. "I saved Max?"

"Well, technically you didn't save his life since he's a bloodsucking walking dead dude," Benny said with a slight grin. "But yeah, you did."

Cisco searched his memories of the nightmare, but all he remembered was pain, hopelessness, and then blessed numbing blackness when he'd finally given up himself and Max. "I don't remember—" His words cut off on a sob.

"That's probably a good thing," Benny said softly. He ran his hand along Cisco's cheek and around to the back of his head, then pulled him into a hug.

Cisco welcomed his friend's gentle touch and strong embrace. He held Benny and let the tears fall. With each one, he purged himself of all the pain, heartbreak, and loss. He cried for what he'd endured, but mainly he cried for the dream Zeke had robbed him of. How long Cisco cried, he wasn't sure, but through it all Benny held him silently, giving Cisco his strength until the last tear fell and he could finally find his own and lift his head.

"I don't know what I'm supposed to do now," he admitted.

"Anything you want." Benny reached over to the bedside table and grabbed a tissue. "You might want to wipe the snot from your nose first."

Cisco accepted the tissue and gave Benny a small, sad smile before wiping the tracks of his tears and then his nose. "That's not what I meant and you know it."

"I know, but it was a good suggestion. Can I give you another?"

"When have you ever asked for permission before giving me your opinion?"

"Well, you look a little fragile so I'm trying to be nice." Benny chuckled and ruffled Cisco's hair. "But seriously, a hot shower would do you a world of good. You really want Max to see you with bedhead?"

Cisco's breath hitched. "Max?"

"Yeah, it's almost nightfall, and if I know him—and I'm beginning to think I understand what you mean to him—he'll be here within seconds of his eyes opening."

"Max is coming here?" he asked more to himself. Jesus, the last thing he'd remembered was losing Max, but was it possible he'd been wrong?

"Yup, so about that shower?" Benny looked down at his watch. "I'm guessing you have about thirty minutes at the most to get your scrawny butt presentable."

Cisco cocked his head, staring at Benny as he slid off the bed and held his hand out for Cisco. "He's really okay? He's coming?"

"Yes, now up you go."

Stunned, Cisco allowed Benny to lead him to the bathroom and get the taps started. *Max is coming?* Cisco had a hard time grasping it. It seemed impossible, and considering he could no longer feel Max's pull, it made it all the more difficult to accept. Long after Benny left the room, Cisco stood beneath the hot spray, but he didn't feel its warmth nor did it help ease the heaviness in his chest or the tension in his muscles. He wasn't only shocked but scared. If Max was alive and he was coming for him, would he ever feel Max's presence as he once had? At the moment he felt like a boat drifting in the middle of the ocean without an anchor, both his heart and soul the only occupants of the lost craft.

TRUE PEACE, something Max hadn't experienced in a long time, was the first thing he was aware of when the grave released its hold. Of course it was followed by a magnitude of unpleasant feelings a second later, the worst of which was shame and guilt. He would never forgive himself for what he'd allowed to happen to Cisco, but rather than let it cripple him, he vowed it would propel him to work twice as hard to keep his boy happy and safe. Cisco deserved nothing less than Max's best.

On every other night since Cisco had entered his world, his first thought was to rush to him, but whereas before he'd had to struggle against his instinct, tonight he found it easier to shower, to dress, and to prepare himself for his meeting with Cisco. Perhaps easy wasn't quite the right word because the unease sure as fuck wasn't easy to deal with. What if the bond that Zeke had severed between him and Cisco was gone forever? No matter what Egnatius had told him, there was still a chance, even a remote one, and it was enough to cause Max to hesitate. If their bond was truly and irrevocably severed, Max would no longer wish to exist. Dressed in black slacks and white silk dress shirt, Max stepped from his chamber.

"Good evening, Max," Angelo and Silas said at the same time. Angelo's smile was broad, no doubt as at peace with Zeke's and Liam's death as he was. Silas, on the other hand, looked anxious.

"Good evening. You okay, Silas?"

"Yes, sir, but if it's all right with you, I'd like to check on Patrick."

"Yes, of course, and be sure to thank him for calling and for leaving the service door open for me. In fact, never mind, you just go enjoy your boy and I'll thank him myself later."

"Yes, sir, thank you," Silas responded and was gone.

"Did I ever mention I hope I never become bonded," Angelo said, shaking his head at Silas's hasty departure.

"Once or twice," Max confirmed. Unfortunately he hadn't hoped for the same thing and it had nearly destroyed Cisco.

"Hey, I know that look, and don't even go there. You being bonded to Cisco is a great thing."

"That remains to be seen." Then a new thought occurred to Max. "If Cisco and I are still bonded, I think it might be a good idea to take him away for a while and give him a chance to heal."

Angelo slung his arm over Max's shoulder. "You are—trust me in this—and I think it's a great idea. Take all the time you guys need. I'll hold down the fort."

"Thanks," Max replied sincerely.

"No problem, just make sure you come back. No way in hell am I taking over your job indefinitely. Understood?"

"I don't know. After what you were able to accomplish with Egnatius—"

"Not going to happen," Angelo said adamantly and then gave Max a shove. "Now go see your boy."

"I think you're a natural. You're already bossing me around." Max chuckled and then traced to Cisco's room before Angelo could protest further. Regardless of what Angelo said, Max knew he'd take over power if something were to happen to Max or even if he chose to step down. Angelo wouldn't necessarily be happy with it, but he would never trust the accomplishments they'd made to anyone else.

Once again, Max hesitated outside Cisco's door, bracing himself for what lay beyond. He'd never been a coward and he wasn't about to start being one now, but he simply had to give himself a moment to lock down his desires. He would never stop trying to find a way to restore their bond if in fact it was severed completely. He'd never give up on Cisco, but it would do his boy no good to be pushed, especially not over what he'd so bravely lived through. No, once again it was Cisco who must come to him and only when he was ready. His need to see Cisco finally pushed Max to open the door and step inside.

Cisco was sitting on the couch next to Benny when Max walked in. Cisco's hair was still damp and his skin flushed from a recent shower. His dark eyes went wide when he spotted Max.

Max closed the door behind him and leaned against it a little, needing the support for his weak legs from the unease and apprehension he caught a whiff of. "Benny, could you give Cisco and me a moment, please?"

"Yeah, sure." Benny pecked Cisco on the cheek. "I'll check in on you later."

Cisco nodded without taking his gaze from Max's.

"Take it easy on him," Benny said as he stopped briefly next to Max. "He's scared."

"I shall," Max vowed without looking away from Cisco. He stepped aside and allowed Benny to let himself out.

The minutes stretched out as they continued to stare at each other, neither making the first move. Max could feel Cisco's apprehension and his gut roiled. He knew one thing with 100 percent certainty: the bond he had with Cisco was even more powerful now. Only he couldn't speak nor could he force his legs to work, even though everything inside him screamed to rush and claim what was rightfully his. He couldn't. Not with Cisco looking so scared and unsure of himself.

A few more painful ticks of the clock and the tension in the room grew to a suffocating level. Then, although Max was by far the stronger of the two physically, it was Cisco, his brave, beautiful boy, who made the first tentative step toward Max.

Cisco came to him and Max laid his hand over his chest with the first hint of a heartbeat. The ghostly thumping got stronger, filled Max's ears when his Cisco lowered his eyes respectfully, fell to his knees, and pressed his face against Max's thigh.

"I know I am not worthy, but please give me a chance to prove I can be your boy again. Please."

"You don't have to ask. You are and always will be my boy, and I will never have another but you."

"Really?" Cisco looked up at Max in surprise.

Although the beating in his chest wasn't real, it couldn't be, it still felt as if his heart would fly out of his chest it swelled so quickly. Max went to his knees in front of Cisco and ran his knuckles gently along Cisco's warm cheek.

"But of course, you are my Francisco, the one I have been waiting for. My Iunctiō Cōpula, the one who will teach me to love again." He then pressed his lips against Cisco's, and as he wrapped his arms around his boy, he knew no one or nothing would ever come between them again. Their bond could not be broken.

# EPILOGUE

THE BLACKNESS stretched out beyond the small window of the private jet that would take him and Max to Egypt, where their quest for Iunctiō Cōpula would begin, and the next chapter of their lives. Cisco was filled with both excitement and trepidation. The past few months had been wrought with danger and pain. It was the moments of happiness, of wholeness while he'd been with Max, that he hoped would be enough to keep the nightmares of Zeke at bay.

Perhaps one day.

So far, he could keep from being haunted by what Zeke had forced upon him while he was with Max. When Max was touching him, when he could see and focus on his Master, nothing else existed. No past, no future, just peace. It was the times when he was lying in his bed alone that the nightmares taunted him. Each day, he was forced to relive the horrors of his time in Zeke's dungeon.

Max had been so anguished when he'd seen the wounds on Cisco's body, he hadn't wanted to cause Max further distress by revealing the scars that couldn't be seen. He didn't want Max to ever learn everything that he'd suffered in Zeke's deep, dark dungeon, but in order for that wish to come true, he would have to deny Max what he wanted most. Life.

This was where the trepidation arose from.

Once they completed the blood bond, Max would be able to read his thoughts and he'd no longer be able to hide the horrors from him. Worse, Max would know he lied to him. He could only hope that in time, Max would forgive him because there was no way he was going to do anything to interfere with Max reaching his dream. A dream that now belonged to Cisco as well. The idea of living peacefully, no wars, no vampire versus human, just he and Max loving and growing old together, was now his dream as well.

"You're awful quiet," Max whispered against Cisco's ear.

Cisco pushed his morose thoughts aside, bringing the images of him and Max growing old together to the forefront and, with them, was able to give Max a genuine smile when he turned to meet his gaze.

"I've never been out of the United States before. I haven't even been out of the state of California before tonight. I can't believe I'm on my way to Egypt."

"It is an amazing country, rich in history."

"Do you think we'll be able to visit Alexandria while we're there? Did you know it was founded by Alexander the Great, and was once considered the crossroads of the world?"

Max entwined their fingers. "You do realize that this trip is not for pleasure."

"Yes, Sir. I realize that, but… I just thought."

Max's smile was gentle as he brought their hands to his mouth and pressed his lips against the back of Cisco's. "I will make sure we find enough time." Max then leaned in and pressed his lips to Cisco's. "There isn't anything I wouldn't do for you."

Cisco kissed him back, melting into Max's touch. "Nor is there anything I wouldn't do for you."

Max sat back and laughed. "That's because you know I'd spank that ass if you didn't."

Cisco tilted his head and gave him an incredulous look. "Now you know that's not true."

Max turned his head, averting his eyes. Zeke had not only taken Cisco's blood, tortured him, and made him relive the horrors through his nightmares, but he'd also stolen something precious between him and Max. Max was no longer able to bring himself to dominate Cisco as he once had, fear of damaging him further making it impossible.

Cisco turned his head and stared back out at the blackness. There was no use arguing about it. No matter what he said, no matter how hard he tried to hide it, Max knew by the way he would tense that he couldn't settle into the right headspace, couldn't let go of the fear.

Max squeezed his hand.

Perhaps one day.

SJD PETERSON, better known as Jo, hails from Michigan. Not the best place to live for someone who hates the cold and snow. When not reading or writing, Jo can be found close to the heater checking out NHL stats and watching the Red Wings kick a little butt. Can't cook, misses the clothes hamper nine out of ten tries, but is handy with power tools.

Facebook: www.facebook.com/SJD.Peterson

Blog: sjdpeterson.blogspot.com

Twitter: @SJDPeterson

Goodreads: www.goodreads.com/author/show/4563849.S_J_D_ Peterson

E-mail: sjdpeterson@gmail.com

With his fauxhawk, sleeve tattoos, and visible piercings, Ridley Corbin has the whole badass vibe going on in spades. The image serves him well as the self-proclaimed protector of the underdog, and he wants nothing more than to be Alex Firestone's hero.

Alex, a mild-mannered library assistant, has moved to Slater, a quiet college town, hoping to hide from his past. He keeps to himself, but that doesn't save him from catching the unwanted attention of the campus bully. But not all is as it seems. Alex's past comes calling, and it's time he becomes top dog.

# www.dreamspinnerpress.com

BEYOND DUTY

SJD Peterson

The repeal of Don't Ask, Don't Tell didn't come soon enough for Gunther "Gunny" Duchene and Macalister "Mac" Jones, career US Marines who met at boot camp in the 1990s. They've been somewhere between best friends and lovers in peacetime and wartime both, but as the clock ticks toward Mac's and Gunny's retirements, the guys have much more to worry about than coming out.

Whether their relationship will survive outside of the closet they've had to shove it into for over two decades is a big question mark. Gunny questions why a hot military man like Mac—who could get any guy he wanted, including a younger, sexier one—would want him. But as Gunny and Mac navigate emotional waters as choppy as any they saw on duty, they just might learn *Semper Fi* applies to more than their careers.

# www.dreamspinnerpress.com

Beyond Duty: Book Two
A Guards of Folsom Story

Gunther Duchene, aka "Gunny", and Macalister Jones, aka "Mac", have overcome the obstacles of coming out and retiring after serving more than twenty years as Marines. Their exit ceremony is behind them, their wedding vows are made, and now it's time for the honeymoon. What better way to kick off their marriage than enjoying the retirement gift Mac gave Gunny? With the leather pants and collar packed, it's off to New York City and the Guards of Folsom club to celebrate—BDSM style.

# www.dreamspinnerpress.com

Carrick Masters and Edward Boyd have already found true love—it's the happy ever after that's eluding them. Between Carrick's job as an orthopedic surgeon and Ed's career as a defense attorney, they have hardly any time to spend together, and what time they *do* have seems to be poisoned by resentment. Carrick and Ed know they need to refocus to make their marriage work, but they seriously need more than a spicy once-a-week date night to get them back on track.

# www.dreamspinnerpress.com

Danny Marshal has always lived his life out loud, but his androgynous appearance is only a small part of who he is. One night at a frat party, Danny meets Lance Lenard, football jock and apparent straight guy. Lance is shocked when he's immediately attracted to Danny's feminine side. Danny is happy to be the subject of Lance's first man-on-man experiment—until Lance begins to struggle with the fact that despite his appearance, Danny is indeed a man.

Lance's whole life has been focused on his goal of playing in the NFL, and he knows those dreams will be smashed if anyone finds out about his little secret. Although Lance has grown to crave Danny's touch, he's not willing to give Danny what *he's* grown to crave: a boyfriend who's proud to love him for every flamboyant and snarky cell in his body.

Life sends Danny and Lance in different directions, each of them focused on his respective Plan A. But the best-laid plans of mice and men often go awry.

# Rival Within
## SJD PETERSON

Officer Thomas Webber made a vow of marriage to his wife, a vow to his God to resist temptation, and a vow to uphold the law. But when Tom is forced to shelter a dark-haired stranger from the tornado raging over the county, long suppressed desires are brought to the surface and he is powerless to resist.

Ben Parker has hidden his true nature his whole life. The laws in 1952 are very clear, and to expose himself would mean rotting in jail, shunned or worse, a possible death sentence. Unable to find a job, he turned to crime. Seven years later, he's still angry and tired of hiding who he really is from the world. After meeting Thomas, Ben can envision himself settling down for the first time. The only problem is, he's already forced Thomas to break the law and become his alibi. And then there's the little obstacle of Tom's wife, family, and commitment to the town of Ramer.

Ben knows what he wants, but in order to get it, Tom will have to turn his back on society and the vows he's made if they are to find the happiness they deserve.

www.dreamspinnerpress.com

*There is underlying beauty in destruction....*

Miah Thade, Finn Reese, and Ritchie Meyer are Resonator, an indie rock band with an edge—best friends turned rock stars, known as the Detroit 3. When Evin Rene appears in their life, none of them can deny he belongs with Rez.

They may have named their first album Ruin Porn because people get off on seeing how Detroit went from deeply loved to thoroughly forsaken, but they're determined to prove that blight isn't the entire story and blight isn't always ugly.

Ritchie, Miah, Finn, and Evin take Resonator to a level no one anticipates. But no prosperity comes without sacrifice, and no secret stays hidden without a trail of lies. As Rez's fame grows, so does the intensity between two of its members… as well as their potential for destruction.

Evin and Finn are about to discover the underlying beauty in their ruin porn.

# www.dreamspinnerpress.com

I am the conductor, leading the sweet symphony of pain and agony.

SPLINTERED

SJD PETERSON

A string of murders targeting effeminate gay men has the GLBTQ community of Chicago on alert, but budget cuts have left many precincts understaffed and overworked. Not to mention, homophobia is alive and well within the law enforcement community and little has been done to solve the mystery. When the FBI calls in Special Agent Todd Hutchinson and his team, the locals are glad to hand the case off. But Hutch finds a bigger mystery than anyone originally realized—seventeen linked murders committed in several different jurisdictions. Hutch's clues lead him to Noah Walker.

Working on his PhD in forensic psychology, Noah has been obsessed with serial murders since he was a child. But coming to Hutch's attention as a suspect isn't a good way to start a relationship. Noah finds himself hunted, striking him off Hutch's suspect list, but not off his radar. To catch the killer before anyone else falls victim, they'll have to work together, and quickly, to bring him to justice.

# www.dreamspinnerpress.com

*Battle Buddy :* At nineteen, Shane Tucker joins the army. Tucker is gay but not ready to be open about it, and Don't Ask, Don't Tell seems like a convenient way to avoid dealing with his sexuality.

The army suits Tucker; he does well from the beginning. Then, during boot camp, he's assigned a "battle buddy," Owen Bradford. Owen is a walking, talking wet dream with no concept of personal space. Tucker only survives the constant temptation by venting to his diary.

Two years later, Tucker—now in the Army Ranger program—is paired up with Owen once again. Getting through training while ignoring the sexual tension between him and his battle buddy might be the biggest test of Tucker's military career.

*Tuck & Cover:* You may have read Tuck's diary entries, but they don't tell the whole story. Tuck will argue the point, but he definitely got a few details wrong—not that I blame him. He was, if you remember, a little sexually frustrated at the time. He probably wasn't thinking straight. I'll never get tired of teasing him about that. Anyway, here's what really happened.

Rangers lead the way! – Owen

# www.dreamspinnerpress.com

# Read more from this author!

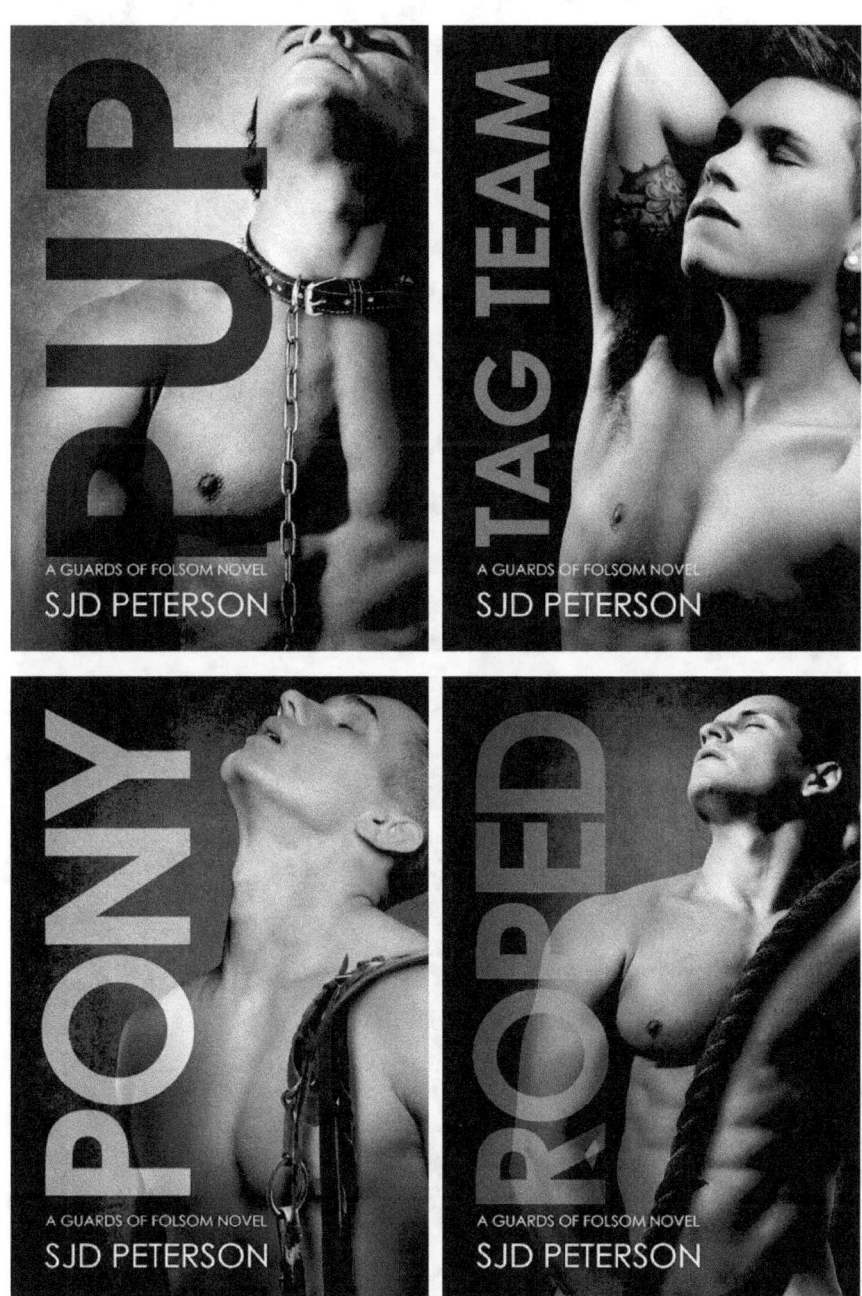

# Read more from this author!

www.dreamspinnerpress.com

A WHISPERING PINES RANCH NOVEL
BOOK IV

CONNER'S
COURAGE

SJD PETERSON

Sequel to *Ty's Obsession*
Whispering Pines Ranch: Book IV

John Price and Conner Burnett have been part of the Whispering Pines Ranch for the past thirty-seven years. A loving couple who have overcome every obstacle thrown at them, John and Conner are a testament to the strength of true love. But now John is in the hospital with a diagnosis of cancer, fighting for his very life.

As his lover struggles, Conner looks back on when they first met. The early seventies wasn't an easy time to be a gay man, especially in a small country town. Considering John's pride, Conner's need to be himself, shame, bitterness, and two stubborn natures, their love story almost wasn't written. But they beat the odds, and Conner will be damned if he'll let anyone take John from him now. He had the courage to stand up for what he wanted in 1974. If need be, he'll go toe to toe with God himself to keep the man he fought so hard to love.

www.dreamspinnerpress.com

A WHISPERING PINES RANCH NOVEL
BOOK V

JESS'S
JOURNEY

SJD PETERSON

Sequel to *Conner's Courage*
Whispering Pines Ranch: Book V

At an early age, Jess Jenkins learned to take care of his family and friends and put their needs before his own. He dreamed of finding the same simple happiness his parents had and followed their example. Then Lorcan James broke his heart and an automobile accident broke his independent spirit. Now that's all Jess is: a broken shadow of the man he used to be, still confined to a wheelchair after six months.

Jess is finally forced to put himself first and accept the help he needs on his journey toward recovery. Though pain, frustration, and depression leave him bitter and eager to push people away, his friends refuse to allow him to wallow in self-pity. Jack has only glimpsed the man beneath Jess's angry shell, but he takes it upon himself to prove Jess isn't broken. And Collin is determined to bring back the sweet man he once knew. The simple, happy life Jess has always wanted is there for the taking—all he has to do is open his eyes and see it.

www.dreamspinnerpress.com

A Whispering Pines Ranch story
A Guards of Folsom story

When Ty left Pegasus for New York, he knew he was falling for Blake but wasn't sure he could trust him. Blake didn't know whether he could be vulnerable enough to take on another boy. Since the move to the Big Apple, Blake and Ty have learned how to live with each other. Now they need to let go of their pasts and take the next steps outside the playroom.

# www.dreamspinnerpress.com

www.ingramcontent.com/pod-product-compliance
Lightning Source LLC
Chambersburg PA
CBHW070114260626
47160CB00004B/1462

# Readers love JOHN INMAN

*Spirit*

"A good storyteller draws the reader in, hooks them and pulls them along till the end. John Inman is a good—no, check that–a great storyteller. His novel, *Spirit*, is compelling and intricate, alternately funny and sad, and wonderfully peopled with realistic characters who wrap themselves around your heart."

—The Novel Approach

"I recommend this book to anyone who enjoys the supernatural, mystery, suspense, intrigue, hot gay men engaging in even hotter sex, cheeky little boys, and good triumphing over evil. Thank you so much, John. I was thoroughly entertained."

—Rainbow Book Reviews

"… This is yet another outstanding book by John Inman. It is hilarious throughout, but yet it does have many serious moments as well…. If you're already a John Inman fan, you'll love this book. If you've never read his work before, I can't recommend it enough."

— On Top Down Under Reviews

"*Spirit* is your typical Inman creation: brilliantly written, fun to read, and impossible to put down."

—Spectrum Books

By JOHN INMAN

A Hard Winter Rain
Head-on
Hobbled
Jasper's Mountain
Loving Hector
Paulie
The Poodle Apocalypse
Serenading Stanley
Shy
Snow on the Roof (Dreamspinner Anthology)
Spirit

Published by DREAMSPINNER PRESS
http://www.dreamspinnerpress.com

# HEAD-ON

## JOHN INMAN

*Dreamspinner Press*

Published by
DREAMSPINNER PRESS

5032 Capital Circle SW, Suite 2, PMB# 279, Tallahassee, FL 32305-7886 USA
http://www.dreamspinnerpress.com/

Head-on
© 2014 John Inman.

Cover Art
© 2014 Reese Dante.
http://www.reesedante.com
Cover content is for illustrative purposes only and any person depicted on the cover is a model.

ISBN: 978-1-63216-005-8
Digital ISBN: 978-1-63216-006-5
Library of Congress Control Number: 2014939166
First Edition July 2014

Printed in the United States of America
ⓧ
This paper meets the requirements of
ANSI/NISO Z39.48-1992 (Permanence of Paper).

*Shattered spirit*
*Shattered heart*
*A shattered life torn apart.*

*From SHATTERED*
—Agnes Snyder-Cousino

# PROLOGUE

"SAN DIEGO'S Most Accurate Weatherman," or so he had been dubbed by the *Union Tribune* in the previous week's Sunday op-ed page, was a little under the weather at the moment. Actually, he was shit-faced.

He tooled down Broadway in his brand-new Beamer, which still smelled deliciously of freshly minted Dakota leather. Not only did the car smell great, but it drove like a dream—even with one finger, which was pretty much how it was being driven at the moment.

He was just coming from a formal dinner with his boss, the head of Channel 10 News, and representatives from the Pacific Southwest Chapter of the National Television Academy, where he had been tipped to the fact he just might be seeing a local Emmy nomination coming his way in a few weeks.

The formal dinner might have been a bit light on sustenance, but it was certainly awash in liquor. Damn, those Academy boys could drink. But what better reason to celebrate, right? As he drove, a tad excited by the possibility of snagging his very own Emmy, "San Diego's Most Accurate Weatherman" was now chattering on his cell phone with everyone he knew. Between conversations, he was texting everyone *else* he knew, because he was too damned excited to let them wait and hear about his good fortune on their own slow-ass timetable.

He had been in the game for less than two years, and this already! If he played his cards right, he might be on his way to snagging a prize even greater than a measly local Emmy nomination. He might find himself a slot as top meteorologist on a *national* affiliate. And wouldn't *that* be a coup! Standing in a New York City studio in a two-thousand-dollar suit, giving a heads-up to the whole damn country about what to expect on the weather front, and doing it behind Brian Williams or Diane Sawyer. And even better than that, doing it at a salary that made his current pay look like peanuts.

Steering with one elbow now, he squirmed around and shrugged out of his tuxedo jacket, simultaneously unknotting the bow tie at his throat and tossing it in the back seat. Once he had accomplished that Herculean feat without mowing down any pedestrians, he went back to texting. This time he sent a happy little missive to his mother, who would be thrilled to death at his good fortune. Anything that even remotely reeked of snootiness appealed to her. And since he didn't really feel like *talking* to the woman at the moment, a text message would have to do.

Fog had been rolling in off the bay for about an hour now, and the tops of the surrounding San Diego skyscrapers were lost in haze from about six floors up.

If he hadn't been so drunk, and if he hadn't been so preoccupied with his cell phone, typey-typing the braggy-ass text message to his mother, who probably wouldn't read it until tomorrow anyway, he might have noticed the car pulling out of the parking structure up ahead.

He might also have noticed he had veered over the centerline.

By the time he did notice these things, it was too late.

Only when the approaching vehicle was less than ten feet away from his shiny new Beamer's front bumper did "San Diego's Most Accurate Weatherman" see the danger. And only then did he spot the two horrified faces in the windshield, illuminated by his own searing headlights stabbing through the fog. Two men. One light haired, one dark. Their mouths agape in silent horror.

But the silence didn't last. Just as he hit the brakes with every ounce of power he could muster, hurling himself into the steering wheel and knocking the wind from his lungs, jarring him down to his spit-shined Pradas—don't think it didn't—a scream pierced the night.

Whether from himself or from one of the two men in the other car, he couldn't distinguish.

The night exploded around him with the ear-splitting sound of metal tearing into metal. His windshield erupted into a supernova of sparkling shards, prisming through the air in slow motion. His cell phone, torn from his grasp by the force of the collision, spun free amid the splinters. And as our weatherman watched that midair ballet of ruin with wonder and awe, and no small amount of horror, the Beamer cartwheeled around him, landing on its roof with a solid *whump*.

It was then, at the precise moment all the remaining windows exploded out around him, that he knew his world had ended.

As light and sound and consciousness abandoned him, he heard again a piercing scream of terror coming from somewhere in the wreckage. Somewhere *close*.

After an unguessable stretch of time—minutes, seconds, hours— he shook himself awake long enough to break free of the seat belt and crawl from the car on his hands and knees. Cold asphalt and slivers of window glass tore at his palms. The reek of hot metal and gasoline filled his nostrils. He staggered to his feet, still reeling from the booze he'd drunk at dinner. The first thing he saw was the young driver of the other vehicle, already lifeless, draped over a bent car door, eyes wide and startled as if amazed by his own demise.

And at that moment, another scream tore through the night from the totaled car in front of him.

This scream seemed to echo forever along the foggy street, ricocheting off the buildings, stunning the very city with its anguish.

Our weatherman swayed on his feet. And just before the darkness took him again, he realized—*he knew*—he would hear the echoes of that scream for the rest of his life.

# CHAPTER 1

GORDON STAFFORD awoke to yet another morning.

Blinking back the California sunshine streaming through his bedroom window, he waited, as he always did, for the sadness to come sweeping through him. He held his breath in anticipation as he waited for that sense of sorrow, that rolling wave of weary defeat, that heart-numbing infusion of *regret* to come thundering in. Every morning when he opened his eyes, *every single morning,* that familiar avalanche of misery buried him alive. This morning would be no different.

Before he could lift his hand to rub the sleep from his eyes, there they were. The horrors. The shame. Piling on, one atop the other. Misery after misery. Digging into him. Eating away at whatever happiness he suspected still might lie hidden, fallow, barely surviving somewhere deep inside the man he once was.

Every morning he fought the same battle. Every morning he tried to reach in and find the happiness before sadness swept it away—simply touch it for one brief moment to prove to himself it was still there.

But every morning, he lost the battle. With each sunrise the sorrow, the defeat, the soul-killing regret, *poured* into Gordon's heart, sometimes before the dreams the night brought had even left his head. Once again, any potential for joy that might still lie hidden inside him was buried, suffocated beneath the appalling crush of memory.

Buried in the guilt of his past. His fucking past.

Gordon heaved a sigh, blinked back the morning light again, and propped himself up on one elbow. Triggered by movement, the jagged stabs of a hangover ripped into his skull. Oh God. How many beers had he drunk last night? He tried to think back, but it was hopeless. He couldn't even remember coming home.

Another blackout. Great. He wondered if it was time for AA yet.

He flung the sheet aside and looked down at himself, naked on the bed. His cock was hard. It always was after a night of drinking. The hangover hots, he called them. He reached down and laid his hand over his dick. Then he reached down a little farther and rearranged his balls, not because they needed rearranging, but because it felt good. With his other hand, he stroked the meager scattering of hair across his chest. Just because that felt good too.

When a third hand came out of nowhere and slid across his stomach, Gordon damn near flew off the bed.

Only then did he realize he was not alone.

Heart thumping like crazy, he gazed down at the man beside him, who was even now rolling over, waking up, his face level with Gordon's hipbone. The man planted a gentle kiss on Gordon's hip, then scooted closer. Gordon felt the man's fuzzy leg drape over his. The guy's dick, just as hard as Gordon's, pressed against Gordon's shinbone.

Gordon dropped his head onto his pillow and closed his eyes, torn between the bliss of the man's lips on his fevered skin and the daggers of his hangover still stabbing him in the head, trying to draw blood.

When the man skimmed his warm tongue along the shaft of Gordon's stiff cock, then slid his hungry mouth over the head of it, taking it in, taking it all in, Gordon pretty much forgot about his hangover and gave himself up to his bedmate's considerable talents.

The guy was good. He sucked dick like he meant it. Gordon's ass kept coming off the bed to meet the man's mouth strokes. He opened his eyes and peeked toward his crotch to see if the guy looked familiar. He didn't. He was a redhead. Gordon didn't really know that many redheads. But apparently this redhead knew him. Considering the way he was going to town on Gordon's dick as if he'd been there before and was really digging the hell out of a second tour, he seemed to know

Gordon very well indeed. At least the lower half of Gordon, from his belly button down.

The trick was good-looking enough, Gordon supposed. He wondered if he should pull his dick out of the guy's mouth long enough to introduce himself. Seemed the polite thing to do. But Jesus, that hot mouth felt so good slobbering all over his cock. Almost as good as that agile tongue fervently probing his glans. And now that the man's free hand had taken over the job of gently rearranging Gordon's balls so Gordon didn't have to do it himself, Gordon lost all inclination to interrupt the process.

Jesus God, the guy was good.

The man freed Gordon's balls and burrowed his hand toward the foot of the bed so he could wrap it around his own cock. Gordon could feel him stroking himself, rubbing the hair on Gordon's shin while humping his own fist and Gordon's leg in tandem.

Gordon used to have a terrier who humped his leg just like that. What *was* that dog's name? Oh yeah. Spike.

Gordon forgot about Spike when the guy whose face was in his crotch suddenly sucked his cock all the way down his throat, making Gordon arch his back and lift his ass about two feet off the bed.

Two seconds later, Gordon gasped, trembled from head to foot, bit down on his own forearm, and shot a shitload of come into the guy's mouth. One thundering jet of heavy cream after another. Come after come after come.

Boy, those hangover hots ejaculations were the *best!*

When Gordon was spent and his ass had collapsed back onto the bed, the redhead freed Gordon's dick from his mouth, happily licking his lips as he did it. He knee-walked up the bed and sat his warm ass on Gordon's chest. Stroking his cock all the while, the man stared down at Gordon with a really sexy smile on his face. There was a big glob of Gordon's come on the guy's chin.

Gordon reached up with a fingertip and pushed the glob of come into the guy's mouth, sort of like Amy Vanderbilt snagging an errant drop of custard. Waste not, want not.

The guy smiled his thanks and continued to stroke his cock, inching a little *farther* up the bed until his nuts were perched on Gordon's chin.

Because he felt he should do *something* to reciprocate for the excellent blowjob, Gordon pushed his lips into the guy's balls and nibbled on them half-heartedly while the guy whacked off.

Apparently, the ball nibbling was a good idea. The guy's thighs suddenly caught Gordon's head in a leg lock, and with a cry of exaltation, the redhead poured come out in a thick, fat stream that soared straight over Gordon's nose and hit the wall behind him with an audible *splat*. The guy came with such force, Gordon half expected to see an organ or two come shooting out with it. Maybe a spleen. Or a kidney.

The total stranger loomed over him and bonked Gordon in the face a couple of times with his still-hard dick just to shake loose the last few drops of come that hadn't soared off into the stratosphere. Gordon graciously let the man rub his plump, dribbling glans back and forth over Gordon's lips, all the while still milking it dry, apparently for Gordon's benefit.

Now that the excitement was over, Gordon's hangover did a reprise. He felt like he had a herd of deranged woodpeckers pecking away inside his brainpan trying to dig out termites.

"You finished?" Gordon asked the redhead, who was still rubbing his dick all over Gordon's face.

The man smiled down at him and seemed a bit surprised when Gordon didn't smile back.

"Something wrong?" the redhead asked, his voice still husky with passion.

"Yes," Gordon said, turning his head away from the still-dripping cock being slathered across his face. "I have to go to work. You have to leave."

The redhead's eyes narrowed. His dick stopped slathering. The huskiness in his voice vanished in a heartbeat. "Well, aren't you the born romantic."

Gordon met that comment with stoic silence.

The guy emitted a rather petulant "Harrumph!" and climbed off Gordon's chest to stand at the side of the bed, looking down. "Mind if I pee before I go?" he asked, obviously not too happy with the way things were turning out.

"Sure," Gordon said. "But make it fast."

If the redhead's eyes narrowed any further, he'd be blind as a bat. "Oh, I will, Fuckface. You can count on it. I might even try to hit the toilet while I'm at it."

And with that he spun on his heels, huffy as hell. Gathering up his clothes from various parts of Gordon's bedroom, the redhead stomped off down the hall.

Gordon just had time to notice the guy had freckled shoulders and a pretty nice ass before he disappeared into the bathroom and slammed the door behind him.

Gordon counted to ten, slowly. Then he kept going. When he hit twenty-three, he heard the door open and footsteps go thumping down the hall in the opposite direction. A moment later his front door slammed shut. Loudly.

Gordon heaved a sigh of relief. He was alone.

He groaned his way to the edge of the bed, took a moment to cradle his aching head in his hands, then teetered up onto unsteady feet to patter naked to the bathroom himself.

Before he got there, the memories engulfed him. A flash of headlights, a glimpse of surprised faces in a windshield. Two men—one blond, one darker haired. As always he remembered a scream but still didn't know if the scream came from him, from the men careening toward him, or from his fevered imagination.

He stood in the hallway, blinded and paralyzed by the slideshow of shadow and light strobing in his head. A chill shimmered through him. His heart grew instantly heavy as that old familiar sadness came rolling in.

He wondered what time the bar opened.

GORDON SCRUBBED himself down in the shower, twice, then brushed his teeth for about twenty minutes since he had no idea what his mouth might have been doing with the redhead the night before. God, he was a slut when he drank.

He flossed, gargled, reflossed, then began brushing his teeth all over again. OCD? *Oh, no,* he thought, *not me.*

While he brushed his tongue and gagged like he was going to heave up his socks, he studied his reflection in the bathroom mirror, which, by the way, could use a good cleaning. Then he remembered the morning's antics and decided his bedroom wall could use a spermicidal scrubdown as well.

Frankly, staring at his reflection, he was a bit surprised he had managed to snag a trick last night at all. He wasn't looking too good, what with the dark circles under his eyes. He was also in need of a haircut and had a cut on his chin from the *last* time he'd shaved with unsteady hands, which was yesterday. Even now, standing in his bathroom alone, he was wearing that same hangdog expression that never seemed to leave his face these days. God, he was pathetic. Gordon's life was spiraling downward at an alarming clip, and he knew it. Unfortunately, simply knowing you have a problem doesn't do much to correct that problem, now, does it?

He spit in the sink, gagging again. And while he was spitting and gagging, he continued to stare at himself in the dirty mirror, trying to blink the red out of his eyes. It didn't work. They stayed red. He had Visine somewhere but didn't feel like searching for it.

He pulled open the left-hand drawer beside the sink and stared at the loaded revolver that had been lying there for three months now, half-ass hidden beneath a stack of washcloths. Gordon stared at the gun for about twenty seconds, then he sucked in a long, shuddering breath and slammed the drawer closed. *Not today,* he thought.

Just as he did every morning.

Gordon Stafford turned his red eyes back to the mirror. He considered shaving the stubble from his face but thought the danger of slicing his throat if he put a razor in his trembling hands too great a risk to take. Besides, he wasn't really going to work, despite what he had told the redheaded trick. He couldn't. He didn't have a job. Well, not a *real* job. Nor did he want one. He had some money in the bank from back in the days when he had a career. It wasn't much money, but it should be enough to last him a few more months. Maybe when the money ran out, he'd take a closer look at the revolver in his bathroom drawer. Maybe then he'd get to know it a little better.

Maybe then he'd let it speak to him. Finally.

Gordon sucked up more mouthwash and gargled until the lining of his mouth felt like it was on fire. He continued to stare at his reflection with those bloodshot eyes and tried to ignore the hangover still eating away inside him.

His face might look like crap, but at twenty-six, Gordon was relieved to see his body hadn't gone to pot yet. A little too thin, maybe, since he didn't eat right, but still erect, broad-shouldered, trim-hipped, long-legged. His curly brown hair, too long at the moment, waved all over his head and hung annoyingly in his eyes. He was forever pushing it off his face. But he also kind of liked it there. That curtain of hair came in handy sometimes, giving him a convenient place to hide.

These days Gordon needed a place to hide. Frequently.

As clean as he could get without resorting to a fish scaler, Gordon dressed in jeans and a white T-shirt, tucked his feet in a pair of tennis shoes, and stuffed some money in his pocket. Out of habit he reached for the cell phone lying on the dresser, then remembered he wasn't using it anymore. In fact, the thing hadn't been charged in weeks. Sort of like his life, Gordon had just let the cell phone wind down like an old clock, not bothering to recharge it, not caring that it no longer connected him to the rest of the world.

Just as Gordon no longer connected with the rest of the world either.

Outside, the San Diego street that Gordon called home baked in the summer sun on this Saturday morning, somnolent and drowsy. Even the neighborhood kids were inside, playing video games and tormenting their mothers rather than tearing up and down the street on bikes and skateboards and screaming their heads off in the heat. It was going to be a scorcher, and everybody knew it.

A couple of die-hard joggers thundered past him as he wended his way toward the bus stop, but Gordon didn't look at them. Even the men in their shorty shorts with their sexy, muscled legs and tight asses didn't draw his interest. Not much, anyway.

Gordon could feel last night's alcohol oozing through his pores under the burning sun. As hot as it was, he let his hair hang in his eyes as he walked so he wouldn't have to nod or say hello to the few people he passed on the sidewalk. One thing Gordon had learned since he turned his back on the world: if you give it half an opportunity, the world is more than willing to turn its back on you too.

And that was just fine with Gordon.

He waited in the hot sun at the corner of Juniper and 30th for thirteen minutes before the downtown bus came trundling along. Felt like an hour. When he climbed wearily on board with his poor hungover head still thumping from the heat, every seat was occupied. All Gordon could do was hang on to a strap about three quarters of the way back and continue to sweat because the air conditioning wasn't working. Someone nearby needed a bath, but he wasn't sure who it was.

Gordon's crotch was at face level with a young guy in the aisle seat next to him. Looked like a college student. Oriental, cute, young. Gordon had his arm above his head, clutching the strap so he wouldn't fall on his face every time the bus took a corner. Since Gordon was only inches away, the guy was happily eyeing Gordon's blue-jeaned package and the two or three inches of bare skin between belly button and belt buckle that Gordon's position left exposed. The student let his eyes wander up to Gordon's face a couple of times, making eye contact, but then those Oriental eyes would slide back to Gordon's crotch a moment later. The guy had a stack of schoolbooks on his lap, and his hand was underneath the stack. Gordon suspected he was playing with himself.

That was a turn-on. Weird, but a turn-on. Gordon could feel his cock lengthening inside his trousers, so just for the hell of it, Gordon took the opportunity to thrust his crotch a little closer to the college student's face as the bus careened around a corner. Gordon gave an inward chuckle as a smile of intrigue crossed the student's face. He thought he might even have heard a pleasant little gasp of surprise from the guy when Gordon's junk came swinging in his direction.

The bus brakes squealed and the bus bumped to a stop in front of San Diego High. The Oriental kid gathered up his books and smiled an "excuse me" up at Gordon, as if to say "this is my stop."

Gordon stepped back. Jesus, the kid wasn't a college student at all. He was in high school!

He felt the blood rush to his head as the kid made a point of brushing his forearm across Gordon's fly while exiting his seat. "Bye," the *high school student* said softly, voice filled with regret.

"Little twerp" Gordon wanted to say but didn't. He merely turned his back on the boy and laid claim to the vacated seat.

*Jesus, they're growing up fast these days. It's bad enough I'm breaking a court order by drinking every night of the week. Wouldn't the judge love to hear about me fooling around with a minor.*

Gordon shuddered at the thought.

Now that he was seated, Gordon realized the old woman with a paper bag in her lap, sitting next to him in the window seat, was the person stinking up the bus. She smelled of urine and rank tobacco. Risking a glance in her direction, he noticed greasy hair, dandruff, and a boil on the woman's neck. She was humming tunelessly as she stared out the window at the blocks rolling by. Her eyes were vacant.

Holding his breath, Gordon immediately pulled himself to his feet and headed for the back of the bus. There were no more seats, so he simply stood by the back steps and clutched another strap, waiting for his stop to come along.

When it finally did, he escaped through the back door, trading the heat of the bus for the heat of the city, and headed south.

Downtown San Diego was a goulash of odd humanity and sometimes odder architecture. The lower end of Broadway down by the bay was modern, clean, the high-rises sparkling. Even the pedestrians were nicely dressed.

The upper end of Broadway, where Gordon alighted from the bus, was a fucking mess. Homeless people sleeping under tarps on the street, doorways puddled with urine, dirty storefront windows smeared with handprints and grime, buildings gone to ruin, pleading for a wrecking ball to put them out of their misery. This end of Broadway exuded little promise, little hope, and little chance for improvement. Sort of like Gordon's life.

He supposed that's why he felt he fit right in every time he climbed off the downtown bus. He needed a wrecking ball to put him out of his misery too.

Three blocks south, in an even seedier part of the city, Gordon passed a long line of homeless citizens standing and sitting, bitching loudly or mumbling insanely to no one or everyone. A couple of homeless souls, pockmarked with meth addiction and looking even worse than Gordon did, reached out as he passed to ask for a nickel, a dime, money for food, money for drink, money for drugs.

Gordon did his own mumbling, muttering apologies. He hid behind his curtain of hair and kept walking. Someone cursed him as he strode away.

Heaving a sigh of either relief or dread, Gordon ducked into an alleyway and tugged open a metal door. He turned his back on the misery outside and faced a whole new world of misery splayed out before his eyes inside.

Mama's Soup Kitchen.

"You're late!" Mama Davis screamed out the moment he walked in the door. Then she grinned a blinding grin and scooped Gordon into her arms. Her face was the color of road tar, her eyes so bright they could stop traffic, her brittle, thinning hair augmented by three hundred dollars' worth of braids, which her daughter sewed onto her mother's head monthly. This month Mama Davis's braids were streaked with gold and had silver beads twinkling at the end. Sometimes when she laughed and threw her head back, you could hear the beads clatter and tinkle around her.

Mama Davis was somewhere between forty and ninety years old. Her braids weren't the only golden thing about her. Her giving heart was golden as well. Golden through and through.

She gripped Gordon's shoulders and pushed him far enough away that her old eyes could focus on his face. "Honey, you ain't lookin' good. You sure you want to work today?"

Gordon dredged up a smile. He wasn't sure where from. He had to work whether he wanted to or not. She knew it as well as he did. "I'm fine. Just didn't sleep good is all."

Mama nodded, her eyes caring and wise. Too wise. She didn't believe a word he said, and Gordon wasn't surprised. She had seen far too many hungover denizens of the street in her day. Hell, there was a time when she had even *been* one. So Gordon wasn't dumb enough to believe she couldn't see the hangover in him.

Mama Davis gently clutched his arm and led him through the bustling kitchen, which was about a thousand degrees inside what with all the cooking going on. She led Gordon into the dining area, where she plopped him down at one of the tables all by himself. He was the only person in the whole establishment sitting down, and that embarrassed him.

"I'm gonna feed you first. Then we'll feed all the poor sheep standing outside my door."

"I'm not hungry," Gordon said.

"Yes, you are," Mama grunted, not taking no for an answer. "Stay here."

Two minutes later she returned with a metal tray stacked with sausage patties, fake scrambled eggs, and three little cartons of milk.

Mama Davis patted Gordon's shoulder and said, "Eat that, then come into the kitchen." She hustled off to see to some disaster or other in the making where all the cooks were preparing the food. There was always a disaster brewing back there somewhere.

After one bite of sausage, Gordon realized how hungry he was. He gobbled down the rest of his breakfast in no time flat. As soon as the food was gone, he guzzled all three cartons of milk, one right after the other.

When he was finished, he fought back a sob at the kindness of one old black lady with three hundred dollars' worth of beaded braids glued to her head. Blinking away a sudden spate of tears, Gordon gathered up his empty tray, utensils, and trash and headed into the kitchen to go to work.

Another day of atonement began.

# CHAPTER 2

AS ALWAYS, the breakfast service in Mama's Soup Kitchen for San Diego's homeless was well attended. The air was so thick with body odor it was about the same consistency as the powdered scrambled eggs, which, by the way, were delicious, and that was more than could be said for the body odor. Only Mama knew how to turn a forty-gallon pot of powdered scrambled eggs into a culinary delight for four hundred indigent people. Unfortunately, only a bar of soap and a good bath could fix a reeking human, and most of the people present weren't exactly on speaking terms with soap and water.

On this Friday morning, as on every other morning of the week, it wasn't just the homeless who partook of Mama's largesse. There was also a good showing of senior citizens from the retirement high-rises scattered around the downtown area, and just to confuse the atmosphere, some of them smelled pretty good. One might spot a regal old lady with blue hair, crisply coiffed and smelling of White Shoulders perfume, tittering in laughter as she stood in line waiting to be served, all the while chatting up the man behind her, a pathetic specimen of humanity who looked like he had slept in a pig sty the night before and was so rattled with delirium tremens he could barely stand upright, let alone carry on a respectable conversation.

Insanity made a fair showing in the mob of waiting diners as well. People mumbling to themselves; people swatting at imaginary flies or leading imaginary dogs; people laughing at unspoken jokes or grumbling at imagined slights; people cursing under their breath at nothing, no one, or everything. Gordon wondered if someday he would be out there standing among them, beaten down, aching from drink, slowly dying from either an exploded liver or some horrific sexually transmitted disease or other. And wasn't that a cheery thought. No, he quickly decided. The revolver in his apartment would see that this fate did not await him. Yes indeed. Gordon would make sure of it.

On this particular morning, Gordon's job was to serve up the sausages. Every time a stainless steel tray slid down the line in front of him in dirty, palsied hands, he dredged up a smile and forked over two patties. Inevitably, the person holding the tray said thank you. There was a big sign on the wall by the front door that demanded it. Never one to mince words, Mama Davis had coined the quote herself.

**Say thank you when God grants a blessing. Otherwise He may stop granting them.**

In this neighborhood, Mama was God, and the poor souls dining here knew it. Every single one of them. Two inches short of suffering delirium tremens himself, and still sick as a dog from last night's drinking, Gordon nevertheless had to retch up an occasional chuckle at the sometimes insincere displays of gratitude tossed in his direction as he doled out the sausage patties. More than once, "thank you" sounded remarkably similar to "fuck you."

As the line of diners rolled past, the tables began to fill. The old warehouse Mama Davis rented at the wrong end of Eighth Avenue began to swell with noise—the roaring hum of hundreds of voices mixed with the clatter of cheap flatware on stainless steel trays bought wholesale from the military. If you wanted ambience, that was the ambience Mama's Soup Kitchen offered. Noise. If you wanted *nice peaceful* ambience for your dining pleasure, you went somewhere else to eat. Of course, then you would have to pay for it.

Along about the time Gordon could stand on tiptoe and look through the propped-open front door and see the tail end of the chow line approaching about half a block away, Mama Davis came up behind him and plunked a fresh pan of sausage patties into the steam table in front of him. Then she gave his rump a friendly pat.

"Honey, I was just doing my paperwork, and you've honored exactly half of your court-ordered hours of community service. Ain't that grand? A few more months and you'll be all done. I'm happy for you. I'll miss your handsome face when you go, I surely will. But maybe you've learned a thing or two, huh?"

She made that last comment as if she didn't quite believe it, considering the hangover Gordon had been suffering when he showed up for work that morning. Mama Davis and Gordon both knew booze was the reason he got in trouble to begin with. Well—booze and poor judgment. The fact he was still drinking showed a less than stellar amount of intelligence on his part, and he kept waiting for Mama to come right out and tell him so. But apparently, she was feeling charitable this morning. He suspected if he did it again, however, she would have him scrubbing pots and pans in the scullery, a job she always reserved for those who displeased her in some fashion or other. Working the serving line and working the scullery were as far from each other on enjoyment levels as rearranging books in a prison library and busting rocks for thirty years with a sledgehammer.

Scullery work sucked. Big time. Nothing could complicate a hangover like scullery work. Gordon decided if he ever did come to work at the soup kitchen with another hangover, Mama Davis would be the last person he'd let know about it.

Gordon gave Mama a reassuring smile, thinking that might display a modicum of good intentions to improve his habits. He doubted she would buy it, but he flashed it at her anyway.

Before she could respond, some sort of kerfuffle broke out near the front door—raised voices, one or two waving hands signaling for help above the crowd, a startled yip from one of the blue-haired old ladies.

Mama took the tongs from Gordon's hand and said, "Go see what that's all about, honey. My arthritis is acting up this morning. I don't feel like getting into a knock-down, drag-out brawl."

Neither did Gordon. But it wouldn't be the first time he had been drafted by Mama Davis into quelling a mini riot or overseeing a truce between combative diners. He supposed he had his youth and his six-foot frame to thank for that, since most of the other people who worked at Mama's Soup Kitchen were about one step away from being as pitiful and downtrodden as the clientele.

Mama plucked a humongous spatula from her apron pocket and pressed it into Gordon's hand. "Take this for protection. Bop 'em on the head if you have to."

Gordon gave a resigned nod and peeled off his rubber gloves before grabbing the damn spatula and stepping out from behind the steam table. He set off toward the mysterious commotion by the front door, dragging the stupid spatula and his stupid hangover along with him.

He had a horrible feeling of impending doom. But then, he usually did.

*AND TO think,* Gordon thought, *I used to be somebody. I used to get forty-dollar haircuts and wear a suit to work every day. Total strangers knew my face and said hello to me on the street. I dealt with people who bathed on a regular basis and weren't crazy. Now here I am, drowning in guilt, jobless for all intents and purposes, wading into a melee of indigents wielding nothing but a spatula to protect myself, and doing it all on the whim of an old black lady whose braids rattle when she laughs and whose respect I want more than anyone else on the planet.*

*Well, shit.*

While his own life might be a bit of a clusterfucked mystery, even to himself, Gordon had the rest of the world figured out completely. At least the homeless world. After six months in Mama's Soup Kitchen, it was a lesson one could hardly avoid learning.

Even here, where the people were barely surviving on a day-to-day basis, there was a caste system. The dregs of the population, Gordon had quickly come to realize, have their elite tier and their bottom rung, just like decent people. The downtrodden masses are comprised of both the kind and the cruel, the givers and the takers, the good and the bad. And yes, even here, in the anus of civilization, the saints were at the mercy of the shitheels. Just as they were everywhere else.

Pushing his way through the crowd, occasionally sucking in his breath to block the stench of one of the filthier residents of the street, Gordon came face to face with both elements. The good *and* the bad. And once again, it looked like the bad were winning hands down.

The three youths Gordon had seen before and knew to be trouble were tormenting a fourth youth whom Gordon had *not* seen before. On closer inspection, Gordon realized the fourth youth wasn't quite as young as he originally thought. In fact, he looked to be about Gordon's age. Midtwenties, maybe. He only appeared younger because of his small stature. The other boys, the ones doing the bullying, were truly teenagers. The only commonality the one on the receiving end shared with his tormentors was the fact that all four of the young men looked like they at least *tried* to keep themselves clean. Not an easy task when one lives on the street.

The poor young man at the center of the fracas was dressed in baggy jeans and a white dress shirt with blue pinstripes he had probably bought or begged from the Goodwill store up the street. He wore a Chargers baseball cap pulled low on his forehead; it all but covered the upper half of his face. He couldn't have been more than five foot five, Gordon decided, slight of frame, with a sprinkle of blond hair on the backs of his hands below his tightly buttoned shirt cuffs. The young man's hands drew Gordon's attention immediately. They were beautiful hands. Elegant, graceful, pale. At the moment, he was shielding his face with them.

The three tormentors were gay. They were also hustlers, perhaps pushed out onto the streets after proclaiming their homosexuality to their moronic, homophobic parents. There were a lot of young men and women like them on the street—trying to fuck their way into enough money to buy a meal, rent a bed, stay alive. Gordon knew these three already. He had seen them off and on over the past few months, unimpressed by the way they interacted with him as he served up their daily breakfast or afternoon meal. Yes, Gordon worked both shifts. And twice a day they raucously cruised him, this trio of gay misfits: made sexual comments, tried to get a rise out of Gordon, once even went so far as to request his attendance in the back alley, where they promised the best three-on-one blowjob he'd ever get in his life in exchange for a couple of bucks.

But Gordon wasn't a fool. While the three hustlers weren't bad looking, Gordon wouldn't have set his dick loose within twenty feet of any one of them.

Nor, apparently, would the young man they were tormenting.

He lay flat on his back on the floor in his baggy jeans and wrinkled dress shirt. On his feet he wore weathered tennis shoes with no socks. One of the three boys, apparently the meanest of the bunch, sat on his chest, holding him down. The other two bullies looked on, laughing.

Their victim was outmatched, but he was mad enough not to care. "Leave me alone! Get off me! I just want some breakfast!"

The teen perched on his chest gave a smirk. "Here, Squirt, I'll give you something to chew on." And he reached for his zipper.

An old lady gasped somewhere behind Gordon, and a couple of veteran homeless gave tsks of sympathy but didn't try to intervene.

There was a streak of blood on the victim's chin, probably from a split lip. Somebody must have already swung a punch, and that was one of Mama's big rules. No fighting.

Gordon grabbed a handful of the teenager's collar and yanked him off the guy. While the kid tried to wiggle out of Gordon's grasp, the other two bullies started cursing at him to let their friend go.

That was Mama's other big rule. No cursing.

Gordon pushed the kid away from him, trying not to throw up the breakfast he had eaten earlier. His hangover was killing him, but now wasn't the time to give in to it. He suspected if he showed weakness around these creeps, they would go for him next.

He pointed to the door. "You three, out! If you can't be civil, you don't eat. Period."

One of the bullies spit up a nasty chuckle and aimed a kick at the young man still lying on the floor, going for his ribcage. The young man groaned and rolled into the kick, clutching his chest. Another bully started spouting obscenities, which caused the old lady somewhere behind Gordon to gasp again. The final bully, the one Gordon had peeled off his victim's chest, straightened his ragged clothes and snarled at Gordon like a mad dog.

"You'll pay for that, fucker." Then he spat on the young man at their feet. "And *you* haven't seen the last of us either, faggot."

The man looked away, ignoring the taunt as best he could, still cradling his bruised ribs. Gordon felt such a surge of sympathy for the guy it surprised him. He extended a hand and helped the man to his feet.

One of the lifelong homeless, an older man Gordon knew as Pistol Pete, finally decided to get involved and started herding the three bullies out the front door. "Pipe down, you three hoodlums, and stop cussing before Mama comes after your skinny asses. She'll take the starch out of your pants, don't think she won't. Get out now. Shoo. You've caused enough trouble."

"Fuck you, old man," one of the teens spat, and old Pete pulled a revolver from his pocket and aimed it at the teenager's head. The teen's eyes grew as big as silver dollars, and when Pete knew he had the guy's undivided attention—he pulled the trigger.

A stream of water shot out of the gun and soaked the kid's face. Then a few more streams of water nailed the other two creeps while Pete pumped away with a vicious grin on his sunbaked face like he was having a real good time.

The people standing around watching were having a good time too, laughing at the three fools who Pete was watering down like a trio of petunias. They had known the old man's gun was fake all along, of course. That's why he was known as Pistol Pete. Every time Pete got mad, he pulled out his squirt gun and let loose. He shot at everything that annoyed him: passing cars, sidewalk-hogging pedestrians, noisy kids. Once, even the mayor found herself in his sights after she voted against funding a homeless shelter through the winter months as Pete figured it was her duty to do. For that little escapade, he spent a week in the city jail, had a spread on the front page of the San Diego Union, and voilà, his name became legend. When he wasn't mad and hosing down his enemies, Pistol Pete sometimes squirted the water down his own throat just to stay hydrated. Pete was big on staying hydrated.

It was the laughter of the crowd more than their fear of Pete or Gordon that drove the three bullies through the front door. But at least they were gone.

Amid a round of applause from the onlookers, Gordon grinned at Pete. "Put that thing away before you hurt someone."

Pete gave him a wink, blew on the barrel of his squirt gun, and stuffed it back into the pocket of his tattered overcoat. Gordon knew he would reload later at the fountain on Fourth and Broadway like he always did.

The young man Gordon had rescued made a move toward the front door.

Gordon touched his arm. "Where do you think you're going? What's your name? Squirt?"

The man pulled his hat lower and refused to look at Gordon's face. "Yeah. You mean I can stay?"

There was something childlike about him. Gordon was surprised to find his nurturing side taking over. Surprising, since he didn't know he still had one. He snatched a napkin from one of the diners eating nearby and ducked down under the brim of the guy's hat to dab the blood from his chin. There was a scatter of blond stubble he had to work through and Gordon felt the oddest sensation when he brushed his fingertips across it—almost a sexual tremor. Gordon wondered where the hell that had come from.

"You hurt, Squirt?" he gently asked.

Gordon was surprised to see a soft smile light the young man's unshaven face. "That rhymed," he said. "You're a poet."

"And don't I know it," Gordon heard himself say like a fool, and the young man smiled even wider. He tilted his head a little higher, and Gordon caught a glint of lively blue eyes beneath the brim of the Chargers hat. The eyes were crystal clear and shone like sapphires behind a curtain of white-blond hair. Gordon blinked in surprise. The guy was a towhead.

"Come on," Gordon said after a brief struggle to find his voice. He took the man's pale hand and led him along the waiting line to one of the tables toward the back of the hall. "You sit here. I'll get you some breakfast. Okay?"

Squirt nodded. "Thank you," he said, looking shy and breathless and a little astounded, as if he couldn't believe what was happening.

Squirt seemed so surprised by his good fortune, Gordon wondered if anyone had ever been nice to him before. And that thought broke his heart a little. Astounded by the sympathy welling up inside him, Gordon felt a blush rise to his cheeks. To hide it, he said, "Stay there," and hurried away to get the guy some food.

He wasn't sure what had gotten into him, but Gordon found himself psyched up about something for the first time in months. He snatched a tray out from under some poor old lady's paw and went down the serving line on the wrong side of the steam tables, gathering up this and that and everything he thought the guy might enjoy. Eggs, sausage, biscuits with extra butter and extra jam, a couple of donuts, and a healthy dollop of bread pudding.

When the tray was full, he glommed on to two cartons of milk and two of orange juice and headed back to the guy's table.

Squirt was sitting by himself, hunched into a protective shell, not looking either left or right but straight down into his lap, where his hands were resting, clenched together. Gordon wondered if he was asleep.

But he wasn't. The young man gazed up as Gordon slid the tray in front of him. He was still periodically blotting the blood from his chin with the napkin Gordon had given him earlier. He gawked at the laden tray of food as if he had never seen anything so beautiful in his life.

Casting his benefactor a sheepish glance, he said, "Wow. Thanks." But he made no move for the cutlery until Gordon practically placed the fork in his hand. That act of kindness elicited another "Thank you."

"Okay, Squirt. You eat now. I'll come back later and see if you need anything. Did your lip stop bleeding?" Gordon had to ask because once again he couldn't see under the brim of the guy's low-slung baseball cap.

"It stopped," Squirt said, his voice barely audible, as if he was embarrassed. Or ashamed. "Thanks for asking."

Gordon laughed and laid a hand on the guy's shoulder. "You don't have to thank me for everything all the time. Just eat your food and that'll be thanks enough for me. Okay?"

"Okay," the guy mumbled. And to Gordon's amazement, he watched Squirt shake out a fresh paper napkin and spread it neatly across his lap. Only when he had it the way he wanted it did he scoop up a forkful of scrambled eggs and begin eating.

Seeing that everything was the way it should be, and his charge was finally sucking up some nourishment, Gordon headed back to the steam table, where Mama Davis was still doling out sausage patties and blessings to everyone who passed. Her old face had a smile beaming all the way across it as she watched Gordon approach.

"That was a fine thing you did, feeding that poor boy. You might just go to heaven for that one day."

Gordon felt himself blush *again*. Jesus, what a morning. He was blushing every time he turned around.

"They were picking on him," Gordon explained. "The gay crowd. You know the ones I mean. They're always causing trouble."

Mama gave a wise nod of her old head, causing her beaded braids to rattle. Gordon was reminded of a rattlesnake. Only Mama Davis was a whole lot nicer. Although she still had a venomous strike or two lying hidden inside her if the occasion called for it.

"If they do it again," she said, "they'll be out of here forever. I give everybody one more chance. The next one'll be theirs. If they don't toe the line, they can eat someplace else. I won't have them tormenting my customers. These poor people are tormented enough."

She handed over the tongs and watched Gordon settle back into serving mode. When she was satisfied everything was as it should be, she gazed back at the lone figure in the dress shirt and baseball cap sitting huddled by himself along the back wall.

"What's that boy's name, Gordon? Did you get it?"

Gordon shook his head. "Nope. Not his real name. They just called him 'Squirt.'"

Mama's face cracked into a broad smile, showing a big-ass pair of dentures lurking behind it. Those dentures were big and white and square and looked like they would be perfectly capable of gnawing down a tree. "He is a Squirt, too, ain't he? No bigger than a minute. Poor little guy." She shook her head and harrumphed a couple of times, like she always did when faced with the madness of the world around her. Mama Davis went from crisis to crisis, day after day, but somehow seemed to enjoy the drama. Gordon supposed her all-consuming generosity and faith in God saw her through it all. Or maybe she just thrived on chaos.

She gave Gordon a gentle pat on the head like she might a poodle. With a chuckle, she muttered for his ears alone, "You did good, white boy." Then she walked away, heading back to the kitchen to make sure things were going smoothly there.

Mama's words made Gordon smile. And as he smiled, his eyes, too, were drawn to the lone figure by the back wall, hunkered over his tray of food. As the young man ate, his knees were bouncing up and down like a kid's. Gordon thought that was about the cutest thing he had ever seen.

Squirt was gobbling up his breakfast at a really good clip, and that realization made Gordon smile again. But there was sadness in the smile too. He wondered how long it had been since the man had eaten a hot meal.

Forty minutes later, after the last rush of diners had wended their way down the serving line and the outer doors were finally pulled shut against any further drop-ins, Gordon cast his eyes to the back wall one more time to see how his charge was getting along.

The table was empty. Squirt was gone.

Gordon stared at the table for the longest time. He finally looked away and went back to work, but he did it with a heavy heart.

When Mama Davis came and told him he had a phone call, he felt his heart sink even deeper inside his chest. Only one person would call him here.

He didn't smile again for the rest of his shift.

# CHAPTER 3

THE GRANT Grill was elegant and stuffy and had been that way for well over half a century. A bastion of male snootiness, it had survived all those decades in downtown San Diego, never once changing location or decor. During most of those years, it reigned as a poster child to sexism, since not until the early 1970s were women allowed on the premises during daylight hours. Buried in the heart of the U.S. Grant Hotel on Broadway and Fourth (just across the street from the fountain where Pistol Pete periodically reloaded his fabled squirt gun), the Grant Grill offered a magnificent menu for the palate but, in Gordon's view, very little nourishment for the soul.

That's probably why his mother insisted they meet there. As far as Gordon had been able to ascertain in the twenty-six years he'd known her, his mother offered very little nourishment for the soul either.

He could see her ensconced at a table in the center of the room, sipping her iced tea and holding court, as it were, speaking in genteel tones to the waiter who appeared rather nervous in the woman's presence. As well he should, Gordon thought. His mother had ended the career of more than one waiter in the popular establishment.

When she looked up and spotted Gordon standing at the door leading in from the street in his T-shirt and jeans, he saw the disappointment on her face immediately. The maître d', whose name escaped Gordon at the moment, apparently saw it too. The man came bustling in to be of assistance.

He whispered in Gordon's ear as he held out a complimentary jacket and clip-on tie for Gordon to slip into so as to meet the dress code. "Don't worry, sir. She looks at me that way too."

Only then did Gordon remember the maitre d's name. Edward. His name was Edward.

"Thanks, Edward," Gordon said with a smile. "How are you today?"

"I'm fine, sir. And you?"

Since Gordon's hangover was still at Def Con 4, his trembling hands couldn't quite handle the clip-on tie. So once again Edward came to his rescue. He stood before Gordon and carefully clipped the tie to the neck of Gordon's T-shirt. When it was in place, the maitre d' buttoned the complimentary sports coat closed to hide the T-shirt and gave Gordon a gentle pat on each shoulder. "There you go, sir. Enjoy your meal. The special today is halibut. It's very good."

Gordon tried to ignore the sympathy on the man's face, but there was no getting away from it. Edward knew Gordon's story as well as Gordon did. There was even a time when Edward might have asked Gordon jokingly about the weather, but those days were long gone, and they both knew it.

"Thank you, Edward," Gordon said again. "I'll join my mother now."

"Of course," Edward cooed. He tucked two menus under his arm and led Gordon to the table in the center of the room, where Gordon's mother sat waiting like a shark. Circling. Circling.

"Here he is, madam," Edward cooed again, this time to Mrs. Stafford. "Good as new."

While his mother ignored the friendly overture, Edward pulled out a chair for Gordon. After tucking him neatly under the table, the maitre d' passed out menus and made himself scarce.

Gordon took in a deep gulp of air and waited for his mother to start bitching. He didn't have to wait long. In fact, he didn't have to wait at all.

"Why must you always embarrass me, Gordon? Where's your jacket? And you look like you've lost weight. You're starting to look sickly."

"Thanks. And my suits are home hanging in the closet. I'm between shifts as you darn well know. I didn't have time to run home on the bus and dress, then hop another bus and get back in time to meet your schedule."

There was a teeny smudge of lipstick at the corner of his mother's mouth. Somehow she knew. A perfectly manicured pinky came up and dabbed it away. "If you would go back to driving your car like a normal person, you would have plenty of time to dress properly."

Gordon felt his heart sink inside his chest like a fucking anchor settling slowly into the frigid depths of an arctic sea. "You know I don't drive now. I haven't driven since the accident. Why must you always bring it up?"

His mother emitted an exasperated huff and took a dainty sip from her iced tea, apparently just to cool herself off. "Excuse me for living," she said, eyeing the other diners scattered about the room, making sure no one was listening in. He saw her give a curt shake of the head to the waiter, indicating she wasn't ready to order yet.

Gordon couldn't stop himself. He had to get a dig in. "Instead of calling me at the soup kitchen, why didn't you just stop in for breakfast?" He gazed around at the rococo trimmings of the Grant Grill. "You could've saved some money and got a free meal to boot."

His mother adjusted her earring. "Very funny. What happened to your cell phone?"

Evasively, Gordon shrugged. "Forgot to recharge it." *Intentionally.* Hoping to avoid more headbutting, Gordon endeavored to lighten the mood. "You look nice today, Mother."

And she did. For a woman in her upper fifties she was trim, petite, and without a line in her face. The truth was if she had one more facelift, her eyes would be in the back of her head and her nose would be stretched flat like Lord Voldemort's, but Gordon decided not to mention that. He wasn't a complete fool.

She was wearing a peach business suit and peach shoes with sensible heels. A string of petite pearls circled her taut neck, and tiny pearl earrings decorated her lobes. Her ash blonde hair, as always, was smooth and elegant, cut in a shoulder-length bob that somehow managed never to look unkempt. It made Gordon conscious that his own hair was probably all over the place, but he didn't really care. He simply pushed it out of his eyes as he perused the menu and waited for his mother to get to the reason for this little tryst. Whatever the reason, he knew it couldn't be anything good.

She seemed to have snagged a thought right out of his head. "You need a haircut. You look like a hippie."

Gordon chuckled. "Sorry, Mother, but the last of the hippies are now sitting in nursing homes sipping Metamucil and praying for a decent dump and an LSD flashback to brighten their day."

If his mother found his comment amusing, she didn't show it. "That complimentary coat and tie are atrocious. Do you need money?" she asked.

"No," Gordon snapped, and his mother flinched. "I'm fine. And my outfit's a freebie. What do you expect?" He tacked that last bit on with a bit more diplomacy, hoping to placate, but he wasn't sure he succeeded. There was hurt in her eyes. Hurt and impatience. She didn't understand what he was going through, and he didn't expect her to. How could anyone know what he was going through? All he knew for sure was that her attempts to buy him out of his misery pissed him off. Did she really think money would make everything all right? Could she honestly be that shallow?

He tried to placate her further, hoping to avoid for a little while longer the subject he most assuredly did not want to talk about. That subject being himself. "How are your orchids doing?"

Gordon's mother grew orchids. Aside from selling real estate—and making a fortune at it—orchids were her only passion. He had always thought it a strange pastime for a woman with so little softness about her. Orchids were delicate, his mother ironclad. From stem to stern. Like a warship.

Still, her face softened a bit at the question. She showed a flash of enthusiasm that he always found disconcerting when it made a rare appearance on his mother's face. She was usually too controlled to show enthusiasm. For anything. Except money. "You should see the array of Phalaenopsis, all in bloom. So lovely. I thought I had lost them for a while, but now they've come back more stunning than ever."

Silence settled over the table, and Gordon could see her pushing herself away from the memory of her beloved orchids. With a dimming of her perfectly mascaraed eyes, she coolly centered her attention back to him. "How are things going with your parole officer?"

The year Gordon had spent in county jail because of the accident was something he tried never to think about. His mother's shame because of it was another thing he tried never to think about. She, apparently, thought of little else. Gordon suspected her shame was now ingrown, like a festering toenail. She could never seem to take a step without it giving her a jolt. It was an inescapable ache inside her every waking moment. Just as it was for him. Only he had accepted it. His mother was still fighting the acceptance of it like a mongoose battling a tenacious cobra.

Gordon's eyes narrowed. "You've talked with him again, haven't you? I told you to stay out of it, Mother. I'm an adult. Whatever shit my life has turned into is my making, no one else's. It doesn't have to wreck your life too. Just stay out of it. Pretend I don't exist, if that's what it takes."

She cast him a dismayed look. "You've obviously never been a mother."

Gordon fiddled with his napkin, his fork, a drop of condensation sliding down his water glass. "And isn't that a brilliant observation."

"Gordon—"

He leaned over the table and brought his face as close to hers as he could get it without actually standing up and climbing over the table. He couldn't decide if the way she pulled away to escape his glare was satisfying or appalling.

"No," he said. "Stop interfering. Time will pass. Everything will work itself out in the end. What I'm going through is no less than I deserve. I killed a man, Mother. Did you think the judge would simply slap my wrist and send me to bed without dinner? Please, don't contact my parole officer again. We can't buy our way out of this. And I don't want to."

At that, his mother's hand fluttered atop her breast, her diamond rings glittering. She immediately gazed around the bustling restaurant to assure herself no one had seen her do it. She lowered her voice to a whisper. "I didn't contact the man. He contacted me. He's worried about you."

"Oh, please—"

"He says it isn't healthy the way you've withdrawn from the world, not tried to find work. He says you seem satisfied with your community service. You need to find a real job, Gordon. Maybe enough time has passed that you can get your old position back. That weatherman they have now is annoying and inept. Everyone misses you. I'm sure they do. And you must be running out of money. You haven't worked in a year and a half. I don't know why you won't let me help you with that, at least. I could write you a check right now, Gordon. It would only take a second."

Gordon fought the urge to just stand up and walk away. That would solve nothing.

"Mother, the station will never take me back. I wouldn't expect them to." He took in a great gulp of air, trying to calm himself. "And my money is holding out just fine. I have plenty. As for my future, don't worry about it. I have it all figured out."

An image of the revolver in his bathroom drawer suddenly filled his mind. And wouldn't his mother be thrilled shitless if she could read *that* thought.

She reached out and laid a hand on Gordon's forearm. Her fingers were cool to the touch. Cool and unfamiliar. He honestly couldn't remember the last time they had touched him.

"I want you to see my therapist. Maybe she can help you work through this guilt you're feeling. Will you at least think about doing that much? I'll pay for the sessions. She's wonderful, Gordon, she truly is. I think she could help you if you gave her a chance."

In reply, Gordon lifted his hand and signaled to the waiter standing by the bar. Gordon made a circling motion over the table with his fingertip to indicate they were ready to order.

"Gordon," his mother said softly, her lips thin, a glint of either hurt or anger sparking her eyes. She clammed up when the waiter approached. Lifting her hand from Gordon's arm, she scooped her menu off the table and smiled her phony Realtor smile at the expectant waiter like maybe he was making an offer on a house she had long wanted to unload.

"The usual," she said, handing over the menu. "Thank you, Ronald."

Gordon sighed, and perused his own menu. "Soup," he finally said. "I'll just have soup."

An onlooker might have seen the mother's sigh perfectly mirror the son's. Genetics in action.

GORDON STEPPED off the bus in one of the poorest parts of town. The houses were run-down, the fences dilapidated. Weeds grew out of the sidewalks. The kids running up and down the street screamed happily in Spanish, many of them born Americans who couldn't speak the language of their own mother country. He smiled as they flew past, those kids. On foot, on skateboards, on bicycles ready to fall apart. Poverty be damned, they were enjoying the hell out of their young lives, taking full advantage of their summer away from school, not caring about the squalor they lived in, knowing only the blind exuberance of youth.

Ducking away from their raucous company and their unbearable happiness, Gordon crossed the street. There he came upon a rusty hurricane fence all but buried in a tangle of ivy. The weeds sprouting through the sidewalk on this side of the street were even more overgrown than they were on the other side. Probably because fewer people walked this side, since it led to the last place anyone in their right mind would ever want to go.

He followed the fence for a quarter of a mile, then ducked through a gateway beneath an arch with the words "Holy Cross Cemetery" rendered in rusty wrought iron high above his head. The macadam driveway that looped through the grounds was recently laid and reeked of fresh tar. Softening under the hot sun, it felt sticky beneath his feet. He quickly stepped off the road and onto the grass as a black hearse and a long line of mourners' cars entered the gate behind him, headlights gleaming dimly in the afternoon sun.

Feeling somewhat silly doing so, Gordon stood in reverence until the funeral procession passed. As he waited, he avoided the stunned gazes and somber faces of the bereaved, tucked away in their air-conditioned town cars, following along behind the flower-strewn hearse, looking out at the new home of their father, or brother, or mom, or nana. Many of them probably wondered when *they* would be making the same trip. And wasn't that a shitty thing to ponder on this steaming August afternoon, when thoughts should have been centered on a barefoot run at the beach or lunch somewhere beneath a big fat umbrella, with the sound of tinkling ice and laughter filling the air instead of the cloying stench of carnations and formaldehyde and the stifled sobs of mourning?

One would think death would be the last thing on people's minds as they went about living their lives beneath that gorgeous cobalt sky overhead. But Gordon knew better. Gordon knew better than anyone.

Death was always there—waiting. Just waiting. To jerk you out of existence or to ruin the existence you had. If not your death, then someone else's. Someone close to you. Or maybe a total stranger.

Oh yes. Gordon knew all about death. Knew everything there was to know about it.

He watched as the funeral procession rolled past. The trail of cars topped a tombstone-studded rise and disappeared from view beneath a stand of pepper trees. The silence rolled back in around him as if resentful of the momentary disturbance and jealously reclaiming its turf. Silence seemed to hold such sway over this place that even the birds in the treetops were voiceless. The overriding presence of death had muted even them.

Around him, Holy Cross Cemetery lay sweltering in the heat, moldering in the summer sun like roadkill at the side of a bubbling highway. Gordon set out across the tussocky grass, imagining he could smell the dead bodies simmering in their own juices, stashed in hot little concrete boxes beneath his feet. Jesus, he *hoped* that smell was only in his imagination.

Just to be sure, he sucked in a great gulp of hot air and dissected its fragrances while standing at the top of a rise. Sweat (his own), freshly mown grass, exhaust fumes from the freeway over the distant hill. No rank odor of corrupting flesh. Just another summer day and the detritus of death left over from his past. Gordon forced himself forward. His expression was grim and his jaws were clenched against the memories trying to fight their way in. He headed toward a spot he could already see in the distance. A place called Guadalupe Circle, one of the cemetery "neighborhoods," named to give the living a sense of camaraderie among the dead. There was a grave there he had come to see. A grave he came to see almost every day.

A grave that he himself had filled.

Gordon kept his mind purposely blank because that was the only way he could deal with the emotions this place evoked. Weighed down with muted grief, he wove his way through a forest of tombstones, most of which had been standing since before he was born, each one marking a life he had never known and *would* never know. He brushed a fingertip over each monument that came within his reach, as if imparting a brief hello to the soul lying beneath. Just a gentle commiseration, a simple moment of respect. An apology of sorts. Yes, even in the death of these poor unknown souls, Gordon could dredge up guilt.

Sweat burned his eyes as he climbed the hillock, which stood in the center of Guadalupe Circle. He could see his destination in the distance—a rectangle of pale, young grass, not yet as green as the acres around it. But it was getting there. Already the rectangular patch of newly seeded grass was less noticeable than the last time Gordon had come here, harder to spot from a distance. In another month he might find himself standing at the very edge of it before recognizing it for what it was.

For what it covered.

Gordon was breathing heavily now, his eyes burning, not from sweat or the scent of cut grass, but from his own emotions. His own weary sadness. He could no longer hold his thoughts at bay. They bombarded him from every angle.

He climbed the last few yards up the hillside like an old man, putting a hand to each knee as he climbed, wearily boosting himself higher, step by suffering step. He left the standing tombstones behind, for this was a new area of the cemetery. Much of the ground was unturned. Unmarked.

Unfilled.

Jeremy Aldritch Booth had been only the second person interred here. And even now there were only a scattering of others. Someday, years away, this area of Holy Cross would be as weathered and timeless as the rest of the cemetery. But for now, the hillside of Guadalupe Circle was like a new wound, still bleeding. Still absorbing pain.

Still hungry.

Gordon stopped with his toes at the very edge of the rectangle of new grass. The headstone was flat to the ground. All the tombstones here were flat to accommodate mowing. It seemed a sad concession to make, to limit the marker for one's existence to a flat piece of rock that lies flush to the earth and cannot be seen from a distance. Gordon ached that Jeremy Aldritch Booth should be inflicted with that final humiliation, that final monument to defeat. After all the young man had lost, this seemed one loss too many to bear.

Gordon wiped the sweat from his forehead with trembling fingers and pressed the heels of his hands to his eyes, hoping to clear the tears from his vision. When he opened them, blinking back the sunlight, he stared down at the flat little tombstone before him.

JEREMY ALDRITCH BOOTH

1988—2012

Asleep In God's Arms

Gordon closed his eyes and, for the millionth time, remembered it all. The screech of tires, the strobing headlights suddenly splitting the night, the flash of two young faces caught in a shard of light and terror. The thunderous boom of the collision clearing Gordon's drunken head in an instant. The dizzying moment of vertigo as Gordon's car spun around him, tipping his world upside down. His cell phone, the cell phone he never should have been texting with as drunk as he was, spinning out of his hand never to be seen again. And finally, that last horrific scream.

As he remembered, he wept.

Gordon sat in the grass at the edge of the grave and reached out to brush a scattering of mown grass from the stone marker. In the distance, off in the direction the funeral procession had gone, he heard a trumpet playing taps. The mournful notes of the horn echoed through the trees and hollows, sliding across the graves as if seeking a way out. When the notes finally ended and silence reclaimed the hill on which he sat, Gordon again reached out to trace with his fingertips the name carved on the stone beneath him.

"I'm sorry, Jeremy," he muttered into the empty air. "I'm so sorry." But as always, only silence answered.

Hours later, with a crescent moon perched high above his head, etched into a blanket of darkness that stretched from one horizon to the other, pierced by a million pinpricks of light, Gordon wended his weary way home along the same weed-grown sidewalk he had trod earlier. He was too tired to block his thoughts now. Too heartsick. He let them come. And they overwhelmed him.

Where there had been children earlier on the dusty sunlit streets, now there were sullen young men, leaning against the side of dilapidated buildings, drawn like moths to the circles of light beneath the few unbroken streetlamps, less impervious to their poverty than the children had been. You could see the angry press of it in the tilt of their heads, the almost desperately regal line of their shoulders as they tried to bear the weight of all they did not own—all they would *never* own. As Gordon passed they watched with leery eyes, while always in the background, Tejano music played from thumping car stereos or dirty boom boxes, filling the night air with the sounds of want and hopelessness. The lonely twang of steel guitars was like the plucking of heartstrings, playing the music of loss and need and never-ending sorrow. A melody Gordon knew all too well.

Not once did the sullen young men huddled beneath the streetlamps in the alleys and on the corners threaten Gordon. Perhaps they saw in him even greater hopelessness than they saw in themselves. Every night they let him pass.

And every night Gordon wished they wouldn't.

He stopped at a liquor store four blocks from his apartment and bought a fifth of the cheapest vodka they had. Mixers cost too much money. He would drink the vodka with water when he got back home.

Gordon carried the liquor home in a paper bag, sipping it along the way because he suddenly decided he couldn't wait. He was drunk by the time he stumbled through his own front door.

There was nothing in his mind but the memory of the revolver in his bathroom drawer. The way it felt in his hand. The heaviness of it. The comfort. But still he pushed the thought away.

He slept drunk another night. And in the morning he again found himself alive.

*Would this be the day?* he asked himself as the first thuds of pain started hammering through his head. He stumbled to the bathroom. And for the first time ever, he was afraid to open the drawer to look in at the revolver lying there.

On this day, he was afraid he would pick it up. And finally let it speak.

# CHAPTER 4

SATURDAY AND Sunday were Gordon's days off from the court-ordered stint at Mama Davis's Soup Kitchen. On Saturday he slept through the daylight hours and did not wake until the sun was just beginning to duck behind the stand of cypress trees overlooking the canyon beside his apartment building. Unknown to him, his bedroom began to darken with evening shadow around him as he dreamed. A welcome breath of night air cooled his naked skin as he lay sprawled across the crumpled bedclothes.

It was the eerie cry of a coyote from down in the canyon, perhaps just beginning its nightly prowl, that first made Gordon stir.

The coyote entered his dream like a madman slipping through an unlocked door. In his dream, it was not a coyote at all, but a wolf. Rabid, insane. The creature stalked him through abandoned city streets where every door he came across was locked against him. Gordon wept in fear as he stumbled naked from block to block, the wolf snapping and snarling at his heels, vile liquid dripping from its slavering jaws. It reeked of sickness and mindless hate. As it trailed behind him down the empty streets, trembling in madness, its gray, insane eyes never wavered. Its fury was centered on him and him alone.

As Gordon ran stumbling, his strength almost gone, the city silence was suddenly fractured by the screech of car tires, the scream and roar of an overworked engine. From the intersection ahead, a black limousine tilted into the turn and came barreling directly toward him, its chrome grille glittering in the sunlight like gnashing teeth. A hubcap rolled away in the midst of the turn and clanged against a parked car. The limo was like a maddened creature itself, with blacked-out windows and black, funereal plumes protruding from the front fenders. It took Gordon a moment to realize it was a hearse. A fucking hearse.

Gordon saw his chance to escape the wolf, and still running toward the approaching hearse, he spread his arms wide and begged it to take him, to end his fear, to set him free from the pursuing beast at his heels. To kill him if that's what it took. Run him flat. Just end his misery and fear and flight right here, right now.

The hearse accelerated toward him with a roar and Gordon smiled. Then the smile froze on his face, as in a momentary flash of windshield glass and reflected light—*or was it a shard of memory?*—he glimpsed two faces staring out at him from inside the speeding vehicle. Insane faces. Laughing madly. Cackling. Their claw-like fingers were clutching the dashboard before them as they peered eagerly through the windshield, waiting, waiting. Their teeth were bared, their horrible feral laughter rang out over the roar of the racing engine.

Behind him the wolf howled in a jealous frenzy, seeing this other creature bearing down on its prey. About to take Gordon. About to snatch him away.

At the eerie sound of the wolf's howl of frustration, Gordon stopped running. He knew he had lost. He stumbled to a halt in the center of the street and waited for fate to deal its hand—waited for whichever creature would take him first. Not caring which it would be. Both the hearse and the wolf would ease his suffering, end his fear. Death was all he wanted. He didn't care who doled it out. Who blessed him with its comfort.

As a scream of terror and helplessness and relief tore from his lips, Gordon's eyes popped open, and his scream echoed futilely through his dim, silent room.

Still weeping in fear, he struggled to a sitting position and looked around with panicked eyes. His heart pounded in his ears. His body was slick with cold sweat. He could smell the liquor on his breath, the acrid sweat on his skin, the stale, unwashed bedclothes beneath him.

He fought his way to the edge of the bed and, jarred by the movement, clutched his head in agony. When the real coyote once again howled from the canyon below, Gordon's heart thundered with terror in his chest.

Then he began to focus. It had been a dream.

He lurched to his feet and staggered from room to room, not sure what he was looking for. Just making sure he was alone. That the wolf was gone.

Clutching the kitchen doorjamb, he stared morosely at the half-empty bottle of vodka sitting on the counter. It was still tucked inside the crumpled paper bag it came in. He was pretty sure he remembered buying the vodka on his way home from the cemetery last night, but for the life of him he couldn't remember drinking it. That he *did* drink it was a no-brainer, of course. His thumping head told him that much.

Gordon stood naked in his dark apartment and felt his entire body tremble in agony. He was so hungover even his morning hard-on was nowhere in evidence, and that almost never failed him.

With a shaking hand, he reached out and plucked the bottle from the bag. He twisted off the cap after a couple of tries because his fingers didn't seem to be working properly, and then he brought the bottle to his lips. The first taste of fire burned his throat and made him gasp. His stomach churned. He leaned over the kitchen sink and vomited bile onto a pile of dirty dishes.

Lifting his head, Gordon stared out the kitchen window through a haze of tears and wondered how this would all end. It couldn't go on much longer, he knew that much. His body wouldn't tolerate the liquor forever.

And with that thought, he tipped the bottle up and took another sip.

*Eat something,* he told himself. *Stop drinking and eat something.*

He almost gagged at the mere thought of food. A third sip of vodka burned the sickness away. A fourth sip eased the shaking in his hands.

The walls of his apartment were closing in on him. He could actually feel them pressing inward. He needed air. He needed light.

He stumbled into the bedroom and snatched his clothes off the floor. They were the same clothes he had worn the day before, but Gordon didn't care. He tugged them on, the same dirty T-shirt and jeans, reeking of sausage grease. He almost wept in desperation as he struggled from one room to another searching for his shoes, mumbling curses beneath his breath, still clutching the vodka bottle and sipping at it now and then because he didn't know what else to do.

He finally found his shoes behind the sofa, where he must have thrown them. The reeking socks he had worn the day before were tucked neatly inside them, so he pulled them over his feet, then slipped into the shoes and tied them snug with fingers that were a little steadier now.

He found a twenty-dollar bill lying on the floor in the hallway. God knew how long it had been there. Gordon crammed it into his pants pocket, rummaged through a dresser drawer until he found another, then grabbed his apartment keys off the foot of the bed, where they were almost lost in a tangle of sheets.

As he crossed the living room and headed for the front door, he averted his eyes from his own reflection in the mirror hanging over the gas fireplace. Gordon didn't need to see how bad he looked. He could imagine. He hadn't bathed or changed clothes in two days. His hair was a mess. His breath smelled like a backed-up toilet. Who cared?

Still unnerved by the nightmare, the wolf, the fucking black hearse, he stepped through the front door into the hallway. He took one final, long swallow of vodka and tossed the empty bottle back into the apartment, where it hit the floor with a thud and rolled under the coffee table, before closing his door behind him.

As he stepped from his apartment building into the San Diego gloaming, Gordon squinted against the glaring orange sunset, tugged his baseball cap low over his face, and headed down the steps to the street on shaky legs.

He had no idea in the world where he was going. He only knew he had to go.

Every few steps he looked behind to see if he was being followed. Twice he stopped and listened hard for the sound of a snarling wolf.

His vision blurred by tears, his heart an aching lump inside his chest, he walked. And as he walked, he wept for all he had lost. And what little he still had left to lose.


THE NIGHT was as black as pitch. Not one light showed anywhere.

Gordon sat in the dirt under a freeway overpass, not quite sure how he'd gotten there. He had no idea where the freeway was located either, but he knew he was under one because of the traffic continually rumbling over his head. A round concrete stanchion, retrofitted against earthquakes with heavy metal bands, pressed hard against his back. It vibrated when the cars passed by above him. The ground beneath his ass was bare earth and scattered scree, as dry as bone dust. He sat perched on a slope, his feet lower than his head.

A cool breeze caressed his face. The breeze smelled of salt water and fish, so he knew he was somewhere close to the beach. It felt good, that breeze, but the darkness was beginning to worry him. He could hear water lapping at the rocks somewhere off to his left.

It took him a moment to realize it wasn't pitch dark at all. He only thought it was dark because his eyes were closed.

Jesus, that was stupid of him.

With a little concentrated effort, he managed to peel one eye open, then after a minute of exertion, the other. He gave a little gasp of pleasure at what he saw. It was the bay. San Diego Bay. It spread out before him in splashes of color and light, like a canvas rendered in sparkling acrylics—dots of yellows and mauves and pinks and startling whites danced across the still water and over the sky as if executed by Seurat. The night in pointillism. Black water cast shattered reflections of the moon overhead. The twinkling shards of moonlight on the water were interspersed with reflected green lights from the Coronado Bridge. The bridge, blue in the daylight but darkly shadowed at night in long ebony brushstrokes, swept over the water from the city proper to Coronado Island in the distance. Gordon began to understand then that he wasn't under a freeway at all. He was under the Coronado Bridge. In fact, he was at the very beginning of the bridge on the city side of the bay.

It took him a moment to orient himself. The Barrio was nearby. Chicano Park. Great. He wondered why he hadn't been beaten and robbed or shot from a passing car or stabbed by a roving band of twelve-year-old Latino schoolkids who were in training mode to launch themselves into a life of crime—if they managed to live long enough to actually embark upon it.

The Barrio was not the best part of town for a white man to find himself in. In fact, it was the worst. Especially at night. Especially *late* at night. And especially late at night when you're drunk as a skunk and weak as a newborn and hungry as hell and you don't even know how the fuck you got there to begin with.

In the darkness under the bridge, Gordon squinted down at himself. The reflected lights on the water were enough to illuminate the area pretty well in a trembly, fluttery sort of way. What he saw wasn't encouraging. His trouser knees were shredded. He must have fallen and torn them. As soon as he realized that, he reached down and touched the bloody scabs on his knees. He hissed with pain and jerked his hands away. Both knees were thrumming like toothaches now. Just what he needed.

His clothes were filthy. And not just with dirt either. His T-shirt appeared to have been vomited on, maybe more than once. His pant legs were wet and cold, his hat and shoes and socks missing completely. Somewhere in the back of his mind, he seemed to remember wading. Wading in the bay. Wading and laughing.

Christ, what the hell did he have to laugh about?

Taking stock of his inner workings, he realized he didn't actually feel too bad. He didn't seem to be suffering from a hangover, at any rate, as he had when he left the apartment. And when was that exactly? Just a few hours ago? A day ago? A week? How long had he been under this bridge? Still analyzing how he felt, he realized the overriding need his body registered was for food. He was starving. He couldn't remember the last time he had eaten. Was it the soup at the Grant Grill when he sat down with his mother for another strafing of guilt? Had it been that long? That was—what? Almost two days ago? Yesterday? Last year?

He pushed the hunger from his mind and tried to focus on more pressing matters. Like what the hell was he doing here?

He remembered reading about a homeless man who had died under an overpass after being bitten in the face by a rattlesnake while he slept. Gordon nervously gazed around but didn't see any snakes. He did see another human, though. He blinked in surprise.

Who the hell was *that*?

The other human seemed to be asleep. He was curled in a fetal position with his back to Gordon maybe ten feet away on the same hillside. He was wearing a ratty sweater and a knit watch cap, half unraveled, pulled low over his face. He had his shoes under his head, using them for a pillow. The toes and heels were out of his socks, which prompted Gordon to wonder why he bothered with them at all. Then Gordon realized the man was better off than *he* was. At least he *had* socks and shoes.

Gordon jumped at the sound of footsteps. They scraped across the slope behind him, setting off a tiny avalanche of stones and loose scree that bounced and slid down the hill toward the water. To his left, Gordon saw legs beneath a flowing overcoat climbing down the hillside beside the place where the ground met the bridge. The legs tripped and slid farther down the hill until the upper body of whoever was approaching suddenly ducked into the deeper darkness under the bridge's rumbling metal and concrete undercarriage.

The figure came quickly to Gordon's side and laid a hand on his shoulder. Gordon almost had a heart attack.

In the dim light, he couldn't make out the man's face. He could only distinguish a brown trench coat, battered tennis shoes, and a baseball cap pulled low. The man was holding something in his hand, but Gordon couldn't see what it was.

"Don't!" Gordon spat in fear, shaking off the hand. "What do you want? What are you doing?"

The man leaned in close and pushed his face in front of Gordon's. In the dim light, Gordon still couldn't see the man's features, but he did have enough light to realize the man was holding his finger up to his mouth, signaling for Gordon to be quiet.

"Don't talk," the man whispered. The objects he held in his other hand, he suddenly laid in Gordon's lap. They were Gordon's shoes. His shoes and socks. The man hissed again, barely loud enough for Gordon to make out the words. "Put these back on. Hurry. We have to get out of here. They're coming."

"Who's coming?" Gordon asked, but the man pressed his hand to Gordon's mouth, silencing him.

"Hurry," the man said again.

Something in his voice, in the tense tilt of his head, relayed the urgency of his words to Gordon's sluggish thought processes. Gordon began to realize maybe there really was a danger approaching and that the man was trying to help him. For lack of a better plan, Gordon began pulling on his shoes. He didn't bother with the socks. He was too scared, now. Just the shoes would have to do.

"Good," the man said, seeing that Gordon was finally following orders. And with a last shushing sound, the man in the trench coat crab walked on his hands and feet across the hillside in front of Gordon and approached the man sleeping there.

While Gordon tried to cram his feet into his cold, wet shoes—he must have had them on when he waded in the bay earlier—the man in the trench coat tried to rouse the homeless guy curled up asleep.

The sleeping man shook him off, just as Gordon had done, but he didn't stop there. He cursed and gave the trench-coated guy a shove down the hill. "Get the fuck away from me!" he spat.

Gordon, in the process of tying his laces with trembling fingers, heard the coated guy whisper, "Fool!" Then he turned his attention back to Gordon.

Once again pressing a finger to his lips to urge silence, he took Gordon's hand and led him away down the slope to the rocks below. They slid and tripped and finally came out on level ground at the edge of the bay. They were separated from the water by a jumble of huge, perfectly square blocks of concrete, dumped haphazardly along the beach to thwart erosion, Gordon supposed. He couldn't think of any other reason for the city to go to the trouble of putting them there.

The man in the trench coat continued to clutch Gordon's hand and pull him away from the bridge. As he did, he ducked down, and in his own fear, Gordon followed suit, still not sure what they were running from, but somehow sensing it was the prudent thing to do.

Gordon still could not see the man's face, but he could see he was short, slight, and had a fringe of blond hair that stuck out from the back of his baseball cap. The blond hair hung over the collar of the trench coat, whipped occasionally by the damp wind coming off the bay. Gordon couldn't help noticing the man's attire was in considerably better shape than his own, and since the guy was apparently one of the city's homeless, that was a disturbing realization. If Gordon hadn't been so hungry and scared, he might have blushed at the truth of it.

Hearing voices behind them, the trench-coated man pulled Gordon down into the jumble of concrete blocks, some as big as Volkswagens. When Gordon tried to speak, the man once again shushed him to silence. As they cowered among the stones, the man kept an arm over Gordon's shoulder. Oddly, Gordon was comforted to feel it there. The man was protecting him. Gordon didn't know why, but he sensed whatever was about to happen wasn't going to be good. If this man hadn't pulled him from beneath the bridge, whatever was about to happen would have been happening to Gordon. Somehow Gordon knew this, and he was grateful.

He tried to whisper a soft "thank you," but the man desperately hissed him to silence.

With the chilly bay water lapping at his toes and once again slipping into his shoes, Gordon hunkered down among the rocks, trembling with cold and weakness. He listened to the voices approach. Male voices. Hispanic.

They were laughing now, and it sounded like there were several. Three or four perhaps. The timbre of the voices changed when they ducked beneath the bridge at the very spot where Gordon had been not more than two minutes earlier. They spoke more softly, their words echoing beneath the bridge, almost lost sometimes among the rumble of automobiles passing overhead.

Gordon peered over the stone in front of him, still glad to feel his rescuer's arm protectively draped across his shoulder. He saw the momentary beam of a flashlight stab through the darkness on the dusty slope, then as quickly go out.

It was too dark to see under the bridge where the voices were, but he suddenly heard a bark of laughter and a curse. The laughter was from one of the Hispanics. The curse was from the homeless man who had shaken away the warning to escape.

Suddenly, within another flurry of laughter, Gordon heard the splashing of liquid and another long, sputtering string of curses from the homeless man. He was not cursing in anger now; he was cursing in fear. A tiny spark of light erupted beneath the bridge. It was the striking of a match. The homeless man cried out, "No!" and before the echo of that cry ricocheted over the rocks to Gordon's ears, there was an explosion of light and flame.

Gordon gasped as the homeless man, engulfed in flames, rose to his feet screaming, and just as quickly sank back to the ground in silence. A group of four or five youths stood a few feet away, their backs to Gordon, watching the man's death throes. One of them was tittering with an eerily feminine laugh. Gordon's attention was drawn to the pathetic, silent corpse huddled on the hillside, burning merrily like a bonfire. There was no movement among the flames now, and Gordon knew the man was dead.

The trench-coated man turned away from the spectacle and pressed his face into Gordon's chest. Surprised by the intimacy of the act from the man who had just saved his life, Gordon found himself draping a comforting arm around his savior and holding him close, giving back a little of what the man had given him. He rested his chin against the blond hair at the man's nape and continued to watch as the flames beneath the bridge slowly burned lower.

When the flames were about to sputter out completely, Gordon heard another burst of laughter coming from the killers beneath the bridge. Anger swelled in Gordon at the sound.

Fighting against the anger because he knew he was in no position to do anything about it, he closed his eyes and buried his whole face in the blond man's nape. The man, seeming to understand Gordon's empathy, pulled Gordon closer, still pressing his face to Gordon's chest.

Gordon thought he felt a shudder in the man's body, and then he realized the man was crying in his arms.

Gordon held him tight, and together they listened as a flurry of footsteps receded. Silence returned, and the final crackle of flame blinked into darkness beneath the bridge. In a matter of one or two heartbeats, it was suddenly as if nothing had happened there in the shadows at all. Least of all murder. Once again, only the gentle sound of water lapping at rocks filled the night around him.

When the reek of charred flesh reached him, Gordon closed his eyes against it, but it didn't help. He pushed his rescuer gently to arm's length and pleaded, "Take me away from here. Please."

The blond man nodded, sniffed, and wiped the tears from his face. "Come on, then," he whispered. "I'll take you home."

Surprised, Gordon asked, "*My* home?"

"No," the man said. "Mine."

"Oh," Gordon said. "I thought—"

"Hush."

They waited in silence for five more minutes, and as soon as they were certain they were alone, that the youths were truly gone, the blond man once again took Gordon's hand and led him from their hiding place amid the jumbled blocks of concrete.

"Thank you," Gordon mumbled, and the blond man nodded.

They walked for almost an hour.

Once, when Gordon's strength was about to give out, the blond man stopped beneath a streetlight, causing Gordon to stumble to a halt beside him. The man clutched Gordon's forearms and said, "They killed him."

Gordon nodded. "I know. I'm sorry." He tilted the blond man's baseball cap back off his face and was surprised to see tears in the man's eyes. And with his first good look at his savior's face, he also saw something else.

"I know you," Gordon said as the young man in the oversized trench coat and the ragged tennis shoes with the longish blond hair straggling over his coat collar stared sadly back. "You're the guy from the soup kitchen. The guy those three jerks were picking on. They called you Squirt."

The tiniest smile twisted Squirt's mouth. A tear slid into the corner of it, and Gordon watched in fascination as Squirt licked it away.

"You fed me," he said. "You treated me like I was real."

Gordon was confused by the words. He thought perhaps he had misunderstood. Before he could think of a reply, Squirt spoke again.

"Are *you*?" he asked.

Gordon was more confused than ever. "Am I what?"

"Real."

Gordon stared at the young and innocent face, at the crystal blue eyes gleaming through the fringe of blond hair. They stood in silence under the glow of the streetlight, alone in the night, as if they were the only two souls alive in the city. It was late. Really late. So late it was almost early. The sun would be up soon. On the silent street, there was no traffic, no ambient noise except for a distant siren splitting the night somewhere far behind them. The only nearby sound Gordon could hear at all, other than the beating of his own heart, was the crackle and creak of palm fronds on a tree across the street as it gently swayed in the wind.

Then he turned his head to better hear the far-off siren. Had they found the burnt body? Did the police know a murder had been committed? Were Gordon and the blond man witnesses?

He couldn't think about that now. It was too complicated. Too— unbelievable. He turned back to the gentle man before him.

"Yes," Gordon said. "I'm real. And you saved my life. That means you're real too."

Squirt tilted his head. Now it was his turn to look confused. "Is that what it means?" he asked.

Gordon laid a hand on the blond man's cheek. At the soothing touch, Squirt closed his eyes and leaned his face into Gordon's hand.

"Yes," Gordon said, touched by the tenderness of Squirt's reaction. "Thank you. You're my hero."

Squirt turned away and looked down the street behind them. "I tried to save the other one, but he wouldn't listen." There was a crack in his voice. When he turned back, Gordon saw a renewed spate of tears in his eyes.

"Did you see what the killers looked like?" Gordon asked. "Could you identify them for the police?"

"No," Squirt said. "Could you?"

"No. They were always in shadow or turned away."

Squirt stared at him with wide, hurt-filled eyes. Gordon thought he had never seen a kinder face in his life. Nor one so sad.

"Don't worry," Gordon said, "It wasn't your fault. You tried to help the guy. You did all you could." After a pause, he added, "You did save my life, though. You saved my life and I don't even know your name. Please. Tell me your name."

The man circled Gordon's hands in his own and gave them a squeeze. Releasing one, but maintaining a grip on the other, he continued up the street, pulling Gordon along behind.

"Squirt," he said, straightening his ball cap. "My name is Squirt. You know that."

Gordon followed along, a head taller, probably thirty pounds heavier, and awed by the simple strength in the man who'd saved him. "I know that's what they called you at the kitchen, but I still don't know your *real* name."

The man didn't look back. "Squirt is my real name. Come on. It'll be light soon. We need to get off the street before the sun comes up. People aren't nice in the daylight."

"They aren't?"

"Not to me," Squirt said, and Gordon pressed his lips together, his heart aching for the loneliness he sensed in the man before him.

"Then take me home, Squirt," Gordon said softly.

And Squirt pulled him along, never releasing Gordon's hand.

As they walked, Gordon slid his thumb over the back of Squirt's hand and felt the blond hairs there bend beneath his touch. He liked the sensation of it so he didn't stop stroking.

Once, two blocks farther on, Squirt giggled. "That tickles," he said.

And Gordon smiled.

IN A section of the city called Mission Hills, Gordon followed Squirt along a dark alley to the back of an electrical shop. Squirt led the way down a flight of concrete steps that sank beneath the edge of the alleyway and opened up in a covered underground hallway between buildings. After rummaging around beneath his coat for a moment, Squirt pulled out a key on the end of a long rawhide cord. It must have been attached to his belt.

While Gordon leaned against the brick wall, ready to weep with hunger and exhaustion, Squirt stuck the key in a heavy metal door and gave it a twist. The door opened wide on squeaky hinges. Squirt reached inside and flipped a switch, turning on an interior light.

Gordon heaved himself off the wall and looked over Squirt's shoulder. "You live here?" he asked. "This is your home?"

Squirt grunted "Yes" and stepped inside. Once again he reached behind to grab Gordon's hand and drag him through the door.

The place looked like a warehouse. There was electrical equipment everywhere. Ladders, fat coils of insulated wire, rolls of soldering copper, shelves and shelves of tools, countless bins filled with sockets and screws and light bulbs and a hundred things Gordon couldn't identify—everything, in fact, the business above their heads would need to operate.

"This is the storage place for the people upstairs," Gordon said.

"Yes. They are my friends." Squirt once again reached out and took Gordon's hand. Like a child dragging his father through a candy store, he led Gordon between long aisles of electrical equipment stacked head high on either side.

While Gordon was too weary to argue, he was also looking around for a phone. All he wanted to do was call a cab and go home. He had no money on him—he had checked on the way—but he did have money at his apartment. At least, he was pretty sure he did. If he could get a cab to take him home, he could pay the driver there. There was food at home too, and dammit, he was *starving*. He would walk, but he was pretty sure he didn't have two more steps left in him.

Gordon followed Squirt down one last long aisle with electrical crap piled high on either side, and at the end they turned left. There, in a sort of alcove, was a makeshift bed. Beside it a table lamp sat atop a wooden crate with a flashlight and a splayed-open book beneath it. A couple of movie posters were thumbtacked to the wall behind the bed, and an old dresser stood there that looked as if it had been glommed from someone's trash.

As poor as the living arrangements were, they were neat and clean and precisely arranged. Far neater and cleaner than Gordon's apartment, in fact, and once again Gordon felt a blush creep into his cheeks.

Squirt removed his hat and hung it on a nail beside the bed. He shook out his pale blond hair and shrugged out of his trench coat. Underneath, he wore a long-sleeved dress shirt with red pinstriping that looked to be about three sizes too big. The sleeves were buttoned neatly at the wrists. Unlike Gordon's shirt, Squirt's was clean. At this point in the evening Gordon was too exhausted to care.

Gordon toed the cold wet shoes off his feet.

"Sit," Squirt said.

Since there were no chairs, Gordon opted to sit on the edge of the bed. As quickly as he did, he cried, "Ouch!" and jumped back up.

"Watch out for the doorknob," Squirt said with a grin.

Gordon pulled the bedclothes away from the edge of the bed and looked underneath. Not only was there no mattress, there was no bed either. It was a discarded door resting on four concrete blocks, with six or seven heavy blankets spread out over it to serve as a mattress.

Gordon rubbed his butt and gave Squirt a sheepish grin. "You have every tool known to man in this place. Why don't you remove the doorknob?"

Squirt shrugged. "I like it there."

"Oh."

"Sit," Squirt said again, and this time Gordon did it with a little more care. As soon as he was comfortable, Squirt sat down beside him.

They sat quietly like that for a scattering of heartbeats, thighs and elbows touching. Both were weary from their long walk and their experiences of the evening. With his tired bare feet flat on the floor and his rear end not so enthralled by Squirt's hard-ass bed, Gordon turned to his host.

"Thank you again," Gordon said.

Squirt merely nodded, then his face brightened. "You hungry? I've got crackers."

Gordon couldn't think of anything he'd rather have, except maybe a shitload of Quarter Pounders with Cheese, but since hamburgers weren't an option, he said, "That would be great."

Squirt reached under the bed and dragged out a black trash bag. He carefully untied the string holding it closed and reached into the bag like Santa about to bestow a gift. He hauled out a simple box of Saltines. Unopened. Then he pulled out a gigantic jar of peanut butter, and Gordon almost passed out in bliss.

"Thank God," he breathed, making Squirt giggle again.

Squirt pulled out a couple of paper plates, two plastic knives, and warm sodas. When it was all laid out before them, Gordon thought he had never seen such a wonderful feast in his life.

"I fed you, now you're feeding me," Gordon said. "Makes us even."

"Does it?" Squirt asked.

Gordon grinned. "Well—as soon as I save your life like you saved mine tonight. Then it will."

Squirt's eyes took on a distant cast. He was remembering. Gordon could see it on his face.

"Poor man," Squirt said. "To die like that."

Gordon nodded. He was remembering now too. The mocking laughter, the crackle of flames, the screams. The smell of burnt flesh.

Still with a faraway look on his face, Squirt softly said, "I think those guys will go to hell for what they did."

Gordon was struck by the simplicity and innocence in the statement. He could also think of no earthly reason to deny the truth of Squirt's words.

"Yes," he said. "I'm sure they will."

"Then they'll burn too. That's called karma." Squirt spoke the word awkwardly, as if he had just learned it and this was the first time it had crossed his lips.

"Karma indeed," Gordon whispered, staring down at Squirt's hand, which the man had just rested on his knee. Gordon laid his own hand over it. "We're safe now, Squirt. You don't have to be afraid anymore."

Squirt nodded. "I know. I'm home. I'm safe."

Gordon looked around the tiny space. "Yes. You're home."

Gazing back at Squirt, Gordon finally spoke the words he had been thinking ever since they left the bridge. "We'll have to tell the police, you know. We have to report the murder."

Squirt turned his stunning blue eyes to Gordon's face, and Gordon found himself lost in their depths.

The stubble of blond beard on Squirt's chin looked as soft as down. Gordon longed to reach out and touch it. So he did. Squirt smiled, obviously enjoying the feel of Gordon's fingertips trailing down his jaw. He did not pull away.

Instead, he said, "Why? I didn't see the killers' faces. Did you?"

"No," Gordon admitted. "But that man. Somebody has to tell the authorities where he is."

Squirt seemed to find that an odd thing for Gordon to say. "He isn't there anymore. He's in heaven. Don't you think he's in heaven?"

"Well—I certainly hope so. After the terrible way he died."

They both sat in silence while the horror of what they had witnessed once again raged through them. But even horror is no match for hunger.

Gordon focused his attention on the food. Right now that was all he could think about. He would consider the police problem later.

He slathered peanut butter over a cracker, slapped another cracker on top of it, and shoved the whole thing into his mouth. Squirt laughed, watching him, then he did the same. They sat there like that for the longest time, eating, crunching crackers, slurping at their warm sodas. Gordon was surprised how comfortable he was in Squirt's presence, as if their friendship had started years ago rather than hours. Squirt seemed to feel the same way.

When the crackers were gone, Gordon asked about a bathroom. Squirt pointed him back the way they had come. Gordon once again weaved his way down the long aisle between shelves of tools. The bathroom was on the opposite side of the door they had entered through.

It was a business bathroom. Tiny. There was no shower or tub, but Gordon found everything else he needed there. Soap, water, paper towels. He stripped down to nothing and bathed himself with a paper towel dripping with soapy water. He dabbed carefully around his skinned knees, blotting up the crusted blood, then dried himself off with another fistful of paper towels. He wished he had a toothbrush, but he didn't, so he made do with rinsing his mouth repeatedly with cold water from the tap.

When he was as clean as he was going to get, he redonned his filthy trousers. The T-shirt he couldn't bear to pull over his head, so he threw it in the wastebasket. With a final wad of paper towels, he wiped down the sink and mirror and cleaned up the mess he had made. Shoes in hand, he wound his way through the aisles again, returning to Squirt's humble abode.

Squirt was still sitting on the edge of his makeshift bed, waiting for him. When Gordon approached, Squirt patted the bed beside him, then stretched himself out on top of the covers that doubled as a mattress. In his wrinkled jeans and too-large dress shirt, Gordon realized Squirt was dressed just as he had been the first time Gordon had seen him at Mama's Soup Kitchen. While Gordon was in the bathroom, Squirt had removed his shoes and socks. His feet were lean with long, sturdy toes. They looked strong and competent and somehow elegant. A forest of leg hair peeked out above Squirt's ankles beneath the hem of his pants, as pale as the hair on his head.

With a gentle smile, Squirt patted the bed again, inviting Gordon to join him. He didn't seem surprised Gordon had returned to him half-naked. "Sleep," he said. "Stay with me."

So in only his filthy jeans, Gordon lay on the narrow bed beside his new friend, pressed up close because there was no room to do anything else. And as soon as his head was on the bed, he relaxed completely. His exhaustion took over from that moment on. Even the hardness of the bed wasn't enough to interrupt how good it felt to finally get off his feet.

He closed his eyes, and when he did, Squirt laid a pale, beautiful hand atop Gordon's midriff. He snuggled close to Gordon's body and rested his head on Gordon's chest.

Surprised, Gordon looked down at him. He felt the stirring of Squirt's breath brush the hair on his chest. Felt the weight of Squirt's warm hand pressing gently on his stomach. With his hat off, Gordon could see how long Squirt's pale blond hair really was. It was straight as string, without a wave in it, sort of like Kevin Bacon's, only blonder.

Gordon gently pushed the hair back from Squirt's face to better see him. When he did, those crystal blue eyes opened wide and gazed innocently up at him. Gordon gave him a wink, and Squirt smiled a pleasant smile.

"What?" he asked.

"Nothing," Gordon said. "Go to sleep."

Squirt closed his eyes once again and burrowed his face even closer to Gordon's naked chest. He did it as a child might have done it—in innocence and apparently without a shred of ulterior motive. He did not seem sexually curious, nor particularly interested in Gordon's body. He merely clutched Gordon as a child might do.

And soon he slept. Gordon could tell by the way Squirt's breathing deepened, the way his long blond lashes stopped trembling. A stillness settled over the man that Gordon found astonishing. It was almost as if the horrors of the night had not occurred at all.

Gently, so as not to disturb him, Gordon lifted his head from the bed and pressed his lips to Squirt's hair. He bestowed a kiss on the man for saving his life, although Squirt did not open his eyes to accept it.

When he bestowed a second kiss, the faintest of smiles graced Squirt's mouth. Even in sleep he seemed to enjoy Gordon's touch.

Gordon dropped his head back and tried to relax. He was startled by a surge of desire that passed through his body, settling in his groin. The desire was centered on the man draped against him. But even that surprising rush of sexual hunger was not enough to keep Gordon awake.

Wearied beyond belief, he was asleep in less than fifteen seconds.


WHEN GORDON awoke, he was alone. He looked around for Squirt, but the man was nowhere to be found. Beside the makeshift bed on an upturned bucket lay a fresh T-shirt, neatly folded. Atop the T-shirt sat two crisp one-dollar bills and two quarters.

Gordon gratefully pulled the T-shirt over his head. It was a little tight, but it fit. He stared dumbly at the money, wondering what he was supposed to do with it. Then it dawned on him.

*Bus fare is two-fifty. Squirt left me bus fare to get home.*

After quickly gathering up his shoes and slipping them over his feet, Gordon made his way to the door leading out to the alley. He was surprised to find another day darkening to twilight around him as he exited. He had slept all day.

Once again he was starving, but now he could go home. He cast a prayer of thanks skyward, hoping somehow Squirt would know it was really meant for him. He carefully locked the alley door behind him and set off for the nearest bus stop.

As he waited there, avoiding the eyes of the people around him because he knew how bad he looked, Gordon still could not completely erase the smile from his face.

The smile came from the memory of the time he had spent with Squirt.

It would not dawn on Gordon until later that this was the first time he had been pulled from his own misery since the night of the accident.

From one night of death to another—from one mangled body twisted in wreckage to another silent body smoking in the dirt, and with a year and a half of heartbreak between them, Gordon suddenly felt an urge to move on. Maybe to reclaim his life.

And it was all because of Squirt.

Standing at the bus stop, Gordon closed his eyes and focused his thoughts away from the fact that he looked like hell and probably smelled like a goat, fully justifying the leery looks being thrown his way. When he did, the first memory to claw its way to the surface was the feel of Squirt's warm breath against his naked chest.

The second realization that came to Gordon was that this was the first day in a year and a half when he hadn't tasted a drop of alcohol. He supposed he had Squirt to thank for that as well.

But more than anything, if not for Squirt, Gordon knew he too would be lying dead under that bridge—a smoldering, gay charcoal briquette.

And a debt like that must be repaid.

He stood at the bus stop wondering how to go about doing that. How could he show Squirt his gratitude? What could Gordon do for the young man? After a while, an idea struck him. Then another. His face gradually brightened. Surprised by his own sudden burst of enthusiasm, he thought he felt a grin creep across his face. He turned to a storefront window to get a glimpse of it and make sure it was really there. Wow. It really, really was.

When the bus finally rumbled to a stop in front of him, Gordon climbed the steps humming. It had been so long since he had heard himself hum the sound was alien to his ears.

# CHAPTER 5

BACK AT his apartment, Gordon first brushed his teeth, then he stripped off his filthy jeans and collapsed naked on the bed. Again, he was asleep in seconds. He awoke at dawn the following morning, refreshed but a little groggy from so much sleep.

Gordon's first waking thought was of the horrible event that transpired beneath the bridge. Not knowing exactly what he should do about it, he called Mama to tell her he wasn't well and needed the day off. She sounded suspicious, but really had no alternative but to agree.

With that weight lifted, Gordon took a long hot shower, shaved, brushed his teeth until he thought maybe they were going to fall out if he didn't stop, then dressed in clean clothes for the first time in three days. He ate a big breakfast with everything he could find in the cupboard that was edible, and then, after opening all the windows to let in the fresh air, Gordon set about cleaning his neglected apartment. Finding a pint of gin under a sofa cushion, he threw it in the trash before giving himself a chance to think about it.

In his bedroom, he stripped the bed and applied clean sheets. While he was doing that, he plugged in his cell phone to recharge it for the first time in weeks.

As he washed up the disgusting pile of vomit-covered dishes in the kitchen sink, he played the TV in the background, wondering if there would be news of the killing under the bridge. He knew he would have to call the police soon, at least to inform them a murder had been committed, in case they didn't already know. But he was hesitant. There would be a lot of questions about why he was under the bridge at that hour. Why he ran instead of trying to help the victim. How he could watch a man set on fire without trying to intervene.

And questions about who he was with at the time.

That last possibility frightened him the most. He didn't want to drag Squirt into this. The man was too fragile, too shy. And really, what could Squirt tell the police Gordon couldn't? Neither of them had seen the faces of the killers. Neither of them knew the assailants' identities. Neither of them could make an identification or pull a face out of a lineup.

But most importantly, how would Squirt cope with the attention? Gordon wasn't sure why Squirt lived the life he lived, what damage had been done to him that brought him down so low in the world, but whatever it was, Gordon felt the need to protect him from any further damage.

Squirt was perhaps the sweetest person Gordon had ever met. Sweet and childlike. And he had saved Gordon's life, for Christ's sake. How would it be to repay him by dragging him into the news and scaring the hell out of him, making him the center of attention?

Three times Gordon snatched up his now fully charged cell phone to call the cops, and three times he changed his mind. What had he really seen in the shadows under the bridge? What could he really tell the police? When he analyzed the question, the inescapable answer was always—*nothing*. He could tell them nothing. Except the location of the body.

Gordon finally admitted the truth to himself. Even if the location of the body was all he knew, he still had to make the call.

For the fourth and final time, he reached for the phone.

And as if God really was up there lending a hand now and then, Gordon's problem was suddenly solved when he saw a report pop up on the noon news. With the Coronado Bridge as a backdrop, one of the local newsmen told of the murder near Chicano Park of a homeless man who was as yet unidentified.

Gordon stopped what he was doing and stared at the TV, soaking in every word. As the reporter told of the arrest of four Chicano youths on suspicion of the slaying, Gordon breathed a sigh of relief for the first time since the murder took place.

They had the killers in custody! They not only knew about the body, they had also caught the killers! Thank God. Maybe he wouldn't have to do anything after all. Justice was being served without him.

The news flattened Gordon with relief. He collapsed onto the couch still wearing his Playtex rubber gloves, a dish towel draped across his shoulder. He buried his face in his hands and almost wept. Until that moment, Gordon had not known how torn up he was about the situation he and Squirt had somehow landed themselves in.

Then his thoughts settled again on Squirt. He lifted his eyes and stared through the living room window at the blazing daylight outside. Squirt was out there right now. Gordon wondered what he was doing. He wondered if he should take a run back into Mission Hills and knock on that alleyway door. And if he did, he wondered if Squirt would answer.

Gordon would like to see him again. Make sure Squirt was all right after the shitty night they had shared. Pay him back the bus fare. Return his shirt. Perhaps try to build an actual friendship.

And at that thought Gordon smiled a wry smile. Wouldn't his mother be thrilled to know her son was broadening his social horizons to include the homeless? Yeah. She'd be chuckling for days over that.

But then Gordon remembered the feel of Squirt's hand encompassing his. The soft, erotic thrill of Squirt's gentle breath stirring the hair on Gordon's chest as they lay on that god-awful hardass bed while trying to unwind after their horrific adventure.

Gordon remembered the cool blue of Squirt's innocent eyes, the soft blond down on the back of his hands, the smell of his hair when Gordon pressed his lips to Squirt's scalp as they lay in each other's arms. The surprise he had felt at the cleanliness of the man. In fact, he had smelled about a bazillion times better than Gordon. And even now he was ashamed to think about it.

Gordon glanced at the clock. It was midafternoon. He tried to imagine what Squirt would be feeling now, what he was thinking. Was he hungry? Was he searching for food? After all, he and Gordon had inhaled all the peanut butter and crackers, and Gordon hadn't seen any other food lying around Squirt's tiny cubicle.

And what about money? While Squirt might have a place to sleep, he was still, for all intents and purposes, homeless. How much money could he have? Hell, maybe the two and a half bucks he gave Gordon for bus fare was all the money he had in the world. It would be like Squirt to offer his last dollar to help someone else. Somehow Gordon knew that for a fact, even if he *didn't* know Squirt very well.

Squirt was not only physically beautiful, but he had a beautiful heart.

And speaking of hearts, Gordon's own heart suddenly began to race. He had to see him! He had to see Squirt! Today? No. Tomorrow. Maybe Squirt would come to the soup kitchen for breakfast. Maybe Gordon would see him there. And seeing Squirt, Gordon could ask to meet him later, when Gordon's shift was over. Maybe spend some time with him. He could thank Squirt yet again for saving his life. And maybe he could even try to figure out how to help Squirt get his life back in order.

And maybe by doing that, Gordon could take a step toward getting his *own* life in order.

If he and Squirt could wade through all those maybes, maybe they really *could* lend each other a hand. Aside from becoming friends, maybe they could go all the way and actually turn their lives around. And wouldn't *that* be a fucking miracle!

And if they couldn't go so far as to resurrect their ruined lives, maybe they could at least find comfort in each other's company. Gordon would like that. Gordon would like that very much. He felt an attraction to Squirt that was kind of weird in its intensity. Even he was willing to admit that. And he thought he understood why.

While he and Squirt were both wounded souls, Squirt had somehow managed to cure his wounds. Those wounds may have damaged Squirt's exterior life, but inside, inside his heart and mind where a person's true character lies, his wounds were healed. Squirt had come to grips with the damage done to him, whatever it was. He had risen above it and still managed to hold onto his inner goodness—his inner well of decency and compassion and kindness.

Gordon's wounds, on the other hand, had not healed at all. Even Gordon's year in county jail had not eased him of guilt as he thought it would. Sometimes, it seems, even punishment and atonement are not enough. In that horrible place, with the endless, silent days plodding along one after the other, guilt simply festered. It ate away at your soul until it strangled the very life out of you. Gordon's guilt had been incarcerated with him. Inside those walls and behind those bars, Gordon's guilt had been inescapable. Just as inescapable as it was now.

No. Just as it was *until* now. *Until* Squirt stumbled into his life.

Squirt had somehow made peace with his wounds. He had learned to heal. He had found the secret. Maybe he could teach Gordon the secret too.

There was an instinctual truth to Gordon's—*well, let's call it what it is,* he told himself—with Gordon's *infatuation* with Squirt. That instinctual truth was this: with Squirt nearby, Gordon was a better person. A happier person. Squirt's goodness and sense of peace radiated outward, encompassing and overshadowing even Gordon's heartache. And now, with Squirt no longer nearby, Gordon felt lost again. He felt empty. Like a doper in desperate need of a fix.

Gordon could feel his guilt moving in to reclaim him. His guilt at taking a human life. Jeremy. Jeremy Aldritch Booth. Twenty-four years old. His life lost because of Gordon's stupidity. Gordon squeezed his eyes shut, pushing the young man's tombstone from his mind, trying not to remember. Trying not to recall the smell of cut grass. The ivy on the cemetery fence. The weeds in the sidewalk. The corpses rotting to ruin underground.

It was the other memories, the other sensations, that were not so easily swept aside. Trying not to hear the screams on that long-ago night, the screams he still could not identify as his own or someone else's. Trying not to listen yet again to that mind-jarring clash of metal. That shattering of glass. That awful feeling of vertigo as the world spun in upheaval at the moment his car flipped around him, turning the universe upside down. The sight of his cell phone tumbling through the air, the unfinished text message still gleaming on the screen, never to be completed. The smell of gas and hot metal as Gordon crawled from the wreckage, miraculously unscathed. The rough asphalt beneath his hands, the uncaring moon still beaming overhead. Approaching the other car with the two men inside on wobbly legs. One man weeping in fear and confusion on the opposite side of the car where Gordon couldn't see him. The other man nearby, lifeless in the driver's seat.

Jeremy Aldritch Booth. Dead on impact. His handsome young face dripping blood as it rested on the window ledge. His brown eyes staring out at the night, at Gordon, in sightless accusation.

Because of Gordon. All because of Gordon.

Gordon gave himself a shake to clear the images from his head. Impatiently wiping hot tears from his cheeks, he desperately pushed back the memories and tried to refocus his mind on Squirt. Gentle Squirt with the white-blond hair and the expressive hands. The simple way he lived his life. The kindness. The sweet smile and heart-stopping beauty. The childlike innocence.

Gordon gave a deep, shuddering sigh, expending all his effort to center his thought on Squirt's face. On Squirt's goodness. And it was as if Squirt helped him do it, pulling Gordon's thoughts toward him. Bringing Gordon closer to Squirt's heat, letting Gordon gather strength and comfort from it.

A moment later, Gordon felt a smile twist his face. If he had harbored any doubts before about the wisdom of what he was about to do, that unexpected smile on his own countenance knocked it into next week.

So. It was settled, then. Tomorrow for sure. Gordon would make the first overture toward friendship *tomorrow*. One way or another, he would worm his way into Squirt's life. Because somehow, that was very important. Somehow, Gordon thought his very survival might hinge on it.

Unbidden, his mind travelled to the gun in the bathroom drawer. He squeezed his eyes shut tight, trying to push the thought away. He forced himself to focus on anything but that.

So. At breakfast. Gordon would talk to Squirt at breakfast. At the soup kitchen.

And it would be that small ray of hope for tomorrow that would carry Gordon through the rest of the day.

That night he went to bed early on clean sheets, and for the first time in months, he went to bed sober. The last thought that touched his mind before sleep overtook him was Squirt's easy smile and crystal clear eyes, as innocent and blue as a California sky. Both exhibited such innocence, such clarity of goodness, it was almost heartbreaking to contemplate them.

And Squirt's warm breath. Caressing Gordon's chest. That was hard to contemplate too. Such hunger welled up inside Gordon's heart when he remembered it, hunger and *desire,* that he pressed his hands to his eyes until the memory passed.

Gordon's sleep was bottomless and deep that night. Once, in a dream, he called Squirt's name. It was long past midnight. He heard his own voice and briefly awoke, but soon drifted off again.

By morning Gordon's dream was forgotten. But Squirt was not.

Squirt filled his mind yet again the moment Gordon opened his eyes.

GORDON WASN'T inside the soup kitchen more than two minutes that morning when Mama Davis descended on him like a great bird of prey, wings outstretched, braids clacking. She grabbed him by the shoulders and gripped them tight as she bored her eyes into his. A smile played at her lips, offering him a glimpse of those boxy, white teeth that looked capable of gnawing down a tree. She emitted a *tut* of happiness, gave him a gentle shake, then released his shoulders. Laying one cool, papery hand to each of his cheeks, she leaned in and gave him a hug. He caught a whiff of Juicy Fruit gum.

"Honey, I thought you were sick?" she asked, pulling back but still holding on, not letting Gordon escape. "But you don't look sick. You didn't drink last night either. I can tell. And you're smiling. This is the first morning in all the months you've worked here that you walked through that door smiling. And without a hangover too. And don't look so surprised. I've been around alcoholics my whole life. I know one when I see him."

Gordon almost gasped. "I'm not an alcoholic."

And Mama gave her smile free rein. "No, honey. For the first time since I've known you, I have to say maybe you're not. What happened? Did you find God, honey? Is He the one who wrought this change in you? Is He the one who made you smile again? He can, you know. He's got it in Him to do that. Oh, yes indeed He does. Tell me, honey, please. Did you find God?"

People were watching the two of them. Gordon could see them trying not to stare, but staring nevertheless. Oddly, Gordon didn't care.

He felt a familiar blush rise to his face, but he didn't care about that either. While Mama stood before him with her papery soft hands pressed to his cheeks, Gordon laid his own hands over hers. To his own amazement, he felt tears burning his eyes.

"Maybe I did find God," Gordon said. "Or the next best thing."

Mama Davis tilted her head, her own eyes misting up now. "What's the next best thing to God, honey? Tell me. I wanna know."

"A friend," Gordon said. "The next best thing to God is a friend."

Mama stared at him in silence for a good ten seconds before slipping her hands out from under his. She yanked a handkerchief from her sleeve and blew her nose with a honk. When she was finished and the handkerchief had once again mysteriously disappeared up her sleeve, she reached out and brushed a tear from Gordon's cheek with her spidery fingertips.

"Keep your new friend close, honey. Don't let him get away. If he can make this change in you then he's got some goodness in him, and that's a fact. Bring him to me sometime. Will you do that? I'd dearly love to meet a powerful soul like that."

"I promise," Gordon said. "I will."

She chucked him gently under the chin. "Good," she said in a fervent whisper. "Now go to work, Gordon. You've got the eggs this morning. And don't overserve. We may not have enough."

Not sure he had a voice left with which to speak, Gordon simply nodded and headed for the steam table, his eyes already fixed on the front door. Looking for a short blond man wearing a trench coat and baseball cap.

It never occurred to him Squirt might not show up at all.

When that turned out to be the case, rather than let it plummet Gordon into depression, it reaffirmed his commitment to get to know Squirt better. And to help the man if he could.


GORDON HAD a free hour between his morning and afternoon shift. He spent the hour roaming the downtown streets and wishing he had time to race up to Mission Hills and rap on a certain alleyway door. He wasn't particularly worried that Squirt hadn't shown up for breakfast at the soup kitchen, although he was disappointed. On the other hand, it gave Gordon time to run a couple of errands that needed to be done before he saw Squirt again, hopefully at the afternoon meal.

His first stop was at the bank, where he pulled three hundred dollars from his savings account. His second stop was Macy's, where he spent the rest of his lunch hour buying shirts and socks and underwear and a couple of pairs of jeans that he thought Squirt might fit into. When he returned to the soup kitchen for the second meal, Gordon stashed his Macy's bags out of the way and went about doing his job, certain this time he would see Squirt come walking through the door.

But as the long serving line snailed its way past and the voices and racket of metal utensils on tin trays swelled around him, Gordon's hopes gradually sank. When Mama locked the outside doors and declared dinner hour over, Gordon knew his worst fear had been realized. Squirt hadn't shown up again.

As Gordon filled the trays of the last straggling diners that Mama had let in before locking the doors behind them, he made plans for what he would do next. He would hop a bus to Mission Hills and deliver the clothes to Squirt personally. That was better than giving them to him here in front of everyone anyway.

A blast of snide laughter caught his attention as the serving line dwindled down to nothing. Gordon looked up at the last bodies wending their way toward him, partially filled trays in hand. His heart sank even deeper than it had been already. This was the last thing he needed.

The three gays who had tormented Squirt the week before were horsing around and complaining about the look of the food and making a general nuisance of themselves, just as they always did. They suddenly seemed to brighten up when they saw Gordon ladling up potatoes au gratin just a few feet down the line.

They snickered among themselves, then centered all their attention on Gordon as they dawdled in front of him.

The three youths were handsome young men, or would have been had they not been so worn down by living on the streets. Still, Gordon could see how certain men would find them attractive enough to pay for their services. And truthfully, their services didn't cost that much. Gay hustlers were a dime a dozen on the streets of San Diego. All you had to do was know where to find them.

While, like Squirt, these three also looked as if they tried to keep themselves clean, there was none of the innocence on their faces that Gordon had seen on Squirt's face. There was none of the kindness in these eyes that Gordon had seen in Squirt's. In fact, there was a coldness on their faces that Gordon could not quite put a finger on, yet could feel the moment they centered their attention on him. Perhaps it was just the worn-down look all prostitutes gradually acquire. The jaded, weary sense of defeat and the slow realization that the world around them is not much better than they are, and that one pretty much deserves the other.

It saddened Gordon to think boys this young could have already come to live their lives in the presence of desperation and not even realize it had taken control of them. But it was there. It was there in the bark of mirthless laughter, the flinty gleam of a cruel eye, the resigned acceptance of whatever life was about to deal out.

When they reached Gordon's place in the line, Gordon almost winced at the chilly, merciless way they scrutinized him. But it was the words they spoke that truly tore at his heart.

The leader was a redhead with freckles and a shirt unbuttoned to his belly button, exposing pale flesh, obviously for sale to the highest bidder. Or maybe even the lowest.

"Well, here he is," Redhead smirked. "Batman. Protector of the downtrodden. Squirt's number one fan. Where's your little blond friend? Home in bed, waiting for Daddy to come home and plow him a new furrow?"

Gordon narrowed his eyes and said, "Just keep the line moving, tough guys. There are others behind you waiting to eat."

One of the other hustlers, a boy who looked about fifteen and who was obviously in the middle of an appalling acne outbreak, but whose body was still beautiful and lithe, prodded Redhead with an elbow. "You know better than that. Squirt's not wallowing in this guy's bed. He's down at the police station getting the shit grilled out of him." He grinned an evil grin when he saw Gordon snap to attention. The kid lowered his voice, one conspirator to another. "I heard it's somethin' serious too. Like murder maybe." Then he howled with laughter.

Gordon's heart leaped into his throat. He dropped his ladle in the potatoes and leaned over the sneeze guard, grabbing Pizza Face's shirtfront and dragging him close. "What the hell are you talking about?"

Pizza Face might have been no more than fifteen, but he had been on the streets long enough to know not to show fear. He gazed coolly at Gordon even while Gordon was dragging him over the sneeze guard and practically into the vat of steaming potatoes.

He looked down at Gordon's fist clutching his shirtfront. "You're wrinkling the merchandise. If you want to manhandle me, you have to pay for the privilege."

Gordon pulled him even closer. "Tell me again what you just said or you'll be digging potatoes out of your ears for the next three weeks."

Redhead and Pizza Face's other friend, a skinny hustler with greenish-blond streaks in his hair that looked like they had been applied with Clorox, were chuckling at Pizza Face's discomfort. They also looked properly impressed with Gordon's butchness. Redhead even reached out and stroked Gordon's bicep. He looked like he enjoyed what he was feeling.

Gordon released Pizza Face and shook off Redhead's hand, repelled by his touch. Redhead snickered and reassumed his role as leader of the pack.

"Your buddy's down at police headquarters, dipshit. Saw him escorted in by two detectives. Word on the street is he had something to do with the old guy who went up like a Roman candle a couple of nights ago down by the bay. You should pick your friends more carefully."

"And you should shut the fuck up," Gordon barked, causing all three of the teens to burst into laughter.

Gordon turned away from the steam table and headed for the door. Mama Davis watched him go. He turned back at the last moment and shot her an inquisitive look across the hall. She smiled a worried smile and waved him on, mouthing the words, "See you tomorrow. Don't worry, honey. I'll lock your bags in the office."

Gordon tapped his heart in thank you. In his desperation, he had almost forgotten about the clothes he had bought for Squirt. With everything under control behind him, he turned and raced through the door, his mind filled with dread.

*Shit. What the hell did the police want with Squirt?*

# CHAPTER 6

SAN DIEGO Police Headquarters was only a few blocks from the soup kitchen, just up Broadway on 16th Street. Gordon was there in ten minutes. He stood outside the front door for a minute, sweating from the run, trying to ignore the rush of terror building behind his eyes.

The terror came from remembering. Remembering the last time he was here. In handcuffs. Confused, frightened, knowing he had just fucked up his life forever. And if all that wasn't bad enough—knowing he had just killed a man.

Simply thinking those last five words brought the old familiar shame and regret thundering through Gordon again. His hands began to shake. His pulse hammered inside his head. He sucked in a great gulp of hot afternoon air, pushed the hair from his face, and tried to block the memories from his mind. It wasn't easy. Those feelings, those memories, had controlled him so long, they were a part of him now. He felt almost empty when they *weren't* inside his head.

Gordon braced himself and lunged forward.

He stormed through the front door and realized immediately he didn't remember the place at all. Then he knew why. The arresting officer almost two years earlier had brought Gordon in through the basement after taking him into custody at the accident site. Gordon had never seen this part of the building before. Even when he left, hours later, again in cuffs, he had exited the building through the basement, where a squad car waited to haul him down to the county jail compound on Front Street, where he would await the filing of charges, and where he would ultimately spend the next year of his life.

He gave himself a final shake in yet another attempt to shed his thoughts and gazed around. He spotted an information desk manned by a female police officer with a bandaged hand. There was no one else in the lobby, and the officer looked bored out of her mind. Since there was nothing else to look at, she centered her attention on Gordon and watched as he approached.

Gordon cringed beneath her stare because he knew, he just knew, what was coming. He knew because he had been living with it ever since his release from jail over a year ago. So when the old familiar light of recognition registered in the officer's eyes, he wasn't surprised. He wasn't surprised by the first words out of her mouth either.

"You used to be the weatherman. Channel 10."

She spoke the words without a smile. She remembered. She remembered everything. Gordon could see that in her eyes too. After all, his trial had been slathered all over the local news shows. He had been a celebrity of sorts once. People love to see celebrities have the rug yanked out from under them.

The officer's eyes were icy. There was no warmth in her voice when she asked, "What can I do for *you*?"

She spoke to him as if he were dirt beneath her feet. But Gordon was used to that too. That's how cops always talk to felons. In a cop's eyes, once a felon, always a felon. If you had a police record, cops rated you just below pond scum. And you retained that rating until you were six feet underground.

He girded himself against the woman's spiteful indifference as he had learned to do time and time again, and concentrated on the words coming out of his mouth.

He again pushed the hair from his eyes—a nervous gesture more than anything. "A friend of mine has been arrested, but it's all a misunderstanding. He didn't do what you guys think he did."

The officer fiddled with the bandage on her hand, seeming to concentrate more on it than on Gordon. She still looked bored shitless. "And what is it we think he did?"

God, Gordon hated cops. He was pretty sure anyone who ever had the misfortune to come under their thumb hated cops. He also wasn't dumb enough to blurt out the fact he and Squirt might know something about the killing under the bridge. Hell, for all he knew, the three twits at the soup kitchen might have got it all wrong and Squirt was actually here for an entirely different matter. If he was here at all.

When Gordon ignored her question, the officer gave him a suspicious look, went through the motions of stifling a yawn like she was speaking to an idiot, and asked, "What's your friend's name?" She painstakingly tapped a few keys on the keyboard in front of her and momentarily turned her eyes to the computer monitor, waiting for Gordon's response.

Gordon blinked. He could feel the blood rushing to his face. My God, he didn't know Squirt's real name! He had no *idea* what it was.

Exasperated, the officer tore her eyes from the monitor and leveled them coolly at Gordon. "Well? Does he have a name? I can't look him up in the system without a name. I'm not cleared for clairvoyance. I have to do stuff the hard way."

Gordon stammered some nonsensical response. Later he wouldn't be able to remember what it was. He finally mumbled, "I'm sorry. I made a mistake."

He stepped away from the desk just as an elevator beeped somewhere off to the right. He turned to see who it was, really for no other reason than simply to avoid the gaze of the cop on the desk. He watched the elevator door slide open even while he walked on shaky legs toward the exit, hoping for a dignified retreat and probably failing miserably. Halfway there, he stopped as if someone had nailed his feet to the floor.

The man stepping off the elevator was Squirt, dressed in khaki slacks that had seen better days, and a black, long-sleeved T-shirt that appeared brand new. It still bore the horizontal wrinkles from the packaging it came in. On his feet, Squirt wore the same disintegrating tennis shoes he had worn the other night. As usual, a Chargers baseball cap perched atop his head, the brim pulled low over his face.

Squirt was accompanied by another man. A cop in a business suit. Gordon instinctively knew the cop was a detective. And if Gordon had to make a guess, probably with Homicide.

Amazingly, the detective had his hand resting on Squirt's shoulder, not in an *apprehension* sort of way, but more friendly-like. He was smiling, while Squirt's expression was hidden by his ever-present baseball cap.

Gordon halted a few feet from the main entrance and waited for Squirt to see him there. While he waited, Squirt and the detective stopped only a few feet away. The detective held out his hand and Squirt shyly took it into his own.

"Thanks for coming in, Jerry. You did the right thing." With his other hand, the detective patted Squirt's shoulder and said, "Take care of yourself, okay? If I need you, I know where to find you. And if you think of anything else, ask for Detective Browning. That's me."

Squirt nodded but didn't say anything. The detective released his hand and turned to reenter the elevator. A moment later the elevator door beeped again, and the cop was gone. Only then did Squirt look up and see Gordon standing by the door.

Squirt's face lit up with a surprised smile. "Gordon," he said, so softly Gordon could barely make out the word.

The smile on Squirt's face eased Gordon's fears considerably. In fact, it caused another rush of blood to suffuse Gordon's cheeks. He stepped quickly to Squirt's side and gave him a hug.

From the corner of his eye, Gordon saw the female officer at the desk shake her head in disgust, but Gordon didn't care. Fuck her. He took Squirt's hand and gently led him toward the exit.

Only when they were standing outside, did Gordon drag Squirt to a halt and duck down to look under the brim of his cap.

"You okay?" Gordon asked. "Why were you here?"

Squirt spoke softly, as he always did. He wore a slight smile on his face, still astounded, perhaps, that Gordon was there waiting for him. "I came because of the man under the bridge. The police needed to know what I saw. It wasn't much, but I still thought they needed to know. Did I do wrong?"

"N-no. Of course not. It was the right thing to do. So what did they say?"

Squirt gave a tiny shrug. "They just said thanks."

"That was it?"

Squirt nodded. "Uh-huh."

"They didn't try to arrest you?"

Squirt ran his fingers over the stubble on his chin as if contemplating the question. "Why would they do that?"

"I don't know."

"Did you tell them I was with you?"

Squirt shook his head. "Didn't figure they needed to know."

Before Gordon could respond to that, Squirt reached out and almost absentmindedly ran his hand along Gordon's bare forearm. Gordon tingled at the touch. "Did you get home all right the other day, Gordon?"

Gordon smiled, laying his hand over Squirt's while it still rested on his wrist. "Yes, thanks to you." Now that they were together, Gordon didn't want to let Squirt go. Not yet. In fact, he suddenly knew exactly what he wanted to do.

"I have something for you."

Squirt's blue eyes twinkled happily. "You mean like a Christmas present?"

"Yeah," Gordon smiled back. "Several of them. Let's go pick them up, and then I want you to come to my apartment for dinner. Will you do that?"

Squirt shrugged again. "Sure," he said. "Why wouldn't I? I'm really, really hungry."

Gordon grinned. "Good."

Gordon was again taken by the way Squirt simplified everything right down to the bare bones, just as a child might do. He equated gifts to Christmas presents. He felt no compunction about reaching out to touch Gordon's skin as if he was mesmerized by the texture of it and totally unashamed of the fact.

And he thought nothing of going to the police to tell what he had seen the night the poor homeless man was set on fire.

Gordon had hemmed and hawed and managed to talk himself out of it easily enough. But Squirt hadn't. Squirt had decided it was his duty to tell the police what he'd seen.

And that, Gordon knew, made Squirt the better person. Once again Gordon found himself humbled by this simple homeless man with the big, generous heart and the straightforward way of dealing with what had to be a rough existence without the histrionics with which Gordon dealt with his. Of course, Squirt hadn't killed anyone. That made a difference, now, didn't it?

"We have to go by the soup kitchen first. That okay?"

Squirt removed his hat and beat it against his leg a couple of times as if to dislodge the dust it had accumulated. While he did, Gordon watched Squirt's pale, pale hair glisten in the sunshine as if it too had been set ablaze. God forbid. Gordon was about to reach out and run his fingers through Squirt's hair, just to experience the fineness of it once again, but by the time he built up the courage to do so, Squirt had redonned his hat.

They set off walking up Broadway. The sun was low in the sky now. They walked slowly, enjoyed the cooler evening air on their faces, breathing it in like perfume. When dusk was in full flower and shadows were finally beginning to deepen around them, the streetlights blinked on. More and more, Gordon saw cars with their headlights gleaming. Night was coming, and the whole wide world was getting ready for it.

Gordon couldn't help wondering what the night held in store. For them.

"Will the people at the electric shop miss you if you come home late?" he asked. "Do they keep an eye on you?"

Squirt seemed surprised by the question. "Why would they? I only sleep there. It isn't my home."

"Where is your home, then?" Gordon asked.

Squirt tapped the side of his head with a lean, elegant finger. "In here," he said. "My home's in here."

Gordon was a little stunned by the naive beauty of those words.

As they walked, Squirt took Gordon's hand yet again. More than one passerby gave them an odd glance, but Squirt didn't seem to mind. And truthfully neither did Gordon. Squirt was clean, he was young and trim, he was beautiful. He didn't look homeless. And even if he had, Gordon liked to think he wouldn't be ashamed to be seen walking down the street hand in hand with him. Gordon liked to think he was better than that.

But he knew he probably wasn't.

As they walked, Squirt tapped each passing parking meter as if saying hello. Just as Gordon had tapped the tombstones as he walked through Holy Cross. Gordon smiled watching him. Then he remembered something the detective had said to Squirt.

"The policeman called you Jerry. Like he knew you. Is that your real name? Jerry?"

Squirt lowered his head and stopped tapping the parking meters. He instantly buried the hand not holding Gordon's in his trouser pocket and left it there. Instead of eyeing the pink sunset overhead as he had been doing, Squirt suddenly watched his feet instead.

"I don't know why he called me that," Squirt said. "He must have mixed me up with somebody else. I don't like it when people call me Jerry. It makes me sad."

"Why?"

"I don't know. It just does." Squirt tore his gaze from his shoe tops and studied Gordon's face. Slowly a smile creased his eyes. He stepped a little closer so that now their shoulders rubbed as they walked. "You came looking for me," he said. "You were worried about me. I could see it on your face when you were standing back there in the lobby."

It was Gordon's turn to shrug. "I thought they'd arrested you. Since I knew you were innocent, I was there to try and get you back. I know what it's like to spend a night in jail. It isn't a nice experience. I would have hated to see you go through it."

"But that didn't happen," Squirt said.

And Gordon smiled. "No, it didn't."

Squirt pointed up ahead. "There's the soup kitchen. Is that where my presents are?"

Gordon laughed. "Yeah. But we can't open them until we get home, okay? They're all bagged up."

"Shoot," Squirt said, obviously disappointed. Then he giggled at the look on Gordon's face. "I was kidding, Gordon. I don't mind waiting. As long as I'm with you, I don't mind much of anything."

And that simple statement tore into Gordon's heart, ricocheted around for a minute, and finally settled into a thrumming sensation that brought another grin to Gordon's face.

"Thanks, Squirt," he said, his voice deep with sincerity. "When I'm with you, I don't mind much of anything either."

Squirt's fingers tightened around his hand, and Gordon smiled to feel them there.


GORDON AND Squirt reached Mama Davis's Soup Kitchen just as the last worker was heading out the door. Gordon grabbed the door before it closed and pulled Squirt inside.

The dining hall was clean and smelled of pine cleaner. Mama Davis was a firm believer in cleanliness. If she hadn't been, the city would have closed her up long ago.

Gordon couldn't see anyone, but he could hear a soft humming coming from the kitchen behind the steam tables in the back of the hall. It was Mama Davis, and she was humming her favorite hymn, "Standing on the Promises." Gordon had heard her hum it a thousand times. When she was happy, when she was mad, when she just didn't have anything else to do, which was rarely, she hummed that song. Never singing the words, just humming. The hymn seemed to be almost a part of the woman. And while Mama Davis was stout and nonsensical and fearless, her humming came out like the most delicate notes of a coloratura—fine, reedy and thin, but always precisely on key. An old woman's voice.

An old woman nobody in their right mind would ever want to mess with.

At the sound of their footsteps, Mama Davis poked her head through the kitchen doorway to see who it was. When she saw Gordon, she flashed her boxy teeth.

"Thank God it's you, honey. I thought the boogeyman was coming to get me."

She stepped forward to meet them, wiping her hands on an apron that looped around her neck and covered her from the bustline to the knees. As always, the wide pockets were weighted down with a variety of objects, making the apron hang funny. She trailed her eyes from Gordon's face and focused on Squirt's. Her features softened.

"I've come for my bags," Gordon said, and Mama nodded, although she didn't take her eyes from Squirt's face.

Gordon glanced at Squirt to see how he was accepting the ogling and was surprised to find a huge smile beaming across Squirt's face.

"Ain't you the pretty one," Mama said, walking straight up to Squirt and folding him into her arms. Squirt hugged her back, all the while grinning at Gordon because he didn't know where else to train his eyes.

When Mama pushed him to arm's length and gave Squirt's ball cap a tilt backward to better see his face, she almost gasped at the sight of his pale blond hair tucked underneath the cap.

"Honey, you're a towhead!" And then she laughed when Squirt ran a hand through his own hair as if wondering exactly what all the fuss was about.

Mama turned to Gordon. "This is your friend, ain't it?"

Gordon nodded. "Mama, meet Squirt. Squirt, this is Mama Davis. She's the lady I work for."

Mama gave Gordon a good-natured slap on the chest. "And a friend too! Don't forget that!"

"And a friend," Gordon humbly added.

Mama studied Squirt's face with a tilt of her head and something warm and knowing in her eyes, as if she was seeing a lot more than his bottomless blue eyes, his gentleness, and the way he had slid his hand into Gordon's as they stood before her.

"I'm pleased to meet you, Squirt."

Squirt blushed, still smiling. "Me too."

Mama studied each of their faces in turn. "Have you boys eaten? I got some food left over. You can heat it in the microwave if it's cold."

Squirt cleared his throat, speaking softly. "Gordon's taking me to his house for dinner. We're going to eat there."

Mama Davis beamed. "Ain't that grand!" She gave Gordon a wily glance. "Bet you've come for your shopping bags." She gave Squirt a pat on the cheek and pointed to a seat. "Honey, you sit there and I'll show Gordon where I stashed his bags. Only take a minute."

Squirt obediently did as she asked, and Gordon followed her into the kitchen.

As soon as they were out of sight of Squirt, Mama turned and pulled Gordon into her arms.

"I won't embarrass you or your friend any more than I already have. I promise. I just want you to listen to me for a minute. That boy's got an angel in him, Gordon. I can feel it. And he's fragile. I don't know what he's been through in his life, but whatever it was, I think it left him pure, if you understand what I'm saying. He's a good but damaged soul, Gordon. Treat him with care. Will you promise me you'll do that?"

"Mama, I—"

The old black woman took a step backward and studied Gordon's face while a smile gradually squeezed the skin of her cheeks and dug trenches around her eyes. "Why, honey, I don't have to tell you any of this, do I? You're smitten by that boy." She placed one hand over her heart and the other over Gordon's heart, as if creating a conduit between the two.

Gordon didn't quite understand what was happening. "No, ma'am, I just—"

Mama laughed a merry laugh, patting Gordon's chest now, just as she was patting her own. "Don't no ma'am me, Gordon Stafford. You can't pull the wool over my eyes. And don't pull it over your own eyes either. I got a feeling you two would be good for each other. Give your feelings some room, Gordon. Let 'em go. Set 'em free. I might be an overly religious old woman, but I ain't so overly religious that I can't see the good in two people coming together, no matter who they are or what body parts they got." She craned her neck around the doorway to study Squirt, who was sitting patiently at one of the tables, spinning his baseball cap in his hands. When Mama Davis turned her attention back to Gordon, there were tears in her eyes. The tears surprised Gordon more than anything.

She stepped forward and pulled Gordon into her arms yet again, just as she had done with Squirt earlier. While she held him in an iron grip, almost squeezing the air out of Gordon's lungs, she whispered cooing words into his ear.

"You treat that boy like gold, Gordon. I got a feeling he's just what you need. He'll bring you back to the world if you let him. I know he will. And I think maybe *you* can bring *him* back too. I surely do. Ain't no misery in the world that can't be overcome, honey. Remember that."

She pressed her cool lips to Gordon's cheek, kissed him there, and gave him a gentle push away. Gordon couldn't speak. Not for a moment anyway. Then he found his voice.

"He's already changed my life, and I don't even know how. I just know I want to be with him."

Mama grinned, flashing those big strong teeth. "Then you be with him, honey. You do what you can for that boy, and I'll just bet he repays you a millionfold."

Suddenly, Gordon felt a stinging behind his eyes. His own tears were on the way now. He should have been embarrassed, but he wasn't.

"He's already repaid me, Mama. Somehow he repaid me the first time I laid eyes on him."

Mama laughed. "Ain't love grand, honey? Ain't it just grander than shit?"

Gordon stared at her, shocked she had said "shit," and even more shocked she had uttered the L-word. Is that what she thought? That Gordon was in love with Squirt? Was that what this was all about?

Mama saw the surprise on his face and chuckled. "You're thinking it's too soon, right? You're thinking you haven't known him long enough."

Gordon could only nod. That was exactly what he was thinking.

Mama grinned. "Love ain't got nothing to do with time, honey. Not a blessed thing. So don't worry. You'll figure it out when you're ready to figure it out." She cackled merrily. "In the meantime, I know what I know. And one of these days, you'll know it too. Just be gentle with him, okay? He already has feelings for you. Don't break his heart again."

Gordon stared across the dining hall. Squirt was sticking his foot straight out in front of him, studying the sorry state of his tennis shoe. When he was finished perusing the left one, he lifted the other leg and studied the right shoe.

"Maybe I should buy him new tennies," Gordon said, more to himself than to Mama.

When she heard the words, she laughed. "Yeah, you do that, Gordon. But there ain't no love involved, right?"

She gave her old head a shake as if wondering why men are always so stupid. When she was finished shaking her head, she dragged Gordon to the back of the kitchen where she unlocked her office door and stepped inside. She pointed to Gordon's Macy's bags piled in the corner.

When Gordon had them in his hands, she gave him a final kiss on the cheek. "As soon as you have it figured out for yourself and you feel the moment's right, you let that boy know how you feel about him. Will you do that for me?"

Gordon gave her a mute nod, still a little stunned by what Mama was implying. When he found his voice, he said, "If what you say is true, I guess I'd be doing it more for me than for you."

"Of course you will," Mama chirped happily, as if Gordon was finally showing a little sense. "Now go. The two of you. Go."

She pulled the ever-present hanky from her sleeve and blew her nose. "Good luck, honey," she whispered as Gordon walked away juggling his armload of shopping bags.

# CHAPTER 7

SQUIRT WAS polishing off his fourth slice of pizza when he looked across the table at Gordon and cleared his throat to speak. "I like your apartment."

"Thanks," Gordon said, wondering how Squirt would feel about the place if he had been here two days earlier when there was crap flung everywhere, dust an inch thick, and a putrid layer of vomit coating the dirty dishes in the sink. "I try to keep it clean," he added, lying through his teeth. He almost never tried to keep it clean. Squirt's basement hole-in-the-wall where he used an old door for a bed was ten times cleaner than Gordon's apartment, and Gordon would be the first to admit it.

Squirt looked good in his new shirt and jeans. Gordon, it turned out, was a pretty good shopper. All the clothes fit Squirt perfectly. In fact, the clothes effected such a transformation on Squirt that Gordon began to imagine how he must have looked before he ended up on the street. Gordon still had no idea what drove Squirt to the life he lived, but it was a safe bet it was neither drugs nor alcohol. Squirt had the clear, healthy eyes of a person who has never overindulged in anything. With his pale hair he looked—*pristine.*

Not to mention beautiful.

In a quiet moment when the eating frenzy was winding down, Squirt sat across from Gordon at the dining room table, staring through the window at the city skyline shimmering in the distance. His hair framed his face like ice framed an eave in winter. The shade of blue of his eyes was the color you see in pictures of the Mediterranean. Azure. Bottomless. Calm.

His voice, when he spoke, was soft. Unhurried. And always unerringly kind. "Gordon?" he ventured.

"Yeah?"

"I like you."

Gordon smiled. "I like you too, Squirt."

Gordon watched as Squirt swung his focus away from the window. Their eyes came together for the hundredth time that day. And every time it happened, Gordon's heart gave a quiet thud inside his chest.

"Thank you for the clothes."

"Squirt, you don't have to keep thanking me. You've thanked me ten times already. You're welcome. And that's the end of it."

"Okay." Squirt fiddled with his fork, then leaned in toward Gordon and asked, "Can I leave the clothes here?"

Gordon didn't understand. "Why would you want to do that? Take them home with you and wear them. That's why I got them for you."

Squirt was beginning to look uncomfortable. Gordon didn't understand that either.

"Do you think we'll see each other again?" Squirt asked.

"Well, sure," Gordon said. "I hope so."

"Here?"

"Sure. I like having you here."

"Then I'd rather keep the clothes here. I can wear them when I come to visit."

Gordon leaned in and laid his hand over Squirt's. He gave Squirt's hand a little shake to get his full attention. "What's going on? What is it you're trying so hard not to say?"

Squirt blushed. He gazed everywhere about the room except directly at Gordon's face. Finally, that was the only place left for his eyes to go. "If I take them to my place, someone will steal them. People are always stealing stuff from me. Customers in the store. They go downstairs to use the bathroom, and sometimes they help themselves to my things. I don't want to lose the clothes you bought me. I don't want to make you mad."

Gordon stroked the hair on the back of Squirt's hand with his thumb. He loved the way Squirt's skin felt. Loved it a little too much, maybe. Mama Davis was way too smart for her own good.

"I don't think you have it in you to make me mad, Squirt. But if you're that worried about the clothes, sure, you can leave them here. Or maybe just wear an outfit now and then when you go home. They don't steal your clothes when you're wearing them, do they?"

Squirt laughed. "Not yet."

Gordon grinned to see him laugh. It didn't happen often, so when it did, it was an occasion. "Then that's what we'll do. The clothes you *aren't* wearing, you can leave here."

Squirt smiled wide. "Good. Thanks."

"And one more thing."

"Yeah?"

"What size shoes do you wear?"

"Size eight. Why?"

"Never mind."

Squirt seemed a little confused by that last round of questioning, but when it was over, he also seemed content to have it settled. His eyes trailed from Gordon's face, down to the hand holding his. He wrapped his slim fingers around Gordon's thumb and held onto it.

"Are you gay, Gordon?"

Gordon was taken aback by the question, but he was relieved to finally hear it asked. It would be nice to get a few things out in the open. It would be nice to know for sure where he stood. And where Squirt stood.

He nodded, hoping he wasn't about to scare the man away. "Yes. I'm gay. Are you?"

"Yes. I always have been."

Gordon smiled. "Me too. I was gay when I was four."

Squirt chuckled. "That's nothing. I was gay when I was *three.*"

"*Two,*" Gordon countered.

Squirt leaned in close and glowered as if trying to be butch as hell. "*One*," he growled. Then he dissolved in a spate of embarrassed giggles. Squirt wasn't exactly built for butch, and apparently he knew it.

Gordon threw his head back and howled with laughter. "Well shit, then, I guess you've got me beat."

At that, they both howled. Squirt's laugh was a raucous, rolling baritone that filled the air like party balloons, all friendly and colorful and warm to the touch. Gordon's own laughter was an ungodly series of snorts and gasps that embarrassed him even while it made them both laugh even louder. For one moment, Gordon's laughter subsided long enough for him to realize it had been months since he had laughed so hard. Through happy tears Gordon watched Squirt's perfect white teeth flash and sparkle in the light of the cheap, apartment-issue chandelier hanging over their heads. Gordon was pretty sure he had never seen a smile so beautiful in his life.

And all the time they laughed, Squirt clung to Gordon's thumb, just like one of those party balloons, afraid to drift away, afraid to catch the currents and rise higher and higher until he disappeared in the distance where he would never see Gordon again.

Watching Squirt, Gordon blinked back a sudden rush of longing. It took every ounce of willpower he had not to throw himself across the table and kiss those laughing lips. But he didn't dare. There was still an aura of fragility around Squirt. Even in the midst of laughter, there was an air of—frailty. As if Squirt could be easily broken. The damage done to Squirt, whatever it had been, had left his life ethereal. Tenuous. It seemed sometimes he barely clung to life at all. Or at least to happiness.

Just the thought of causing Squirt more injury scared the hell out of Gordon. He understood injury. He understood barely hanging on to life. He understood taking about all you can take and having nothing left with which to fight. If he ever thought he was the one who pushed Squirt over the edge to a place where he could never claw his way back, Gordon would never forgive himself. Never.

Pushing those thoughts away, Gordon held out the pizza box and waved it under Squirt's nose. "One piece left. Eat it. I'm stuffed."

"You sure?"

"Yeah."

Squirt snatched up the slice without further comment, causing Gordon to grin. For a little guy, Squirt sure could eat.

While Gordon sat watching Squirt polish off the pizza, still comfortably content in his company, Gordon had one more surprising thought pop up during the course of an evening that had already offered several.

His car. It was still parked twenty feet below his ass in the underground parking lot beneath the building. It had been sitting there since he bought it upon his release from jail. Gordon had driven it from the dealer's lot on that first day of his renewed freedom since his last car had been totaled in the accident, and two miles down the road, he had suffered such a severe panic attack, he barely made it the rest of the way home. The car had been sitting in his parking space ever since. Occasionally, Gordon would go downstairs and crank her up, letting the engine idle for a while because he felt he should, but he hadn't actually driven the car since that day. Something his mother didn't understand at all. Unfortunately, it wasn't something he could explain to her either. The fear. The cold sweat. The horror he would do something wrong, something stupid. Cause another accident.

*Take another life.*

Gordon turned away from Squirt to stare at the old rolltop desk in the corner. His car keys were in the top drawer. He knew somehow that now was the time to let that fear go. It was time to start driving again.

Later in the evening, when the pizza was long gone and Squirt's luscious eyes were looking sleepy after he and Gordon spent a quiet hour sitting on the sofa holding hands, Gordon finally spoke the words that probably meant very little to Squirt, but meant the world to him.

He leaned in to give Squirt a hug. They did not kiss, although Gordon wanted to. Gordon swept the hair from Squirt's forehead and ran a gentle thumb across Squirt's brow, causing the young man to close his tired eyes as if he enjoyed the touch.

"It's been a long day, and you're about to conk out," Gordon said. "When you're ready I'll drive you home."

Squirt nodded. Both men stood, and Gordon was surprised when Squirt walked directly into his arms. "Thank you," he whispered against Gordon's shoulder.

"No," Gordon whispered back. "Thank *you.*"

He pulled Squirt close as his head filled with the sound of his own thudding heart. Gordon could never remember a man who fit so perfectly in his arms.

Ever.

"I can hear your heart," Squirt said.

And Gordon smiled.

"Good."


GORDON DROPPED Squirt in the alleyway at the back of the electrical shop. With a bashful last wave, Squirt dug into the pocket of his new jeans for the key and let himself in. Gordon waited until Squirt was safely inside before driving off.

The car felt good beneath him. He hadn't realized until tonight how much he missed driving. He rolled down all the windows and let the wind whip through his hair as he maneuvered along the city streets. When he found a freeway ramp, he goosed the accelerator and merged into swiftly moving traffic headed south.

The night was balmy and the car responsive in his hands. It seemed to be as relieved as Gordon to be back on the road again, almost anticipating his every move, knowing where it wanted to go even before Gordon did.

As the miles rolled by, Gordon relived every second of the evening, every snippet of conversation. His heart still soared from the hours he had spent with Squirt. A soaring heart was a new revelation for Gordon. But although the feeling was new, Gordon wasn't dumb enough not to know what it meant. He remembered what Mama Davis had said to him back in the soup kitchen and wondered how the woman got to be so smart.

When the speed of the freeway traffic began to bother him and he felt that old familiar panic beginning to settle in his gut, Gordon exited and prowled the city streets instead, trying all the while to think of only the present, not the past. And he succeeded in keeping the memories at bay by remembering Squirt: how he spoke, how he ate, how he reached out so often just to touch. The kindness in his eyes, the softness of his voice, the warmth of his hand. As the night grew later and the miles on the odometer increased, Gordon slowly wound a roundabout path back to his apartment building, where he eased into his parking space, glad to be home safe and sound. As he switched off the engine, he leaned forward and rested his head on the steering wheel, closing his eyes. His body was tired, but his mind was going a mile a minute.

"Thank you, God," he whispered into the darkness behind his eyes. "Thank you for what you've done." *Squirt,* he thought soundlessly. *Thank you for sending me Squirt.*

Gordon opened his eyes and stared through the windshield into the unknown years that lay ahead. What did he need to fill those years? What was the most important thing he required to live a decent, productive life?

A job, he supposed. Sooner or later he would have to find a fucking job. But in meteorology? The only field he knew anything about? Doubtful. Unless it was a position in the background, away from the cameras. His days of being a local celebrity weatherman were over and he knew it. No one would hire him now for on-camera work. Not when the whole city knew his story.

So as far as looking for work, maybe he wasn't quite ready yet. Not until he thought it through. Not until he mapped out a plan. He had enough money to last a while longer. So for now maybe he should concentrate on the second thing he needed to lead a decent, productive life. And that second thing was a whole lot easier to figure out.

He needed someone to *share* the life he was about to carve out for himself. Someone he wanted to be with, and someone who might want to be with him. And for this immediate goal, there was no hedging. No wishy-washy hemming and hawing. No putting it off. He knew exactly what he wanted. He knew exactly *who* he wanted. And tomorrow he would start to make it happen. Full court press.

Climbing from the car and pocketing his car keys, Gordon grinned a sleepy, mischievous grin as he whistled his way up the stairs to his apartment.

Poor Squirt. The guy wouldn't know what hit him.

# CHAPTER 8

THUS BEGAN an odd courtship.

While Gordon rediscovered the joy of being sober—grateful to have survived all the alcohol he had poured into his body over the past year with a minimum of lasting physical damage, or so he sincerely hoped—he also rediscovered contentment. His nightmares vanished. He began eating properly. He gained a few pounds, which made him happy. He looked better, felt better, and Gordon even found a smidgeon of religion in the way he looked to the heavens to thank whoever was up there for giving him this second chance, and to a kind providence for passing on to him a set of genes strong enough to bypass alcohol dependency with a minimum of trauma.

While the memories of his past still tore at him, he learned to sidestep the pain by concentrating on other things, other people. Mama Davis, for instance. Or Pistol Pete. Even thoughts of his mother could be used to push his sins to the back burner for a while. If those thoughts failed to steer his attention away from himself, he had the Mount Everest of distractions to fall back on.

Squirt. Squirt could snag his attention every time. Squirt's face became the greatest weapon in Gordon's arsenal of tricks for self-preservation. The memory of Squirt's sapphire eyes, or towheaded locks, or the way their hands fit so perfectly together, invariably eased Gordon's shame, his heartache, his guilt, at least for a while. When his head was *completely* filled with memories of Squirt, he would oftentimes simply stop whatever he was doing and close his eyes to lock the memories inside. When he did, he would always feel a lightness settle through him where before there had been that old familiar crush of shame. And when that lightness settled in, deep inside, he would feel a smile begin. Every time.

It was during one of those smiling moments of remembering Squirt's goodness, Squirt's sweetness, Squirt's sexiness, that the gun in Gordon's bathroom drawer was banished to a shoebox, and the shoebox was stuffed all the way to the back of the top shelf in his bedroom closet. He breathed easier with the gun out of sight. Often he went hours without thinking about it at all.

Just as Gordon noticed a change in himself, others began to see a change too. Mama Davis particularly. When around Gordon, she invariably had a merry twinkle in her eye for she understood the change in him, even if he didn't. If Gordon thought he was fooling anyone, he was sorely mistaken when it came to Mama Davis. She saw everything.

Aside from all these overt changes in his life, there was one more change he experienced, and this one was not so overt. The change was this: Gordon's heart was once again beating with a purpose. Oftentimes, it didn't just beat, it *thrummed.* It might be buried deep inside his body where it couldn't be seen, but it could sure as hell be felt.

And Gordon had Squirt to thank for that thrumming heart, which brings us back to the odd courtship he now embarked upon—the odd courtship, in fact, the young men *simultaneously* embarked upon. For if one was smitten, so was the other. Yet they edged carefully toward each other in a strange sidling dance, each irresistibly drawn to the other, but each gun shy, afraid of rejection, leery of being hurt. Gordon had experienced how happiness could be so swiftly snatched away in life. He was fairly certain Squirt must have an understanding of loss too, although Squirt was not one to speak of his pain. In fact, he rarely spoke of himself at all.

So Gordon took things slowly.

Gordon was drawn to Squirt in such a way, and with such intensity, that even he couldn't explain it. It wasn't just sexual attraction, although that was certainly a part of it. But it had more to do with Squirt's aura of innocence. His simplicity. The fact that he always seemed to be teetering on the edge of either great happiness or great distress, but never really fell into either. There was a calmness to Squirt. It soothed Gordon's mind and eased his fears. That tranquility was like a drug, and as time went by, Gordon found himself craving it more and more.

Aside from the embarrassing high school crush Gordon had on Squirt, which was exactly what it felt like, Gordon had another incentive for wanting to spend time with his new friend. His life had been aimless for so long, now he thought he might actually have a chance to help someone. To help Squirt. To lift Squirt up from the life he was leading. A chance for Gordon to finally do some good in the world after all the harm he had caused.

It seemed to Gordon that Squirt's motives for wanting to spend time with *him* were far simpler. He liked Gordon. Gordon knew this because Squirt told him so. Often.

Every day now Squirt came to the soup kitchen for breakfast, and every day, well fed and smiling, he waved good-bye to Gordon and waited outside the alley door for Gordon's shift to end. Then the two would walk, simply walk, up and down the city streets until Gordon's afternoon shift began. Sometimes they hardly spoke. Sometimes they never shut up. Sometimes they laughed a lot and sometimes they didn't laugh at all. But always, *always,* Gordon felt content to be in Squirt's company, and he was pretty sure Squirt felt the same.

On quieter streets, when fewer pedestrians crowded the sidewalks, they would step closer together and let their shoulders brush as they ambled along. At other times, when there was no one around at all, their hands would migrate toward each other and clasp together, swinging idly as they walked. Those were the times Gordon liked the best.

In the evenings, when Gordon lay alone in bed in his apartment overlooking the canyon, he would pick vignettes from the day and relive them in his mind:

Gordon playfully pulling the ever-present baseball cap from Squirt's head and plopping it on his own, just so he could see Squirt's pale, pale hair glisten in the sunlight....

Squirt's careful capture of a tiny dog who had slipped his collar and run out into traffic, scaring his old lady owner half to death. The tears of thank you in the old woman's eyes as Squirt cradled the dog in his arms, then handed it back to her after giving it a gentle kiss on the head....

Although Gordon loved the silences they sometimes shared, it was the words they exchanged that he remembered the most.

Once, on a day that threatened rain, Squirt smiled at Gordon and said for the hundredth time, "I like being with you."

Gordon smiled back and stepped closer, letting their shoulders touch. "I like being with you too."

"Don't your other friends miss you?" Squirt asked.

"What do you mean?"

Squirt gave an uncomfortable shrug. A worried shrug. "I mean, they must miss you since you spend so much time with me."

Now it was Gordon's turn to look uncomfortable. "Squirt, I don't have that many friends. And even if I did, I would rather be with you."

"Really?"

"Yes."

And Squirt never mentioned Gordon's other friends again.

Another time, when the sidewalks were so hot it was like walking on coals, Squirt ducked into a convenience store as they passed and bought two sodas, handing one to Gordon.

"I wish I had known what you were going to do," Gordon said. "I would have bought the drinks myself."

Squirt took a long pull of his Coke and sighed happily. Then he rolled the cold can across his sweaty forehead. "I like doing things for you."

"I know," Gordon said. "But you don't have much money. Next time let me buy."

Squirt seemed to find that funny. "I have money. I work."

This was news to Gordon. "Where do you work?"

"At the electrical shop. I clean up the place and sweep the floors and rearrange the shelves when people come along and put stuff back in the wrong place. They pay me and give me a place to sleep. So there. See? I have money."

This was the first glimpse Gordon had into the mystery of Squirt's survival on the streets. And once again it caused Gordon no small amount of embarrassment. Squirt was working. Gordon wasn't. Squirt really was a better person. Kinder, more giving, and trustworthy.

He held down a job while Gordon didn't, unless you wanted to call a court-ordered stint at Mama's Soup Kitchen a job. Squirt had even shown the common sense to go to the police about the murder under the bridge when Gordon kept putting it off and hoping he wouldn't have to get involved at all.

"I stand corrected," Gordon finally said, conjuring up a smile. "So thanks for the Coke."

And in answer, Squirt rolled his ice cold can over Gordon's forehead for a change, laughing happily when Gordon sighed in bliss because it felt so good.

Gordon bought Squirt a bus pass, although Squirt didn't want him to, and on weekends, Squirt would visit Gordon in his apartment. They watched movies on TV, played Monopoly at the kitchen table, tested Gordon's cooking skills, which were meager, and sometimes simply sat and spoke softly of inconsequential things until it was time for Squirt to go home.

One evening they took a crack at Trivial Pursuit, and Squirt beat Gordon three games in a row. This was the first time Gordon realized how intelligent Squirt really was. While his social skills were minimal, his thinking processes were a hell of a lot less muddied than Gordon's. And the guy was smart. Really smart.

This discovery thrilled Gordon no end, and his high school crush revved up a notch. He began to look at Squirt in a different way. He looked at him more as an equal than a community project. He was less intent on *improving* Squirt's life, and more intent on simply getting to know him better.

And getting closer.

Every day Gordon longed to take their friendship to the next level, and every day he sheared away. His hunger for Squirt had not lessened one iota, but Gordon did not want to push himself onto Squirt. He wanted Squirt to make the first move. That was the only way Gordon could be sure Squirt was really ready and truly *wanted* a relationship with Gordon that went beyond the boundaries of friendship.

Many nights, rather than look back on the things they had said or done that day, Gordon would let his mind travel all the way back to the beginning. To the first, and only, complete night they had spent together. Lying together on Squirt's god-awful, rock-hard bed in the basement beneath the electrical shop, both of them exhausted to the core after the horrors they had seen under the bridge.

But it wasn't the horrors Gordon remembered. It was the feel of Squirt's cheek resting atop Gordon's bare nipple. It was the feel of Squirt's sleeping breath stirring the hair on Gordon's chest. The memory of Gordon's hard cock wanting more that night. The urges he experienced imagining what it would be like to strip Squirt of everything he wore and savor the true man beneath. The heat, the softness, the hunger flowing both ways. The sexiness of the man's kindness. The humble smile that made Gordon long to taste his lips.

The need Gordon felt to take Squirt all the way to whatever sexual awakenings they chose to explore.

And as time passed, Gordon's hunger for Squirt grew. And not just the sexual hunger. His feelings grew as well.

The day Gordon learned Squirt shared the way he felt was the happiest day of his life. And it changed them both forever.

It all came to a head the evening Gordon's microwave oven exploded.


GORDON AND Squirt stood in Gordon's kitchen breathing in the heavenly aroma of buttery popcorn popping away in the microwave. In the living room, a DVD of the director's cut of *The Exorcist*, which Squirt had never seen, was waiting to scare the shit out of them. It was Halloween night, and they both thought a spooky movie would be perfect for the night's entertainment.

"Is it gory?" Squirt asked, referring to the film.

Gordon grinned. "Gory as hell."

A sly look dimmed Squirt's incredible blue eyes. Just the hint of a sneaky smile twisted the corners of his mouth. "Will you hold my hand if I get scared?"

Gordon tilted his head and felt a rush of excitement stir his body.

They had been seeing each other daily for over a month now. Gordon had taken care to keep the relationship on a strictly friendship basis, never going farther than holding hands, and lately that decision was irking the hell out of him. He wanted to move things forward. He knew someday he would, but he was just waiting for the perfect time to do it. However, the last thing he wanted to do was scare Squirt away.

Now, with the bag of microwave popcorn banging and clattering in the background and Gordon's heart suddenly banging and clattering in the foreground, and that sneaky little grin making Squirt's face even cuter than it already was, Gordon didn't hesitate to finally make his move. Apparently, the fates had convinced him the time was right, and who the hell was he to argue with the fates?

He took two steps forward without a beat of warning and folded Squirt in his arms. Their bodies came together just as Gordon witnessed Squirt's eyes open wide in surprise.

Standing almost a head taller, Gordon tucked Squirt's head under his chin and kissed his snowy hair. He smiled to feel Squirt's hands hesitate only a moment before sliding up Gordon's back and hugging him in return. Gordon smiled and closed his eyes when he felt Squirt's lips press against his throat.

"You don't have to be scared of a stupid movie," Gordon whispered, shooting for playful but not quite carrying it off. His voice was far huskier than he intended. God, he was turned on. "I'll protect you."

"And I'll protect you," Squirt whispered back, teasingly, but not so teasingly either, tilting his head up to gaze into Gordon's face.

Squirt's breath was sweet. They had been eating Halloween candy earlier. M&M's, Baby Ruths, Kit Kats, Rolos. While they tore into the candy bowl, they had turned out the porch light to discourage trick-or-treaters, and their ruse seemed to work. Not once did the doorbell ring. After they had made a pretty horrific dent in the candy bowl, they were craving salt. Thus the popcorn popping in the microwave.

Gordon bent his head and took a gentle taste of Squirt's smile, rather like a wine connoisseur testing a new vintage with the daintiest of sips. The moment their lips came together, Squirt's warm hand moved up to caress the side of Gordon's neck. Gordon closed his eyes and lost himself in the kiss. His heart was pounding like crazy, and he could hear Squirt's heart hammering too. Gordon could feel someone's knees begin to shake, but they were standing so close together and holding each other so tightly, he couldn't tell if it was him or Squirt doing the shaking.

When Gordon felt Squirt's tongue worm its way into the kiss, gently asking to be let in, Gordon parted his lips enough to let Squirt go where he wished to go. The taste and heat of Squirt's tongue on his own made Gordon's heart hammer louder.

They were both hard now and Gordon felt Squirt press himself closer. Confined in fabric, their two cocks did an intimate little dance of their own. Squirt's hand slid under Gordon's shirt and laid its warmth across his ribcage. Gordon shuddered at the touch.

And just as Gordon thought of reciprocating, of reaching beneath Squirt's shirt to explore the wonders hidden there—the microwave exploded!

*BOOM.*

Squirt and Gordon jumped two feet into the air, hard-ons and all. Their kiss died a bone-crushing death when their heads banged together in midair. Gordon cast an immediate prayer skyward, thanking God he hadn't bitten off his tongue. Or Squirt's.

Squirt apparently had a different set of priorities. He quickly shoved the microwave aside and yanked the cord out of the wall, while Gordon simply stood there like a goon trying not to poop in his pants. That *BOOM* had startled the bejesus out of him.

"Holy crap!" Gordon barked.

Squirt turned to Gordon, and his eyes crinkled up, first in laughter, then in something else. *Not* laughter, was the closest Gordon could get to nailing it down.

"Did my heart blow up?" Squirt asked. He didn't seem to be completely joking.

"No," Gordon said, pulling Squirt back into his arms. "But I think my nuker just nuked itself out of existence. We may have to forego the popcorn. You okay?"

A sudden stench filled the room. Gordon and Squirt swiveled their heads to see a puff of black smoke billow from the vent in the side of the machine. Then the microwave spat up a cough that sounded eerily human, along with a couple of clicks and a teeny series of thumps, as if a stuttering, dying heart were winding down to silence. They could hear a sizzling noise that sounded like bacon frying in a skillet.

Gordon grimaced. "Death rattle."

At that, Squirt did laugh. He did it with his mouth pressed to Gordon's throat again. Gordon could feel Squirt's smile against his skin, and Jesus, he had to close his eyes to fully experience the sensation. By the time he was finished experiencing, Gordon was smiling too.

"Got a screwdriver?" Squirt asked, his hands once again sliding beneath Gordon's shirt and caressing his back. Gordon had to close his eyes *again.* This time he felt a tremor rattle his body from head to toe at the feel of Squirt's fingers on his skin.

Then Squirt's words sank in. He opened his eyes and gazed down into Squirt's sweet face. "What do you want a screwdriver for?"

"To fix your microwave."

"Surely you jest. We'll fix it with a credit card."

"How can you do that?"

"We'll buy a new one."

Squirt giggled. "Gee. And you look so butch. Where's the screwdriver?"

"You're serious."

"Well, yeah."

Without stepping from Squirt's arms, Gordon freed one hand and pulled open a kitchen drawer less than two feet away. Still staring fondly, and a little daringly, into Squirt's incredible eyes, he rummaged around by feel until he pulled a screwdriver from the mess.

"Junk drawer?" Squirt asked.

"You bet. You didn't think I had an actual tool box, did you?"

Squirt dragged his lips over Gordon's chin. "Uh, no. Probably not. Do you have pliers?"

"No, but I have tweezers. Will that do?"

"No. And I'm not even going to ask why you have tweezers."

Gordon grunted. "That's probably wise."

Squirt pulled himself from Gordon's arms. "This won't take long. Can you remember where we were? You know, kissing and hugging and all."

"Fuck, yeah," Gordon said. "I'll never forget it."

And at that Squirt's face softened, his eyes delved deeper into Gordon's. He slid his fingers along Gordon's jawline, and when he spoke, his voice was as soft as his eyes. "Right answer," he said.

Then, all business, he turned to the microwave oven, which was still sitting there on Gordon's countertop sizzling and spitting out smoke. Squirt released the oven door and, using the tail of his shirt for a potholder, pulled the blackened bag of microwave popcorn out of the machine and tossed it into the sink.

Gordon watched as Squirt, using real potholders Gordon handed him this time, extracted the revolving plate from inside and laid it carefully in the sink as well. Squirt then picked up the microwave and carried it to the kitchen table, where he plopped it down face first, exposing the back.

Squirt's eyes opened wide. "Dust much?"

Gordon hastily grabbed a fistful of paper towels and wiped the back of the microwave clean. "Don't be a wise ass."

Squirt bit back a grin. "Sorry."

In fifteen seconds or less, Squirt had the back off the machine and was looking at what lay underneath, his brow furrowed in concentration. Then he flipped the machine over onto its newly exposed back and pried off the front panel that held the window and keypad.

Gordon leaned over Squirt's shoulder, more to feel Squirt's heat than to really see what was going on. Still, he thought he should at least *act* interested. He pointed to a mass of wires and teeny tiny knobs. "What's that?"

"Circuit board. Hooks to the keypad on the outside."

"What's it do?"

"Everything."

Gordon pointed to something else. "What's that?"

Squirt grinned. "Fan. Sucks the air in through the vents to cool the circuit board while the cavity is heating."

"Cavity?"

"The inside of the oven. Where you put stuff to cook."

"Oh." Again he pointed. "What's *that*?"

"That's another fan. Sucks the heat out of the cavity and blows it through the opposite vent to the outside to keep the rest of the machine cool."

Gordon pointed to something else. "Oh. And what the fuck is that bizarre looking contraption?"

"That's the magnetron. The big Kahuna."

"Important, huh?"

"Well, yeah. It's the generating device for the microwaves that do the cooking. Since microwaves won't penetrate steel, it shoots them through this little mica window into the cavity, and voilá, popcorn, or pizza, or coffee, or whatever the heck you're cooking." Squirt gave a little sigh. "Do you want me to fix this thing or do you want to continue the tour?"

"Cranky," Gordon smirked, running an imaginary zipper across his lips.

Since Gordon was still standing close behind him peering over his shoulder, Squirt scooted his ass across Gordon's crotch by way of apology. "Sorry."

Gordon wasn't sorry. Gordon almost fainted. He pressed his lips to the back of Squirt's head, and Squirt giggled when Gordon slid his tongue over the nape of his neck.

"You're not helping," Squirt tittered.

"Not you maybe, but it's doing wonders for me." His finger came out again and pointed at the guts of his poor dismantled microwave. "What are those?"

"Capacitor and diode. Work together as an electrical pump to send some serious volts of electricity through the magnetron."

"And that's what makes it cook?"

Squirt nodded. "That's what makes it cook. Basically."

"How the heck do you know this stuff?"

Squirt shrugged. "Not sure. Just do. *Born* knowing, I guess."

"That's impossible, Squirt. Nobody is born knowing how to dismantle a microwave oven. It's not like—you know—a fucking genetic memory."

Squirt was piddling with the diode, or the magnetron, or whatever the hell it was. Gordon wasn't sure. He didn't much care either.

Gordon had two questions he wanted to ask. One was a hell of a lot more important than the other. He decided to get the silly question out of the way first.

"So, can you fix it?"

"Yes, but not today." He pointed to a tiny glob of melted rubber in the circuit board. "See that? The circuitry shorted out. I need a soldering gun to fix it. I'll bring it with me next time I come over."

Gordon was impressed. He had never seen a soldering gun in his life. Wasn't even entirely sure what a soldering gun was. "You mean you have one of those?"

"Actually, I have two."

Gordon slapped his own chest as if a sudden palpitation made him giddy. "My God, that's sexy." And Squirt burst out laughing.

While Squirt was laughing, Gordon thought it might be a good time to ask the second question. The *important* question. He reached around and cupped Squirt's chin in his fist, dragging Squirt's eyes to his.

"Baby, I can't do this anymore. My circuit board is melting too. Will you come to bed with me? Tonight? Right now? Can I—can I please make love to you?"

Pinned as he was between Gordon's chest and the kitchen table, Squirt squirmed around in Gordon's arms to face him. His eyes narrowed in concentration as he studied Gordon's face, only inches from his own. The tip of Squirt's tongue came out and licked at his own burgeoning smile. He reached up to push the long hair from Gordon's eyes. His thumb stroked Gordon's temple, while he cupped Gordon's cheek in his other palm. His hands were warm to the touch. Gordon could feel them branding his skin.

Squirt dropped his head to Gordon's chest. "So you do want me that way," he whispered into Gordon's shirtfront.

"God, yes," Gordon answered, gathering him close. "Baby, I want you every way there is."

"I wasn't sure."

Gordon pressed his lips to Squirt's hair, inhaling the scent of it, relishing the softness against his face. "I know. I'm sorry. I've wanted you since that very first night. But I was afraid I'd scare you away. I'm nuts about you, Squirt. I want to be with you. I want you to—*like* me."

Squirt lifted his face and gazed into Gordon's eyes. "Is that really what you want? For me to like you?"

And Gordon faltered. But the faltering only lasted a second. The kindness, the hope, the *excitement* he saw in Squirt's eyes gave him the courage he needed to take one further step forward. To open his heart just a little bit more. "No," Gordon said. "That isn't what I want at all. But it's all I have the courage to ask for tonight. Will you let that be my answer for now? Will you?" Gordon closed his eyes, unable to look at Squirt's face another second. Afraid of what he would say. Afraid of what he would do.

Squirt stood on tiptoe and touched his lips to each of Gordon's eyelids. He slid his lips down Gordon's cheek to Gordon's slightly parted mouth. He pressed his own mouth there, and while their lips were together, Squirt whispered, "It's been a long day. Shower with me first. If you still want me, then we'll go to bed. Will you do that?"

"What do you mean, if I still want you?"

"You'll see."

Confused, but elated, Gordon nodded.

And immediately, Squirt took his hand and led him through the apartment. At the bathroom door, they both kicked off their shoes. Again, Squirt stood on tiptoe and with his mouth brushing Gordon's lips, his pale fingers began unbuttoning Gordon's shirt.

Gordon reached out with trembling hands to do the same for Squirt.

# CHAPTER 9

GORDON KNEW this memory would never leave him—this memory of the two of them standing in the hallway of Gordon's tiny apartment, each reaching out to undress the other. But what should have been a wonderful moment for Gordon was tempered by the somber expression on Squirt's elfin face. He would not meet Gordon's eyes, nor would he smile. He concentrated solely on unbuttoning Gordon's shirt.

Gordon tugged at the last button on Squirt's oversized dress shirt and sucked in a tiny breath when it fell open for the first time, giving Gordon a glimpse of what lay beneath.

Squirt was beautiful. His chest hairless and pale but more trimly muscled than Gordon had expected. Gordon rested his fingertips on Squirt's smooth, warm stomach. He slid them upward, and as they glided over Squirt's white-hot flesh, Gordon swept Squirt's shirt back, opening it wide.

"You're beautiful, baby," Gordon muttered, but still Squirt would not meet his eyes. Gordon bent to press his lips to first one, then the other, of Squirt's small brown nipples.

Squirt tensed at the first sensation of Gordon's mouth on his skin, then seemed to relax into the kiss. He tipped his head back until the tendons on his neck stood out. His lips parted slightly. Then he opened his eyes and pushed Gordon's shirt off his shoulders, watching it slip down Gordon's back with the merest rustle of fabric and fall in a heap at Gordon's feet. Gordon's shoulders were strong and unblemished. A brush of dark hair lay scattered across his chest. Squirt leaned forward and breathed in the heated scent of Gordon's skin, his eyes open wide, taking in everything.

Squirt trembled as Gordon pushed his shirt away from his pale, beautiful chest. It slid down Squirt's back but did not hit the floor. The buttons at the cuffs held it in place. Gordon tore his eyes from the alabaster skin of Squirt's torso and dropped to his knees to take each cuff in his hand, awkwardly undoing the button that was holding up progress. When both sleeves were unbuttoned, Squirt's shirt slid away.

On his knees before Squirt, Gordon gazed up at Squirt's face while Squirt looked down at him and buried his hands in Gordon's long hair.

It was then Gordon saw the scars. On the inside of Squirt's arms. Both arms. Countless white ripples of flesh, whiter than the flesh around them. Squirt's forearms were scored, crosswise, from elbow to wrist, countless times. Gordon turned Squirt's arm in his hand to get a better look. Then he did the same to the other arm. He ran his fingers gently over Squirt's ruined flesh. The ridges of scar tissue felt bumpy beneath his fingertips.

Gordon gazed up into Squirt's face, his eyes sad. Wounded. "Baby, what happened?"

Squirt could only shake his head, his face red. He was embarrassed, which wounded Gordon even more.

"I don't know," Squirt sighed. "I don't remember. I—I don't remember a lot of things."

Gordon draped his arms around Squirt's hips and pulled him close, pressing his face into the heat of Squirt's belly. He kissed Squirt there, just above the navel. A tremor ran through both of them when he did.

Gordon dragged a smile from somewhere deep inside and looked up into Squirt's face. His smile was an offering. "Do you remember you like me, Squirt? Do you remember that much?"

And Squirt answered Gordon's smile with one of his own. His eyes crinkled happily. "Yes, Gordon. I remember it every time I turn around. I—I remember it every time I breathe. Every time my heart pumps a beat. I remember it every time I touch myself thinking about you."

Gordon's breath caught. Again, Gordon pulled Squirt closer, burying his face in the pale, lean stomach, inhaling the scent of Squirt's skin. Longing for more. Longing for everything. He slid his hands up the wales of Squirt's ribcage until his thumbs brushed the tiny nipples, causing Squirt to shiver at the touch.

Gordon's voice was a husk of sound. He was so turned on he could barely vocalize his thoughts. "Do you do that, Squirt? Do you lie on your little bed and really touch yourself when you think about me?"

Squirt nodded, his hand cupping the back of Gordon's head, holding him tight against him. He didn't speak; he simply gazed down into Gordon's eyes and nodded.

Gordon was hard in his trousers. He could feel his cock straining against the fabric, begging for release. Gordon almost gasped out the words he wanted to say.

"Do you come when you think of me? Do you touch yourself until you come?"

Squirt swallowed. Again he nodded. "Sometimes," he said. Then he stopped himself. "No. Always."

Gordon smiled. He pressed his lips to the scars on Squirt's forearms. First one arm, then the other. Squirt tried to pull away, but Gordon wouldn't let him. Finally, Squirt gave in to Gordon's kisses, offering his injuries up completely. Gordon could sense him trying not to be ashamed. Trying to allow Gordon free rein to go where he wanted to go, do what he wanted to do.

"Are they ugly?" Squirt asked softly. "Are my scars ugly?"

Gordon reached high to lay his fingers over Squirt's lips, not to silence, but to feel. To caress the words. "No," he whispered. "The scars are part of you. That makes them beautiful." After a beat of hesitation, Gordon said, "I have scars too, Squirt. It's just that mine are way inside where people can't see them."

To Gordon's surprise, Squirt kissed his fingertips and gave his head a sad little shake. "You're wrong. People can see them. I did. I saw them the first day I met you." Squirt took a long shuddering breath. "We can shower now if you like."

Still smiling, and aching with hunger, Gordon reached for Squirt's belt buckle and tugged it open. Squirt's baggy trousers immediately slid to the floor.

Squirt stood naked and hard before him.

THEY STOOD close in the tiny shower cubicle, each soaping his own body because he was too shy to attend to the other. At least at first. Only when Gordon felt the heaviness of Squirt's erect cock brush against his leg did he free himself from all restraint and dive right in to the moment.

He slipped his soapy hand around Squirt's hardness and bent again to press his lips to Squirt's chest. Squirt rose on tiptoe and pushed his dick into Gordon's fist, and Gordon thought it was the sexiest thing anyone had ever done to him. Squirt's slight body and big dick created a perfect storm of beauty in Gordon's eyes. Gordon wanted Squirt in every way he could imagine. He wanted all of the man.

When Squirt's fingers gently circled Gordon's own cock, just as Gordon was touching him, Gordon closed his eyes and damn near melted.

Gordon reached overhead and grabbed the shower nozzle, aiming the spray directly at them.

"We're clean enough, dammit. Rinse off. I want you in my bed. Now."

Squirt emitted a bubbling giggle since the water was aimed directly at his face. "I won't be much good to you drowned."

So Gordon moved the spray to let him breathe. Seemed the least he could do. He wasn't in the mood for chitchat or niceties. At that particular moment, he had never wanted anyone as much as he wanted Squirt.

When both were soap free, Gordon pushed open the shower door and grabbed a towel off the back of the bathroom door. With his hair dripping everywhere, and while Squirt stood obediently before him, hard and beautiful, Gordon ran the towel over Squirt's body, drying him off. He briskly toweled Squirt's hair until it stood up all over his head. Then, more gently, he lovingly dried Squirt's genitals, enthralled by the weight and heft of Squirt's erect cock. Squirt was uncut, and Gordon thought he had never seen anything as scrumptious in all his life. Like a supplicant come to worship, he lowered himself to his knees. With the deftest of movements, he carefully eased Squirt's foreskin back to dry him completely. It took every ounce of willpower Gordon possessed not to take that perfect cock into his mouth right then and there.

When Squirt was as dry as he would ever get, and Gordon was so turned on he thought he might spontaneously combust in another minute or two, Gordon perfunctorily dragged the same towel over his own body and through his own hair.

When he was finished, Gordon flung the towel over his shoulder and tugged Squirt through the bathroom door and into the bedroom to the sound of Squirt's laughter. At the foot of the bed, he turned to gently pull Squirt into his arms. Their mouths came together as each body pressed hard against the other. The kiss was sweet. Gordon didn't open his eyes even once through the long tasting. The sensation of their two cocks, hard and eager, bumping heads down below, made Gordon a little weak at the knees. When Squirt's leg came up to hook around Gordon's calf, and Squirt's cock pushed even harder into Gordon's flesh, Gordon took him by the shoulders and eased him around until his back was to the bed. Then Gordon lowered Squirt gently down onto the mattress.

And it was at that moment, with Squirt perched on the edge of the bed and Gordon standing naked before him, that Squirt proceeded to make every one of Gordon's dreams come true.

Squirt cupped Gordon's heavy balls in his hand and, leaning forward, slipped his mouth over Gordon's straining cock. Gordon closed his eyes at the sensations coursing through him. Every muscle in his body tensed. Unable to stop himself, he pushed himself deeper into that velvet mouth. Squirt dragged him closer, Squirt's fingers pulling at Gordon's ass, fingertips brushing Gordon's sphincter when he did.

When Gordon gave a shudder that almost knocked him over, Squirt laughed around his cock and pulled him completely down onto the bed on top of him.

Gordon straddled Squirt's chest, his cock eagerly plumbing the heated depths of Squirt's hungry mouth. Reaching around behind him, Gordon scooped up a fistful of Squirt's magnificent cock. When Squirt gasped at the touch, Gordon freed his cock from Squirt's mouth long enough to position himself beside Squirt on the bed in the 69 position.

Once there, he pulled Squirt close. Squirt echoed the movement and then took Gordon's cock into his mouth again. Gordon found it was his turn now to worship the cock before him.

Squirt's dick was beautiful, as hard as stone and heavily veined. Despite his erection, the foreskin still buried Squirt's glans in its satiny folds. Fascinated, Gordon gently placed his fingertips near the head of Squirt's cock and slowly eased the foreskin down, exposing the plump and eager glans beneath.

The glans was perfectly formed, bulbous and pink. A shining crystal dewdrop of precome shivered at the tip of it. With his heart thundering in his chest, Gordon carefully lapped the precome away, closing his eyes as he relished the sweet taste of it. He watched wide-eyed as Squirt's hips rose off the bed to meet him, as he gave himself up completely to Gordon's need.

Gordon smiled at Squirt's reaction. With his free hand, he stroked Squirt's lean flanks, his strong legs bristling with pale hair. Gordon's own body shook with the ministrations of Squirt's hot mouth surrounding his dick. With his eyes wide open and his hunger for the man beside him growing into a living, pulsing creature inside him, Gordon slipped his lips around Squirt's glans and slid that long, fat cock as deep into his mouth as he could get it.

Squirt pulled Gordon closer as he engulfed Gordon's iron cock all the way down to the root. His mouth played a melody of desire that stirred Gordon to new heights.

When Squirt's fingers tore into Gordon's hair and Squirt's cock pushed ever deeper into Gordon's throat, his whole body trembling with need and urgency, Gordon gave himself up to nothing but meeting Squirt's desires. He pulled him in, as deep as he could take him, and with touch and the movements of his mouth and tongue, Gordon let Squirt know that he wanted Squirt's release as much as Squirt did.

And finally it came.

As Squirt's back arched wildly into him and Squirt cried out Gordon's name, his fat cock erupted inside Gordon's mouth, releasing jet upon jet of hot, sweet cream. The torrent poured out so thick and fast Gordon could barely keep up. Ropes of steaming come leaked from his lips and poured down his chin. When the torrent lessened a bit, but the surge of come had still not stopped, Gordon pulled Squirt as close as he could and drew that long heaving cock deep into his mouth, extracting every last drop of sweet elixir, not willing to waste another drop—not letting Squirt collapse back onto the bed replete until Gordon knew for sure the man had nothing left to give.

When Squirt's body finally collapsed, Squirt reached down with a trembling hand and caressed Gordon's cheek for a moment, thanking him. And with his heart still pounding so loud that Gordon could hear it and feel the percussion against his skin, Squirt once again turned his attention to Gordon's cock, which had slipped from him, almost forgotten, at the moment of his own ejaculation.

With his face still pressed to Squirt's groin, still inhaling the scent of Squirt's balls and tasting Squirt's sweet, thick come on his lips, it took Gordon only a very few minutes to reach his own point of no return.

Squirt seemed to relish the game. He hunched into Gordon's body, his legs pinning Gordon down, his hands moving in a constant motion over Gordon's heated skin. Squirt's tongue dragged a hungry dance around Gordon's cock as his hot mouth circled, and caressed, and stirred the juices in Gordon's body, forever coaxing, taunting, begging Gordon to let himself go. Just as Gordon had craved the rush of Squirt's come down his throat, had ached to experience Squirt's orgasm filling his mouth, marking him for his own, Gordon could now sense Squirt's desire to taste Gordon's juices. To control *him*. Savor *him*. Laying his own claim on Gordon, just as Gordon had done to him.

Gordon closed his eyes and felt the churning inside his groin that heralded release. His body was a mass of live wires, trembling now and shuddering at Squirt's slightest touch, Squirt's tiniest urgings. Every flick of Squirt's tongue made him gasp, every finger stroke on his skin made Gordon plead for more.

Because he couldn't bear not to, Gordon arched his back into Squirt, just as Squirt had done to him, and the moment he did, he felt the come surging upward. Surging out.

"Yes, baby, yes," Squirt mumbled around his cock, and Gordon felt his own release explode from him.

Squirt gasped and laughed as the buckshot load of hot come tore from Gordon's cock and splattered the back of his throat. Squirt sucked and urged and pleaded, while Gordon trembled and lunged beneath him. The come filled Squirt's hungry mouth, and Gordon could almost sense Squirt's stubborn refusal to lose a single drop of the precious cream.

Squirt pulled Gordon into him as his lips drew everything from Gordon's body they could extract. Every taste. Every drop. Every tremor of excitement and every shuddering lunge of passion his mouth could stir. If there was one driving need in Squirt at that moment, and Gordon could sense it with every fiber of his being, it was to make Gordon happy. To give Gordon a moment he would never forget, and in doing so, do the same for Squirt. For Gordon understood inherently that Squirt was enjoying his orgasm even more than Gordon was. And that was a hell of a thing to realize.

As the last drops of come were reverently drawn from him like water from a blessed well, Gordon relaxed his body against Squirt's incessant urgings. And the moment Squirt released him from his mouth, Gordon pulled Squirt into his arms, shifting him around in the bed, dragging him down atop him, tucking Squirt's face into the crook of his neck and burying his own face in Squirt's shower-damp hair.

Squirt burrowed into Gordon's arms with a soft sigh, and Gordon closed his eyes and simply—held on.

They awoke sometime in the middle of the night. After Gordon tried to make sense of the tangled bedclothes, and finally succeeded, Squirt slipped back into his arms as if he were exactly where he wanted to be. And exactly where Gordon wanted him to be.

As Gordon lay there peacefully, enveloped in Squirt's scent, held protectively in Squirt's slight, pale arms, he knew he had found love for the very first time in his life. He knew if he was ever to be a happy, complete man, he would have to make Squirt his own.

He watched the stars through his bedroom window until he had drifted beyond awareness of the night around him, but not beyond the sensation of Squirt's gentle breath stirring the hair on his chest, the feeling of Squirt's heavenly pale arms holding him close, clutching him tight.

Gordon buried his lips in Squirt's wintry blond hair, Squirt's smell filling his head. He could feel their two hearts pumping more calmly now, one against the other. Squirt reached up to rest his cool fingers softly against the side of Gordon's neck, and Gordon turned his head and pressed his lips to the scars on Squirt's forearm.

"I'm sorry about the scars," Squirt mumbled.

"Don't be," Gordon whispered back, draping his arms more securely around Squirt's warm back, holding him close, holding him safe. "Never be sorry with me. You have nothing to be sorry about. Okay?"

"Okay, Gordon," Squirt sighed against him, his eyelashes brushing Gordon's chest like butterfly wings. "I'll try."

Just before sleep finally took him completely, a smile found its way to Gordon's mouth, and he knew it would remain there through the whole long night.

When the rays of the rising sun plucked Gordon into morning, stirring him awake with a gentle rush of excitement to discover Squirt was still in his arms, smiling at him drowsily, Gordon knew his life had changed.

It was the very first thought that entered his head.

# CHAPTER 10

GORDON STOOD at his kitchen window and gazed out onto the street, waiting—waiting. Then it happened. Half a block away, Squirt turned to see if Gordon was watching, and when Squirt saw Gordon at the apartment window, his face lit up. He smiled and waved and touched his fingers to his lips as if to send a kiss Gordon's way. Gordon grinned and waved back. He tapped his heart for Squirt to see, and Squirt's smile widened. His teeth flashed in the sun. Then Squirt turned away. Head high, he jauntily strolled toward the bus stop down the street, wearing one of the outfits Gordon had bought him. Going home. Gordon couldn't hear it, of course, but he somehow felt certain Squirt was whistling a merry tune as he strode along. At least he hoped he was.

Gordon missed him already.

Even after Squirt could no longer be seen, Gordon found it impossible to wipe the grin from his face. *What a night.*

He stared at the corner Squirt had disappeared around, waiting to see if maybe Squirt would reappear for some reason or other. When he didn't, Gordon finally turned from the window and began straightening the apartment. He grabbed up some dirty clothes and threw them in the hamper. Then he wended his way toward the bedroom and began making the bed. As he did, he suddenly found himself standing like a statue in the middle of the room, clutching Squirt's pillow to his face, inhaling Squirt's scent. Then he lay down on the bed and buried his face in Squirt's side of the bed. The sheets still carried the musky, heady smell of the man. Gordon lay there and breathed in the mixed aromas of soap and sex and heated, sleeping flesh until he began to feel like a perv. Then he hopped up and finished straightening the bed.

*Sweet Jesus, what a night.*

Gordon's only regret was that Squirt hadn't allowed Gordon to drive him home. He said he could just as easily take the bus—after all he had a bus pass now—and that would give Gordon some time to himself before he had to begin his day. Gordon didn't care about having time to himself. He would rather have had the few extra minutes with Squirt that driving him home would have given him. But Gordon didn't want to seem cloying either. He didn't want to smother the guy. He still had a pretty horrific fear of scaring Squirt away, and that wouldn't do at all.

Gordon was already making plans in his head. And scaring Squirt out of his life would have dropped a bomb on every one of those plans.

Bed made, head still filled with memories of the night, Gordon jumped when his cell phone rang. It had lain on his dresser uncharged for so long, Gordon had almost forgotten the sound of its ring.

He snatched it up knowing full well who was on the other end. And he was right. Oddly enough, he was almost glad to hear the familiar voice harping, "Hello? Hello? Answer me dammit. Hello?"

"Hello back, Mom," Gordon chirped.

There were a couple of beats of silence. Obviously, his mother hadn't expected the phone to be answered. Hadn't expected the damn thing to work at all. Gordon wondered how many other times, on how many other mornings, she had stood across town listening to a recorded voice saying "That number is not available. Please try again later."

When she finally did speak, Gordon's mother sounded fairly amazed. "My God, Gordon, you charged your phone. You charged it and you actually answered it when it rang."

Gordon grinned. His mother couldn't see the grin, but that was probably a good thing. "It's true. I did."

His mother sounded equally amazed, or maybe even *more* amazed, when she said, "And you sound happy. Good grief, Gordon, the last time you sounded happy, I think you were six, and your front tooth had fallen out, and you thought you'd make a killing from the tooth fairy. I remember I stuck a five-dollar bill under your pillow, and you still thought you were gypped."

Gordon tried to think of himself at six, but nothing came, so instead he thought of Squirt in the throes of a mighty ejaculation. And boy wasn't that a pip of a thought. He couldn't stop the words from escaping his lips. "If you had had the night I just had, you'd sound happy too. And five dollars for an actual body part *is* a gyp."

All this good cheer seemed to have taken his mother aback considerably. On one of the rare moments Gordon could remember, she was almost at a loss for words. "Well, that's good, honey." She stumbled a bit around the sentence, still sounding a little thunderstruck. "I mean, about your wonderful night. I don't suppose in all this euphoric bliss and rapture, you've actually started driving again. That would be too much to hope, right?"

Gordon couldn't remember the last time his mother called him honey. "As a matter of fact, I started driving yesterday."

"Holy shit," his mother said. "Maybe you'd better tell me about this miracle night you just experienced. And I don't believe I just said holy shit."

Gordon laughed. It wasn't often he caught his mother off guard, and he was enjoying the hell out of it. Then he laughed even harder when he realized he had just caught *himself* off guard enjoying this moment with his mother. He tried to ratchet down the happiness before she had his ass committed. "Was there something you wanted?"

Gordon could hear the smile in his mother's voice when she answered. "There must have been something, but I'll be darned if I can remember what it was."

"Maybe it's time to drop another few hundred bucks on your therapist." Gordon grinned.

He couldn't see it, of course, but he could feel the woman grinning back. "Maybe it is."

Suddenly Squirt began filling up the corners of Gordon's mind again, and with a smile splitting his face from ear to ear, Gordon, said, "I have to run, Mom. I'll meet you for dinner one of these nights. Maybe I'll bring a friend for you to meet."

His mother's voice dropped an octave, but still she sounded pleased. "Oh, so that's what this is all about. Well then, good, darling. Anybody who can knock you off the Morbid Train and make you smile again is one of my favorite people already. I'll look forward to dinner."

"Love you," Gordon said before he could stop himself.

His mother took a long moment to let that soak in. When she responded with a stuttering "I—I love you too," Gordon could hear the emotion in her voice.

He decided he'd better disconnect before he killed her completely. When the cell phone was silent in his hand, he carefully laid it on the dresser and collapsed onto the bed like someone had just shot his legs out from under him.

*Squirt did that,* Gordon told himself. *He's not even here in the room, and he made two people happy.*

Gordon closed his eyes and pondered the wonder of it all, ignoring the fact his cheeks were starting to hurt from smiling so hard. He reached out in the darkness behind his eyes and pulled the memory of Squirt into his arms.

The memory was nowhere near as good as the real thing.

GORDON'S PAROLE officer sat across the desk shuffling papers. Gordon perched on a straight-backed chair in front of him, patiently waiting for the guy to stop piddling around. They were in the county administration building at the foot of Broadway, not more than a hundred feet from the bay. The Coronado Bridge, where Gordon and Squirt had witnessed the murder of the unfortunate homeless man, was a couple of miles away on the other side of downtown.

Gordon's parole officer didn't know anything about Gordon witnessing a murder, and Gordon planned to keep it that way.

Through the office window, propped open with a fat law book of some sort, Gordon could hear a ship's horn blaring from the channel, perhaps prodding a sailboat out of its path. There wasn't much of a breeze wafting through the window, but what breeze there was smelled of seawater and warm churros from a vender down on the street. There was always a party atmosphere on the waterfront during the summer in San Diego, what with all the cruise ships and tour boats taking on and dropping off vacationers every five minutes. The festive air even occasionally penetrated the staid and dusty probation office, where

Gordon's parole officer, and countless other county minions, plied their assorted trades.

Tom Rhiner was in his midfifties. He had a shockingly gorgeous head of steel gray hair, looked fit and trim in his tie and shirtsleeves, and to Gordon's amazement, he also seemed a bit disconcerted at the moment. Gordon couldn't imagine why since he had just told Mr. Rhiner he was now ready to start looking for work, which was what the man had been urging Gordon to do for the past six months.

The paper shuffling was obviously a ruse to cover Mr. Rhiner's discomfort, although Gordon still didn't know what his parole officer had to be uncomfortable about.

Finally, Gordon thought he should come right out and ask. "Is something wrong? They're not going to throw me back in the slammer, are they?"

Mr. Rhiner jumped like someone had poked him with a pin. Then he laughed at himself. "No, Gordon. You're doing great. And I'm glad to hear you've decided to start looking for work. It's past time for you to rejoin the human race."

"Then what's the problem?" Gordon asked.

Mr. Rhiner stared at him for a few heartbeats while his face slowly reddened under Gordon's gaze. He ran a hand over his five o'clock shadow (the day was almost over), then turned his eyes to the window to look outside. Seeing no means of escape in that direction, Mr. Rhiner turned his eyes back to Gordon with all the enthusiasm of a man about to suffer his first root canal.

"Gordon, I was wondering.... Well, it's come to my attention that—no, wait. I um, well um, I'd like to ask a favor....Well, no, it's not a favor.... Oh, crap!" Mr. Rhiner's face was so red now Gordon began to wonder if he was about to have a stroke.

Gordon leaned forward and rested his hands on the desk. "Geez, Mr. Rhiner, just spit it out. Since the worst thing I can imagine is them sending me back to jail, and since you tell me that's not the problem, then I'm pretty sure I can handle whatever it is you're trying to wiggle out of telling me."

"Of course, son," Mr. Rhiner said, shocking Gordon down to his toes. The last thing he expected Mr. Rhiner to do was call him "son."

Mr. Rhiner sucked in a great breath of air, like he had been swimming underwater for the past ten minutes, and then he ran a hand through his hair. When he pulled his hand away, his steel gray hair was sticking straight up off the top of his head like a dead hedge.

Gordon was holding his breath now, wondering what the hell the man was trying to get at.

He didn't have to wonder long.

Still as red as a stop sign, Mr. Rhiner finally got the courage to say what he was trying to say.

"Gordon, I wonder if you would consider it a breach of ethics for me to ask your mother out to dinner?"

As soon as the words were spoken, Mr. Rhiner collapsed back in his chair like someone had just pulled his plug.

Gordon sat there blinking. Once. Twice. Then a grin spread across his face from ear to ear, and Mr. Rhiner, seeing it, became even redder.

Finally, Gordon found his voice. "She told me the two of you had spoken. I just assumed it was about me."

If Mr. Rhiner got any redder, he was going to go up like a Roman candle. "It *was* about you, Gordon. She's concerned for your welfare. We both are."

Gordon studied his parole officer's face just long enough to make him a little more uncomfortable than he already was, then decided to cut the man some slack. "Hell, Mr. Rhiner, go for it! I'm not sure you know what you're getting yourself into, but if that's what you want, hell, yes. Give it a shot. My mother needs a man in her life. Maybe then she'd leave *me* alone." And after a moment of consideration, he added, "Joke. That was a joke."

Mr. Rhiner tugged his tie loose. Maybe he was trying to drain some of the blood out of his face before it started seeping out of his ears. "Really, son?"

"Yep," Gordon said. "It really was a joke."

Mr. Rhiner was chewing on a pencil now. The guy was a wreck. "No, Gordon, I mean is it really okay if I ask your mother out?"

Gordon laughed. "As long as you aren't already married, or suffer from some horrible STD, or are hiding the fact that you're actually an alien from another planet come to take over humanity and boil us down to bouillabaisse, shit yeah. You have my blessing."

Mr. Rhiner stammered, wide-eyed, "I'm a widower."

Gordon clucked in sympathy, then decided it was stupid to cluck so he nodded instead. "Well, good. All the better. My mom's a widow. You have something in common already."

With that out of the way, Mr. Rhiner tried to pull himself back into probation officer mode. He was still pink, and he looked like he knew it, but he no longer appeared to be on the verge of going up in flames. He slid a slip of paper across the desk.

"Take this, Gordon. It may be your best shot. I wish you all the luck in the world. I really do."

Gordon stared at the paper, almost afraid to pick it up. "Why? What is it?"

Mr. Rhiner smiled a warm smile. The warm smile was almost as surprising to Gordon as the fact that his parole office wanted to date his mother.

Mr. Rhiner tapped the paper with a fingertip, then slid it a little closer to Gordon's side of the desk. "This might just be your best opportunity to become a weatherman again. It's not at your old station, but it's still local, and I know the man personally. He promised me he would give you every consideration just as soon as you got your head out of your ass and—I mean, as soon as you made up your mind to go back to work and stop texting while you're driving drunk."

Gordon's eyes popped open wide. He must have looked startled and hurt because Mr. Rhiner backtracked.

"I'm sorry, Gordon. That was meant to be a joke. Guess it wasn't funny."

"Not funny at all."

"I'm sorry, son. I'm still a little rattled about the mother thing."

Gordon nodded absentmindedly, but he still did not take the piece of paper. "Did my mother set this up?"

"No, Gordon. I did. What happened to you two years ago might have happened to any of us. You did nothing malicious. You simply practiced bad judgment. Driving drunk and texting on top of it was a boneheaded thing to do, and I'm sure you know that now. In fact, I doubt if anyone knows it better than you do. I shouldn't tell you this, but I've done the very same thing myself on occasion. At least, I used to. Since meeting you, I certainly don't do it anymore."

"Why didn't you tell me about this job before?"

Mr. Rhiner leaned forward. Some of the blood had drained from his face. He had even patted down his mop of gray hair so he didn't look so insane. Of course, Gordon figured after a few dates with his mother, Mr. Rhiner would probably start looking insane all over again. Poor bastard. But he would let the man figure that out for himself.

"I'm sorry, Gordon. I didn't tell you about the job earlier because I knew you had to want it. You had to be ready to get back in the saddle, so to speak. Ready to climb back up on the horse."

Gordon gave a good-natured grimace. "Clichés always help."

Mr. Rhiner's face softened into a grin. Some of the blood shot back into his cheeks. "Sorry."

Gordon nodded. "Me too."

Gordon struggled to push away all thoughts of what happened to him on that night two years ago when his life fell apart, and the moment he did, he began to feel a rush of excitement building in his stomach. Then that tiny rush of excitement clawed its way upward and spread his lips apart into a smile. He still refused to touch the slip of paper. He still couldn't bear to let himself hope that what Mr. Rhiner said was true. That he actually had a chance of going back to his old profession.

"I don't know what to say," Gordon stammered. "I don't know… how to thank you."

Mr. Rhiner beamed back at him. "Just claim the job as your own, and I'll be happy. And maybe put in a good word for me with your mom."

Gordon laughed. "I'll praise you to high heaven. She'll think you're Jesus Christ himself by the time I get done with her."

Mr. Rhiner blushed again. "Well, don't get carried away." But he looked happy when he said it.

He stood and stuck out his hand. "Good luck, Gordon. If you get the job, we'll find another way for you to satisfy your community service. I'll arrange it with Mama Davis at the mission. Is that all right with you?"

Gordon nodded, still not quite believing his good fortune. Of course, he didn't have the job yet, but at least he had a chance. And that was good enough for the moment.

"Sure," Gordon said, clasping Mr. Reiner's hand. "But if I do get the job, I'd like to tell Mama Davis myself. She's been wonderful to me."

Mr. Rhiner gave him a sly smile. "According to your mother, whom I spoke to this morning, you also have someone else you might like to talk to about all this."

Now it was Gordon's turn to blush. "She told you?"

Mr. Rhiner nodded. "I think it's great, Gordon. Everybody needs a little love in their life." Then he blushed again.

Gordon was too thrilled to notice. With his free hand, he slid the paper off the desk with a fingertip and stuffed it in his pocket. With his other hand he continued to shake Mr. Rhiner's paw.

"Thank you," Gordon said, and Mr. Rhiner nodded.

"You can go now, Gordon. Keep me posted. And your next appointment with me is on the 15th. Don't be late."

"I will. I mean, I won't. And—"

Mr. Rhiner held up his hand. "No more thanks. Just wish me luck too. I think maybe we're both going to need a little help from the fates."

Gordon laughed, and because he couldn't seem to stop himself from doing it, he leaned over the desk and pulled Mr. Rhiner into a hug.

Then, before the surprise departed his parole officer's face, Gordon spun on his heel and left the office, gently pulling the office door closed behind him.

As prearranged, he found Squirt sitting on a piling at the edge of the bay, feeding potato chips to a gathering of sea gulls, who were squawking up a storm and trying to snatch the chips right out of Squirt's hands. Squirt was laughing at their antics.

When Squirt looked up and saw Gordon approaching, his smile hit high beams.

Not caring what anybody thought, Gordon pulled Squirt into his arms. "Hi, Baby."

Squirt tilted his ball cap back out of the way and peered under Gordon's curtain of hair. "Take me home," he said softly. "I want to make love."

Gordon nodded, his heart so big in his chest there was barely room for anything else.

"Home it is," he whispered back.

GORDON STROKED Squirt's bare back as the smaller man squatted over him on the bed. Squirt was hard and his cock lay hot against Gordon's stomach. Both men were naked, their bodies slashed by planks of light as the rays of the setting sun blasted through the bedroom window, spilling out across the bed.

Squirt's lips were pressed to Gordon's mouth, tasting, exploring. Gordon closed his eyes as Squirt foraged over him. Gordon was so excited his hands were trembling at the touch of Squirt's skin, so hot and smooth and welcoming. Squirt's pale legs clasped him tight as Squirt slid his cock over Gordon's flesh. While Gordon's hands were trembling, Squirt was trembling all over. Gordon could feel the raggedness of his breath in their kiss.

Squirt pulled his lips away and scooted down on the bed, dragging his mouth over Gordon's chest while Gordon buried his fingers in Squirt's hair. Gordon arched his back as Squirt's lips travelled farther south, brushing his stomach. Squirt tugged playfully at Gordon's pubic hair with his teeth.

When Squirt pressed his mouth to Gordon's balls, sucking first one testicle, then the other, into that moist, hungry cavern, Gordon breathed, "Oh, God," and arched his back higher.

Squirt released his balls and slid his lips along Gordon's shaft. Gordon was so hard he thought maybe his dick was going to explode, and if Squirt kept doing what he was doing, he *knew* it would.

Squirt gently surrounded Gordon's glans with his silken lips, and ever so slowly, he slid his mouth further down Gordon's shaft until

Gordon's entire cock was buried in that heavenly moist heat. As Squirt worked his magic on Gordon, his hands played along Gordon's chest, testing and teasing every ripple of flesh, every underlying rib, every sizzling speck of heat.

Gordon was never quite sure where it came from, but when Squirt released him from his mouth, he immediately began rolling a condom down over the length of Gordon's iron cock. Gordon opened his eyes and gazed along the length of his body to watch. Squirt saw him watching and smiled a sexy smile, once again pressing his lips to Gordon's balls as he finished rolling the condom all the way down to the base of Gordon's dick.

Satisfied, he squeezed Gordon's glans gently with his fingertips and smiled all the broader when Gordon's hips again came off the bed to meet his touch.

"Close your eyes, baby," Squirt cooed, and Gordon did, relishing the feel of his condom-wrapped cock being stroked and squeezed by Squirt's talented fingers.

The sudden scent of lotion filled the room, and the next thing Gordon knew, Squirt was once again ranging up his torso, tasting Gordon's skin along the way, until he pressed his mouth to Gordon's lips, his tongue begging to be let in. His body now trembled so violently that Gordon began shaking too. Just knowing how excited Squirt was, was a turn-on of the very first magnitude.

Even with his eyes closed while they kissed, Gordon could tell by Squirt's motion he was doing something down below. Something to himself. When Squirt gasped, Gordon understood. Squirt was entering himself with a fingertip.

"Let me," Gordon mumbled around their kiss, and easing Squirt to the side, he laid him gently on the bed, face down.

Gordon threw his leg over Squirt's pale, perfect body, and now it was his turn to take control. He kneaded Squirt's lean back and flanks as Squirt buried his face in a pillow. Gordon smiled as he touched the silken skin of Squirt's buttocks and oh so gently spread the cheeks apart. There was lotion there Squirt had applied moments before, and with his heart beating like crazy because he was so damn turned on,

Gordon traced a fingertip around Squirt's pink opening, grinning when Squirt spread his legs wider to give Gordon better access.

Applying pressure, Gordon slid a fingertip through the tightness and heat and slowly buried it in Squirt's opening. Squirt lifted his ass to meet Gordon's gentle piercing and his legs opened even wider. The muscles of Squirt's calves and the back of his thighs were knotted and quivering.

Gordon pressed a kiss into either inner thigh, and then, with his finger still buried deep and moving in and out gradually, he positioned himself over Squirt's body, pushing his lips across Squirt's ear.

"Tell me what you want, baby," Gordon whispered. "Tell me what you want."

And Squirt reached around to pull Gordon close. His ass rose higher to meet the pressure of Gordon's hard cock against the small of his back. Squirt was gasping now in anticipation. Gordon could hear it, could sense Squirt's need for him. His hunger.

"Fuck me, Gordon. Please. I can't wait anymore."

Squirt twisted his head around and found Gordon's mouth with his lips, and as they kissed, Gordon slipped his finger free. Circling Squirt with his arms, he felt Squirt reach below and lead him home.

Squirt positioned Gordon's glans against his sphincter, and as Squirt forced himself to relax completely, Gordon helped by pushing gently forward. With a gasp from both of them, Gordon found himself entering the well of heat. His cock slid, ever so slowly, deeper and deeper into the depths of Squirt's core, and as he lost himself in the sensation, he pressed his mouth to the back of Squirt's neck and tried not to cry out his pleasure.

"Oh God," Squirt mumbled with his lips buried in the hair on Gordon's forearm. He nipped Gordon there as he arched his back higher and accepted Gordon all the way inside. As Gordon began to move his hips, gently at first, afraid of causing pain, he opened his mouth wide and sucked at the nape of Squirt's neck. He was so turned on by the taste of the man and by the eroticism of the penetration that the pounding of his frantic heart filled his head as if nothing else existed.

"Oh God," Squirt repeated as Gordon pulled his cock almost free before slowly burying it again, then again.

Long minutes of gentle pounding passed. When they were both crying out, clinging hard, happily taking and being taken, Gordon knew he could not go on. His come was roiling in his balls, begging for release. His heart was hammering so hard he thought it might tear loose from its moorings and go bouncing across the floor like a fucking basketball.

Squirt rolled his head from side to side, signaling how lost he was in the sensation of Gordon's cock buried deep inside him. He continued to arch his back into Gordon's thrusts, groaning with pleasure at each new penetration.

As Gordon came closer to orgasm, Squirt seemed to know. "Yes," Squirt gasped. "Finish it. Come for me. Please, Gordon. Use me. Come inside me."

And in reply, Gordon drove his cock harder into Squirt's eager ass. Time and time again. And as he did, he saw Squirt slide a hand under himself and felt the rhythm of Squirt stroking his own cock to completion. When Gordon finally cried out, filling the condom with his seed, Squirt's ass rose high into the air to meet Gordon's thrusts yet again, and then it was Squirt's turn to cry out. Gordon slid his hand under Squirt's belly just in time to feel Squirt's hot come spill out into the palm of his hand.

Gordon pulled Squirt more tightly into his arms, and as the last drops of his own come oozed from him, filling the condom, Squirt once again craned his neck around and sought out Gordon's mouth. Their lips came together as their bodies spilled the last of their passion. The passion Gordon knew they shared. The passion they shared for each other.

"Thank you," Squirt mumbled into the kiss, his body trembling yet again. He seemed to relish the feel of Gordon's arms holding him close, the sensation of Gordon's cock softening inside him, as much as Gordon did. Squirt shuddered a final tremor that spoke to Gordon of overpowered nerve endings rippling over Squirt's skin like waves of electricity.

"Thank you," Squirt said again, but so softly Gordon could barely hear the words. He could feel Squirt's lips roam over his, lingering, savoring.

Gordon pulled back just enough to study Squirt's face. Amazed, he watched a tear slide down Squirt's flushed cheek. Touched, Gordon pressed his forehead to Squirt's as he scooped the man even tighter into his arms.

"Stay with me," Gordon whispered. "Stay with me forever."

Squirt struggled unsuccessfully to find his voice. Instead, he pressed his face into the crook of Gordon's neck and nodded.

Gordon felt Squirt's hot tears on his skin. Only then did he realize they were mixed with his own.

# CHAPTER 11

WHILE SQUIRT, freshly showered, went to rummage through the fridge for something to eat, Gordon grabbed a quick shower himself—to cool off as much as anything. While he showered, he pondered.

Sex with Squirt was like a road trip to heaven. Gordon stuck his face in the cool spray and smiled at the memories of the hour he and Squirt had just spent together.

And at the words they had spoken at the end of it.

Gordon couldn't quite believe he had done what he did. He had practically asked Squirt to move in with him. Hadn't he? And Squirt had said yes. *Hadn't he?*

But that wasn't the most bizarre aspect of it. The most bizarre part of the whole episode was the fact that Gordon was head over heels in love with a man whose name he didn't even know!

Now that was a fucking wonderment. Wouldn't Gordon's mother be thrilled about that!

Christ.

Well, Gordon would have to set this straight right away. He cranked off the shower, gave his head a massive shake to disperse the water from his too-long hair, and stepped out of the shower stall to dry off. That done, he donned a pair of boxer shorts and padded through the apartment to find Squirt sitting at the kitchen table eating a bologna sandwich.

Squirt jumped up when Gordon entered the room. "You want a sandwich? I'll fix it for you."

"No, Squirt," Gordon said around a smile. "You sit down and eat. I want to talk to you."

Squirt was naked. The only thing he wore was a rubber bracelet in the colors of gay pride he had found on Gordon's dresser. Gordon thought he had never seen a more beautiful human in his life—the pale clean lines of his slight body standing perfectly erect, muscled just enough to be stunning; the brush of blond hair on his sexy legs, matching the pale thatch of hair on his head; his heavy cock, even in repose, swinging delectably in the air. Gordon watched in some sort of lovesick awe as Squirt flung himself back into the kitchen chair and resumed eating his sandwich. Gordon wasn't sure, but he thought he detected a hint of trepidation in Squirt's countenance. Just a glimmer of unease.

Gordon suspected he knew what the unease was all about. Squirt was wondering exactly what it was Gordon wanted to talk about. Maybe he thought Gordon was going to backtrack on the words he'd uttered as they lay in each other's arms just a few minutes earlier. Determined not to let Squirt feel apprehensive another second, Gordon dove right in. Best to get everything out in the open right now. Then they could both relax and enjoy each other's company.

"Babe, I meant it when I asked you to stay with me. I didn't just throw the words out in the middle of sex because it seemed like the right thing to say. I want you here with me. I'm nuts about you. I want us to be a unit. A family. Lovers. I want us to be lovers." Gordon swallowed hard. "I love you, Squirt."

Squirt set his sandwich aside and reached across the table to lay his hand atop Gordon's. His fingers intertwined with Gordon's and Gordon brought Squirt's hand up to his face and pressed it to his lips.

"Tell me you feel the same way, Squirt. Please."

Again, a film of tears blurred Squirt's eyes. He stared into Gordon's waiting face for a long, long moment from the depth of his floating sapphire eyes, and when he finally spoke, he squeezed Gordon's fingers between his own.

"I do," Squirt said. "I want to be with you every minute. And— and I know you love me, Gordon. I knew it before you spoke the words just now. I can sense your love for me every time we're together. You said you want us to be lovers, but I think we already are. I think in my heart we were lovers the first time we saw each other. That day back at Mama's. Remember? That day you rode in on your white horse and rescued me from those bullies. I think we were lovers then. I think every day since then I've grown to love you more."

Gordon realized Squirt was right. Squirt had held a place in Gordon's heart ever since that very first meeting.

And wonder of wonders, Squirt felt the same way he did! Squirt cared for him too!

"I need to tell you some things first, Squirt. There are things you need to know about me. And… and…."

"And what, Gordon?"

"And there are things I need to know about you."

Squirt slipped his hand from Gordon's grasp and rose to his feet. He carried his plate and the knife with a smear of mustard on it to the kitchen sink. He stood there, nude and unashamed, his back to Gordon, and washed and rinsed the plate and knife before carefully placing them in the strainer by the sink. When he was finished, his back still to Gordon, he stared through the kitchen window. The day was waning. It would be dark soon. Gordon realized if they were going to turn the lights on, they would either have to get dressed or he would need to close the curtains. Those were Gordon's mundane thoughts.

Squirt's thoughts seemed to be more serious.

Quietly, Squirt spoke to the window as if addressing the setting sun. "There are a lot of things I can't tell you, Gordon. I can't tell you, because I don't remember them. Something happened to me. Something… bad. But I don't know what it was. I—I've been living like this for a while now. Someday maybe I'll remember. The doctors tell me I will, anyway. Someday maybe I can tell you all the things you want to know. But you'll have to be patient with me." Squirt finally turned from the window in all his naked beauty and stared at Gordon sitting at the table watching him. "Can you do that, Gordon? Can you wait for me to remember?"

Gordon didn't understand, but he believed what Squirt said. He had read of such things in college. If something in Squirt's past had been so horrible that he felt he needed to block it from his mind, then Gordon would be patient, just as Squirt had asked him to be. He loved Squirt enough to do that. Didn't he?

Gordon's smile was meant to reassure. To understand and reassure. "Yes," he said. "I can wait. I can wait forever if I have to."

Squirt crossed the room to where Gordon sat at the kitchen table in his boxer shorts. He eased himself down onto Gordon's lap and draped his arms around Gordon's shoulders, laying his cheek to Gordon's stubble—they both needed a shave—and as Gordon draped his arms around Squirt to drag him close, Squirt pressed his lips to Gordon's shoulder.

"I don't think I've ever loved anybody like I love you, Gordon. I don't think I *want* to. It's been too hard loving you and not having you completely. It's been too hard thinking I knew how you felt but not really knowing for sure because you never actually said the words."

Gordon pressed his face into Squirt's neck, inhaling the luscious scent of the man, loving the heat of him, the softness, the *life* he offered of himself. "I've said the words now," Gordon whispered. "You don't have to wonder anymore. Okay?"

Squirt nodded. "Okay."

"And I don't have to wonder either. Right?"

Squirt pulled back enough to gaze into Gordon's eyes. "No. I love you too, Gordon. I love you more than anything."

Squirt's face blossomed into a rosy hue and Gordon grinned at him. "Not used to saying those words, are you?"

Squirt grinned back. "Nuh-uh."

Gordon swept his fingers through Squirt's pale hair as he stroked the fluff on Squirt's thigh with his other hand. He was getting aroused, and since Squirt was sitting on his dick, he was pretty sure Squirt was aware of the fact.

"Now that you've said the words out loud, it's not so bad, is it?" Gordon gently asked.

Squirt gave his head a tiny shake. "I'm glad we said them. I feel like we're—I don't know—*complete* now. As if we've sealed a deal or something."

"We have sealed a deal. We're together now. I'm yours. You're mine. I want you to move in right away. All right? I'll help you get your stuff from the shop. Everything but the fucking door you use for a bed. That stays. Doorknob and all."

Apparently, Squirt had more common sense that Gordon did. He didn't even bother giggling about the bed. "What are we going to live on? Neither one of us has much of a job."

Squirt scooted back in Gordon's lap and slipped his hand between his legs to take hold of Gordon's erection. He did it seemingly without ulterior motive. He simply wanted to hold it in his hand. When he did, Gordon closed his eyes for a second because it felt so good, then he laid his own hand in Squirt's lap, where lo and behold, another erection had popped up. Gordon slid his cool fingers around it, sliding back the foreskin as he did so. He brushed a gentle thumb over Squirt's slit and was repaid for his action by Squirt quivering in his arms.

Gordon smiled. "I have a lead on a job, and if it pans out, we'll be set. You're no dummy. I think we can find a better job for you than cleaning up the damn electric shop and sweeping up other people's messes. Even the wonderful world of fast food would be better than that. Whatever happens on the job front, I have enough money to get us through for a while. So don't worry about it, okay? Let's just concentrate on each other for a while. And let's concentrate on getting you well. My mother has a therapist that might be able to help. We can see her if you—"

Squirt tensed in his arms. "I've done all that. I still do it, Gordon. It hasn't helped."

Gordon cooed him to silence. "Then we'll figure out something else. Just don't worry. We both seem to be a little damaged. But put us together and we make a really spectacular whole. Don't you think?"

The apprehension in Squirt's eyes faded. While his lips turned in a tiny grin, his fingers moved with a bit more urgency as they stroked Gordon's cock, so Gordon did the same.

Gordon laughed. "We're going back to bed, aren't we?"

"I certainly hope so," Squirt said, looking down, watching Gordon's thumb redistribute the first drop of precome to seep its way free across the head of his dick.

With wide eyes, they focused on each other's faces. Their lips came together, sweetly but urgently.

"My legs are going to sleep," Gordon muttered through the kiss.

Squirt giggled. He leapt to his feet and pulled Gordon from his chair, hard-on and all.

"Then come to bed, old man. I'll do what I can to get your circulation going again."

Gordon looked down at their two erections and grinned. "I think you already did."

As the darkness at the end of the day began to claim the apartment, their two bodies once again molded themselves to one, and for the first time in his life, Gordon made love to a man he had declared love for. Not a stranger, not a trick, not a one-night stand. A man he loved with all his heart. And a man who loved him back.

Gordon knew he would never be the same again.

Later, as they lay sated, blanketed in darkness, Gordon asked the question he had long wanted to ask.

"Please, Squirt. Tell me your name. Just once. Tell me that much. Let me hear it from your lips."

Squirt lay cuddled next to Gordon, his cheek on Gordon's chest. Silence filled the darkened room. The silence went on and on. Squirt was pretending to be asleep. Gordon knew he wasn't really sleeping by the brushing of Squirt's eyelashes against his skin.

He pressed his lips to Squirt's hair, glorying in the scent and softness of it. As a few heartbeats thudded past, Gordon allowed the silence to claim the room. Letting the question remain unanswered.

For now.

Later, in the wee hours of the morning, both men found themselves awake. Restless.

"Let's go get my stuff," Squirt said. "There won't be anyone at the shop to ask me questions. We can be in and out of there in twenty minutes. I'll explain it to the boss when I go to work tomorrow to clean the place up. Can we do that, Gordon? I don't want to have to explain myself to anybody tonight."

"Are you ashamed to tell your boss you're gay?" Gordon asked. "Is that what it is?"

"N-no," Squirt stammered. "He already knows that. But, well, he's real protective of me. He's not going to like it that I'm leaving. I want to talk to him about it after my stuff is gone. It'll just be easier that way. So can we do that? Can we go now while there's no one there?"

Gordon could think of no reason not to. "Sure," he said. "Let's get dressed."

As they pulled on their clothes, Gordon suddenly stopped with one leg in the air, the other inside his trousers, frozen in place like a half-dressed statue. "I love you, Squirt."

Squirt blinked back happy surprise. Then a melancholy tenderness softened his beaming face. "I love you, too," he echoed, reaching out to stroke Gordon's cheek. "I honestly do."

Gordon closed his eyes to better relish the touch.


SINCE SQUIRT owned almost nothing, his belongings didn't even fill Gordon's trunk. He and Gordon were in and out of the basement storeroom in half of Squirt's twenty-minute estimate.

"How can you live like this?" Gordon asked, bewildered, packing the third and last box in the rear of the car.

"Sometimes we have to do what we have to do," Squirt answered, his voice a somber monotone.

They were standing in the alley behind the electrical shop, the street lamp casting an eerie yellow light down on them through the fog that had rolled in off the bay. Gordon looked up at the sad inflection in Squirt's voice. Only then did he realize he shouldn't have said what he said.

"I'm sorry, Squirt. I didn't mean that the way it came out."

Squirt nodded. If embarrassed, he was trying to hide it. "I know."

Gordon took the last bunch of clothes from Squirt's arms and tossed them on top of the boxes in the car, slamming the trunk lid down on the lot. He immediately turned and pulled Squirt into his arms.

"I never want you to live like this again. I'm going to take care of you now, Squirt."

Squirt relaxed in Gordon's arms. "We're going to take care of each other," he said softly. "You won't be ashamed of me, Gordon. I'll get a proper job. I promise. I'll make you proud to be with me. I will."

Gordon pressed his lips to Squirt's forehead. "I'm proud to be with you already."

Squirt tensed in Gordon's arms.

Gordon stepped back to look into his eyes. "What is it, baby? What's wrong?"

Squirt mumbled something unintelligible, then made a visible effort to make himself understood. "It's my boss. He worries about me. Just for a while, if it's okay, I'd like to keep getting my mail here at the shop. All right? Then my moving away won't seem so permanent to him."

"He must like you a lot," Gordon said.

And Squirt nodded. "He's been like a father to me. I don't want to hurt his feelings."

"Then do whatever you think is right, Squirt. It doesn't matter to me. It's you I want, not your mail."

Squirt sighed, obviously relieved.

A pigeon cooed somewhere in the eaves above their heads. Then it cooed again. They both looked up but couldn't spot the bird.

"We're disturbing the wildlife," Gordon said. "Did you lock the shop door?"

"Yep. All locked up."

"Then let's go home."

"Home," Squirt echoed. "I like the sound of that."

Gordon ushered Squirt around the car, opening the passenger door like a proper gent.

"So do I, baby," he said. "So do I."

# CHAPTER 12

GORDON AND Squirt settled in as live-in lovers without a lot of fuss and with even fewer doubts. They both knew living under the same roof was the right thing to do. After all, they were crazy about each other. Why *shouldn't* they live together?

It didn't take long for Gordon to realize Squirt was a loving and generous partner. The umbrella of uncertainty and shyness under which they had begun their relationship was quickly lost in the shuffle of moving in together, never to be seen again. The quiet hours they spent, softly talking, sharing, planning their future, were only topped by the hours they spent naked in each other's arms. Sex became more to Gordon than just sex. It became a five-star experience. One he never tired of. Just the thought of Squirt's hands on him made Gordon ache. The memory of Squirt's mouth, tasting, drawing, coaxing him into orgasm, made him tremble in his boots, no matter where he happened to be—on the street, in the car, doling out bacon to a string of homeless vagabonds. Recalling the many times his hardness slipped into Squirt, and the many times Squirt cried out in pleasure at the piercing, his pale body shivering beneath him, was a never-ending wonder to Gordon. Those were his favorite moments, to be captured and held in his thoughts to drag out whenever he pleased. And he pleased a lot.

To say they never tired of each other would have been an understatement. They were addicted. Happily, unquestionably addicted. They couldn't get enough.

"Ain't love grand?" Gordon asked one night as they lay in each other's arms, hearts hammering down, bodies languid, the sheen of come still shimmering on their lips.

Squirt nodded, seeking his voice. "Yes," he finally mumbled, his mouth on Gordon's throat. His favorite spot. "Oh, yes."

For a while, Gordon continued to work at Mama's Soup Kitchen. Even he knew what he was doing, of course. He was vamping to the music of the desultory life he had been living the past two years, afraid to really crawl from the protective shell he had made for himself. He had opened himself up enough to let Squirt in, but he was still afraid to give the world another shot at him. As the days rolled by, however, his happiness with Squirt and Squirt's happiness with him, began to take a toll on Gordon. It changed him. For the better. He began to be a little less afraid of the world—a little less afraid of himself. His self-confidence grew.

While Gordon remained at the soup kitchen, Squirt continued to work as a janitor at the electrical shop. They did not speak of changing jobs, but in Gordon's mind, that fact seemed to always be there in the background just waiting for them both to resurrect it and finally set about making it happen. Still, there seemed to be no rush. It was funny how life's uncomfortable truths could be camouflaged by love. Yet even love could not hide all truths. For instance, Gordon's money was running low, and he knew it. Something would have to be done soon, or *both* men would find themselves out on the street.

Still, they had a little time, and Gordon let the gradual gathering of courage take him forward at its own pace. When the time was right to act, he would know it. When he was ready to face the world again, he would know that too. He didn't doubt it for a minute.

Squirt was nervous about meeting Gordon's mother, so Gordon promised him some time to get used to the idea before he paraded Squirt out for his mother's approval. Happily, his mother was preoccupied with a certain Mr. Rhiner, whom she found to be interesting and a pleasant change from her real estate cronies.

She spoke of him occasionally on the phone, and that was enough to set Gordon's alarm bells clanging. His mother was the most secretive person he knew. If she liked Gordon's parole officer well enough to actually mention him on the phone, Gordon figured she must be smitten.

Gordon was rather surprised to find himself happy for her. And for Mr. Rhiner too. Although he still wasn't sure the poor man knew what he was biting off, getting into a one-on-one with Gordon's mother.

But Gordon was a little too wrapped up in his own earth-shattering love affair to worry too much about his mother's. Put simply, he was far too happy with his own life to really give a shit about hers.

There was still guilt eating at Gordon, and it took him a while to realize exactly why. The truth came to him one morning at the very moment when he opened his eyes to a new day with Squirt nestled snugly in his arms, their bodies satiny and warm from sleep.

Gordon slipped quietly from bed, letting Squirt sleep on. He stood at the bedroom window and gazed out on the canyon below through sleepy eyes. He remembered the wailing coyote months before that had prompted the nightmare about the wolf. All his past mistakes suddenly slid back into place in Gordon's mind as he stood naked at the window with Squirt snoring softly in the bed behind him. That old familiar pain settled into Gordon's heart just as it had before Squirt had come along to fill his heart with love instead. Even with Squirt's heavenly scent still on his skin, Gordon knew immediately where the guilt came from.

It came from that tiny patch of new grass, shimmering in the distance on the hillside in Holy Cross cemetery. The place that never completely left Gordon's mind. Ever.

That day, between his morning and afternoon shift at the soup kitchen, Gordon drove his car to Holy Cross and trudged along the tussocky grass to Guadalupe Circle, where Jeremy Aldritch Booth lay moldering in the hot ground, baked by the California sun burning overhead.

By the time Gordon reached the flat stone with Jeremy's name carved into it, the tears were flowing down his cheeks. Too weak and too heartsore to care if anyone was watching or not, Gordon dropped to his knees at the foot of the grave and buried his face in his hands.

When he had a semblance of control over his emotions, he took his hands away and thumbed the tears from his eyes. He rested his hands in the sun-warmed grass and spoke in a whisper to the young man asleep below.

"I have no right to ask this—" Gordon began. But his voice gave out, lost in a sob.

He cleared his throat, wiped a new spate of tears from his face, and tried again.

"Jeremy, I've come to ask your permission to—to finally let you go. I have to move on with my life now. If I don't, I never will. I found love where I never thought I would. I discovered happiness, which I know I don't deserve. But—but—I need your permission to give myself up to it. I know I can never pay the price for what I've taken from you, but please, my pain won't bring you back. It never could. I know that now. Please be the bigger man here and let me try to make something of my life again. I will never forget you. I know that. And I will never forgive myself for what I did to you. But please. Please, Jeremy. Let me have this. Let me have Squirt. Let me have—*love*."

Gordon's voice broke yet again, and with a final "Please," he once again buried his face in his hands. He wept softly until he managed one more time to pull himself together.

And at that moment, a wonderful thing happened.

A cooling breeze stirred against his skin. He opened his eyes. He lifted his head and let the air soothe his fevered face. Looking down, he watched a tiny ladybug crawl across the carved stone in front of him. Jeremy's stone. The clean scent of newly cut grass suddenly filled his nostrils.

Staring up at the azure sky, he blinked back drying tears and pulled himself to his feet. He stepped forward and, leaning down, brushed his fingertips over Jeremy's tombstone—the tombstone of a man he had never met in life but knew intimately in death. The moment his fingers touched the stone, the ladybug unfurled her wings and flew away.

"Good-bye," Gordon whispered. And turning from that tiny patch of pale grass on the hillside where his soul was also buried, Gordon headed back to his car on wobbly legs.

The emptiness he felt was new. It wasn't the emptiness of not caring. It was different somehow. But did it mean what he hoped it meant? Had he been forgiven?

One day he supposed he might know. But not today. And hell, perhaps never.

Days passed. Peaceful days. Gordon's life continued. His happiness with Squirt went on. Somehow his inner turmoil had been quelled. At least for a while. For whatever reason, either wishful thinking or actual forgiveness from the man lying dead in the ground, Gordon took up the reins of his life with a lighter heart, a clearer purpose.

Three weeks later, Gordon finally dredged up the courage to do what his parole officer suggested. He picked up the phone and punched in the number on the little slip of paper Mr. Rhiner had given him. The call was answered on the second ring.

A meeting was set.

Too unsure of himself to boast of all the possibilities that might result from this one simple meeting, Gordon told no one. Not Squirt. Not his mother. No one. He barely dared to think of it himself.

Finally, the day came. Gordon wore his best suit and tried to stay calm. The job interview lasted two hours. When it was over, Gordon stood on the sidewalk outside Channel 9 Studios and closed his eyes, inhaling a huge gulp of hot summer air that was redolent with the scent of honeysuckle. Squinting into the sunlight, he looked around, finally spotting the source of the smell. There was a hurricane fence at the back of the parking lot awash with blooming honeysuckle vines, and Gordon thought he had never seen anything so pretty in his life. Or anything that smelled as sweet.

Of course, even Gordon believed he should be forgiven his effusive frame of mind. After what had just happened, who *wouldn't* be effusing like crazy?

The truth was, Gordon couldn't quite believe it. The job interview had gone exceedingly well. That fact was brought clearly home when Gordon looked down at the sheaf of papers in his hand. A contract. Unsigned as yet, but still a contract. The offer was on the table. Gordon simply had to accept it.

Jackson Price, the KTSI station manager, a chain-smoking middle-aged guy with a paunch and a receding hairline that was just on the verge of poofing out like a spent candle to leave him as bald as a bowling ball, had been friendly, open, and enthusiastic about Gordon's prospects. The offered pay was reasonable, although nowhere near the salary Gordon had earned at Channel 10. The time slots offered him for his weather reports were primetime all the way, and while it was still up in the air, he might even be offered a short weather spot on the channel's morning show, *A.M. San Diego,* with an accompanying boost in salary.

While all this was great news for a guy who had spent the last six months of his life ladling out instant scrambled eggs and sausage patties to a bunch of derelicts and senior citizens, even Gordon had to admit there was a time in his life when he would have been appalled by the prospect of working at this particular San Diego news affiliate.

The truth was, had Gordon been offered a job as meteorologist at Channel 9 before his own life self-destructed, he would have laughed at the very idea. Channel 9 was the poor kid on the block as far as local San Diego news stations went. For the most part, their anchors were people like Gordon, people who couldn't find a news job anywhere else—people who had either had their shot at fame and blown it, or people who had stayed too long at the fair and perhaps had sprung for a few too many facelifts trying to stay viable. It was common knowledge in the business that John Q. Public wasn't too hot on the idea of having news or weather reports thrown in his face at dinnertime by a bunch of old fucks. John Q. Public preferred to get his news from folks who were at least halfway pleasing to look at.

Channel 9 San Diego was the only station in town to buck that trend.

In other words, Channel 9 News was almost entirely staffed by people on their way out of the business for one reason or another. Age, personal problems, ineptitude. And oddly, in spite of all that, they still put out a pretty good news show, if you weren't too aesthetically snooty to watch it. They had even garnered a couple of local Emmys along the way to prove it.

But to show how humbled Gordon had become after all the horrible crap he had put himself through during the past two years, what with a heart-wrenching vehicular manslaughter trial culminating in a year of jail time and all of it topped off with months and months of guilt and shame and innumerable visits to the cemetery to mourn the man he killed, not to mention the untold hours he had spent staring at that goddamn revolver in his bathroom drawer just before toddling off to the soup kitchen to dole out food to the downtrodden—phew!—in spite of all this, Gordon found himself feeling only gratitude that Channel 9 was willing to take him on at all.

Now, with the job securely his if he chose to accept it, at least for a year, his would be the youngest and best-looking face on the Channel 9 news team, or so Mr. Price had informed him. Gordon's youth and good looks would be enough to get his foot in the door of public opinion. Then it would remain to be seen if the news-watching public could be cajoled into overlooking his past.

And that really was a big if.

While Jackson Price didn't say it in so many words, Gordon understood that any extension of his first one-year contract with the station would hinge entirely on whether the viewing public could be persuaded to take the high road and forgive Gordon his past transgressions. After all, San Diegans knew Gordon's story hands-down. The news-watching public had been bombarded with daily updates during the course of his trial, and later bombarded again at the time of his release from jail. Any television celebrity, even a small-time celebrity like a local weatherman, is always at the mercy of the people on the other side of the TV screen. Gordon knew that better than anyone.

"Frankly," Mr. Price didn't actually come right out and say, although he might as well have, "it will be entirely up to you, Gordon, to charm the public enough to pull off your own resurrection."

"If you can get people on your side," Mr. Price *did* say, "you might very well have a home with Channel 9 for as long as you want."

Remembering those words, a silly grin stretched Gordon's lips. That's right ladies and germs—as long as he wanted! That's what the guy said!

Such a burst of adrenaline suddenly shot through Gordon, he gave a whoop and raced for the car. He had to tell Squirt the good news.

On his way home, even as excited as he was, Gordon kept the car well under the speed limit, on both the freeway and city streets. He wouldn't have touched his cell phone for a thousand-dollar bill, no matter how many times it chirped and buzzed and vibrated in his trouser pocket. It could have crawled out of his pants and slapped him in the face with a wet fish and he *still* wouldn't have answered it. And texting? Forget it. He hadn't endured the past two years without learning *something*.

His overabundance of caution went straight out the window once he pulled into his parking space under the apartment building. He flung himself from the car, hurled himself up the stairs, contract in hand, and threw himself through the front door.

"Squirt! Baby! Where the fuck are you? I've got news!"

But Squirt wasn't there. Gordon checked every room.

He grabbed the phone from the kitchen wall. Maybe Squirt was working at the shop. Gordon figured he'd just give him a call and tell him the news over the phone. He had to tell somebody. He *had* to.

While Gordon dialed the number, an open newspaper on the kitchen table caught his attention. Gordon's eyes burned into two pictures on the front page.

They were pictures of Gordon. Side by side. Mug shots. Both front and side views. Grainy, as newsprint photos often are, taken on the night of the accident two years earlier. There he stood, unkempt, bleary-eyed, in a total state of shock, his ninety-dollar tuxedo shirt torn at the collar, his hair a fucking mess. He held a placard under his chin with a booking number on it. There was a cut on his right cheek, which had been covered with a Band-Aid by a paramedic moments earlier.

The pictures had been taken less than an hour after the accident— the accident that killed Jeremy Aldritch Booth and turned Gordon's life into a walking shipwreck.

Staring at the photo now with wide, horrified eyes, he felt the phone slip from his hand and clatter to the floor. The contract in his other hand drifted from his grasp, forgotten. Only then did Gordon see the smear of food on the wall. The shattered plate on the floor in the corner.

His excitement morphed to fear in a heartbeat. Gordon tore his eyes from the mess and grabbed the newspaper off the table.

# CHAPTER 13

GORDON STARED at the paper, his mind so packed with conflicting emotions whirling around, he didn't know where to begin to sort them out. In the maelstrom raging between his ears, not one coherent thought seemed capable of rising to the surface.

Finally, one thought *did* make itself known. And it was horrible.

"Oh, no."

Crumpling the paper in his fist, Gordon raced through the apartment to the bedroom and flung open the closet door. Squirt's clothes were still there, neatly hung among his own. He yanked open the dresser drawers. Squirt's underwear was where it always was, still neatly folded, unlike Gordon's stuff that was jammed in any old way with no sense of order whatsoever.

Atop the dresser, Squirt's money, a few crumpled bills and a smattering of change, lay in a ceramic dish, right where it always lay when Squirt was home.

Gordon breathed a sigh of relief but it was short-lived.

He spotted Squirt's tennis shoes, a newer pair Gordon had bought a few weeks earlier, sitting under the bed. It was the only pair of shoes Squirt owned. Gordon had tossed the others in the trash when he bought the new ones.

Confused even more, Gordon tried to think. What had just happened here? He stared at the shoes. Why would Squirt leave without his shoes? Gordon's spark of concern blossomed into a flame of fear.

*Where the hell was Squirt?*

And then his mind wandered back to the crumpled newspaper in his hand. He looked down at it, trying to ignore the dawning terror stuttering through him.

The newspaper was two years old. Gordon had a stack of old newspapers buried deep in the back of the closet, stuffed in a pillowcase. They were newspapers chronicling the trial. Gordon's trial. The paper in his hand was one of them. The booking photos that had snagged his attention in the kitchen still made him sick to his stomach every time he looked at them.

Gordon hated those pictures. And everything they brought to mind.

He strode back to the closet and slid the clothes aside. Sure enough, the pillowcase was there on the floor, but the papers were spilled out. Scattered. Rifled through. Everything bad that had ever happened to Gordon was chronicled in those damn newspapers. Everything about the accident. Everything about the aftermath of the accident. His public shaming. The loss of Gordon's job at Channel 10. The retraction of his upcoming Emmy nomination. Jail time. Stories about the man Gordon had killed. Everything.

And Squirt had seen it all! My God, would it be enough to destroy Squirt's love for Gordon? But that was stupid, wasn't it? Their love wasn't that fragile, was it? Gordon had meant to tell Squirt everything long before this, of course, but somehow time had passed and Gordon's past had remained buried from the eyes of the man he loved. Conveniently? Maybe. Gordon hadn't wanted to tell Squirt about the horrible thing he had done. Who would? But he *should* have told him. Gordon should have sat Squirt down and made him listen. But he hadn't. And now maybe it was too late.

But they had both had secrets they didn't want to share, hadn't they? Gordon's past. Squirt's own past. Even Squirt's real name. Squirt had avoided that topic just as assuredly as Gordon had sidestepped his own humiliating truths. And Gordon had let him do it.

Only now did Gordon begin to wonder about a few things. Why did Squirt insist on still getting his mail at the electrical shop where he worked? Why did he turn away at the least mention of his real name? If Squirt had a shameful past that he was hiding, Gordon would have understood. Hell, how could he *not* understand? If they were both living lies, how could one blame the other for what Gordon himself was also guilty of?

Gordon glanced over the scattered headlines at his feet, each one of them causing an ache in his heart. Local Weatherman Charged With Vehicular Manslaughter. Local Weatherman's Trial The Hottest Ticket In Town. Stafford's Victim In Third Year Of Law School—Top Of The Class. Weatherman Found Guilty—Justice Served. Stafford Sentenced To One Year In Jail. Prosecuting Attorney Says Weatherman Got Off Easy.

Gordon squeezed his eyes shut, blocking out the words. He could feel the blood rushing to his face. Even now the shame of all that had happened was almost too much to bear. The only thing that had made it bearable the past few months was Squirt. The love they had discovered for each other had given Gordon his life back.

Was that over now? Was this too much for even Squirt to deal with?

*Was he gone for good?*

For the first time in weeks, Gordon raised his eyes to the shelf above his head—the shelf where he had stashed the gun.

The fucking gun.

His pulse hammered in his ears. He raised his hand, not toward the shelf, but to grab the closet door. He slammed it shut, locking the gun—and his past—inside.

Gordon pressed the heels of his hands to either side of his head and tried to think. He couldn't give up this easily. He had to find Squirt. That was his first priority. He'd worry about this other shit later.

First he had to find Squirt.

Gordon grabbed the car keys off the kitchen table and headed out the door. On the way to his car he poked his head in the laundry room to make sure Squirt wasn't there. He wasn't, dammit.

Gordon began a slow drive through the neighborhood, peering around corners, down alleys, checking the sidewalks and storefronts. No Squirt. The day was winding down. It would be dark in a couple of hours. Gordon drove, gnawing his lower lip, heartsick to think he had kept his life a secret from Squirt. Even if Squirt had done the same to him.

How could two people love each other as much as he and Squirt and still not open up about *everything?* It's as if they had spent every waking moment together living only for the present, shunting their pasts into a corner, leaving their histories out of the relationship completely. Why would they do that? Their histories made them who they were. If you profess to love someone, you need to know everything about them. Don't you? Otherwise you're living—and loving—a lie.

Gordon knew Squirt had emotional problems in his life. There were a lot of things he didn't remember, Squirt had said. Gordon wasn't sure if Squirt meant things from his childhood or things that had happened later. And Gordon had never pressed Squirt to find out. Why was that? Was Gordon so terrified that delving into Squirt's past would open up his own?

Then there was the matter of the horrific scars on Squirt's arms. Obviously self-inflicted. Squirt had spoken of them with shame when their relationship began but then never mentioned them again. There was a doctor somewhere helping Squirt deal with his memory loss— Gordon knew that much—but he didn't know how to get hold of her. He only knew Squirt visited her in an office downtown twice a month. Gordon didn't know the doctor's name. He never saw the bills. He had no idea where the office was.

Jesus! How could Gordon be so stupid? How could he tell Squirt he loved him in one breath, then turn away from the problems Squirt battled as if they meant nothing? What kind of lover would do that?

But getting back to more pressing matters, how far could Squirt go without shoes and without money? But even more importantly than that, *where* would he go? Gordon could think of only one answer.

The electrical shop. The place he had once called home. Apparently, he had friends there. And once again, they were friends Gordon had never met. Had never *tried* to meet.

Even if Squirt hadn't offered, Gordon should have done something about that.

He steered the car toward Mission Hills, checking the clock as he drove, wondering what time the place closed. Hell, he didn't even know *that.*

Gordon banged the heel of his hand on the steering wheel. Shit shit shit.

He drove faster. Getting worried now. Getting *really* worried.

When he spotted the shop, crammed between a deli and a tiny bookstore, its neon sign burning bright in the evening light, Gordon breathed a sigh of relief. At least they were still open. Squeezing into the first parking space he could find, he raced to the shop, car keys jangling in his hand. He was so on edge, he jumped when the little bell over the door announced his entrance.

He had never been in this part of the business before. Only in the basement. It was another part of Squirt's life he hadn't bothered trying to share.

An older man behind the counter looked up when Gordon came through the door.

Gordon felt the man's disapproval before he took two steps into the store.

And it stopped him in his tracks.

IT WASN'T the first time Gordon had seen dislike on the faces of strangers. He remembered the female cop at the police station that day when he was searching for Squirt. This guy had the same look, same expression. Leery. Suspicious. Cold. Like he knew Gordon's past and didn't approve of it. One. Little. Bit. And Gordon accepted that. He had seen it too many times before to let it throw him now.

On the clerk behind the counter, however, the look of cold suspicion had already twisted itself into one of pure hatred. And it happened before Gordon had taken three steps into the building. The intensity of it lay on the air like the stench of rancid meat. Gordon could almost see the newsreels playing inside the guy's head recalling the whole sordid story of Gordon's downfall. He could even see the imagined headline being fabricated on the spur of the moment by the overactive interchange of synapses sparking through the man's brain cells. Conceited Overpaid TV Celebrity Acts Like An Ass And Kills Somebody Doing It.

Good headline, Gordon thought. Covered the facts nicely.

He braced himself against the man's glaring eyes and resumed his approach toward the counter.

The clerk threw his hand in the air like a traffic cop. "I've got nothing for you here. Best just turn around and go out the same way you came in. We're closed."

Gordon saw two customers speaking to another clerk in the back of the store. *Closed my ass,* he thought.

But he decided to shoot for honey. Vinegar never did get him anywhere.

"I'm not here for your services. I'm looking for someone."

The man cocked his head to the side, his dislike peppered now with a little confusion. "Who the hell could you be looking for in here?"

"Squirt," Gordon answered, still not understanding the intensity of the man's suspicions. "I'm looking for Squirt."

The reaction he got was so over the top, it was almost funny. Gordon didn't think the clerk could have jumped much higher if Gordon had dropped a cattle prod down his pants.

Mightily confused now, since the man's reactions were so far beyond anything Gordon had seen from anyone else, he actually took a step back when the clerk came rushing from around the counter.

The clerk stomped across the store on long legs. He was a big guy. In his fifties, maybe, but there didn't seem to be much fat on him. If things deteriorated into a fight, Gordon knew he would have his hands full. But before Gordon could really do anything about it, his arm was clasped in an iron grip and he was being propelled toward the front door. Apparently the guy actually intended to toss him out on his ear, like some cheesy-ass movie villain.

That pissed him off.

Gordon jerked his arm away and shoved the man to get some space between them. "What the fuck do you think you're doing?"

If the man was surprised to find Gordon fighting back, he didn't show it. He took a fistful of Gordon's shirtfront and yanked him close. "Don't you think you've done enough to that boy? Now get the fuck out of here. And if I ever see you around this place again, I'll rip your fucking head off. Do you understand me? You're not welcome here. You'll *never* be welcome here, Mr. Stafford. Now get the fuck out!"

Again, Gordon tore himself from the man's grasp.

Confused even more than he was before, he tried to understand. "I get it. I'm not your favorite person. Believe me, I get that a lot, so don't think you're hurting my feelings or anything. But goddammit, I need to find Squirt. It's important. I think something may be wrong. All you have to do is tell me if he's here. Maybe he's downstairs on his shitty-ass bed. If he is, I'd like to see him. Squirt and I need to talk."

All the while Gordon spoke, the man's eyes grew bigger and bigger, like he couldn't believe the words coming out of Gordon's mouth.

"How do you know about Squirt's bed? And how do you know he used to live in the basement? And what the hell is any of it to you, anyway?"

Gordon didn't want to get Squirt in any trouble or anything, but this was getting ridiculous. This pit bull motherfucker was protecting Squirt like Gordon was out to kill him or something.

"I probably know more about Squirt than you do. *Sir.* We share an apartment together, if it's any business of yours. I'm surprised he didn't tell you. Now something has happened, and—"

Now it was the clerk's turn to take a step backward. *"You're* the man Squirt's taken up with? *You?"*

Gordon still didn't understand what was going on. "Yes. He and I—"

But that's as far as he got.

The color drained from the man's face. He looked like he was about to topple over. Gordon flashed on the words the man had spoken earlier: "Don't you think you've done enough to that boy?" What the hell did he mean by that?

The store clerk seemed to have worn himself out. He looked around for a place to sit and finally rested his ass on the edge of a barrel filled with sale items. There seemed to be a little of everything in that barrel: light bulbs, sprockets, penlights, screwdrivers, rolls of electrical tape. Dusty odds and ends that had been sitting on the shelves too long, maybe, and were now reduced to collecting even more dust in a dollar barrel by the front door.

Gordon pushed his hair out of his face. His hand came away wet. He was sweating.

"What the hell is wrong with you?" he asked. "What the hell did I ever do to you? *Or* to Squirt, since you seem to be so appalled that we know each other."

The man gaped at Gordon. Just gaped. Then he rubbed the palms of his hands on the knees of his work pants. Maybe he was sweating too.

His face took on a look of amazement. When he spoke, his voice was just as amazed. "My God, you don't know, do you? You don't know who Squirt is."

"No, I—"

"Shut up, Mr. Stafford. Let me think." The man scrubbed at the bristles on his chin. He needed a shave.

Now a little rambling monologue took place with the clerk talking more to himself than to Gordon.

"And Squirt doesn't know who you are either. How could he? He's blocked everything out. He doesn't remember any of it."

"Remember what?" Gordon asked. "What is it Squirt doesn't remember?"

The man settled his eyes on Gordon and breathed a deep sigh, as if forcing himself to calm down. "It's not that he doesn't remember, Mr. Stafford. It's that he *chooses* not to remember. The doctors call it selective amnesia. But you don't know about any of that, do you?"

Gordon shook his head. "No. He told me he had problems with memory. He told me about his doctor. But that's as much as I know. He never told me—why."

"Why," the man echoed, shaking his head in disbelief. There was less anger and hate in his eyes now. He looked merely weary. "No, I don't suppose he did tell you. That's because the why of it all is exactly what Squirt has selectively blocked from his mind. I'm a little less sure about the other why."

"The other why?"

"Yes, Mr. Stafford. Why you would choose not to tell Squirt the truth about *you*."

"But—"

"You should have told him. Even if he didn't understand it."

"Understand what, for Christ's sake?"

The man merely stared at him.

"Look," Gordon said. "If you want to explain it all to me, great. But before you do, please, tell me if Squirt is downstairs. He left without money or shoes or—"

"No," the man said. "He isn't here. I'd know if he was. I guess we'd better go find him, then."

Gordon was confused even more by that statement. "We?" he asked.

"Yes, Mr. Stafford. We. And while we search I'll fill you in." As if an afterthought had struck him right between the eyes, he gave Gordon a befuddled perusal. He spoke to himself more than to Gordon, and Gordon knew it. "How the fuck did you two ever come together?"

The question sounded rhetorical so Gordon didn't even try to answer it. His priorities were elsewhere. "If we're going to look for him, let's do it now. It's getting dark."

The clerk nodded. "Yes. All right."

He heaved himself off the edge of the barrel and called out to the other clerk still rattling off information to the two customers in the back of the store while pointing to a selection of porch lights hanging on the wall. "Dan! I have to leave. If I'm not back by closing time, lock up for me."

Gordon watched Dan nod and go right back to schmoozing the customers. Porch lights don't sell themselves, after all.

"Come on," the clerk said more softly, eyeing Gordon anew with a little less suspicion now, but not by much. "Let's go find Squirt. My van is out on a call. We'll have to take your car if you have one."

"I do," Gordon said, heading for the door.

The little bell over the shop door heralded their leaving. This time Gordon didn't jump when it jangled about his head. In fact, he didn't even hear it. He had too many other things on his mind.

The clerk followed Gordon onto the street, lighting a cigarette as he went. He still looked none too friendly.

# CHAPTER 14

GORDON EASED into rush hour traffic. "Where're we going?"

"I don't know," the man said. "Let me think. Just drive."

So Gordon drove.

The man slid his side window down to let the smoke from his cigarette escape. He didn't bother asking if Gordon minded if he smoked. And Gordon didn't much give a shit. He was still trying to figure out the answers to more important questions.

"What's your name?" Gordon asked. "And what's your relationship to Squirt?"

The man cast a cool glance in Gordon's direction, then took a long pull on his cigarette while he apparently decided whether he was going to answer or not. Finally, he did.

"Jerry worked for me."

"Jerry?" Gordon remembered the cop at the police station calling Squirt Jerry. He had suspected that was Squirt's name, but when he broached the subject at the apartment, Squirt had turned away, changing the subject.

"Yes," the man said. "His name is Jerry. I'm Sam."

He didn't offer to shake hands, and neither did Gordon.

Gordon eased around a stalled car just as the streetlights up and down the boulevard blinked on, heralding the approach of night. "And you hired Squirt to clean up your place of business and gave him a place to sleep. That was a good thing to do. Thank you."

Sam impatiently flipped his cigarette stub through the window. "I didn't hire Squirt to clean up the shop, Mr. Stafford. He just fell into that when his other skills—*left him.*"

"His other skills?"

"Yes. His other skills. The skills he plied until you came along and ruined his life."

It was Gordon's turn to do the cattle prod jump. "I didn't ruin his life! We love each other. We're lovers. I'm sorry if you didn't know he was gay like Squirt said you did, but—"

"I knew he was gay," Sam softly said. "But you still ruined his life, whether you know it or not."

Gordon could feel the back of his neck heat up. He was getting mad. It was also getting dark, which seriously lessened any chance they would have of spotting Squirt on the street. That made Gordon even madder. He flicked on the headlights. "Squirt and I have been nothing but good for each other. I don't care if you believe that or not. But I would like to know how it is you think I ruined his life. Fill me in. Give me the full brunt of your insight on the subject, Sam. I'd love to hear your version of events."

Sam twisted around in the seat, unbuckling his seat belt to do it, so he could stare at Gordon directly.

"Fasten your seat belt," Gordon said. "I don't want a ticket."

Sam gave a snicker and left his seat belt unhooked. "No, I don't suppose you do. You've had enough problems with the law, I guess."

Gordon saw no reason to deny it. He knew the man had recognized him the moment he walked into the shop. If he recognized him, then like every other newspaper reader and TV junkie in San Diego, he knew Gordon's story as well. "Yes," he snapped. "More than enough."

Sam's voice was lower now. Almost disbelieving. "You really don't know who Jerry is, do you?"

"No, goddammit, I don't. And I don't know what skills you're talking about either. I don't know *anything* apparently, except that I love him and I'm worried about him and if you have any ideas on where to look for him then I wish you'd tell me! It was your idea for us to look. So let's fucking look instead of arguing this bullshit back and forth."

"Jerry is an electrician, Mr. Stafford. He's worked for me for four years. Two years as an electrician and two years as… as you see him now."

Gordon remembered that day in the kitchen. He mentally slapped himself in the forehead. Of course. "He fixed my microwave," Gordon said, recalling how sure of himself Squirt had been that day. How knowledgeable. "He brought his tools to the apartment and fixed my microwave. I should have known."

"There are other things you should have known, Mr. Stafford. For one, you should have known to leave Jerry alone. Not to get your life mixed up with his. You've inflicted enough damage on the boy. He is what he is today because of you."

"Yes. He's a good person. A kind man. Notice I said man, not boy. And above all that, he's my lover. That's what he is. I don't care if you believe it or not, Sam, but Squirt and I are happy together. We love each other very much. We're trying to get back on our feet and move forward with our li—"

"Jerry can't move forward because his mind won't let him. And you're not helping!"

Gordon slammed his fist into the roof of the car. "But *why*, goddammit?"

No answer. Gordon turned to see what Sam was doing. He was staring through the windshield, apparently lost in thought.

"What is it?" Gordon asked. "Do you think maybe you know where Squirt might be?"

Sam slowly turned his eyes to Gordon. There was no longer anger on the man's face. Merely weary concern. "Yes. Turn right. It's a couple of miles up this street."

Gordon turned as he was directed. Once he was headed east he realized this was the same street he always took to Holy Cross Cemetery. Fear bit into him that he couldn't explain. He gripped the steering wheel tightly and drove. Teeth clenched. A dribble of sweat suddenly skittered down his ribcage beneath his shirt.

"You know where we're going now, don't you." Sam said. It wasn't a question.

"Y-yes. I think so. But I don't know why."

Sam lit another cigarette, flipping the spent match through the window. Gordon saw its little trail of sparks scatter in the darkness in his rearview mirror like a tiny fireworks display.

"I'll explain when we get there," Sam intoned.

Gordon only nodded. Suddenly he wasn't mad anymore. He was scared.

IT WAS dark in the massive cemetery. There were no lights to show the way. But it didn't matter. Gordon had traveled the weaving pathways so many times, he knew them by rote. He also knew the custodian would lock the gates soon. They couldn't linger long. He and Sam needed to hurry.

But Sam didn't seem to have any hurry in him.

Gordon crept along the winding lanes between the tombstones, the darkened landscape around them echoing an eerie, plaintive silence. Gordon couldn't bring himself to head directly for the stone on the hillside he knew so well. That required too much thinking. Too much... dread... to contemplate. He simply drove. Aimlessly. Down one winding lane, slipping onto another, turning on a whim, heading off in the opposite direction. Never stopping. Just moving forward. Like a bird afraid to light. Hoping against hope that Sam had another destination in mind altogether, other than that same pale patch of sod Gordon had been watering with his tears for what seemed like forever. And surely Sam did have another destination in mind. He had to.

What could Jeremy Aldritch Booth possibly have to do with all this?

And all the while Gordon asked himself that question, he felt the old misery settling into his soul. He tried to ignore it, but it just kept getting worse, like a bitter taste that simply won't go away.

The moon was huge. It sat like a spotlight on the horizon, beaming down, causing the tombstones to gleam as if carved from ivory. Those stones glimmered over the rolling fields like a mob of angels come to life, awakened, perhaps, by the crunch of car tires easing over the macadam paths. They lifted their heads and seemed to wave out a warning as the car's headlights stabbed through the shadows, illuminating them one by one by one.

Sam didn't seem particularly interested in pointing Gordon in the right direction. He simply used the cocoon of sound and dark inside the car as a backdrop to tell his story as Gordon silently listened.

When he spoke, Sam's voice was sad: a heartache thumping out a quiet, endless pain in this wasteland of finished lives. Gordon might not understand what the man was driving at, but he understood pain. He had lived it long enough to recognize it for what it was.

"Let me tell you about a young man I used to know," Sam droned from the shadows beside him. "Let me tell you about Jerry."

"All right." Gordon breathed the words while his own heart pounded in his chest. In his ears, his heartbeat seemed impossibly loud, as if it echoed over the forest of tombstones surrounding them. The night was cool, a blessing after the long hot day. It was scented with the cloying smell of old, forgotten flowers—the flowers left to wither on the graves just as the corpses were left to rot beneath the ground. A tribute to the dead, perhaps, those flowers, or just a sop to the living to let them know they were still alive and magnanimous in their manufactured grief.

Gordon closed his eyes against that thought, pushing it away.

"Tell me," he said quietly. "Tell me about… Jerry."

Sam lit another cigarette, the match illuminating his doleful eyes as he stared out at the fields of dead.

"He came to me four years ago," Sam began. "And I liked him right away. He was a good electrician. Learned it in the Navy, he said." Sam smiled. Gordon could sense it in his voice. "He was such a little runt, but my God that guy could eat."

Now it was Gordon's turn to smile. "Still can."

"He was a good worker too. One of the best electricians I've ever seen. And I've been in the business my whole life, Mr. Stafford. I've seen a lot."

Sam took a breath. Gordon could smell the stale smoke on his breath from across the car. The older man settled himself more comfortably in the car seat, as if readying himself for a long tale. "I never dreamed he was gay until he took it into his head to tell me one day. Casually. Over lunch in the backroom. Said he had found someone he loved and they were moving in together right away, so if I called his new number and someone else answered, I would understand."

Gordon watched silently as Sam started rummaging through the dash, touching it here and there, prodding with a fingertip. It took Gordon a minute to realize he was looking for the ashtray. By the time Gordon figured it out, Sam had located the damn thing and smashed out his cigarette butt in it. Maybe he didn't want to defile the graves by tossing it out the window like he had done all the others.

"Go on," Gordon said softly.

Sam rattled out a cough and spit through the window. Gordon guessed he didn't think he was defiling anything by spitting on the graves instead.

"Jerry had some rough waters ahead because of his gayness. Not from me, mind you. I'm used to gay people. Got me a brother that's queer as a three-tailed cat. Other relatives too. Some alive, some… gone. Nicest people in the world, gays. Like I said, I'm used to 'em. But Jerry made the mistake of telling his folks he was batting for the other team, and they immediately showed their true colors by disowning him completely. So at the ripe old age of twenty-four, or thereabouts, Jerry suddenly found himself without a family. It's a good thing he had his new partner to see him through it. I knew him, you know. I knew him well. He was a good man, Jerry's lover. Crazy about Jerry he was too. They were good for each other. They were… happy."

Sam pointed to the side of the macadam lane. "Stop here," he said. "Turn off the engine."

With a rush of new fear mingled with the old, Gordon pulled the car to a stop at the base of the hill leading up to Guadalupe Circle. The same place he always parked when he came to Holy Cross in the car. He switched off the headlights and let the darkness roll in, swallowing them whole but for a red spot of still-burning tobacco smoldering in the ashtray between them. When Sam saw it, he used the twisted cigarette butt to tap the ember out properly.

Gordon tried to set his fear aside and concentrate on what Sam had told him. "So that's what he meant when he said he had no family," Gordon muttered, more to himself than to Sam.

"What's that?" Sam barked. "What did you say?"

Gordon sighed. "Squirt told me he has no family."

"And he was right," Sam snapped. "He doesn't. Not really. He has a bunch of homophobic fuckhead relatives who dropped him like a hot potato the minute they learned he was gay, but that's not what I'd call a family. Would you?"

Poor Squirt. "Uh, no. I guess not."

"Heartless bastards," Sam mumbled through the window, staring out at the stones in the moonlight.

To Gordon's surprise, Sam popped the door handle and stepped out of the car. Gordon squinted against the sudden glare of the interior light.

"I need some air," Sam said. "Come with me, Mr. Stafford."

Gordon yanked the car keys and meekly followed.

Sam kept his eyes to the ground as they walked. While the moon was bright overhead, it was still a treacherous place to stroll, with the soft tussocky earth and the stones and the many items of condolence left behind to honor the dead: real and plastic flowers in legged vases stabbed into the ground, figurines of the Virgin Mary here and there, and on one dark patch of granite sitting atop the grave of a child, a phalanx of toy cars neatly arranged as a border around the stone.

The atmosphere seemed to soften Sam's voice. It would have softened anyone's. "You know, Mr. Stafford, all the time Jerry's family was tossing him from their lives, they spouted Bible verses at him. I'm sure you've met a few people like that. Religion is their sole purpose for living. Worshiping a God that nobody can prove exists mattered more to them than protecting the son they had borne into this world and could see with their very own eyes."

"I'm sorry," Gordon said, stepping carefully around a stone vase filled with what looked in the dark to be plastic lilies. He bent to touch one and realized it was real. "It must have been hard for Squirt to be suddenly alone like that."

"Yes. Well, like I said, he wasn't entirely alone. He had friends at the shop. And he had his lover." Again, Sam's voice relayed the presence of a smile. It was an odd accoutrement to wear in a place such as this, Gordon thought.

A question entered Gordon's head and he immediately tried to push it away. He wouldn't ask that question of Sam. He couldn't. His heart was sinking fast enough as he saw where Sam was leading him. They were already climbing the hill toward the center of Guadalupe Circle. Gordon had walked through these same stones not more than a week ago. He knew many of the carved names by heart. Jacobs. Styles. Mendoza. Blaine.

Gordon's pulse was pounding in his head as they drew ever closer to the summit. The armpits of his shirt were cold and clammy with sweat. Off in the haze of distance, he spotted the San Diego skyline, glimmering like a desert mirage. Behind it, he knew, the vast Pacific Ocean sprawled out endlessly, following the very curvature of the earth until it reached its opposite shores, worlds and worlds away.

Gordon tore his eyes from the beauty of that sparkling horizon. He pointed to a patch of shrubbery surrounding an area of the cemetery filled with the tiny graves of infants. "Let's go that way," Gordon said.

Sam shook his head. "No, Mr. Stafford. Let's go *this* way." And he gripped Gordon's arm to propel him forward. Gently, but not so gently either.

With his heart a cold lump of steel in his chest, Gordon followed the man up the grassy hill. Already, in the moonlight ahead, he could see where the familiar grave lay. The grave of the man he had killed. Sam was walking straight for it.

"Why are we here?" Gordon quietly asked. "I thought we were looking for Squirt."

Sam didn't answer. He merely plodded on, his fingers a vise on Gordon's arm. Gordon let himself be drawn forward, trying not to think. Trying not to think at all. Of Squirt. Of himself. Of what lay ahead among these stones of the dead that he knew so well.

Trying not to ask himself why Sam was bringing him here.

That question, Gordon most *certainly* did not try to comprehend.

Two stones away from the patch of pale grass, which in the moonlight, looked as green and lush as the grass around it, Gordon stumbled. He tripped forward, landing on one knee. Immediately the wet grass soaked through his pant leg. The caretakers must have just watered. Gordon shuddered at the clammy moisture on his skin.

Sam stood over Gordon, hand extended to help him up. "We're not quite there yet. Don't stop now."

Gordon took the hand and pulled himself upright. When Sam turned to walk on, he did not release Gordon's hand, but kept it firmly clasped in his own great weathered paw.

Sam stopped at the edge of the grave Gordon knew so well, the very place he knew Sam was leading him all along. There was no point blocking the truth from his mind any longer. He felt a sob rise in his throat, clawing its way to the surface. His eyes burned with surfacing tears.

Once again Gordon stumbled to one knee, this time in grief. In shame. "No," he muttered, his hand coming to rest on the grave's wet grass. This time the grass felt cool and comforting against his skin. As cool and comforting as death might feel.

Sam said nothing. He stood beside Gordon. Stoic. Mute. He did not reach out to comfort Gordon. Nor did he seem surprised to hear Gordon weeping in the darkness beside him.

Gordon tried again to staunch the rising sobs. He squinted through the tears that rippled his vision.

The moon gazed down at the two men by the graveside. If it held any interest in what was happening below, it showed no sign. A gust of wind blew through the surrounding stones, rattling the leaves in the tall eucalyptus tree on the crest of the hill. And as soon as the wind freshened, a wisp of dark cloud slid in place to dim the moon.

In the sudden darkness, the tombstone was unreadable. But Gordon knew what it said. He had memorized its words long ago.

JEREMY ALDRITCH BOOTH

1988—2012

Asleep in God's Arms

Gordon fell forward, sinking *both* hands into the wet grass. He closed his eyes against the darkness, even while he was grateful for its presence. He didn't want to weep in front of this man. He didn't want to weep in front of God, if God was watching. Not again.

But the weeping came. It tore out of him like lava from a rent in the earth. Hot, gushing, furious.

"Oh, God," he stammered. "I—I understand now. It was Squirt I heard screaming inside the car that night. Squirt was the passenger I couldn't see. It was his... *his lover* I killed." He looked up at Sam standing stone still beside him. "Wasn't it?"

And beyond all expectation, beyond all imagining of sympathy coming from the man standing beside him, Gordon felt Sam's hand come down gently on his shoulder.

"Yes, Mr. Stafford," Sam said, the words clipped and businesslike, his voice as cool and emotionless as the wet grass at Gordon's fingertips.

"And the other man in the car was my son."

# CHAPTER 15

GORDON'S HEART stuttered in his chest. The old shame came rolling in. But this time the shame was so profound he thought it would sweep him away completely.

"Your son—"

Sam turned his back to Gordon and slowly knelt to his knees at the side of the grave. He brushed at the damp grave marker with his fingertips, sweeping away a dusting of mown grass. "Yes, Mr. Stafford. Jeremy Aldritch Booth was my son. Aldritch was his mother's maiden name."

Almost blinded by tears now, Gordon groped outward with his hand until it rested on the heel of Sam's shoe. The shoe was damp from the grass. He clutched Sam's heel and tried to get his voice under control.

When he wiped away his tears, he saw Sam staring back at him, his tired face doleful and sad in the moonlight.

"I'm so s-sorry," Gordon stammered. And his pleading seemed in his own ears such weak words to speak, his weeping began again. Uncontrollable this time. Still clutching Sam's heel like a man clinging to a cliff, Gordon buried his face in his other hand and fell forward. He pressed his forehead into the earth at the foot of the grave.

The grave holding this man's son. The man Gordon had killed in an act of stupid drunken recklessness almost two years earlier.

Gordon sucked in a shuddering gasp of air and opened his burning eyes to see the hatred he deserved.

What he saw instead was pity. And it took his breath away.

Gordon breathed out the only words he could find. "I'm sorry," he said again. "I'm... sorry."

Sam's voice was husky with emotion, but still he did not shed a tear. Perhaps his tears had been spilled already. Perhaps he had none left. "I know you are, Mr. Stafford. You said it at the trial too. Do you remember? You wept on the stand and said you were sorry. I sat in the back of the courtroom because I couldn't allow myself to get near you for fear of what I would do. After that day, after you accepted what you'd done and pleaded forgiveness for it in front of that courtroom full of strangers, I still spent a lot of time hating you. A natural reaction, I guess. But slowly, as I watched your grand life turn to crap, I realized you had paid an awful toll for your actions that night. Not as great a toll as my son, but a toll nevertheless."

"You watched my life?" Gordon sighed. "I don't understand."

Sam groaned his way to his feet, pulling his heel from Gordon's grasp and rubbing his knees from bending too long. "Can't squat like I used to. I have to stand up. Arthritis. Crawled around under too many houses in the course of my career."

"C-certainly," Gordon stammered.

Sam gazed down to where Gordon still cowered on the ground, and he seemed to be doing it with sympathy. But how could that be?

"Mr. Stafford, everybody in this city knows your story. I watched the news every time your name was mentioned, as you can imagine. I'm afraid you were a bit of an obsession with me for a while. I know everything you went through. I know how difficult it was for you in jail. I know how you lost your career, how you've spent the last few months working in a homeless shelter, tending to the poor, how you drank too much, maybe still do for all I know. I know how you lost your fine house and had to take a tiny apartment instead. It's all chronicled in the news stories. All of it. You only have to know where to look to find it. And since I had more reason than most to look, I did."

Gordon opened his mouth to speak, but Sam waved him to silence.

"Let me finish." Sam looked out at the same city skyline glimmering in the distance that Gordon had gazed at earlier. While his voice was gruff, his face was pensive. Weary. "I was finally beginning to let the hate I felt for you dissipate, Mr. Stafford. I saw that you were paying a continuous price for the horrible thing you did, and I knew I would have to be satisfied with that. It was small revenge, but it was better than nothing.

"Then you walked through my door today and suddenly I knew I still hated your guts. Maybe even more than I had before. Seeing you healthy and strong, while my boy's bones are lying under this fucking hill, cold and still and lifeless forever, would be enough, I guess, to make any father hate you. But now that I've had some time to think, I'm beginning to realize maybe I was being… unfair."

"You weren't!" Gordon cried. "I deserved your hate. Oh, God, I'm—"

Sam held up a hand. "Don't say you're sorry again, sir. It doesn't help. Let me finish what I'm trying to say. With no wife still living and my boy now gone, I've sort of focused all my attention, well, all my *love,* on Jerry. After all, my son was crazy about him. And I've come to be a little crazy about him too. I'm not blind, you know. I saw the change in the boy over the last few months. I knew he had found someone he cared about, and I thought it was a good thing. I even hoped maybe it would be enough to get his life back on track. To break through the brick wall he's constructed inside his head regarding that night. That night you killed my son."

Gordon flinched at the words, and once again buried his face in his hands. But he listened. He listened to every word Sam said. Hungry to hear it all. Hungry for words of forgiveness. Or hatred. Or condemnation. Whatever words this man wished to throw at him, Gordon was willing to accept. If they were words of hatred, Gordon most certainly deserved them. As for forgiveness, he could not yet believe that was being offered. How could it be?

Sam cleared his throat as if not used to speaking so long. "After the accident Jerry tried to commit suicide. You saw the scars, I guess. I don't suppose he told you where he got them."

"No," Gordon said, awash in grief all over again. "He couldn't remember. At least that's—"

"And it's true," Sam interrupted. "He doesn't remember. Losing my son was hard on the boy. It almost stole his mind away completely." Sam settled his eyes on Gordon. "And now—with you—Jerry has been happy again for the first time since I don't know when. When he moved out of the shop, I was worried, but I thought it still might be the best thing for him. I didn't try to stop him. I thought he deserved a little happiness. He deserved to have love in his life again. And love can cure a lot of ills, Mr. Stafford."

"Yes," Gordon breathed, his spent tears cold on his cheeks. "Squirt cured me. He made me want to live again."

Sam tapped a cigarette from the pack in his shirt pocket, and Gordon watched his face suddenly flare into existence in the light of the match he snapped to life with a flick of his thumbnail. He shook the flame out and took a long draw on the cigarette. When he spoke, his words were mixed with smoke.

Sam's voice grew stern, but not unkind. "Why did Jerry leave you, Mr. Stafford? Today. What made him run?"

Gordon was finally calming down. Now suddenly he fought the urge to weep again. "I think he found out who I am. I think he found out the truth. The truth even I didn't know until you just told me. There were clippings. I had hidden them in the closet. Hidden them from myself, actually, not from Squirt. He saw them. I think he's finally beginning to understand that I'm the one who killed his—his lover."

Sam stared down at Gordon, his cigarette dangling from his lips. He plucked it out and flicked the ash away. "I was afraid of that."

"Please," Gordon rasped, his voice hoarse, his throat raw. "Tell me why Squirt doesn't remember. His name, his job, anything. How can that be? And now that he's seen those news stories, does his running away mean his memory's returned? Is he out there somewhere now, hating me?"

Sam stared down at him, silent. Then he gazed back at the sparkling skyline in the distance. "I can't answer your last question, Mr. Stafford, because I just don't know. But as for the rest of it—as for how it can be—it's called selective amnesia. It's caused by mental or physical trauma. Jerry loved my son very much. To see him die in front of his eyes made Jerry lose his grip on reality just enough to block that night from his memory completely. Unfortunately, when he blocked that night, he also blocked a lot of his own past with it. He didn't do it on purpose. He didn't plan it out. When the doctors brought him around after his failed suicide attempt, his memory was just gone. All of it. Kaput. He had lost a lot of blood. Maybe that had something to do with it. I don't know. Or maybe it's just the way the human mind sometimes deals with tragedy. With grief. And sometimes the cure is worse than the problem."

"Wh-what do you mean?"

"I mean it can get worse, Mr. Stafford. If Jerry is forced to face the truth before he's ready, it could steal his mind away completely. He could become either completely disconnected from reality, or he could shut down altogether."

"How do you know this? His doctor?"

"Yes," Sam said. "I speak to his doctor often. We've become… friends, of a sort. Actually more like war buddies, I guess, fighting the battle together. Trying to keep Jerry safe." Sam took another long draw on the cigarette and blew the smoke at the moon. "I wonder if Jerry told her about the new love in his life. And if he did, I wonder why she didn't tell me. Afraid to, probably. Afraid I'd go ballistic."

"Maybe," Gordon said. "But whatever you think about it, you have to believe me when I tell you it isn't wrong. It's not a bad thing. Squirt loves me. I know that much. And I love him."

"Yes. I suppose you do. But sometimes love isn't enough to cure the world. Sometimes it takes a little strength. When Jerry lost my son, it seems to have taken most of his strength away. And so far it hasn't returned."

"Why did you bring me *here?*" Gordon asked, gazing around at the forest of gravestones surrounding them. "Did you think he'd be here?"

"Yes. He comes here sometimes. I suspect so do you. Or am I wrong?"

Gordon's shame returned with a rush. "No. You're not wrong. I came here almost every day before I found Squirt. Now I come… less."

Sam stared down at him. "If I had known you were the one Jerry had taken up with, I would have stopped it, you know."

Gordon nodded, and when he did he felt a tear skid down his cheek. "I suppose you would have. But you'd have been wrong to do it. Squirt and I can still save each other. I know we can."

After a beat of silence, Sam tilted his head to the sky as if seeking out the words he wanted to say from among the stars above his head. It took Gordon a moment to realize that wasn't what he was doing at all. He was trying to keep the tears inside his eyes, trying not to let them fall.

For Gordon, Sam then uttered the most surprising words of the night.

"I think you're right, Mr. Stafford. I would have been wrong to keep you two apart. And I think you're right about something else. If there's any hope for Jerry at all, I think it will come from you. And the love he feels for you."

"Sometimes maybe love *is* enough," Gordon ventured, hoping against hope. Longing for the warmth of Squirt's arms around him even now. Even with everything that was happening. His mind suddenly bloomed with visions of Squirt's pale hair, pale eyes, pale skin. His strong hands. The scars on his arms. The gentle way he made love. The easy, contented smile that lit his face when he spoke of love, of life. Of Gordon.

"Maybe." Sam ceded the word like it was the last he had to give. "Maybe it is enough."

A night bird chortled in the eucalyptus tree over their heads. Sam stared up into the dark treetop, following the sound. "It's my fault, you know. My fault you didn't recognize Squirt."

"What do you mean?"

Sam turned to gaze at him. "You never saw a photograph of the other man in the car, did you? It was never in the papers. That's because I kept it out. When Jerry's mind snapped I had him confined for a while."

"Confined?"

"Yes, Mr. Stafford. Confined in a place where they were trained to handle patients like that. They did a good job too. They took care of him until he was capable of making it on the outside. With a little help at least."

"A little help from you," Gordon said.

"Yes. But the facility served another purpose too. It kept him out of the public eye. Away from the press. I didn't want his picture slathered all over the papers like yours and my son's were. At least I managed that much. I kept Jerry safe." Here Sam gave a quiet, disbelieving chuckle. "I also set it up for the two of you to get together. There must have been a lot of coincidence involved in it, but the fact that you didn't recognize Jerry certainly didn't hurt either. So here we are, with you in love with the lover of the man you killed. And the lover of the man you killed loving you back." He spat up another wry laugh. "The world's a funny place. No two ways around that."

"I think I would have loved him anyway, Sam. Even if I'd known who he was."

Sam gave a shrug. "Maybe you would. Who the hell knows?" He seemed to have used up his last ounce of energy. He brushed a hand across his face as if he could wipe the weariness away like a layer of dust.

Gordon watched him. When Gordon spoke, the words sounded torn from his throat, even to his own ears. "Where is he, Sam? He isn't here. Where could he have gone?"

Sam shook his head. Lost for an answer.

And in the midst of a growing silence between the two men as each of them contemplated their own thoughts, their own miseries, Sam's cell phone rang out loud and clear from his trouser pocket. Atonal. Blaring. Strident.

Above their heads, the night bird in the eucalyptus tree complained about the racket.

Fishing for the phone, Sam muttered to himself, "I hope this is who I think it is. Maybe he went to her. He might have, you know. It's possible."

"Her?" Gordon asked.

But Sam had turned away, hunched inward, his ear pressed to the phone. "Yes?" he said softly. "Yes. It's me."

*Let him be found,* Gordon silently pleaded to whoever might be listening. God, maybe. If God existed. *Please God, let Squirt be safe.*

Gordon held his breath. Waiting.

Finally, Sam said into the phone, "Yes. I can be there in twenty minutes." And after a pause, Sam said, "We don't have to contact him, Doctor. He's here with me."

He turned and gazed at Gordon. When he did, Gordon struggled to his feet, his trouser legs soaked from the wet grass, clammy against his skin.

Sam spoke into the phone one last time. "Don't worry," he said, his voice an empty chuckle. "I haven't killed him yet."

With that, he tucked the phone into his pocket.

"Let's go," he said. "Jerry's at Mercy Hospital."

"Is he all right?"

"That's what we're about to find out."

Sam set off down the hill toward the car. With a final glance at the gravestone at his feet, Gordon anxiously followed.

THE HOSPITAL was a hive of activity. The woman rushing toward them through the crowded entryway was dressed in slacks and a suede vest, her shirt-sleeves white and billowing around her. Everything about her screamed *lesbian*. Everything about her also screamed *smart and caring*.

Gordon liked her immediately.

She was calling out to them while still ten feet away, her voice tense but businesslike. Her eyes were focused on Gordon as she strode toward them. "The police found him by the bay. Lying under the bridge. He had my card in his pocket, thank God, so they called me. I instructed them to bring him here. I think they would have anyway."

Upon reaching them, she nodded to Sam and held her hand out to Gordon. "We meet at last," she said. "Jerry told me you were his new love. He didn't make the connection, of course, but I thought one day he might. I guess that day has come."

"Yes," Gordon said, stunned by her bluntness and still not sure what was going on. "Where... how is he?"

She gave him a weak smile. "Two questions at once. Economical. I like that." She turned her attention to Sam, taking his hand. "Hello,

Mr. Booth. Don't look at me like that. I'm sorry I didn't tell you who Jerry had taken up with, but frankly I figured nothing good would come of it if I had."

"You were probably right," Sam muttered.

She gave him a lazy smile. "I know I was right."

And somehow, hearing Sam's last name, the same last name as the man Gordon had killed two years earlier, all but broke Gordon's heart all over again. He felt himself swaying on his feet. Before he knew what was happening, both Sam and the doctor were steering him toward a bank of chairs in the reception room off to the right.

When Gordon was seated, the doctor leaned in to look at his eyes. "Feeling better? I guess this has all been a pretty big shock for you."

Gordon was embarrassed to be mollycoddled like this. After all, he was the bad guy here. No point trying to deny that.

"I'm fine. I just… got dizzy."

The doctor smiled. "Yes. Well. That's understandable, under the circumstances."

"C-circumstances?"

She ignored him. "Jerry is on the fifth floor. The psychiatric wing. He's safe and comfortable." She straightened, giving Gordon a last reassuring pat on the shoulder, and turned her attention to Sam. "What happened?" she asked. "He's in the state I warned you about a year ago. Something must have happened to push him into it."

Sam rested his eyes on Gordon. They were neither kind nor unkind. They were simply eyes. "Ask *him*," Sam said. "He can explain it better than I can."

The doctor turned her eyes to Gordon once again. "Well, Mr. Stafford? Can you tell me what happened?"

But Gordon had a question of his own. "What state? What state did you warn him about a year ago?"

The doctor's cell phone beeped. She dug it from her vest pocket, looked at it, then pressed a button before stuffing it back in her pocket. She sat in the chair beside Gordon and rested her hand on his arm. "There have always been three possible outcomes of Jerry's mental illness, Mr. Stafford."

"Call me Gordon."

She smiled politely. "Gordon. I'm Dr. Stark." She gave Sam a brief glance before continuing. "Those three possible outcomes are these: He could go on being the same way he is now, with the memories blocked forever. He could suddenly reacquire his lost memories with almost no residual effects at all and just get on with his life like a normal human being. Or he could reacquire the memories, find they were too much to deal with, and shut himself down completely as a way to protect himself from them."

Gordon nodded, trying to think. Trying to ignore the fear rising through him. "You mean like a catatonic state where he doesn't know anything?"

"Yes, Gordon. Exactly. A catatonic coma."

Gordon tried to stammer out a question but the words would barely come. Besides, he knew the answer already. *He knew it.* "And which of those three possibilities has happened?" he finally uttered, bracing himself for the truth.

Dr. Stark twisted a wedding ring on her finger. She looked down at her hand while she did it. Then she raised her eyes to Sam before focusing her attention back to Gordon.

"Jerry has done the last, I'm afraid. He is unresponsive. They found him that way, lying under the bridge by the bay. He isn't hurt in any other way. No one… bothered him. But I'm afraid he has shut himself off completely. He flipped the switch, Mr. Stafford. Well, *he* didn't. His brain did. I was always afraid it would."

Gordon watched a man wheel a young boy across the crowded lobby. The boy had a brand-new cast on his leg, and the man was bitching loudly about a goddamn skateboard that was on its way to the trash and what a pain in the ass it was to raise a kid. Father of the year.

"The switch," Gordon mumbled. When he looked into the doctor's eyes, then up at Sam's, Gordon felt himself deflate like an old balloon. Every ounce of life just seemed to leak right out of him. He fought back tears because he finally understood that tears wouldn't help. They wouldn't help anybody. Least of all Squirt.

With an effort, he found his voice. "He discovered my newspapers, Doctor. The ones about me. About the accident. The trial. All of it. I found them scattered in the—in the closet. He read them all,

I think. That's why he's the way he is. It's my fault. I ruin everything I touch. I should have known I didn't deserve happiness, and I should have known I couldn't atone for what I did to Sam's son without hurting someone else. I thought Squirt and I could help each other. I thought we loved each other enough to do that. But he's just another one of my victims now. Another life I fucking ruined. I just keep racking them up, don't I? Victims? They just keep piling up at my feet."

Dr. Stark gave him a petulant glower. "Your feeling sorry for yourself isn't going to help Jerry. This doesn't have to be a permanent state, you know. A few are, but not most. He can awaken tomorrow, for all we know. Or next year if we're not so lucky." She looked up at Sam standing over them. "Sam, sit down. You're making me nervous."

With a surprised look, Sam dropped into the chair on the opposite side of Gordon. Only then did Dr. Stark take a firm grip on Gordon's chin and drag his face around until they were staring into each other's eyes.

"Just because Jerry's mind has suffered a setback, it doesn't mean he loves you less, Gordon. It doesn't mean he's given up on you. And you shouldn't give up on him either. And stop this self-flagellation. It's not going to bring Sam's son back and it's not going to help Jerry either."

She took Gordon's hand. "Now, then. If you're through feeling sorry for yourself, let's go visit my patient."

For the hundredth time that day, Gordon fought back tears. "He won't even know I'm here."

The doctor smiled. "We don't really know that, Gordon. Some experts argue that patients with catatonia know everything that goes on around them. Others claim they are impervious to all outside stimuli."

"And which do you believe?" Sam asked, before Gordon had a chance to.

Dr. Stark used a businesslike finger to adjust a tiny pearl earring in her lobe. "I believe it depends on the patient. With Jerry, we won't know until we try. But we can be absolutely certain of one thing."

"What's that?" Gordon asked.

She gave him a sly smile. "If we don't try, we'll accomplish jack shit."

Dr. Stark rose and beckoned them to follow. "Now, let's go see Jerry. And for Christ's sake, try not to be so morose. Both of you. That *certainly* isn't going to help him."

Sam and Gordon meekly followed her to the elevators. As they waited for one to arrive, she again gently patted Gordon's arm.

"Love can do wonderful things, Gordon. Don't ever let that truth escape you. Be strong for Jerry now, just as I'm sure he would have been strong for you. Wouldn't he?"

With that one simple question, Gordon knew she was right. If the tables were turned, Squirt would have been there for him.

"Yes," Gordon whispered, more to himself than to her. "Absolutely." Gordon doubted many things in his life. But not that. That he believed completely.

The doctor smiled a benign smile when she saw the truth register on his face. As the elevator bonged and the doors slid open, she ushered both Gordon and Sam inside.

"Let's go see Squirt," she said, pushing the button for the fifth floor. "Isn't that what you call him, Gordon? Squirt?"

She was humming softly as the elevator rose.

# CHAPTER 16

IT WAS a sobering walk through the Mercy psych ward, with its heavily meshed windows and air of melancholy hopelessness. The drab green walls were chipped at face level from the clawing nails of frantic inmates, which Gordon only realized when he saw one of the patients doing exactly that. The mindless stares on the faces from the beds on either side of the center corridor that traversed the huge barracks-like room made Gordon look away. As vacantly desperate as those gaping looks were, they were somehow accusatory too. Not of Gordon, but of Gordon's health, of Gordon's functioning mind. Walking among these damaged people made Gordon feel shame at being whole. And he could see his own shame mirrored back in the empty eyes around him.

The mournful weeping of the afflicted, the barely disguised stench of waste and urine and soiled bedclothes, the occasional cackle of laughter bombarding him continually from one direction or another, all brought the truth smashing down on Gordon.

Squirt was a patient in this horrible place. And it was Gordon's fault he was here.

Gordon, and an equally appalled Sam, followed Dr. Stark's businesslike steps as she clacked over the faded linoleum floor of speckled green and tan on her sensible two-inch heels. The ward seemed to go on forever. After a while Gordon found it easier to just watch his own feet rather than look around. It was easier on the heart that way. Easier on the… guilt.

The windows looking out onto the world of the sane, if one wanted to call it that, were heavily fortified with steel mesh and bars. The mesh was so thick and had such tiny holes, one could barely see through them to the night outside. The bars were wrapped in rubber to protect the occasional confused head that came into contact with them, either purposely or otherwise, from cracking itself wide open and letting the insanity spill out all over the floor.

Twice during the trek down the long ward, they were forced to wait while locked doors surrounded by heavy wire that stretched from one wall to the other and all the way up to the ceiling, were unlocked by attendants to allow them access to continue on. Gordon supposed the partitions separating the long tunnel-like ward gave the staff a better chance of keeping things orderly if, God forbid, some sort of uprising occurred. Or perhaps it was for the safety of the patients themselves, since this way they had fewer insane peers to contend with.

Squirt lay in the last bed on the left-hand side, abutting the back wall. Gordon saw him from a distance, and the second he did, he felt a chill creep into his heart. He involuntarily stopped, just for a moment, before he could find the courage to go forward. Squirt looked so small and helpless and still, lying there surrounded by such mindless mayhem, that Gordon didn't quite know how to process it all.

For some reason, Gordon had expected to find Squirt strapped in with leather restraints on his wrists and legs, but he was not. Squirt lay peacefully with his head on a faded hospital-blue pillowcase. A wool blanket was pulled neatly to his chest and tucked under the mattress all the way around. The first thing Gordon did was touch Squirt's chest through the blanket to see if there were restraints underneath the covering. There were not.

"He's not tied down, if that's what you're wondering," Dr. Stark said softly.

Not caring what anyone thought, Gordon leaned over the bed and pressed his lips to Squirt's forehead, brushing Squirt's pale hair aside to do it. No one was surprised when Squirt did not react to his lover's kiss, least of all Gordon.

"How will they feed him?" Gordon asked. "A stomach tube?"

"Hopefully not," the doctor said. "For now we can get by with an IV of nutrients. If the coma goes on too long, however, we may have to resort to a tube. I'm hoping that won't be necessary."

Gordon slipped his fingers under Squirt's still hand, which rested atop the blanket. His skin was warm to the touch, his hand as light and airy as a feather. And as still as death.

To Gordon's surprise, Sam dragged a chair from against the wall and positioned it beside the bed. "Sit," Sam commanded him. "You still look like you're going to fall over."

Gordon sat. Squirt's face was pale and calm. Gordon could faintly hear him breathing. His white hair was a bit damp, as if perhaps he had been bathed when he was brought in to the hospital, and his fine, pale hair had not yet completely dried.

Dr. Stark pulled up a chair on the opposite side of the bed facing Gordon while Sam propped his back against the wall by the headboard, arms folded over his chest. Sam had a worried expression on his face. His eyes skittered continually from Gordon to Jerry to the doctor. He fiddled with the cigarette pack in his shirt pocket but never pulled it out. The toes of his shoes were still sprinkled with grass cuttings from the cemetery lawn.

Dr. Stark leaned forward, resting her elbows on the edge of the bed like she might have leaned them on a desk. She studied Gordon's face.

"You still don't fully understand, do you?"

"No," Gordon sighed. "I…. How can his mind completely shut him down like this? How can the brain do that?"

Dr. Stark sighed in return. "Excellent question, Gordon. Unfortunately, I don't know anyone who can satisfactorily answer it. The brain is probably the least understood part of the human body, but still we know some things. Memories are stored in two separate parts of the brain." She tapped her skull as if testing a melon. "Those two parts are the hippocampus, the normal seat of memory, and the amygdala, one of the brain's emotional centers. Gordon, some scientists now believe human memories are rewritten in the brain every time they are activated. Like a rat in a lab test learns to relate pulling a lever with receiving food. But if you block a certain chemical process during the execution of pulling the lever, the memory can be forgotten as quickly as it's learned. Do you understand?"

"No."

She grinned. "In medical parlance, it's called lacunar amnesia. In Latin, lacuna means gap. In other words, when the chemical process is interrupted, a hole in the memory is left behind."

Gordon longed to feel Squirt's fingers tighten around his hand, but they remained motionless. If there was life in them, he couldn't feel it.

He gazed at the doctor. "And Squirt's body somehow interrupted that chemical process to block out the night... Sam's son was killed?"

"Yes. The trauma of seeing his lover die before his eyes—" Dr. Stark glanced up at Sam standing behind her. "I'm sorry, Mr. Booth. If you don't want to listen to this—"

"I'm fine," Sam said, his voice determinedly bland. "Go ahead."

Dr. Stark nodded curtly and turned back to Gordon. "The shock of seeing his lover die before his eyes caused Jerry to block the image, the whole episode, from his mind. In Jerry's case, he seemed to have blocked almost everything that came before it too. He has not only blocked Jeremy's death, he has also blocked Jeremy. Completely. He doesn't remember him at all. Not yet anyway. I tried repeatedly to introduce Sam's son into our sessions, but Jerry fought me every step of the way. At least, his mind did. But there's still hope. Like I told you earlier, the memory loss could end at any time, and the memories could quite easily come flooding back in all at once."

"And then he'd wake up?" Gordon asked.

She too reached over to brush Squirt's hair from his forehead, smiling down at his sleeping face with gentle eyes. "Presumably. Or the memories may remain lost forever. We won't know until he is able to speak to us again."

"If he ever can," Gordon said, so softly that the words were barely tangible.

But the doctor heard them. "Yes," she said. "If he ever can."

She reached over Squirt and rested her hand atop Gordon's. "Gordon, you have to remember something. Jerry has more than one battle ahead of him. He has the battle he's fighting now with his mind, but he also has an entirely different battle to fight when he wakes up."

"What do you mean?"

The doctor gave Gordon's hand a gentle squeeze. "If he wakes with his memory restored, he'll then have to decide what his new knowledge requires of him. He'll know who you are, Gordon. He'll know you're the reason for everything that has happened to him. And for what happened to Jeremy. Do you understand? He may not be able to cope with it. He may leave you. God forbid, he may even hate you, Gordon." She pulled her hand away and readjusted her pearl earring. Gordon realized it was a nervous gesture. She didn't like what she was having to say. "You may lose him over this, Gordon. You have to be ready for that possibility. I'd be remiss if I didn't warn you. All right?"

Gordon nodded. He had thought of it himself, but somehow hearing the words come from the doctor's mouth made the possibility all the more terrifying.

He forced himself to speak, to sound matter-of-fact, to nod his head. "I understand," he said.

She bestowed a gentle wink on his worried face. "It's only a possibility, Gordon. It hasn't happened yet. Probably, it never will. Don't despair."

Gordon cradled Squirt's fingers in his hand. "He loves me," he said. "He'll understand. He won't leave me over this. I know he won't."

The doctor gave him a hearty smile, but it never quite reached her eyes, as if maybe she didn't fully believe the words Gordon had just told her, or what *she* was about to tell *him*. "In that case we have nothing to worry about," she said, dragging a smile into play.

Immediately, she molded her face into a more businesslike expression. "Getting down to brass tacks" she seemed to be saying as she sat up, straightened her vest, and gazed around the wing. "I'm going to arrange with the staff for you to have visitation privileges any time you like. You are, in my eyes at any rate, Jerry's spouse. If a human presence can make any difference to him at all, I would think yours could do the most good."

Dr. Stark craned her head around to look at Sam. "You too, Mr. Booth. You can visit Jerry any time you like. I guess we all know his family isn't likely to come around, and I'm glad they aren't. The only people I want next to my patient right now are the people who love him. And that means the two of you. All right?"

Sam nodded. Mute.

Gordon muttered, "Yes."

The doctor studied each of their faces in turn. "Are you two all right with each other? If there are animosities between you, and I'm sure there are, can you keep them under wraps around Jerry? Like I told you both earlier, we don't really know how much outside stimuli gets through. But if there's a lot of anger and quarreling going on, I don't want it seeping into his head. Do you understand me? If I get wind of it, I'll throw you both out on your ears and have you barred completely from this wing. Got it?"

This time Sam and Gordon both nodded.

And the doctor nodded in reply. "Good." She pulled herself to her feet. "I'm going to grab some coffee in the cafeteria. Would anyone care to join me?"

"I will," Sam said. "Coffee sounds good."

"I'd rather stay here," Gordon said. "If it's all right."

"Of course," Dr. Stark said, smiling down at him. "Take care of him, Gordon. You may just get him back before this is all over. I hope you do anyway."

Tears filled Gordon's eyes yet again. "So do I," he said softly, trying desperately to keep his voice on an even keel.

Without saying another word, Sam and the doctor set out on the long trek back the way they had come, through the Mercy Hospital Psychiatric Ward, where all manner of misery thrived, to the hospital cafeteria somewhere in the bowels of the building where they could sit around and sip a cup of coffee in peace without seeing some maniac trying to claw down the wall around them.

Gordon watched them walk away, and when they had gone through the first locked partition, and that first door was relocked securely behind them by a nurse in white, Gordon turned his eyes to Squirt, lying in the bed before him.

"I'm sorry, baby," Gordon whispered.

He laid his head on Squirt's chest and closed his eyes.

Squirt's heart thumped faintly in Gordon's ear. Squirt's fingers lay still and distant in the palm of Gordon's hand. If there was any love for Gordon still beating inside the man, Gordon couldn't feel it.

He squeezed his eyes shut, trying to block the fear rising up inside him. Gordon had the horrible sensation that though he had found Squirt at last, Squirt was lost to him anyway.

Gordon rested his forehead on Squirt's arm, closing his eyes against the pain, against his own imaginings. He quietly wept until Squirt's blanket was damp to the touch.

The next time he opened his eyes, a tall male nurse with a gigantic ring of keys jangling on his belt, was gently shaking him awake. The ward was closing to visitors for the night.

Gordon struggled to sit up, wiping the sleep and dried tears from his eyes.

"I'll go, then," he muttered to the nurse.

The nurse smiled kindly. "Visiting hours begin at nine in the morning. I imagine we'll see you then. If you need anything, ask for me. Nate. My shift starts at six."

"All right. Thank you, Nate."

Gordon looked around. From what he could see, he was the only visitor still on the premises. He didn't see Sam or Dr. Stark again that night. He wasn't sure how Sam made it home.

Forlorn and heartbroken, he went to his own empty apartment and tried not to think about having a drink. He succeeded, but barely.

He spent the night tossing and turning on the sofa, unable to lie in the bed because he could smell Squirt's sweet scent still on the sheets.


GORDON CONTINUED to work at the soup kitchen in the afternoons. Mama Davis gave him the mornings off to visit Squirt. That went on for a week, until Gordon realized it would just postpone the day when his court-ordered community service could end. The next morning he showed up at the soup kitchen for his regular morning and noon shift and limited his hospital visits to the afternoon and evenings, where he stayed until the end of visiting hours every day.

The unsigned contract from Channel 9 News lay on Gordon's kitchen table, a never-ending reminder of the life he had to reclaim if he ever wanted to make anything of himself again.

But he couldn't face that now. He hadn't the heart for it. Until Squirt's sickness was resolved, he knew he would never have the heart for it. He phoned Jackson Price, the KTSI station manager, and told him he needed more time to think about the offer. Mr. Price seemed surprised but didn't push Gordon into a decision. Gordon knew then and there that if he failed to call Mr. Price again, Mr. Price would not follow up on the job offer. The ball was in Gordon's court, and Gordon knew it. He also knew his time was running out. Mr. Price would no doubt rescind the offer unless Gordon came back with a definite answer soon.

Still, he could focus only on Squirt. Until Squirt was well, the job would have to wait.

One day, as Gordon returned from his late morning walk between shifts at the soup kitchen, he spotted a mannequin in a downtown store window dressed in the gaudiest pajamas he had ever seen in his life. With a broad smile lighting his face for the first time in days, Gordon rushed inside and bought three pair, all in different Day-Glo colors. Each set of pajamas had a different Looney Tunes character on the shirt pocket: Bugs Bunny, Daffy Duck, and Marvin the Martian.

While in the store, he also bought bright colorful bedding for Squirt's bed so he wouldn't look so pale and forlorn lying there in the clean but faded hospital sheets and blankets they supplied him with. Gordon bought two sets of sheets for Squirt. One with teddy bears all over it and one with fruit. *Tons* of fruit. Melons, apples, bananas, pineapples. For a blanket, Gordon found a bright yellow throw with butter-yellow sunrises sprinkled across it and a host of SpongeBob SquarePantses, traipsing through fields of black-eyed Susans, strewing petals and rainbows.

How gay was that?

Now when Gordon began his long trek down through the psych ward, he could spot Squirt immediately. Squirt's bed, with Squirt gaily attired in it, stood out like an exploding fireworks factory shimmering in the distance.

Two more weeks passed. And while his pajamas and bedding changed daily, Squirt remained the same. He had yet to open his eyes. He had not moved. His skin looked even paler than it had before.

Gordon tried desperately to remain hopeful. He began reading to Squirt as he lay in the bed. He read softly at first, so as not to annoy the other patients. Then one day he spotted three patients edging closer to hear what Gordon was reading, and when he realized what they were doing, Gordon read a little louder so they could hear. In a few days, Gordon found he had acquired a loyal audience whenever he read to Squirt (he was reading Tom Sawyer)—six or seven lost souls who apparently looked upon Gordon's reading time as the highlight of their day.

Those six or seven lost souls never once had a visitor that Gordon could see, which was sad, so they began to look at Gordon as their very own.

Gordon didn't mind at all.

Time passed. Gordon began to know the hospital staff by name: Lucy, the head nurse; Jill, the RN who worked weekends; a couple of candy stripers who brought books and magazines around for the patients who had the wherewithal to read or look at pictures; and the physical therapist, Miss Dennis, who sometimes gave Squirt massages to keep the blood flowing to his unused limbs as he lay in bed unmoving. All were friendly and generous with their time, and Gordon thanked them more than once for taking such good care of the man under the SpongeBob SquarePants blanket.

Gordon also struck up a quiet friendship with Nate, the only male nurse on the ward and also gay. Being a gay man himself, Gordon came to know Nate better than all the rest. Nate seemed a bit in awe of Gordon's devotion to Squirt. Gordon suspected Nate had no love in his own life, although he should have. He was certainly good-looking enough.

In the third week of Squirt's hospital stay, as Gordon sat beside him reading aloud, still from the same book, he heard footsteps approaching. Gordon marked his page and closed the book. (Tom and Becky Thatcher were lost in the cave and their candle had just gone out!)

"Oh, don't stop now," one of the patients muttered, but they all fell silent when a man and woman entered their midst. When they realized the couple had come to visit the man in the colorful bed, the other patients politely scurried away to return to their own drab, colorless reveries, worrying, perhaps, in their mindless way, about Tom and Becky still lost in that horrible cave and wondering how it would all turn out.

Gordon was stunned to see who the visitors were. "Mom! Mr. Rhiner!"

Perhaps he was even more stunned when his mother leaned over him and kissed the top of his head as Mr. Rhiner looked proudly on. When his mother straightened and studied the patient in the bed for the very first time, she slipped her hand in Mr. Rhiner's. The action was not lost on Gordon. He may have even smiled a little to see it.

Both Gordon and Mr. Rhiner followed his mother's eyes to the man in the bed.

"So this is him," his mother said, smiling as she spoke. "My goodness, he's a towhead. His hair is beautiful."

Gordon leaned in to brush an eyelash from Squirt's motionless cheek. When he was finished, his fingers lingered long enough to stroke a strand of Squirt's hair where it lay splayed out on the pillow. "Yes," he said, "it is."

Mr. Rhiner stepped forward and presented his free hand to Gordon. Gordon took it and gave it a friendly shake. As they released their grip, Mr. Rhiner, Gordon's parole officer, and apparently now his mother's main squeeze, trailed his eyes back to the man in the bed.

"I recognize him from the photos at the accident scene, Gordon. He was hardly scratched that night. Neither were you. It seemed Mr. Booth took the full brunt of the collision. I've never fully understood that."

"He was the only one not wearing a seatbelt," Gordon said. "But still...." Both his mother and Mr. Rhiner knew what he had chosen not to say.

"But still it was your fault anyway," Mr. Rhiner said, gently easing the words into the open.

Gordon nodded. "Yes. Still it was entirely my fault."

Mr. Rhiner stepped back just as Gordon's mother reached out a hand to caress Gordon's cheek.

"Thank you for leaving me a message, Gordon. For letting me know what's going on. I've been worried about you. You're never home."

"I've been here," Gordon said simply.

His mother's eyes were swimming with tears. She didn't seem to mind that they were about to wreak havoc on her perfectly applied mascara. "Has there been... any improvement?"

"No." It almost wore Gordon out just to speak that one simple word. He didn't embellish it with excuses or explanations. He let it hang in the air like a dusty, battered flag on a windless day.

His mother's eyes skimmed the surrounding beds, the hideous linoleum, the puke green walls. They finally came to rest on the book in Gordon's lap.

"You're reading to him," she said gently.

"Yes."

She sidled a little closer to Mr. Rhiner, as if for support. He rested a possessive hand against the small of her back, which seemed to give her strength.

"You're looking haggard, Gordon. Come to dinner with us. Please. You look like you haven't had a decent meal in weeks."

"I'm sorry," Gordon said. "I just ate downstairs in the cafeteria." It was a lie. He hadn't eaten since noon. "You guys go ahead without me."

His mother tilted her head and studied his face. "You're afraid to leave him. You're afraid he'll wake up while you're gone. Aren't you?"

"Yes." It was Gordon's greatest fear. He had to be here to explain things the minute Squirt opened his eyes. He had to plead his case before Squirt's heart closed against him when he realized who Gordon really was.

"Can we sit with you a while?" his mother asked kindly.

Gordon nodded, surprised by the gratitude he felt that his mother would offer to do such a thing.

Mr. Rhiner toddled obediently off to scavenge two plastic chairs from various parts of the ward and carried them silently back to Squirt's bed. He placed one chair next to Gordon's for his mother, and placed the chair for himself against the wall on the opposite side of the bed.

"No, Tom," Gordon's mother told Mr. Rhiner. "Sit by me."

And so Mr. Rhiner did, dragging his chair close beside her and once again, when he was settled, taking Gordon's mother's hand. It was the first time Gordon had heard the man's first name. It somehow made him more human in Gordon's eyes.

Gordon knew then and there his mother and Tom Rhiner loved each other, and he was glad to see it. Gordon had learned a lot about love since Squirt came into his life. He had learned even more about love on the day Squirt closed his eyes against the world, leaving Gordon behind.

They stayed until closing, keeping Gordon company, much to the chagrin of the six or seven patients who were dying to find out how Tom and Becky were getting along in that cold dark cave.

At nine o'clock, they left the ward with Gordon. At the front steps of the hospital, before they parted to retrieve their separate cars, Gordon said the words he had wanted to say all night.

"I'm glad you two found each other."

His mother blushed.

Mr. Rhiner beamed. "Thank you, Gordon."

With a gentle kiss on his cheek, Gordon's mother said good night. "Stay strong," she whispered in his ear. "And I like your man. He's beautiful."

"Thank you," Gordon said.

Gordon watched them walk away, hand in hand, shoulders brushing. When they rounded the building to where their car must be parked, Gordon turned to find his own. It was parked on the street two blocks over, somewhere in *that* direction. He set off in search of it. He grinned in the light of a streetlamp as he thought of his mom and Mr. Rhiner. Well, good. He was happy for them both.

Gordon never suspected that the very next day his world would change again.

And this time it would change forever.

# CHAPTER 17

THE CALL came at 7:00 a.m. Gordon wrestled with a tangle of sheets before he could manage to reach the phone and answer it.

He didn't recognize the voice on the line.

"Gordon? Mr. Stafford? Is that you?"

Gordon squinted at a beam of sunlight slanting through the bedroom window. It was too early for sunlight. Wasn't it? "Yes," he said. "That's me. Uh, who the hell is this?"

"It's Nate. The nurse at Mercy. Are you awake? I need to know you're awake."

Gordon sat up, his heart plummeting in his chest. Nate. The psych ward nurse. What the hell did he want?

"I'm awake, Nate. What is it? What's wrong?"

"I think you'd better get down here right away."

"You mean *now?* Visiting hours don't start for a couple of hours. I'll call in to cancel work and I'll be there promptly at nine. That okay?"

"No, Gordon. Come now. I really think you should come *right this minute*. Don't worry about visiting hours. I'll let you in. The duty doc is asleep in her office and won't start her rounds until later. I'll watch for you and let you in when you get here. All right? Will you come?"

"Uh, yeah. I guess so. I'll be right down. Is Squirt—I mean Jerry—is he okay? Nothing's happened, has it? It's not time for the feeding tube to be put in, is it? They aren't prepping him for surgery or anything, are they? I think we ought to talk about that goddamn feeding tube before—"

"Just come, Mr. Stafford. Come now."

"All right, Nate. I will. I'm on my way." And Nate disconnected.

Gordon blinked himself awake. He wondered if he should call his mother to meet him at the hospital. If something bad had happened, he wasn't sure he was ready to handle it alone. If he did call her, would Mr. Rhiner be chewing on her neck in bed, slurping and grunting? God, Gordon wasn't ready for that. And what could he tell her anyway? He didn't have a clue what was going on!

Nope. He was an adult. He didn't need his mother. He'd handle this alone.

He threw the bedclothes aside and started yanking on clothes. Once he was dressed, he took two precious minutes to brush his teeth and pee (simultaneously) before crashing through the front door and down the stairs to his parking space. Once in the car, he glanced at his reflection in the rearview mirror and almost screamed. His hair, long overdue for a cut, was sticking up everywhere. He spit in his hand and tried to press the unruly clumps flat to his head, then decided *fuck it* and started the engine.

Craving coffee, but in too big a rush to stop, he was at the hospital in less than ten minutes. By a stroke of good fortune, he found a parking space less than fifty feet from the front door. He jogged through the entryway, discovered an open elevator, slammed the heel of his hand on 5, and about the time he realized he hadn't zipped his pants and quickly did, he was standing at the entrance to the psych ward.

Nate was there waiting for him. He was grinning. "You look like shit."

"Thanks. Why did you call? What's wrong?"

Nate's eyes drifted down the long ward with the mesh partitions separating it into three sections. From the main entrance one could see all the way to the back wall, where Squirt's bed stood.

Gordon followed Nate's glance and his eyes popped open wide. He took a step closer to get a better view.

Squirt's bed was empty.

"Oh, God," Gordon said. "Where is he? They haven't taken him to surgery, have they? It's too soon for that damn tube. Sam and I told them yesterday not to—"

Nate gripped his shoulder. "Calm down, Gordon. Calm down and follow me."

Instead of heading toward the first locked partition into the fifth-floor ward, Nate did an about-face and led Gordon back into the hall.

"Where are we going?" Gordon asked. "Can you leave the ward like this? Aren't you on duty?"

"I'm on my break. Come on."

Gordon followed Nate's long strides back to the elevator where Nate pressed the button for the first floor.

"Where's Squirt, Nate? Answer me."

Nate smiled. "Hang on a minute and you'll be knowing everything you need to know."

A cold chill settled in Gordon's spine. "Oh, God, Nate, we aren't going to the morgue, are we?"

Nate burst out laughing. "Jesus, you've got a morbid streak."

They stepped from the elevator and Nate pointed to an arrow on the wall. The arrow led to the hospital cafeteria.

"No, Nate. I'm not hungry, dammit. You do know you're pissing me off, right?"

Gordon had never seen Nate so happy. He seemed to be enjoying a private joke that he wasn't quite yet ready to share with the man trailing along in his wake.

"It's not all about you, Gordon. Other people might be hungry too."

"I'm sure, but—"

Just before they reached the cafeteria doorway, Nate stopped and faced Gordon in the middle of the hall.

"Good thing I have my comb with me," he said. And with that Nate pulled a comb from his back pocket and proceeded to wrestle the tangles out of Gordon's hair.

"Ouch," Gordon said. "What the hell are you doing?"

"Sprucing you up. And tuck in your shirt."

"My shirt?"

"Yes. Tuck the fucker in."

Gordon tucked. Heaving a massively discontented sigh, he said, "Nate, please, just tell me what's going on. I'm about to clock you."

"Testy," Nate cooed, giving one final yank to a really nasty snarl on the top of Gordon's head, after which he gazed at the comb and said, "Oops. Pulled that one right out."

Gordon didn't notice. He had spotted someone through the door of the cafeteria. The someone was sitting at a booth in the back by the windows, through which the morning sun was only now cresting over the trees in the distance. The table where the someone sat was piled high with food on half a dozen separate plates. From where Gordon stood, he could see a breakfast plate with eggs and bacon and a stack of pancakes, a plastic basket piled high with fried chicken, a platter of fries with a hamburger perched on the side of it, and at least six cartons of chocolate milk scattered around, some unopened, some crumpled up and empty.

The someone sitting at the booth was Squirt, and he was going from one plate to the other, tasting this and tasting that. He wore wrinkled green pajamas, the ones with Daffy Duck on the pocket, and his hair looked even worse than Gordon's. Under the table, Squirt's feet were bare. He was enjoying the food so much his toes were curled.

Gordon had never seen anything more beautiful in his life. His face split into a broad grin, and just as quickly as it popped up, the grin disappeared.

Had Squirt's memory returned?

Gordon gripped Nate's arm. "Is he... well? Is his mind okay?"

Nate still wore a smile, although he looked a little confused by the sudden fear that scarred Gordon's face.

He prodded Gordon toward the door. "Go see for yourself," he said. "I told him you were coming."

"Did you?"

"Yes," Nate snapped. "That's your lover sitting over there, isn't it? Go say hello to him for Christ's sake. What are you waiting for?"

Gordon chewed his cheek, watching Squirt shovel down food. The restaurant was bustling. Squirt hadn't noticed him yet.

A lump as big as a chicken egg formed in Gordon's throat. He was scared to death. He clutched Nate's arm like a drowning man grabbing a tree limb. "What did he say when you told him I was coming?"

Nate cocked his head to the side and studied Gordon with no small amount of sympathy. "He asked if you'd been to see him."

"And what did you tell him, Nate?"

Nate stuck a fist on his hip and rolled his eyes. "I told him the truth. That you'd been here every day. Every. Single. Fucking. Day."

"What did he say to that?"

Nate grunted. "You're stalling. Go see your lover right now, or I swear to God, I'll throw you over my shoulder and cart you to him like a sack of potatoes."

"All right!" Gordon snapped. "I'll go!"

And like a man headed for the gallows, Gordon crossed the cafeteria on wobbly legs until he stood before the table where Squirt sat shoving french fries in his mouth.

Squirt looked up, saw Gordon standing there, and blinked. With considerable effort, Squirt swallowed the mouthful of food he was chewing, and as soon as his voice box was open for business, he said, "You've come."

Gordon nodded.

Squirt gazed around at the other diners for a moment before focusing his attention again on Gordon. "You can sit if you want," he said quietly.

Gordon nodded and eased himself into the booth beside Squirt. The food smelled delicious, and Gordon was starving, but he couldn't take his eyes from Squirt's face, striving to see an emotion there. Happiness? Hatred? Uncertainty? But there was nothing. If Squirt had come to any epiphanies concerning the two of them during the month he had been in a coma, he was keeping those epiphanies to himself.

Gordon sat mute, not sure what to say since he didn't know where he stood in Squirt's eyes.

The silence lasted so long, Squirt finally shoved the basket of chicken in Gordon's direction. "You want some chicken?"

"Sure," Gordon said. "Thanks." He snagged a drumstick with trembling fingers.

Squirt cleared his throat. He seemed to have accepted the fact that if there was going to be conversation, it would be up to him to get it jump-started, since Gordon was apparently stuck on mute. "They tell me I've been asleep for weeks."

"Yes," Gordon said.

Squirt's eyes softened, but he didn't smile. "And I still look better than you do. How long was I out exactly?"

"Thirty-one days. And thanks. I just woke up."

"Me too. You counted?"

"Counted what?"

"The days."

"Yes. Continually."

"I missed you," Squirt said.

And this brought the teeniest smile to Gordon's lips. "No, you didn't. You were asleep."

"I mean I've missed you since I woke up."

"Oh." Then the meaning of the words sank in. "Did you? I mean are you? I mean have you? Missed me, I mean?" Gordon asked in a rush.

"Yes. The doctor just left. Did you see her?"

"No. You mean Dr. Stark?"

"Susan. Yes. She's been with me since four o'clock. I guess one of the nurses called her when I came to. She drove right down."

"You look good," Gordon said. But in truth he thought Squirt looked drawn and bleary. Understandable, he supposed. There were dark circles under Squirt's eyes, and his lips, when they weren't wrapped around something to eat, looked tight and thin. He also appeared rather stiff in his movements. Gordon was always as stiff as a poker after a good night's sleep. He couldn't imagine how stiff he'd be after sleeping for a month. Even so, Gordon had to admit Squirt looked better than he did.

"You must be starved," Gordon said, staring with wonder at the massive array of food before them—very little of which seemed to have actually been eaten, however. Maybe Squirt's eyes were bigger than his stomach. "Did the doc say it was a good idea to eat yourself right back into the coma you just climbed the fuck out of?"

"I didn't ask. And why are you swearing?"

"I'm nervous."

"Oh." Squirt eyed the food on the table, as if wondering what he'd been thinking when he ordered it. "The doc told me I could order what I wanted, but I wouldn't be able to eat much. I thought she was crazier than me."

"Was she?"

"No." Squirt looked sad when he said it. "She was absolutely right. I guess my stomach shrank while I was out. And I'm still kind of weak."

"And your memory?" Gordon ventured, fearing to know but needing to ask anyway. "What about—"

Squirt didn't wait for Gordon to finish the question.

"I remember everything. Almost. What hasn't come back, some day will, or so the doctor tells me."

"So the accident is… well, you know what happened on that night when… well, I mean you know about…. Oh, crap." Gordon stumbled to a halt, too afraid to continue.

Squirt carefully laid his fork on his plate and tucked his hands under the table. He turned his head to look through the window at the morning unfolding outside. He seemed to enjoy the view. Gordon supposed mornings were pretty cool if you hadn't seen one in a while. "I remember, Gordon. Most of it, anyway."

Gordon's heart was pounding so hard he thought he could feel it in his feet. "And the papers in the closet back at the apartment? Do you remember finding those?"

"Y-yes. I was confused at first. Then I thought I understood what it all meant. After that I don't remember what happened. They say they found me under the bridge. The same bridge where those boys set fire to that man. Do you remember, Gordon? We were there that night he was killed."

"Yes. I remember. I'll never forget it. Sometimes at night I still hear him screaming."

Then the memory of another scream filled Gordon's head. The screech of tires on asphalt. The clash of metal on metal as that other scream filled the air around him. Squirt's scream. Squirt's scream as his lover's body crashed through the car window, tearing his life away in an instant.

Leaving Squirt behind.

Gordon remembered the gnashing of a wolf's teeth as it snapped at his heels, trying to reach him, trying to pull him down to feed. No. Wait. That was a dream. That wasn't real. Or was it?

Gordon wiped the exhaustion from his eyes and tried to focus. Squirt looked so beautiful sitting there. His pale hair glistening in the sunlight streaming through the window. A tiny smudge of ketchup on his lower lip. His blue eyes glimmering like crystal, finally open again, taking in the light after long weeks of darkness.

Gordon tentatively stretched out his hand beneath the table and rested it on Squirt's leg. Squirt looked down at it, eyes appraising, as if he wasn't sure what Gordon was doing, or why he had done what he did. When he lifted his head to study Gordon's face there were tears blurring his blue eyes. A tiny tremor jarred his chin.

At that moment, Gordon knew he was wrong. Squirt understood why the hand was there. He understood it perfectly. Squirt understood what was happening better than Gordon did.

And his next words proved it.

"Do you still love me, then?" Squirt asked. "You and me together, that wasn't a dream, was it, Gordon? You still love me. Right? You never left me?"

Gordon clutched Squirt's hand beneath the table. "No, baby. I never left you. You left me. You got sick and you left. It wasn't your fault. You weren't well." Gordon tried to order his thoughts. He coughed up a pitiful laugh at his own expense. "I love you so much I can't think straight."

Their eyes held each other for a heartbeat, then Gordon said, "It was never my love for you that was in question, Squirt. It's your love for me I've been worried about. After all I've done to you, I need to know. Can you still love me like you said you did before? Before… you went to sleep. Before you found out who I really am. You do know now, don't you, Squirt? You know who I am, don't you?"

Squirt's hand lay unmoving in Gordon's. It felt as it had when Squirt lay sleeping on his gaudy bedclothes back in the ward. Still. Unresponsive. Lifeless. Squirt's hand felt the same as it had when Squirt's mind was a million miles away. When the coma had taken him. Was he now leaving Gordon again? Would Gordon ever be able to get him back? Or would Squirt find his own way back? Did he even want to?

Squirt studied Gordon's face. He looked solemn doing it. "You tell me who you are, Gordon. I think I need to hear it from you."

A fire began in the back of Gordon's eyes, and in moments the heat brought tears to blur his vision. He knew the feeling well, that burning heat. It was the heat of shame. But there was another ember bursting into flame there too, searing his mind, dredging up the tears, causing his throat to tighten.

It was the flame of fear. Fear for what he was in jeopardy of losing.

"Tell me," Squirt said again, prodding gently. He spoke as if addressing a child. Simply. Beseechingly. "Who are you, Gordon? Make me understand who you are. Who you are and what you want. Tell me what I mean to you, Gordon."

The voices in the cafeteria were lost to Gordon's mind. Every particle of his attention was focused on Squirt sitting there beside him looking so innocent. Looking so… patient. And so wounded.

"I'm the guy who loves you, Squirt. I've loved you since the first time I laid eyes on you. I didn't know who you were then. You have to believe that. I would never have had the nerve to approach you if I'd known."

"Known what? Who I am? So tell me. Tell me who you think I am. Tell me who you want me to be. Can you do that?" Squirt asked, the food before him seemingly forgotten. His eyes as blurred with tears as Gordon's. Asking Gordon to say things he was afraid to say. But he had to, didn't he? Gordon had to get things out in the open sooner or later or there was no hope for them at all.

So Gordon began, his heart thundering anew.

"I was in the other car that night. You know that, don't you? It was me, Squirt. I'm the one who killed your lover. Every bad thing that has happened to you since that night is because of me. But I'm so stupid, Squirt. I never knew. I never knew you were there that night at all. I never found out until you left the apartment the day you found the papers in the closet. That day you learned the truth, I learned it too. I-I went to the electrical shop looking for you. I met Sam. Jeremy's father. He told me everything. We looked for you, Squirt. We went to the cemetery where Jeremy is buried. We talked for hours. Just as I didn't know who you really were, Sam didn't know who you had moved in with. The whole lot of us were skirting the truth all over the place, Squirt. But now it's time to lay out the truth once and for all."

Gordon's tears finally broke free. They slid an unhurried path down his cheeks while Squirt stared at their flight. He sat so still he seemed to be unbreathing. Unalive. But Gordon could see a pulse tapping in Squirt's throat beneath the skin. When he swallowed, Squirt's Adam's apple bobbed up and down in his pale throat.

Silently, Squirt waited. Waited for Gordon to speak the words he needed to hear.

"Squirt. I'm sorry for what I did that night. I was a fool. I was careless and drunk and stupid. I've hated myself ever since. I hated myself right up until the moment I met you. At the soup kitchen. Remember? Then suddenly, I felt like I had a reason to live again. To be with you, Squirt. That's my reason to live. It's the only reason I need. Please don't take that away from me. Please don't... hate me." His voice gave out. He swallowed hard.

Squirt took a shuddering breath. It rose from that place he had gone to while listening to Gordon's words. To Gordon's pleas.

"I've never hated you," Squirt said. "I don't think I'd know how."

"Good." Gordon sighed, closing his eyes, trying to settle back to earth. Trying to understand exactly what was being ironed out here.

Squirt stared across the cafeteria to Nate, who still stood by the door, watching.

"I asked the nurse to call you, Gordon. I don't know his name. Did you know I asked him to call you?"

"No," Gordon said. "He didn't tell me that. And his name is Nate."

"Is it?"

"Yes."

Gordon edged closer, his hands still clutching Squirt's hand beneath the table. A man a few tables away watched them, then turned away as if realizing he was intruding on something that did not concern him.

Squirt's voice was as soft as cotton on the air. "What happened that night was an accident, wasn't it, Gordon? You didn't mean for any of it to happen? Did you?"

Gordon paled. "Of course not."

"The doctor told me you spent time in jail over it."

"When did she tell you that?"

"Tonight. Is it true?"

"Yes. I spent a year in jail. It should have been more. I got off easy. I know that now."

"But it ruined your life. She told me so. Is that true too?"

Squirt pulled from Gordon's grasp and wiped the tears from Gordon's cheeks with the cuff of his pajama shirt. Afterward, he tucked his hand back in Gordon's grasp.

That small reassuring movement gave Gordon more hope than anything else that had happened. Still, he could feel how close he was to losing Squirt. It was as if he were balanced on the edge of a knife and could fall either way—into happiness or back to hell where he was before Squirt came along to save him.

"Yes," Gordon said. "After the accident my life was ruined. I didn't want to live anymore. I couldn't see any reason to. That lasted until the day I saw you. Believe it or not. It's the truth. Meeting you gave me my life back. Loving you gave me a reason for living it."

"I believe you," Squirt said quietly.

"Do you, baby? Why?"

Squirt smiled a sad little smile. "Because my life was the same. You changed it. You gave it back to me."

"But I was also the one who took it away."

And Squirt looked down—at the food on the table, at the mess in front of them. But none of it seemed to register. He gazed out at the people in the cafeteria, milling around, scarfing down food, paying their bills to the girl at the counter. None of that seemed to register either.

"It's funny, Gordon. I was never able to face the truth. Then seeing those papers in your closet, reading about everything that happened, it sort of cleared my head. Erased the fear. I can't explain it, but I think it all happened for the best. If it wasn't for our past, yours and mine, we wouldn't have a future. We would never have met. And even if we had, we would not be the people we are today. I might not have loved you, then, at first sight. You might not have loved me. We might not have fit so well together."

"No," Gordon said. "I suppose that's true."

"I loved Jeremy," Squirt said, biting back a fresh surge of tears. "But he's gone now. I'll never forget him again. But I can never forget you either. I can never let myself... lose you. What happened back on that street corner that night so long ago wasn't planned. You didn't do it on purpose. You didn't set out to ruin our lives, mine and Jeremy's. And you also didn't set out to lay the groundwork so the two of us could be happy for the rest of our lives either. It just happened. All of it. Everything in our lives today, the good and the bad, came about from that one moment in time when you looked away. When you were careless. Jeremy died because of it. But we didn't. We're still here. And we found each other because of it."

Gordon squeezed Squirt's hand. "Oh God, Squirt, does that mean you can forgive me? Does it mean you still love me?"

Squirt blushed. "I guess it does." Then his shy smile broadened. "I *know* it does."

Suddenly Squirt's face turned ashen.

Seeing it, Gordon gasped. "What is it? What's wrong?"

Squirt clutched his stomach. "I think I ate too much."

Gordon was so relieved he almost fell out of the booth. He laughed, then thought maybe he really shouldn't. He motioned Nate over and together they led Squirt from the cafeteria and back to the ward. There, Squirt crawled under his SpongeBob SquarePants throw and was sound asleep before either Gordon or Nate could tuck him in.

Satisfied his patient was safe, Nate said his good-byes, and before he left the ward to go home from his shift, Gordon pulled him into his arms.

"Thank you, Nate. Thank you for calling me."

"It was Jerry's idea."

"I know. But thank you anyway." *Squirt still loves me*, Gordon wanted to scream to the heavens. *He almost said the words. If it wasn't for a bellyache, he would have.*

Nate gazed down at Squirt on the bed. Squirt's pale, pale hair was tossed about his face like a scattering of snow. With his eyes closed, Gordon thought, one would never know the beauty of Squirt's crystal blue irises. The way they caught the light. The way they looked at Gordon whenever a rush of love came into his heart. Or a rush of hunger for Gordon's body. But Gordon knew.

Gordon always knew.

"Are you two going to be all right?" Nate asked. "The two of you, I mean. I know you've had… problems."

Gordon blessed the man with a lopsided smile. "All the problems we had were of my own making. But yes, now I think we're going to be all right. Maybe the past is finally buried. No. Not buried. Out in the open. I hope so anyway. Squirt has forgiven me, I think. And he still loves me. That makes me the happiest guy in the world."

Nate's expression was sober and sweet as he gazed first at Gordon, then down at Squirt's peacefully sleeping face. "I've admired the way you cared for him, Gordon. If I ever find a lover of my own someday, I hope it will be someone like you. Squirt's lucky to have you."

"No," Gordon sighed, touched by Nate's sincerity. "I'm lucky to have *him*."

"Then never take him for granted," Nate said, looking uncomfortable all of a sudden, as if wondering if he had said too much.

Gordon saw the look and knew exactly what it meant. He pulled Nate into his arms to ease his embarrassment. "Thanks again, Nate. I owe you one. And don't worry that it will get you in any trouble, calling me like you did and all that. I won't tell anyone. Your secret's safe with me."

Nate nodded. And just before he walked away, he hugged Gordon back.

"Good-bye," he said softly.

With that, he hurried off on his long legs. Gordon raised a hand to wish him well and thank him yet again, but Nate didn't turn to see it.

A little sadly, Gordon watched him go, wishing him the best. And when he and Squirt were finally alone, Gordon tugged the battered copy of *Tom Sawyer* out from beneath Squirt's mattress where he had hidden it the evening before.

Immediately, a handful of patients began edging toward him, coming from everywhere, eyeing the book, eyeing Gordon. Excited. Eager.

Gordon glanced at Squirt, once again sound asleep in his bed, just as he had been for the past thirty-one days. Only this time Gordon knew he would wake.

And better yet, when he did wake, Gordon knew Squirt would still love him. Just as he always had. Just as he always would.

That thought brought a smile to his face, and as the patients crept persistently closer, Gordon laughed quietly at the hopeful expressions on their faces. He pressed a finger to his lips, imploring silence, and they each did the same, shushing themselves and shushing each other like a bevy of mad librarians.

Gordon perched on the edge of the bed and opened *Tom Sawyer* to a dog-eared page deep inside the book. In the faintest of whispers, so as not to disturb Squirt, he read, "Chapter thirty-one. Found and lost again."

In the mellow hush of his voice, his audience of the insane settled contentedly around him. Drifting to the floor like autumn leaves, they harked to every word Gordon uttered as he led Tom and Becky safely from the cave.

And all the while he read aloud, Squirt snored softly in the bed beside him, his hand resting gently at Gordon's back.

# EPILOGUE

"YOU BUSY tomorrow?" Gordon asked. It was an offhand question. His mind was really on other things. Like balancing three poinsettias and an umbrella in his arms while plodding up the hill to Guadalupe Circle to decorate Jeremy Aldritch Booth's grave.

Squirt was balancing poinsettias too, but he somehow managed to look a little more graceful doing it. And he hadn't bothered with an umbrella. That helped. "Rewiring a house in Kensington. Sam says it's an all-day job. I'll probably be home late."

Gordon grinned. "I'll keep the sheets warm."

"Slut."

"Oh, wait," Gordon said. "I have to check the numbers on this storm for the evening weather report. Sally's great on camera, but she can't read the Doppler for shit. I'll probably be late myself."

It was Squirt's turn to grin. "Then I'll keep the sheets warm for *you*."

"Goody."

"Since you'll probably be later than me," Squirt said, "I'll pick up the suits from the dry cleaner for the wedding. Your mom will kill us both if we aren't dressed at our best. And the boutonnieres too. I'll pick those up at the florist."

Gordon rolled his eyes. He had forgotten the boutonnieres entirely. "Thanks. Maybe marriage will mellow the woman out."

"I doubt it."

"Me too. Poor Mr. Rhiner."

"No shit."

The air was cold for San Diego. Squirt's hair was tucked under a wool watch cap, which made the clean architecture of his face stand out as if etched in marble. *No two ways around it,* Gordon thought. *The man's a looker.*

Squirt shot Gordon a sidelong glance. There was a smirk on his face as he did. "You're cruising me," he said.

"You betcha," Gordon answered.

As the crest of the hill approached, Squirt said, "I'm sorry I went overboard on the flowers, but Jeremy really loved poinsettias. Covering his grave in them seemed like a good idea at the time. Didn't think about lugging them up the hill on the coldest, rainiest day in recorded history."

Gordon cocked his head and snickered. "It's forty-five degrees and barely sprinkling. Hardly the coldest, rainiest day in history. I'm a weatherman. I know. God, San Diegans are wimps."

"Thank you, Mr. Sweater-Coat-Gloves-Two-Scarves-Earmuffs-Galoshes-and-Umbrella."

"Well, you need to be prepared."

"Oy," Squirt said, although he wasn't Jewish.

Without really thinking about it, Gordon edged closer to Squirt as they trudged up the final slope to the grave. He had been surprised when he realized he did that under all kinds of circumstances, the sidling close, and Squirt did the same, seemingly unconsciously. Gordon thought they just functioned better at touching distance. Then again, they loved each other like crazy. Maybe it wasn't so surprising after all.

It had rained for days and the ground was soggy beneath their feet. Jeremy's tombstone had been washed clean and looked sparkly new nestled in the wet green grass. Squirt and Gordon looked down at it, still cradling their poinsettias, their heads filled with their own private thoughts.

The melancholy this place had always infused in Gordon had lessened of late, although it still stirred a tear now and then, often when he least expected it. At the moment, however, he was feeling good about being here. It was, after all, a nice thing they were doing. Although certainly not enough to right wrongs. Nothing would ever be enough for that.

"I still miss him," Squirt said softly, his face peeking out from a tangle of red poinsettia leaves. "Sometimes when we make love, I imagine you're him." His eyes popped open wide as he turned to study Gordon's reaction. "I probably shouldn't have told you that, huh?"

"It's all right," Gordon said. "Sometimes when we're making love, I imagine you're tall."

Squirt blinked, then barked out a laugh. "Tit for tat, then."

They first arranged the poinsettias over the grave from tombstone to foot, burying the entirety of it in red plumage. When that didn't look right, they clumped the poinsettias in a scattered mass around the stone marker. They both liked that arrangement better.

"Jeremy says thank you," Squirt softly said, making a final adjustment to the pots.

And Gordon smiled, reaching out to take Squirt's hand. Unsatisfied, he released Squirt's hand, tugged off his glove, then clasped Squirt's hand again, skin on skin. That was better.

"I wish I could have known the man," Gordon said.

Squirt gazed at him. His nose was red from the biting wind slipping over the hilltop, burrowing under scarves and jackets, making a general nuisance of itself. Squirt's hand tightened in Gordon's grasp as he said, "Jeremy has filled your mind for almost three years, Gordon. I doubt there has been a single day he wasn't there. I don't think anyone knows him better than you do."

"Three years," Gordon mused, amazed by the passage of time, as mortals always are. "That means we've been together almost a year. Our anniversary's coming up."

"I know."

"It's funny, but every day I wake up in your arms, I love you more."

Squirt offered a sweet smile. "I know that too."

Connected by hands and hearts, they gazed down at the grave together, satisfied. It was a happy grave now, alive with color and life and beauty and Christmas, which was just around the corner.

"Final touch," Squirt said, pulling a fistful of silver tinsel from his coat pocket. He bent and carefully weaved the tinsel over and through the poinsettias. When he was finished, the grave was gleaming, the tinsel shooting out sparks of light as it stirred in the wind.

Gordon grinned. "I take it Jeremy liked glitz and glitter and sparklies galore."

"What gay man doesn't?"

When the rain began to pepper down a little harder, Gordon opened his umbrella and Squirt ducked under it with him. They stood at the grave a moment longer, Squirt's hand tucked into Gordon's coat pocket. Shivering a little now in the cold, they finally turned to make their way back down the hill to the car.

Gordon pointed to the Coronado Bridge on the horizon. Both men stood in the drizzle for a scattering of heartbeats and stared at it through the curtain of falling rain.

"We spent our first night together under that bridge," Gordon said.

Squirt nestled closer. "The night the man was burned."

"Yes." Gordon considered that long ago night, the good of it and the bad. Squirt looked surprised when Gordon said, "I want to drive over it. Now. Maybe we'll have lunch in Coronado. I'm hungry for seafood."

"All right," Squirt smiled. "Whatever you want."

Because of the weather, the traffic was light. The cars on the bridge were scattered and far apart.

As Gordon reached the highest point at which the bridge arched over the bay, Gordon slowed the car and took the lane to the right nearest the edge. He fumbled under his seat and extracted a black parcel, wrapped in plastic and tightly taped.

He handed it to Squirt. "Hold this a second."

Squirt took it, hefting it in his hands, fingering the shape of it under the plastic while Gordon lowered the car window at Squirt's side, letting in the cold air and rain.

"What is this?" Squirt asked, leaning away from the open window to avoid the wind. "It almost feels like a gun."

"It is a gun," Gordon said. And taking the package from Squirt's hand, he flung it through the passenger window, where it arched out over the concrete rail of the bridge and disappeared into the mist.

Casually, Gordon rolled the window up to once again seal out the rain and cold, and then he settled himself behind the wheel as if nothing odd had just happened.

"Want to tell me what that was all about?" Squirt asked, twisting in his seat to look back at the spot in their wake where the mysterious package had sailed off into oblivion.

Driving down the far slope of the bridge into the City of Coronado, Gordon eased the car toward the first off-ramp.

"I'd rather not," he said, a feeling of freedom burning behind his eyes. "Not today at any rate. Let's just go eat instead."

Squirt stared at him for a moment, then finally nodded and let it go. "All right, Gordon. If that's what you want." He reached out to brush his fingertips over Gordon's coat sleeve. "Prawns would be nice, don't you think?"

"Then prawns it is," Gordon said, reaching out to stroke Squirt's cheek.

The wipers beat a rhythm against the rain, and the car heater threw out a delicious blast of warm air as Squirt pressed his lips to Gordon's gloved hand. As content in Squirt's company as Gordon had been since the first day they met, and as sure of Squirt's equal contentment, he guided their talk to little things as the San Diego skyline bleared in the distance across the bay.

Squirt leaned across the seat and playfully lifted the earmuff from Gordon's ear. "I love you, you know," he said.

"Thank you, Squirt. And I love you." Gordon smiled when he spoke the words because they tasted delicious on his lips.

And later, the prawns were delicious too.

JOHN INMAN has been writing fiction since he was old enough to hold a pencil. He and his partner live in beautiful San Diego, California. Together, they share a passion for theater, books, hiking and biking along the trails and canyons of San Diego, or, if the mood strikes, simply kicking back with a beer and a movie. John's advice for anyone who wishes to be a writer? "Set time aside to write every day and do it. Don't be afraid to share what you've written. Feedback is important. When a rejection slip comes in, just tear it up and try again. Keep mailing stuff out. Keep writing and rewriting and then rewrite one more time. Every minute of the struggle is worth it in the end, so don't give up. Ever. Remember that publishers are a lot like lovers. Sometimes you have to look a long time to find the one that's right for you."

You can contact John at john492@att.net, on Facebook: http://www.facebook.com/john.inman.79, or on his website: http://www.johninmanauthor.com/.

Also from JOHN INMAN

http://www.dreamspinnerpress.com

Also from JOHN INMAN

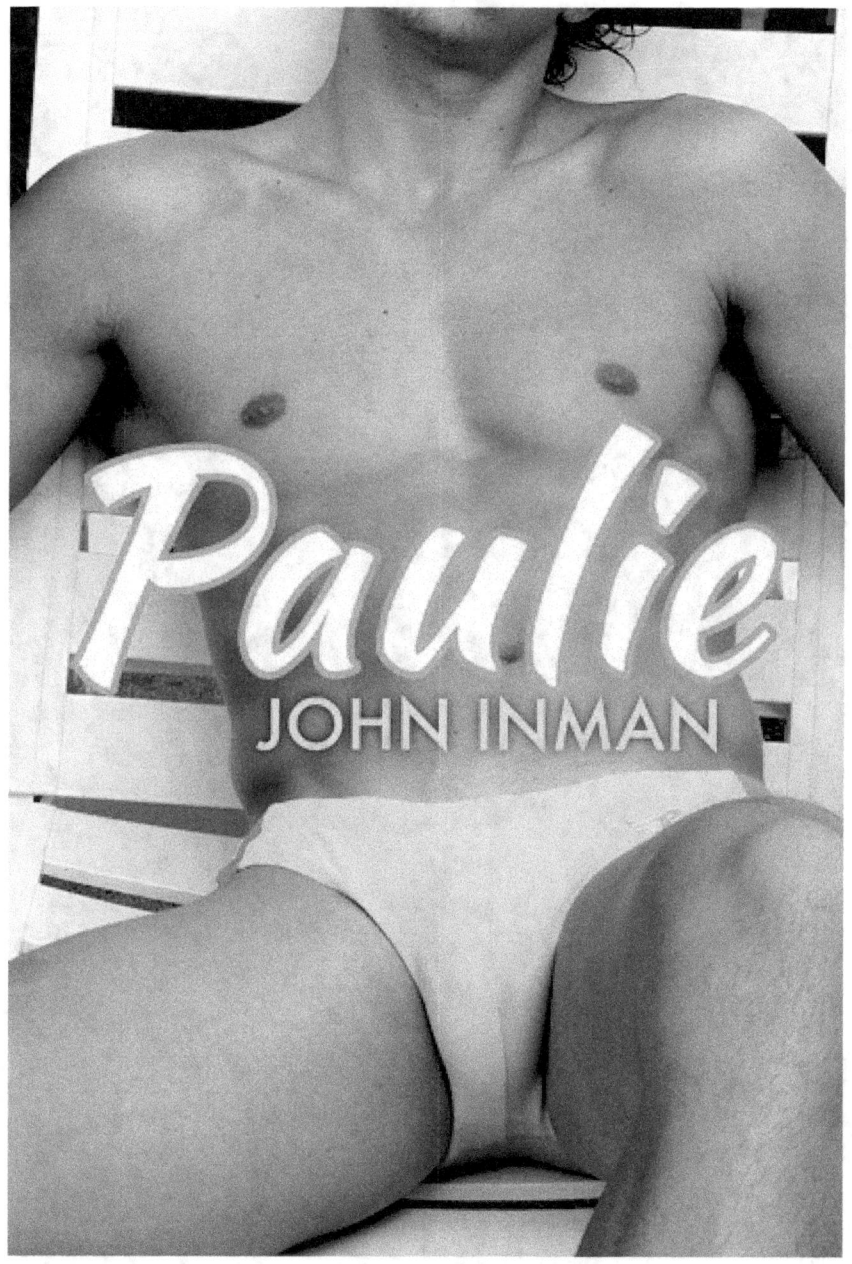

http://www.dreamspinnerpress.com

Also from JOHN INMAN

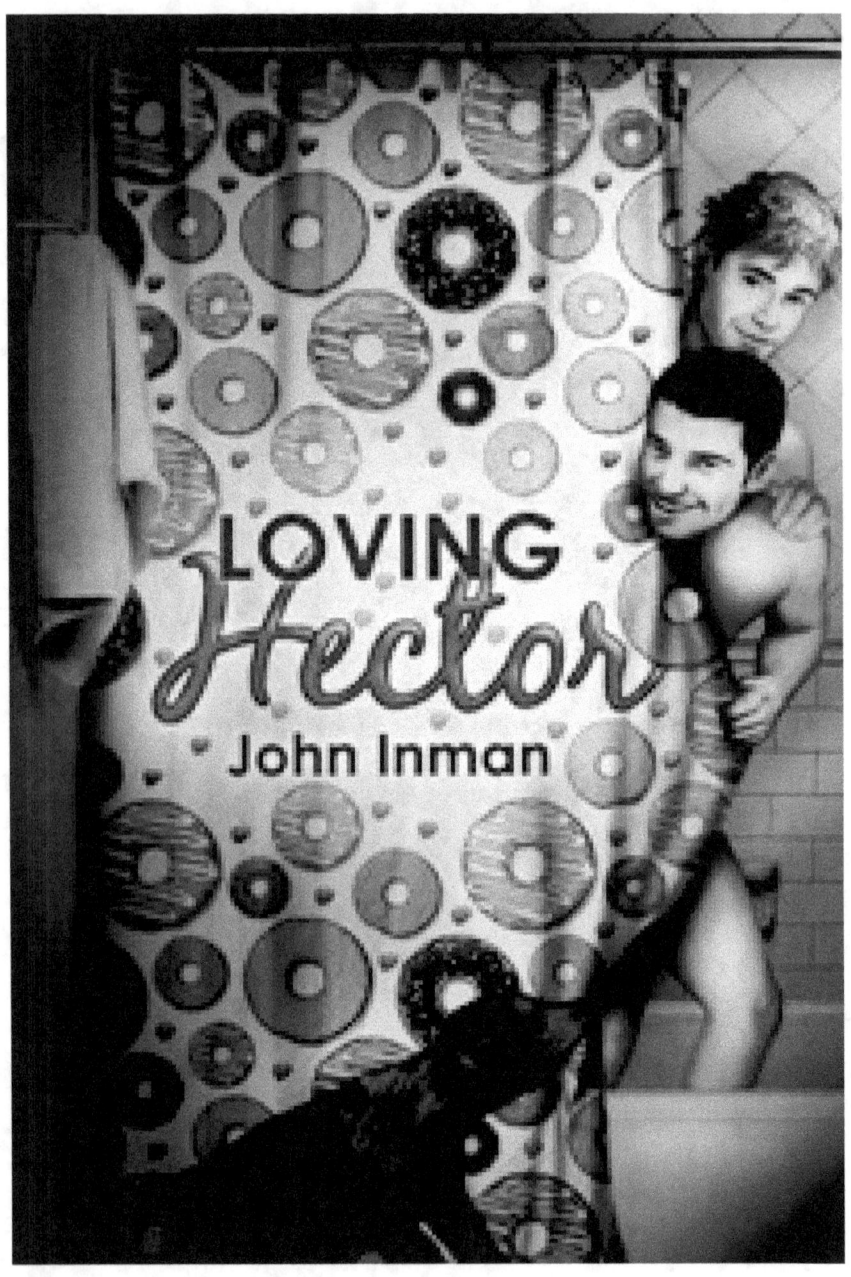

Also from JOHN INMAN

http://www.dreamspinnerpress.com

Also from JOHN INMAN

JOHN INMAN
HOBBLED

Also from JOHN INMAN

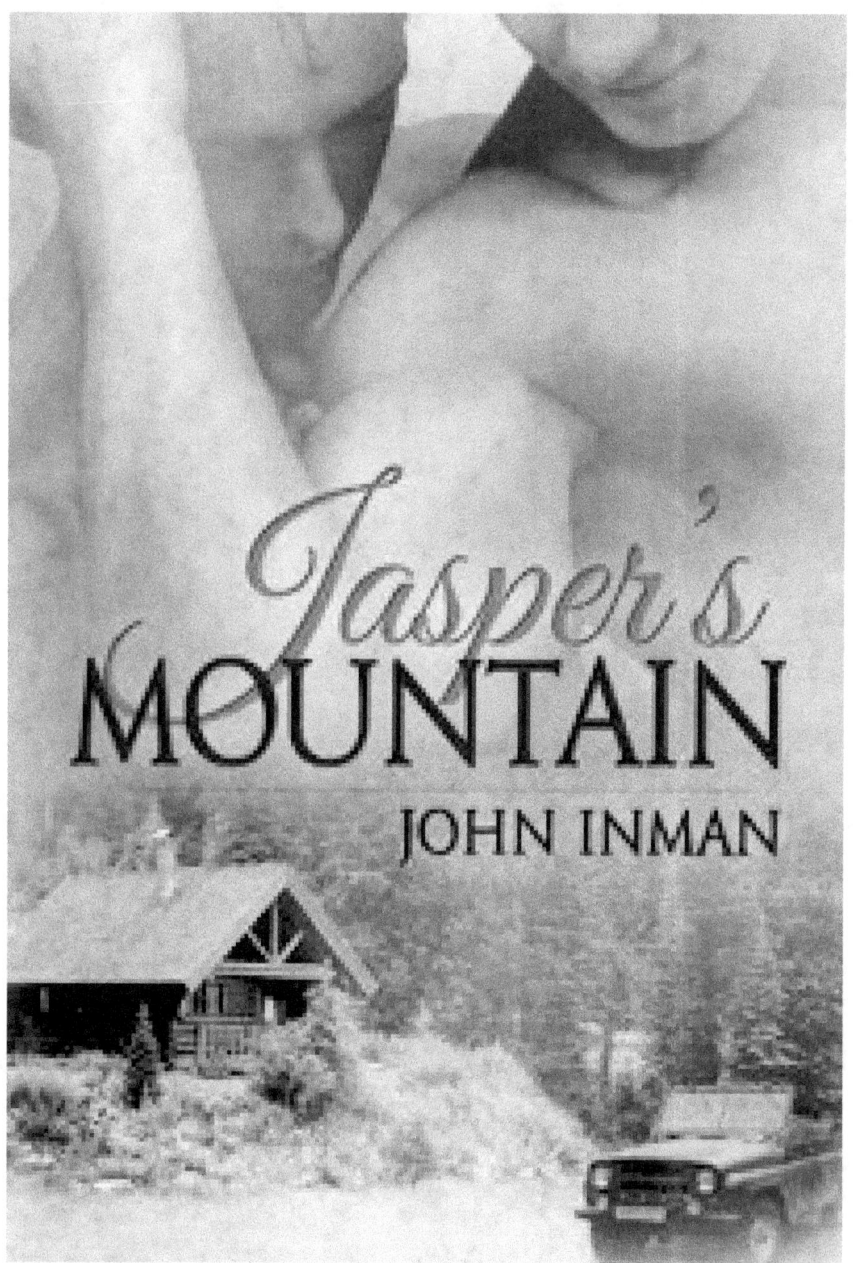

*Jasper's*
MOUNTAIN

JOHN INMAN

http://www.dreamspinnerpress.com

# Also from JOHN INMAN